Island of Bones

IMOGEN ROBERTSON

headline
review

First published in Great Britain in 2011
by HEADLINE REVIEW
An imprint of HEADLINE PUBLISHING GROUP

First published in paperback in Great Britain in 2012
by HEADLINE REVIEW

2

Cataloguing in Publication Data is available from the British Library

ISBN 978 0 7553 7204 1

Typeset in Poliphilus and Blado by Ellipsis Digital Limited, Glasgow

Printed and bound in Great Britain by
Clays Ltd, St Ives plc

Headline's policy is to use papers that are natural, renewable and recyclable products
and made from wood grown in sustainable forests. The logging and manufacturing processes
are expected to conform to the environmental regulations of the country of origin.

HEADLINE PUBLISHING GROUP
An Hachette UK Company
338 Euston Road
London NW1 3BH

www.headline.co.uk
www.hachettelivre.co.uk

To my parents, Mark and Celia

ACKNOWLEDGEMENTS

Thank you as always to the friends and family who support me all through the process, then kindly go out into the streets to rugby-tackle strangers and recommend the novels: my apologies to anyone they've harassed in a bookshop. Also, many thanks to those people who have written to me, or spoken to me at signings and events to say kind things about my first two Westerman/Crowther novels. It has been a continual source of encouragement as I wrote this book, and is much appreciated. Huge thanks, as always, to Flora and everyone at Headline; to Annette, David, and to Goldsboro Books; and to Richard Foreman and all his angels, and the friends and allies I have made through him.

As usual I have gathered material from just about everyone I've spoken to in the last year and a half. Particular thanks go to Bob, Faye and all at the retreat in Bridport (especially Walt and Bis) for letting me handle and shoot longbows; to Lottie Tyers for the use of her name; to Andrew for our discussions on folk medicine, and to all those who have been kind enough to talk to me about the grief of losing someone very dear to them. Also, thanks to the people of Keswick, whose reputation for friendly hospitality is as well deserved in the twenty-first century as I'm sure it was in the eighteenth.

And of course I'm particularly grateful to Ned for making all things possible and everything a great deal more fun.

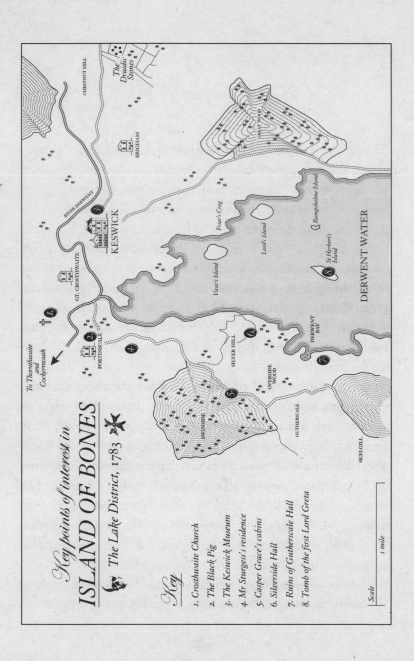

Key points of interest in
ISLAND OF BONES
The Lake District, 1783

Key

1. Crosthwaite Church
2. The Black Pig
3. The Keswick Museum
4. Mr Sturgess's residence
5. Casper Grace's cabins
6. Silverside Hall
7. Ruins of Gutherscale Hall
8. Tomb of the first Lord Greta

Scale

1 mile

To Thornthwaite
and Cockermouth

CHESTNUT HILL

The Druidic Stones

BRIGHAM

RIVER DERWENT

GT. CROSTHWAITE

KESWICK

PORTINSCALE

Friar's Crag

Vicar's Island

Lord's Island

Rampsholme Island

St Herbert's Island

SWINSIDE

OVERSIDE WOOD

SILVER HILL

DERWENT BAY

GUTHERSCALE

SKELGILL

DERWENT WATER

PROLOGUE

THERE WAS A PECULIAR HUSH around the Tower the night before an execution. The mist from the river shushed the streets and people moved quietly. The guards nodded to each other, stamped their feet and wished for dawn, then thought of the man in the Tower; they looked at the light showing faintly from his rooms and shivered again.

The fire could do little against the damp air of a February night, and nor could the wine warm the two men keeping vigil in the white-washed cell. They had been silent a long time. It was clear they were brothers — they had the same hooded eyes, the same slender figure — but they were turned away from each other, thinking their own thoughts. The younger of the two, Charles, glanced sideways at his brother without turning his head. Lucius Adair Penhaligon, 2nd Baron Keswick, was shivering and flushed; his silk waistcoat was undone and his hands were working one over the other as if he were trying to wash something from them. Charles looked back into the yellow flames, a little nauseated.

The fire cracked and Adair started at the noise; then, as if

1

woken suddenly, he looked around at the plain walls with an air of disbelief.

'What a little life I have had, Charles,' he said. 'And now I am afraid to lose it.'

Charles picked up the decanter and filled his brother's glass again. His own was still full. He set it back down on the table between them and returned to his contemplation of the fire without replying.

'How can it be I shall be dead tomorrow at this time? I cannot imagine it – I cannot.' Adair then downed the contents of his glass. His voice quivered. 'Can nothing be done? Can *you* do nothing?'

Charles shook his head and heard his brother begin to snivel.

'I did not murder him, Charles!' Adair shook his head slowly from side to side, as if trying to shift some weight across the floor of his mind. 'No one believes me, but I did not, I swear I did not. Where is Margaret?'

'You have had her letter. She is in Ireland now.'

Adair looked around the room as if the matter was not settled, as if their sister might appear in the shadows. 'Yes, of course. And has no one else come, Charles? Have none of my friends come to sit with me tonight?'

'No.'

The sound of his weeping grew louder, and Charles wished he could block out the noise. The stones around the fire were charred black with the ghosts of other flames. Charles watched, willing the sparks to fly free of the grate and consume it all – his brother, himself, then the whole city – and leave not a trace of them or their history behind them. The flames continued feeble and sullen. Very well, if he could not burn away his past, he would abandon it. Once the estate was sold, he would sign himself into the student roll of the University of Wittenberg and lose himself there and in his studies; after that, Padua perhaps. Then he could forget the gothic horrors of his family, the blood and money. Finding himself thinking of his own future, he glanced back at his brother. The sobbing had eased. Adair wiped his face and snuffled into his handkerchief.

'What will they say of me when I am gone, Charles? Will they say anything, as they lose the money they won from me at the card table? Perhaps they will laugh. They used to laugh at me. I would be so sure of winning, I wore my coat turned inside out for luck, and each night they would ask if I were certain of my success, then laugh at me – but I *was* sure, I was sure every time. I only needed a hundred, and it seemed like such a simple thing. Oh God! Will it hurt, Charles?'

Charles turned away. 'If the hangman knows his job, it will be quick.'

Adair scrambled suddenly to his feet and ran to the corner of the little room where a jug and ewer waited and bent over it. Charles heard the splatter of his vomit on the porcelain, the dry heavings of his stomach. After some moments Adair returned to the fire to find his glass full again. He could hardly hold it to his lips, so violent was his trembling.

'Charles, do you think there is a God? The priest tells me I shall be saved if I repent.'

His brother did not answer him.

'You think I am a coward?'

'You fear what every man fears.'

Adair suddenly stood again and threw his glass with a

cry. It smashed, and the last of the wine dripped down the wall.

'For God's sake! Will you not weep for your brother, Charles? How are you so cold? I was no better a brother to Margaret, yet her letter was so sodden I can hardly read it. Do I not deserve your tears? Can you weep? Are you a man at all?' Adair dropped back into his seat as if that small act of outrage had exhausted him entirely. When he spoke again, it was as if he was talking to himself. 'I did not kill him – and yet no one believes me. It was the other man, the man with a hundred pounds. It was not my fault. Why does no one believe me?'

Charles stared at his cuffs and would not look up, willing the time to pass.

'Oh, leave me to the priest, Charles. He will weep, if only because it is his pleasure to see a man pray.'

Charles stood and turned towards the door.

'Charles?' Adair tumbled out of his seat and on to the brick floor at his brother's feet, grabbing hold of his hand. Charles felt the soft damp flesh on his own and was revolted, but Adair's grip was too desperate for him to be able to pull free. 'I swear I am innocent of this! The old man wanted to see him alone, and I needed the money – what was the harm? Father was dead when I found him! I took the knife out of him, but he was gone, then I ran. I was afraid. Oh God! I am innocent and now they are going to kill me, and you shall let them. Why don't you believe me?'

Charles looked down for a moment, then crouched beside him. 'I don't believe you, Addie, because you have always been a bully and a liar. I don't believe you because you were found with the knife in your hand, and confessed the crime . . .'

'I only meant I had *caused* it by arranging for the man to meet him! Please, Charles, I am begging you . . .'

Charles felt Adair's fingers kneading his own.

'I don't believe you because you had the money you stole from our father's notecase in your coat. It was bloody, Addie, our father's blood was on the bills.'

'I found him, and I pulled the knife out and then I meant to throw the money away so it got bloody from my hand . . .' his voice was whining, 'but I needed it, Charles! I could not throw it away. It was the other man, the—'

'The man whom no one has seen.' Charles's voice was hard. 'No one, Addie! The man you only conjured in your mind when you found you had neither the courage to take your own life, nor stand trial for the crime. If you had not retracted your confession, there might have been some mercy for you.'

'But I didn't do it!'

His grip relaxed. Charles pulled one hand free and put it around his brother's neck, then with his thumb lifted Adair's face till they could look each other in the eye. Adair's face was soaked with tears and his nose dripped; his eyes were bloodshot and a thread of bile hung from his lip.

'Yes, you did, Addie. May God forgive you, and I shall forgive you for it if I can.'

He let Adair's head drop again then stood, reached into his pocket and drew out two gold guineas. These he placed carefully before his brother on the cold floor. 'Give these to the hangman when you reach the scaffold. Goodbye, Addie.'

He opened the door to the outer room where two guards looked up from their cards, then turned back. Adair remained kneeling on the floor, the fire making silver on the silk of his embroidered waistcoat, gold in the expensive weave of his britches, jewels across his close-cut coat with its porcelain buttons. He was staring at the coins in front of him. The only thing left in the world he could buy was a quick death. Charles closed the door and was escorted out into the dark and stench of the city.

The following day, Tyburn on the edges of London

THOMAS GOFFE, a rather nervous gentleman in a bad wig, shot to his feet.

'Carmichael! Over here, man!'

Such was the crush on the stands that Goffe had to resort to standing on the rickety bench and waving his hat to attract the attention of his friend.

He was spotted, acknowledged, and soon joined by an extremely handsome man who carried himself with such an air of superiority that his neighbours almost climbed on top of each other to give him all the room they could.

The open fields below them were thronged with a great mass of people. Here in the stands a considerable number of gentlemen sat tightly together and chattered with a slightly feverish excitement, but those who could not afford this elevated view joined the swarm of people below, churning the field to a mud bath. Hawkers wandered through the crowd selling chap-books of the most popular last confessions for a penny, others offered filled pastries from covered baskets. All around, a competing chorus of street singers declared their territory with their damp lungs like cockerels and stamped their feet against the cold as they sang. Jugglers and fire-eaters sweated for pennies at the edges of the crowd and a little army of pickpockets danced among the unwary for handkerchieves and shillings.

It was carnival.

'Where did you get that monstrosity?' Carmichael asked. Goffe was confused. He touched his hat; Carmichael gave a tiny shake of his head. Goffe then touched the white curls of his wig, and with his face falling into childlike dismay, watched Carmichael raise an eyebrow.

'Thompsons on the Strand, Carmichael. You recommended them yourself.'

'Did I? Their standards have declined considerably.' Goffe dropped his chin into his collar. 'How long have you been here?'

'Lord, an hour at least, or I should never have found a place.' The pride of having done so brightened Goffe. He dragged out from between his feet a basket, which he uncovered with a flourish to show three promising-looking bottles and a number of cold pies. Carmichael smiled, and Goffe went a little pink as he handed one of each to his friend. Carmichael was an easy man to disappoint. 'So, did you see him?'

Carmichael drank deeply from the bottle before replying. 'A glimpse, no more. What's to see? A landau getting more and more covered with the muck the people throw at it, a dozen men-in-arms, and a coffin. I came the back way. The crowd is pressing all along the route from the Tower. He'll be here in half an hour.'

Goffe gave a little high-pitched giggle and bit into his pie. 'How will he take it, you think, Carmichael? You must be willing to guess, having been his friend so long.'

7

Carmichael brushed flakes of pastry from his sleeve. 'Yes, poor Lucius Adair. I once met his father, you know. Lord Keswick was a clever man with money perhaps, but brutalised by all those years spent beyond the reach of civilisation. If he had been *my* father, I might have killed him.'

Goffe slapped his thigh so hard, gentlemen on the bench above heard the vibration. 'Oh, oh Carmichael! You could teach the Devil himself new tricks!' He slid his eyes over Carmichael's fine blue coat and wished he had one like it. 'You'll miss Adair's pockets though,' he added quietly.

Carmichael shrugged and sucked at the bottle again before looking up and becoming suddenly still. Goffe noticed the fixity of his attention. He craned his neck to look the same way, swallowing once or twice. 'What is it? Are they coming?'

'No, not yet. See that man on the end of the bench, three below with his back to us?'

Goffe wiped his mouth and peered. 'What, thin fella? Looks like a parson? He'll get no kind of view from there.'

'That man, my dear Goffe,' drawled Carmichael, 'is Charles Penhaligon now, and will be the new Lord Keswick before I have finished this pie.'

'No!' Goffe said in delight. 'The brother! Did you ever meet him then?'

'Once or twice. An odd sort of creature. He can play the gentleman, but always seemed a little touched to me. Cuts up dead animals and calls it natural philosophy.'

Goffe shuddered. 'Disgusting – the whole bunch of them. Oh look! They've spotted the carriage. Not long now till we see how nicely Adair dances the Tyburn jig.'

The excitement of the crowd had deepened, and as the first

of the spectators caught sight of the soldiers leading the procession from the Tower a wave of jeers and whistles broke and rolled over them. The jugglers and singers paused in their work and struggled for a view with the rest. Goffe noticed a pretty, hard-eyed woman near the bottom of the stands, her skirts tucked up. Her hands were clenched into fists and her red mouth was open and snarling. Goffe licked his lips.

'It does bring out the whores, doesn't it?'

Carmichael nodded. 'The hanging of a nobleman? Why, of course. High holiday for us all.'

Charles did have something of the parson in his manner. It was his dark-coloured clothing and the severe planes of his face, his cold eyes that made even those passing him in the street feel examined, judged, and keen to pass on. A woman, swinging her fat hips down from the highest benches, also noticed him, his hands lying empty on his lap before him, and took the chance, as she reached the lower level on which he sat, to thrust one of her pamphlets between them.

'That's a penny, lover.' He looked up at her, and she was struck by the bright blue of his eyes in his pale face. A firm chin, dusted with dark stubble. Sharp bones in his cheeks, a young man. 'Every word gospel – all writ down at the trial. Horrid murder! He sliced up the maid too, you know. Near killed her.' She tried a wink.

'I do not want it,' he said.

'Come on, sweetheart. Only a penny.' She touched her hair.

He turned his eyes towards her again and something in them made her step back; they had a violent glitter to them. 'I do not want it.'

'All right, lover,' she said, plucking it from between his fingertips and hurrying over to a red-faced countryman who held his coin in the air as summons. She couldn't help looking back at him though. His stillness was so strange in the fevered flurry of the crowd.

The thin man folded his hands on his lap again and studied his cuffs. The roar of the crowd told him that the coach was approaching. There were jeers and laughter flowing from every side. Then a hush fell, spreading out from the gallows like a wind. Charles lifted his chin.

His brother Lucius Adair stood on the back of the hangman's cart, looking small at this distance. In front of him stood the priest from the jail. Addie's lips were moving as if in continual prayer, then he lifted his voice.

'Good people . . .' he began. Charles wondered if Addie had spotted him in the crowd. No matter. He had said he would attend and he had kept his promise. His eyes were fixed on the little figure. Addie had always liked to be looked at. Well, he had his wish now. 'I go to my death a guilty man.' There was a great roar, and Adair had to strain to make himself heard again. 'But not of the crime of which I am accused.' Stamping and swearing from all quarters. Charles had not expected him to admit it now. The crowd hallooed and mocked. Charles's contempt for his brother was absolute. He had made their family an entertainment, like a chained bear. There had been a woman playing a hurdy-gurdy in the crowd as Charles found his seat. He thought now that fairground music would follow him for his whole life.

His brother continued: 'I have sinned. I blame no man but myself, and so may God have mercy on my soul!'

Only at the last did his voice quaver and rise. The crowd was divided between cheers and curses. Loud laughter rocked and swayed over the people in places. Addie offered his hands to be tied and seemed to stumble a little. Charles swallowed. There was a man in the crowd who kept looking at him. Escape was impossible for Adair now, but might it be possible for Charles to flee? He could abandon the title that would fall on him when the hangman had done his work, and choose another name. Yes, it was possible.

The hangman had to hold Adair steady and whispered something to him as he slipped first the hood and then the rope around over his head. To Charles, it seemed at once as if the hood had covered his own face. He saw the fierce triangle of the gallows, the thousands around him, but at the same time it seemed that everything had disappeared – that he saw only black cloth, felt the pinch of the ropes on his wrists behind him, the weight of the slack noose round his neck, his own panting breath drawing the weave to his lips. Its stink that of the sweat of other frightened men.

The rope snapped tight and Charles felt his own breath choked out of his throat as his brother's legs began kicking free in the air. He put his hand to his collar and struggled to breathe. All around him was this impossible noise, the elation of the crowd. Its roar became one with the rushing of his blood in his ears. His mouth tasted bitter. The hangman grabbed onto Adair's legs and pulled hard. Charles felt his throat constrict still further; it was as if some invisible beast had its thumbs pressing down on the hyoid bone of his neck and was waiting for the snap. Two minutes, perhaps three. All eternity.

The struggling ceased, the people cheered and whistled, and

Charles gasped in air again. He lowered his face, waiting for his heart to slow. The body was cut down, and at once the hangman began to divide the rope into portions and sell them to those in the crowd who had managed to push close enough to reach him.

When Charles could look up again, he saw the body being rolled into the coffin. A man he knew vaguely from the College of Anatomy took a seat on its lid like a dog guarding a bone. Would the men he knew feel troubled about dissecting the body of his brother? Perhaps a little, briefly. But bodies were valuable. He had taken no steps to prevent their taking it. Adair had been wearing the same buff coat and silk waistcoat he had worn the previous evening; they would belong to the hangman now.

Charles took a deep breath and stood. Already the crowd was thinning out. The spectacle was over, so the usual day-to-day business resumed.

A man tapped him on the shoulder. 'So that makes you Lord Keswick now, sir?'

Charles turned his blue eyes on him. 'What?'

The man looked unsure and glanced over his shoulder to the place where Carmichael and Goffe had been sitting. 'Fellow up there said you were the brother – the heir to all that money. It's an ill wind, your lordship.' He shook his head. 'Still, that's some bad blood to inherit.' There was a gleam in his eye, a certain wet hunger in his lips.

Charles drew on his gloves, his hands shaking only very slightly. Interesting, the strange effects on the physical body the emotions could have. If he could draw his own blood now, at this moment, what would he find in it, he wondered.

'They were mistaken,' he said, looking at the man very steadily. The man's smile faltered and he began under that gaze to look almost afraid.

'My apologies, sir. And forgive my asking. Only natural to be curious, I'm sure you'll agree. Such a tale.'

'Indeed, and I pity Lord Keswick that he must be associated with it.'

'Of course, sir. My apologies again, sir.' Charles took a step away, but the man raised his voice. 'Your name then, sir?'

Charles paused for a second. 'My name is Gabriel Crowther,' he said, and disappeared into the crowd.

The summer of 1783 was an amazing and portentous one, and full of horrible phenomena; for besides the alarming meteors and thunderstorms that affrighted many counties of this kingdom, the peculiar haze or smoky fog, that prevailed for many weeks in this island and in every part of Europe, and even beyond its limits, was a most extraordinary appearance, unlike anything known within memory of man. By my journal I find that I had noticed this strange occurrence from June 23rd to July 20th inclusive, during which the wind varied to every quarter without making any alterations in the air.

Gilbert White *Natural History and Antiquities of Selborne,*
1789

The universities do not teach all things, so a doctor must seek out old wives, gypsies, sorcerers, wandering tribes, old robbers and such outlaws and take lessons from them . . . Knowledge is experience.

Theophrastus von Hohenheim (1493/4–1541), called
Paracelsus

PART I

I.1

Tuesday, 1 July 1783, St Herbert's Island, Derwent Water, Cumberland

'AN EXTRA BODY? What do you mean, an extra body?'
Mrs Hetty Briggs spoke a little more loudly than she had intended and her voice echoed in the stillness of the ruined chapel. Her steward lowered his head. He could not think of what else to add. They were silent a moment, and the hot wind that had so troubled them this summer shook the trees together. In spite of the warmth, Mrs Briggs shivered. She touched her steward's sleeve and said more quietly, 'My apologies, Gribben. You had better show me, I think.'

Turning away from him, she remembered the lady and gentleman who had accompanied her here to this little island, part of her husband's estate amongst the lakes and hills of Cumberland. They had stood a little apart from her while she spoke to her man, but were now frankly staring at her. The gentleman was the local magistrate, Mr Sturgess, and Mrs Briggs was suddenly very glad indeed that he had decided to come with them. The lady, very beautifully dressed for a trip across the lake and a visit to a ruin, was her house-guest for the summer, the Vizegräfin Margaret von Bolsenheim. Her lips were slightly parted and there was a shimmer in her eye.

'That is,' Mrs Briggs added, 'perhaps you should show us all.'

Mrs Briggs had always considered her ownership of St Herbert's Island as accidental. It was just another feature of the estate her husband had purchased, like the walled garden behind the main house of Silverside, or the lawns that dropped down in front of it to the lake, and like them she regarded it as purely ornamental. The island was a pleasant spot for a picnic and known for its magnificent views of the surrounding hills. In addition, the ruin of the old chapel added something romantic and picturesque for visitors to the area to discover. It was known that Mrs Briggs had no objection to local people, or travellers from elsewhere, drawing their boats up onto the shingle, therefore many took advantage of her generosity and arrived sketchbooks in hand to sample the scenery. Her one nagging concern about the island had always been that the chapel, disused for a hundred years before Mr Briggs acquired the land, still contained the altar-tomb of Sir Luke de Beaufoy, 1st Earl of Greta, and his wife. There they had lain since the middle of the fifteenth century while the walls decayed around them. On the one hand Mrs Briggs did not think it right that they should be disturbed after resting over three hundred years in one place; on the other she knew the walls of the chapel must give way at some point and when they did, the tomb would be smashed and their bones ground back into the clay. That did not seem fitting either.

She had given the thought voice one evening a few days

previously while playing Quadrille at Silverside with the Vizegräfin, the Vizegräfin's son, and Mr Sturgess. The Vizegräfin declared she had always thought the place absolutely perfect for a summerhouse. '*So* medieval that the local people persist in calling it the Island of Bones,' she had said, laying down her cards. 'Let the First Lord Greta and his wife be moved to Crosthwaite Church – far more suitable – then they can call it something nicer. Briggs Island, perhaps,' she added, and sniggered a little into her cards. Mr Sturgess had supported the Princess wholeheartedly. The Vizegräfin's son, Felix, had contributed nothing to the conversation but a yawn.

Mrs Briggs had presumed the subject would be forgotten as the cards were laid down, but the following morning Mr Sturgess had called at Silverside to tell them that the vicar of Crosthwaite would be happy to receive the tomb and the bones it contained, and to give Sir Luke and his wife a home on consecrated ground. The Vizegräfin began to draw plans for a summerhouse. Mrs Briggs was still not convinced about the necessity of rebuilding, but at least the nagging guilt about the First Lord Greta's mortal remains would be removed, and she was hopeful that the Vizegräfin and her son would leave Silverside before she had to commit to constructing any of the gothic wonders that now decorated that noble lady's sketchpad.

The Vizegräfin moved swiftly towards the tomb, leaving Mrs Briggs to follow her. As she passed, Mrs Briggs noticed spots of colour on her guest's cheeks. She bore down on the two labourers whose efforts had finally dislodged the cover from the tomb. Thin-faced, mean-looking men, they stood behind the opened tomb like penitents with their heads lowered and their caps in their hands. The Vizegräfin's dark-blue skirts brushed over the stone flags, stirring last autumn's dead leaves. She walked with a straight back and a quick even step that had been perfected by a number of expensive dance masters in her youth, so she gave the impression of floating from one place to the next in time to some unseen music. To the men at the tomb, it seemed as if one of the prettier saints had broken free of the stained glass in Crosthwaite Church, but she aged as she approached through the shadows of ruined masonry and overhanging foliage. The young and graceful female became, as she drew closer, a woman something over forty whose dress and deportment were perhaps a little more hopeful than wise.

Mrs Briggs glanced at the effigies of Sir Luke and his wife. Their stone faces had become washed and worn with rain and snow. They looked weary and ready for a warmer bed. Their hands were held over their chests in attitudes of prayer. At the lady's feet, a greyhound was curled with its alabaster nose tucked into its tail, and its ears flat; at the gentleman's sat a tiny lion, its mane carved in carefully tumbled locks. It reminded Mrs Briggs of the style Felix von Bolsenheim had of arranging his hair. He had avoided their party, calling his mother morbid, and taken his longbow out to hunt rabbits on the fells instead. The Lady had apple cheeks; the Lord was bearded and had a long nose. Mrs Briggs had recently donated, from the collection at Silverside Hall, a portrait of this gentleman to the new museum in Keswick. She had always felt that the portrait disapproved of her and had been glad to be rid of it, having deserted it in an upper corridor for thirty years. The painted face seemed to her always to be stiff with outrage that his lands were now in the possession of a man who had started life as a clerk.

The Vizegräfin reached the lip of the tomb and looked down into it, then gave a little screech and hastened away. Mrs Briggs approached more carefully and took in the sight with less eagerness and greater calm, Mr Sturgess at her side. There were two wooden coffins within, as had been advertised by the effigies, and though worn and rotten, their structures had held. But across the two coffins lay this extra body, a corpse incongruous even in a tomb. It was curled head to knees, its flesh turned leathery, its clothes faded, its mouth pulled wide open. There was a dry, almost sweet scent to the air. Even Mr Sturgess looked pale and Mrs Briggs so far forgot herself as to bite the side of her thumb. She thought the Vizegräfin noticed and frowned at her.

They were silent a moment. Mrs Briggs could hear the call of the lapwing on the Walla Crag, and the regular beat of the woodsman's axe in the park on the opposite side of Derwent Water.

'How very odd,' she said at last.

'What are we to do?' the Vizegräfin questioned, glancing between them. 'Mr Sturgess, as magistrate here, can you advise us? Who is this man?'

'I cannot possibly tell you, madam.' He stepped away, considering. 'This body may be nearly as ancient as those on whom he lies, or he may have died within five years. Who can say? But perhaps the body might rest at Silverside Hall while some enquiries are made, Mrs Briggs? One of our older residents may remember a man gone missing, though I myself cannot recall any such matter in my time here. If not, then I suppose

Crosthwaite Church may give him a Christian burial. I cannot see what else might be done.'

'Perhaps we should summon my brother Charles,' the Vizegräfin said quietly, then, as she found the others looking at her: 'You know he has become quite renowned at ferreting all sorts of information from a body. It might interest him. Will you be so kind as to invite him, Mrs Briggs? And there is a woman, a widow now who seems to involve herself in his interests. You had better invite her too. They might arrive in time for your party if you are willing to go to the expense of an express.'

'They would be very welcome at Silverside Hall, Vizegräfin.'

'I understand from the newspapers that my brother lives in Sussex now, and goes by the name of Gabriel Crowther. The woman's name is Harriet Westerman.'

I.2

Monday, 7 July 1783, Caveley Park, near Hartswood, Sussex

GABRIEL CROWTHER RODE UP to Caveley Park at a furious pace and handed his sweating horse to the stable lad without a word. On being shown into the salon where Mrs Harriet Westerman was at work at her accounts, he took advantage of long friendship by throwing himself down on the sofa at the far end of the room and staring at her carpet with an expression of loathing. If he noticed that Mrs Westerman's young son and his tutor were in the room and working at their lessons within a few feet of him, he gave no sign of it. Harriet had looked up from her papers long enough to mark him and his manner, but she continued to write as she spoke.

'Mr Quince. It seems Mr Crowther is not in one of his sociable moods. Perhaps you and Stephen may continue this morning's work in the library.'

Mr Quince, who resembled nothing so much as an egg that had learned the trick of tying a cravat, stood and gathered his pupil's books, made his bows and headed for the door at once. Stephen followed him, but reluctantly, looking back at his mother. She noticed and smiled at him. 'Off you go, young man. And work hard at your sums. I feel the lack of such learning today.' He sighed noisily, and though his shoulders slumped he followed Mr Quince dutifully enough.

As Harriet turned back to the pages in front of her she noticed she had smudged the ink of her last entry with her sleeve. 'How did I become so clumsy with my pen?' she said, as much to herself as her companion, and tried to dab at the mark with her handkerchief. It seemed to spread. 'At least when I was in full mourning the marks were not so visible. Now Mrs Heathcote finds a new one to scold me over every week.' Seeing that Crowther was still intent on her carpet she tucked one of her red locks behind her ear. 'The most current *Advertiser* is under the cushion to your right, Crowther.' She looked back down at the accounts in front of her.

Harriet Westerman had been a widow for some twenty months now and was beginning to become accustomed to her grief. She had put off her mourning clothes with regret a year after her husband was murdered. Her dresses had continued muted in their tones another six months, but as the spring of

1783 had shown itself in the bright green fuzz on the silver birches, and the hawthorn had begun to star the hedgerows around Hartswood with white, she had felt she was required once more to adopt the colours she had worn as a hopeful wife and mother. It was necessary. Her husband's success as a Captain in the Royal Navy had earned him a handsome estate. Now it needed to be managed, and Harriet realised that her steward came to her more readily when he did not fear he would be interrupting her grief. She had two children, Stephen and his sister Anne. She wanted them to grow up cheerful and active, and knew that they therefore needed an example of cheerfulness and activity in their mother. Her mourning ring she kept on her left hand alongside her promissory ring. It was small enough to feel like a purely personal indulgence and she tried to check her habit of twisting it to and fro on her finger when alone or in deep thought. The residents of Hartswood, her family and friends, began to congratulate themselves and each other on her apparent recovery.

In their sympathy and attempts to offer comfort and consolation, her acquaintances had often hurt her. Harriet had never realised quite how dull-witted some people could be. Some had suggested that widowhood would be easier for her to bear as her husband's duties had often kept him at sea for long periods. It was as if they expected she would forget from time to time that he was dead at all. Others intimated that her husband would be pleased she was still young and handsome enough to attract a man who might take his place. She had managed not to let her temper rise on such occasions, at first because in the desperation of her loss she had hardly heard the words. Later she had found she could bear to keep a resigned smile on her face and her tongue still if she drove her nails into her palm as such people spoke to her. She already had a reputation for unconventional behaviour, and though letting loose her tongue would be a relief, society would begin to distance itself from her if her manners in company were not impeccable, and to some degree her estate, her family and her friends would suffer.

Such social niceties had never troubled Gabriel Crowther. He visited only two houses in the neighbourhood, Caveley and Thornleigh Hall, home of the young Earl of Sussex, his guardian and his family. There Crowther found people whose company he could tolerate, or even enjoy in moderation, but he would trouble himself with the local gentry no further. He ignored them, and when that was insufficient he was rude. It was an effective strategy that gave him the leisure he required to continue his anatomical studies in peace.

Harriet completed another column of figures in her firm neat hand, then frowned when they did not add up as she expected and twisted her mourning ring. Crowther had noticed Harriet's habit of driving her nails into her palm when the local ladies fluttered about her; he had told her sharply not to be foolish. A week later, a matron of Pulborough was unfortunate enough to quote an improving passage on grief to Mrs Westerman in his presence. It was a passage she had been to the trouble of memorising for the poor widow, and she was rather proud of it. When she was done and blinking damply into Harriet's face, waiting for her reaction, Crowther had put his fingertips together and in a cold drawl began to speak. For anyone other than the families of Thornleigh Hall and Caveley to hear his voice was a novelty, but from between his thin lips there emerged such a devastating critique of her logic, and of the literary quality of the passage, that the matron wished he might be struck dumb again at once, and her husband thought he might have to issue a challenge.

Mrs Westerman's sister, Rachel, and the Earl of Sussex's guardian, Mr Graves, tactfully intervened. Such were their skills, the company could convince itself no insult had been offered and the matron's husband was allowed to return to his discussion of the current sport. The story of the encounter must have spread, however, for no one was seen pressing improving books and quotations on the widow again, at least not when there was any danger of Mr Crowther overhearing.

Harriet heard a snort of contempt from the sofa and looked up again. Crowther was reading the page in front of him with arms extended and lip curled.

'I conclude you are reading the letter from Paris about the causes of this strange weather we are suffering under.'

'I am, madam.' He paused. She remained looking at him. 'Do you wish to explain your fortunate guess?'

Harriet raised her eyebrows. 'It was no guess, Crowther. News of the war with the French you read without feeling, news of the court or the arts you do not read at all, news of death or crime you read with weary disdain. Only an individual offering conclusions you think faulty in the natural sciences could rouse you to anger.'

Crowther looked back down at the paper in front of him, and said sullenly, 'I have reason to be angry. This correspondent begins well enough. Listen: *"The multitude therefore may be easily supposed to draw strange conclusions when they see the sun of a blood colour shed a melancholy light and cause a most sultry heat"*. Very well, and so they may do — but so does this man. To leap from there to "*This, however, is nothing more than a very natural effect from a hot sun after a long succession of heavy rain,*" is nonsense. Any child knows a damp fog. This summer has nothing of that in it.'

Harriet stood from her desk and moved towards the French windows that gave her a view of the lawns and shrubbery to the west of the house, putting her hand to the base of her spine. The grass looked yellow and feeble. She felt this summer that her home was becoming small and pinched after the pleasant cool of spring. She was breathless, confined, and there was no clean air; the season seemed to pant with its little hot winds and lash out with sudden lightning like a child with a fever.

'It has been a foul month, with the heat, and this dry wind that seems to parch the leaves and claps the doors, but gives no relief from this mist.' She turned away from the window and began to walk up and down the length of the salon. 'I have had three workers collapse in the heat, yet the sun itself is hardly visible. If you scorn this gentleman's explanation, what is your own?'

Crowther shrugged. 'Because I cannot give you an alternative does not mean I have to swallow any pap that is offered to me. However, accounts of earthquakes in Italy this year make me suspect that the matter thrown up from the earth on such occasions may be the cause. Think of this sulphurous tang in the air.'

Harriet paused in her walking and sniffed the air above her head a moment before replying, 'True. Mrs Heathcote believes it to be the smell of the Devil come out from Hell to breathe on the land. She tells me so every morning when she gives me my coffee, and complains that the brass fittings of the house are tarnishing as quickly as she can make the maids polish them. But can foreign earthquakes also produce the storms we have been victim to?'

Crowther buried his chin in his chest. 'We English *must* make such a mystery of our weather. There are storms every year, yet we always think them harbingers of the Apocalypse and act as if we saw lightning for the first time. Because two things happen at once does not mean they originate from the same cause.'

Harriet put her hand to her forehead. 'They have been unusually severe, but very well, sir. I shall not hide under the altar of the church as yet. But if someone gave me a witching cure for this weather, I would try it. It pushes me down so, Crowther. I feel as if I am carrying a body across my shoulders every step I take. Yet I must always seem cheerful.' She noticed he was looking at her from under his hooded lids with careful attention. She restarted her walk and said in a lighter tone, 'But tell me what has caused you to come to us in such an unpleasant mood this morning.'

He put the paper down. 'I had the pleasure of seeing my house pointed out to a party of pleasure-seekers this morning, and found myself, in my own parlour, being identified as a curiosity of the area like a bearded woman at the county fair.'

She turned again on the carpet and her skirts rippled, falling over themselves in an attempt to keep pace with her. 'You *are* a curiosity, Crowther,' she said, folding her arms across her bodice. 'You should have waved your scalpel at them. They would have drunk all of the best brandy at the Bear and Crown to recover their nerves and you could have charged Michaels a commission on the sales.'

She dropped into a seat opposite him with a rustle of silk and leaned back, trying to pull the warm air of the room into her lungs. Her conscience was still a little troubled by her role in forcing Crowther out of seclusion. Three years previously, she had persuaded him to become involved in her enquiries into the affairs of Thornleigh Hall. There had been deaths, and Crowther's own history of family scandal had been thrown into the light and picked over in the newspapers. Yet they had managed to protect the current Earl and his sister, and seen them take possession of the Hall in the care of their guardians. It had cost them both, and neither were the people they once had been, but she could not regret those decisions made.

'Yet *we* are fortunate. Graves and Mrs Service have to allow parties of ladies and gentlemen through Thornleigh Hall half the days of the week and watch them examining the floorboards for bloodstains.'

'Let them lock the gates then.'

'Crowther,' Harriet said, 'how could they? It is their duty to be stared at.'

Crowther's further thoughts on the troubles suffered by the Earl of Sussex's family were lost as the door to the salon opened and Mrs Heathcote entered with a letter on a tray. She presented it to the gentleman rather abruptly. Mrs Heathcote had been housekeeper of Caveley since its purchase, and regarded both Mrs Westerman and her sister as a good pair of girls who only needed proper managing. It was a sign that he was accepted almost as part of the family that she now regarded Mr Crowther in a similar light.

'There we have found you, Mr Crowther! An express arrived for you and Hannah thought you would have come here, you having left your own house in such a temper, and so she has brought it along. I would offer you coffee, but it has such a stimulating effect. Perhaps you had better have some of Miss Rachel's Nerve Drops until you are in a better humour. Now, will you take your dinner here, or must Hannah have something by for your convenience?'

Crowther realised he had probably been brusque with Hannah, his own housekeeper, before he left his home and recognised that he was now being punished for it. He took the letter and unfolded it, trying to ignore both Harriet's stifled laugh and Mrs Heathcote's stony gaze.

'I can forego the drops, Mrs Heathcote,' he said, with his eyes cast down. 'My thanks and apologies to Hannah. I shall dine here, if I am welcome.'

Harriet waved her hand with a smile and Mrs Heathcote, encouraged by this display of Crowther's improved manners, nodded. 'There now. Very good, sir. You know she has enough to manage at the moment.' With that she swept out of the room like a 40-gun frigate under full sail.

When the door closed Harriet laughed hard enough to bring tears into her eyes while Crowther read his express. When she had recovered sufficiently she asked: 'What extra work are you giving poor Hannah, Crowther? Has she finally begun to regret entering your service?'

'At times, I am sure she has,' he replied, continuing to read. 'I have had several samples from London arrive in a despoiled state due to the heat. They had lost all interest scientifically and I am informed the smell of decay was very difficult to remove from the drapery.'

This confession was enough to send Harriet into a further

fit of laughter, so it was some time before she could ask what was the matter of the letter Crowther held in his hand. His reply soon quieted her. His expression was rather wondering, his eyebrows lifted, and he reread the message with his head tilted to one side, as if unsure of what he was seeing on the paper in front of him.

'I am requested, and the invitation is extended to yourself, to go into the Lake Country near Keswick. My sister, the Vizegräfin Margaret von Bolsenheim, is staying in our former home with her son as guests of the current owner. And they have found a body.'

Harriet left Crowther shortly afterwards to dress for dinner, and to inform her sister that she intended to journey immediately into Cumberland. The invitation had delighted her. She had never seen that part of the country, and in the heat her household duties had become ever more irksome and confining. Yet every pleasure had a price on it. In this case the price was, she was certain, about to be extracted by her sister.

Rachel Trench was the darling of the neighbourhood. A paragon of everything a young woman should be, she was pretty and charming with a lively manner that never went beyond what was proper to her situation in life. She read novels, but did not talk about them too much. She appreciated music and sang rather well, but never gave long displays of her talent. Only her somewhat unusual sister was regarded as a slight blot and some had worried that even Miss Trench's excellent character might be tainted by sharing a home with her so long. However, in 1780, the year that Harriet had first forced her acquaintance on Crowther, Rachel had met a young and very handsome lawyer from Pulborough by the name of Daniel Clode. He had had some share in the adventures of the family since that time and had been present in Captain Westerman's last moments. The mutual affection between Rachel and Daniel had been plain throughout, and when Harriet put off her mourning clothes, their engagement was announced. The neighbourhood breathed a sigh of relief. Some thought that perhaps Miss Trench might have found a better match, but all agreed it was best that she be removed from Caveley. Mr Clode came from nowhere, his parents were barely respectable, but now he handled so much business for the estate of the Earl of Sussex, he was more and more noticed in society, and it was hoped marriage to Rachel might put the final polish on him.

Rachel, while modest about her own qualities and proud of her sister's bravery, was painfully aware of local opinion. Harriet knew she did not worry on her own account, or not greatly, but rather was concerned about her nephew and niece, and wondered what effect their mother's reputation might have on their prospects. Harriet found the burden of this rather wide-eyed concern intensely irritating. Particularly because, as Crowther had occasionally pointed out to her, her temper was always more likely to fly when she felt herself in the wrong. Harriet knew it hurt Rachel to see her the subject of any number of lurid pamphlets, and it made her tremble to be introduced as 'the sister of *the* Mrs Westerman'. It was unlikely, therefore, she would welcome the news that Harriet intended to abandon her household on a moment's notice and travel hundreds of miles to view a corpse.

Harriet found Rachel in her chamber writing a letter. Harriet suspected it was to her fiancé. She was happy to see that their affection – for it was an acknowledged love match – was so warm that although they met every other day, their letters still flowed back and forth. Fixing on the correspondence as a chance to delay mentioning her trip, Harriet asked what was the subject of her letter.

Rachel smiled at her sister and said briskly, 'Daniel is eager to set a date for our marriage. I write to ask him to be patient.'

'Why, for heaven's sake?' asked Harriet. 'The household is out of mourning. Marry him as soon as you may. I have always thought late September a fine time for a wedding. Then you may spend your first winter locked up together before you have had time to tire of each other's company.'

Rachel put down her pen. 'I hope I may never tire of his company.' She crossed to the armchair where her sister was seated and took her place at her feet, reaching up for her hands and taking them between her own. Harriet looked down at her, more golden in her colouring where she was red, and wondered unkindly if her looks would fade as she aged. 'But Harry, I cannot leave you alone yet. Little Anne is so young and I know you miss James still. And Stephen will be going away to school soon. You are used to having people about you. I shall ask Daniel to wait a year or two longer. He will understand.'

Harriet removed her hands and frowned into the carpet. 'Rachel, I shall miss my husband every day until my death. If you put off your marriage for that reason, you and Daniel will die of old age before I am done grieving.' She waited a moment till she could be sure her voice was steady again. 'You are not even leaving Hartswood, for goodness sake. I know

Clode has made enquiries about the Mansel House in the village – Michaels told me. Once you have returned from your wedding trip we shall meet every day. Crowther is often here, and the family from Thornleigh. Do not play the martyr out of pity for me.'

'But Harry . . .'

'Set the date, Rachel. But I fear I shall have no time to assist in the arrangements for some time. Crowther and I leave for Cumberland in the morning. His sister has discovered a desiccated corpse there and we mean to go and see it.'

Rachel flushed. 'This is some joke!'

Harriet smiled tightly. 'No joke at all. We are invited by Mrs Briggs, the most respectable owner of Silverside Hall. I have never seen the Lake Country and yet I am constantly being told how charming it is. Do you remember when the Rollinsons went there last summer? All the women in the family were driven into verse by its charms. I only wish they had confined themselves to nature poetry rather than composing odes on the anniversary of James's murder. As for the other matter, I have never seen a desiccated corpse before either. It has all the novelty of the landscape, and there is no danger of it inspiring poetry – a great advantage. Someone took the trouble to place it in a tomb, you know. Someone else's tomb, I mean. On an island. It's most intriguing.'

Although Rachel had turned away, Harriet could see the colour on her cheek. She might have a reputation for her sweet nature, but she had courage to match Harriet's when it was called on, and a stubbornness that was no less powerful for being better concealed. 'And what is to become of us, while you are gone?' she demanded now. 'Stephen, baby Anne and myself? I am grieved we do not provide sufficient novelty, Harry, but you cannot simply throw a dust-sheet over our heads when you wish to be somewhere else.'

Harriet hesitated for a moment, and then said: 'I shall not leave you and my daughter here alone. You may all decamp to Thornleigh Hall and Mrs Service can chaperone you in my stead. As to Stephen, I intend to take him and his tutor with me. I am sure the visit will be most instructive.'

'You wish to show him the corpse?' Rachel said, shocked.

'No, of course not. I mean the mountains and lakes, and so forth.' Harriet waved her hand in the air to describe the extent of the educational possibilities available. 'Though there is no point in being too precious with Stephen. If he continues in his wish to enter the Navy, he will see corpses enough before long.'

'He has already seen his father's,' Rachel murmured, and the air left Harriet's lungs rather suddenly. 'I suppose you may dispose of us as you wish, Sister.'

The bitterness in her voice was such Harriet held out her hand again, but Rachel would not take it. She continued instead, 'You seem very courageous to some, Harry, but you and I both know you are simply running away. When did your home become such a prison to you?'

Harriet found she had no breath to reply, so unwillingly adding weight to her sister's words, she got to her feet and left the room.

I.3

Tuesday, 15 July 1783, Keswick, Cumberland

STEPHEN WESTERMAN ENJOYED the preparations for the journey from Sussex to Cumberland immensely. At nine years old he was unencumbered by the necessity of taking any part in planning the arrangements, so was at perfect liberty to enjoy all the fuss taking place around him. The trip had been prepared for in a single night. The house at Caveley, so quiet since the death of his father, had been thrown by his mother's sudden decision into a state of busy confusion. Firstly the family at Thornleigh Hall were consulted, and a warm invitation to Rachel, little Anne and her nurse was immediately extended and gratefully accepted. Her family thus dispensed with, Harriet had set about her arrangements. The rooms became busy with orders and requests, the scratching of pens and the creak of leather bands tightening round chests and boxes. It made a stirring in Stephen's heart. He ran from room to room, fetching and carrying until his feet were sore.

Years of service with a family used to the demands of the Royal Navy had made the servants quick and efficient packers. However Mr Quince, Stephen's tutor, was not used to such sudden changes of residence and Stephen could not help noticing his mother's eyes begin to flash and her foot start to tap as the man tried to slim down his library of leisure reading and instruction manuals to a size suitable for travel.

The candles had burned all night, and in the confusion no one remembered to send Stephen to bed until midnight had passed. This, and watching his shirts packed flat and the lid slammed shut over them confirmed him in the idea that he was about to embark on a great adventure. He had often been told that travel and exploration were in his blood. His parents had circled the globe before his birth and he himself had been born at sea. However, his own experience of travel was confined to the occasional visit to London, and once going to meet his father at Portsmouth on the return of his ship to home waters. Now at last he was going to see the world, or at least some other part of it. The only thing that gave him pause was realising that his favourite possession, an elaborate model of his father's last command, HMS *Splendour*, was too large and delicate an object to take on a journey of this sort. He consoled himself by finding it a station on the table in the nursery where its tiny crew could examine the park beyond the window in his absence.

The following days of travel were crowded with novelty. He slept soundly in a number of strange beds and ate with relish whatever was put in front of him at the inns where they stopped to change horses. His mother spent part of each day travelling with him, his tutor and the majority of the luggage in the second carriage, and they competed to point out elements of the landscape to each other as the countryside began to subtly shift its shape. It was a delight to have so much of her time, and she laughed more often than she had been used to of late. The accents of the postilions and servants in the inns began to change, then change again, and under the guidance of his tutor and mother, Stephen began to get some creeping sense of the variety of his country.

The final day of the journey had begun very early, and as his mother was travelling with Mr Crowther, Stephen slept deeply as only the young can in a jolting carriage. So he found himself being gently shaken awake by Mr Quince as the carriage began its approach to the ancient market town of Keswick. His tutor smiled at him and told him to look out of the window.

'That river you see is called the Greta,' the young man said. Stephen hauled himself forward and peered out of the window. Mr Quince consulted his guide to the area, a present from Thornleigh Hall. 'Greta is the name of the family who used to own much of this land in the past. Do you remember our discussions of the Rebellions of 1715 and 1745, Stephen? Can you tell me anything of them?'

Stephen yawned. 'In 1715 the Old Pretender landed in Scotland but was driven off by the Duke of Argyll. Then in 1745 Bonnie Prince Charlie had a try at it and Cumberland did for him at Culloden in 1746. Why do you ask, sir?'

'Lord Greta joined the Old Pretender in 1715 and was tried for treason the following year. He escaped into exile. I think it was after that, that Mr Crowther's family came into possession of this land.' He looked as if he wished to press Stephen on his history further, but the boy quickly pointed upwards.

'What is the name of that mountain, Mr Quince?'

Mr Quince checked in his book. 'That is the mighty Skiddaw.'

It was mighty indeed, Stephen thought. The huge flanks of the mountains rose up around him like fairytale giants, their sides mottled and softened with bracken, becoming more broken as they rose with rocky outcrops. It was as if a massive stone fist were gradually tearing through a green mantle. He gripped the edge of the window and stared for a moment, then turned back to Mr Quince. 'Do you think there are dragons living there, sir?'

His tutor smiled, deciding that further discussions on the Rebellions would have to wait. He was a young man, modest and sober in his habits and manners, but still able to share something of Stephen's pleasure at the landscape. He closed his guide.

'It looks like the country for them, does it not? We shall have to search for them.'

Crowther had not enjoyed the journey so completely as Stephen, but then he did not think to. Any suggestion that he might delight in the variety or be discomforted by the quality of his accommodation would be met with incomprehension. He had what was sufficient to his needs and there his interest in his material comforts ended. He found it perfectly possible to read as the carriage surged or jolted forward according to the state of the roads and so he passed his time reasonably contented. However, on the morning that they began their final approach to Keswick he found his book no longer held him. He closed it to find Mrs Westerman observing him.

'Crowther, when did you last visit this town?'

He chose to look out of the window as he replied, 'In 1751, madam. The estate was sold in that year to the current owner, Mr Briggs; I came to sign a number of documents and provide for the staff of the estate in my father's name, though I never met the gentleman. The sale was made within three months of my brother's execution. He murdered our father in the late autumn of 1750, and was hanged in the February of the following year.'

The events of Crowther's past were seldom spoken of between them. Crowther had used the wealth he had inherited to bury his personal history deeply, and turn his youthful interest in anatomy into expertise. He had taken his current name and studied under it in Germany, Italy and London, withdrawing finally into Sussex, his wish to avoid any larger world and dedicate his time to the mysteries of how life exists in the actuality of flesh, bone and brain. His involvement with Mrs Westerman and the corpse she had found on the edges of her estate in the summer of 1780 had pulled him from his candlelit study into the public glare of day, and though his bloody heritage had been discovered and exposed, still he kept the name and manners of Gabriel Crowther, the man he had made himself, a man without connections, a free man. It was an uneasy accommodation, and his former name, his former title and place in society could still itch at him from time to time, or rear up growling. No doubt they would do so even more fiercely here.

'And what became of your sister at that time, Crowther?' Harriet said. Crowther looked at the woman opposite him for a moment. Widowhood had not altered her as much as he had feared it might. His sister would be some ten years her senior, he supposed, and might have already made that transition from womanhood to matron that had yet to begin with Harriet.

His sister. She was an infant the age of Anne Westerman when he had left Keswick for his schooling. His visits to the family home had been infrequent from that point. They had met as strangers at the funeral of their mother early in 1750, and when, on his father's murder, a family of Irish cousins had offered to give her a home, he had accepted the proposal at once and with relief. He had thought to write after their brother's death on the scaffold but had abandoned the attempt. She became part of a past he wished nothing of. When his lawyers told him of her marriage, the birth of her son and her separation from her husband he had instructed them to make the proper financial arrangements, and there he felt his obligations ended. Her son would be something of Rachel's age now, and was heir to his wealth and rejected title as well as those the young man would inherit through his own father, a man of minor nobility in one of the Prussian Courts. Crowther wondered, if he had known a Harriet Westerman at that early stage in his life, would events have unfolded differently, but at that time there had been no person so ready, like her, to ignore his wealth, his habit of chilled command as to question him. He had done what best suited him, and never thought of doing otherwise.

'She went to some of my mother's family in Ireland. I have not seen her since then. I told my lawyers not to inform her as to either the new name I took at that time, or my address, though I do not think she ever enquired.'

Harriet turned her ring. 'I am interested to meet her, Crowther. Are you?'

He looked out of the window. 'I do not know, Mrs Westerman.'

She waited for him to continue, but when he did not, said brightly, 'So, sir. We have known each other three years and waded through a great deal of blood together. Would you think me impertinent to ask you for your given name?'

He smiled. 'I was born Charles William Gabriel Penhaligon, and at the moment of my brother's hanging became the Third Baron of Keswick.'

Mrs Westerman considered a moment, then shrugged and said, 'I think we are reaching the outskirts of the town, my lord.'

The little town of Keswick was becoming accustomed to the elegant coaches of strangers appearing in its midst. Since it was founded it had known times of prosperity and poverty. When the hills were discovered to be rich sources of metals in Henry and Elizabeth's day, the inhabitants had found their numbers swelled by German prospectors, and forges and mills had crowded round the rivers. When the mines began to weaken, these buildings had been left to rot and the population had dwindled once more, returning to the ancient agricultural practices of the region while Keswick had hunkered down to wait for better times.

Now the fells and hills were proving to be a source of wealth once more, though in a different fashion. Since the poet Gray's account of his time in the area, the curious had begun to find their way to the town over the improving roads, wishing to see for themselves the landscape of which he had written in such high style. Other descriptions of the area had appeared from time to time, and nowadays few visitors arrived to take rooms at the Royal Oak or Queen's Head without Mr West's guide to the area in one hand, and a Claude glass in the other, eager to be awed by the scenery. The natives of the area were pleased to show off their home and take the guineas of these romantic travellers, so had gained a reputation as generous and friendly hosts. Many had become adept at moulding their histories to the inclinations of their individual guests. To some they pointed out the peaks; to others they spoke of the bogles, fairy people, lost treasures and giants; to others they showed druidical stones and sites of ancient castles built to defend against raids from the borders. In this way, what had been earlier in the century a rather poor little town dreaming of former days of glory had begun to thrive again and take the pleasures of its visitors more seriously with a variety of entertainment and new buildings.

As the carriages passed through the main square, Mr Oliver Askew, one of the prime instigators of these improvements, watched them with interest from the front door of his new museum. The occupants had money enough, he could see that by the comfort in which they travelled, but the equipage was rolling past the better inns towards Portinscale and Silverside Hall. More guests for Mrs Briggs, perhaps. He thought of the skeleton recently discovered in the tomb on St Herbert's Island and rubbed his hands. He had commissioned and received a dramatic, if purely imaginative, sketch of the grisly discovery and was keen to hang it, but he was nervous of the Vizegräfin's reaction to her portrayal. She had heard of his display of pamphlets, cuttings, sketches and curios related to the death of her father and her brother's execution within a day of her arrival at Silverside, and had sent a note to ask that they be removed from display for the length of her stay. Mr Askew was a naturally pugnacious man, and liked to boast about his habits of plain speaking with manly pride, yet something in the tone of the note had snapped his will like a reed and the display was now boxed up in his storeroom till the Vizegräfin might take herself abroad again. For the time being, the picture of the discovery of the skeleton lay under baize to be exhibited to the curious on request, and only when he was sure those making that request were unacquainted with the residents of Silverside.

He turned back into the museum and was glad to feel its relative cool. The little space was lined with all manner of things, his own maps of the area, stuffed animals both foreign and domestic, a collection of mineral samples, an arrow head and a stone axe discovered in a field adjacent to the stone circle. His visitors' book lay open on the counter, ready for the signatures of any person of quality that might wish to see them.

He began to examine the various corners and cabinets for signs of dust. His maid had broken her ankle some weeks ago, and though it looked as if she would mend, he had not been able to find anyone else so neat in her absence. He ran his finger over the frame of an oil painting of *The Luck of Gutherscale Hall*; his finger came up clean, so he stepped back with a small grunt of satisfaction to admire it. *The Luck* was a jewelled cross which had seemed to disappear into the air when the last Earl of Greta joined the rebellion in 1715. Legend said it did not wish to leave the lake, so deserted him and slipped from his saddlebag. The picture hung next to the portrait of the 1st Earl with the Luck in his hand, and the artist had used the portrait as his source and added a few more rubies and an extra diamond or two. It was painted against black, and the artist had been of sufficient skill to make the jewels seem gleaming and alive.

Mr Askew's fairer visitors always sighed over the picture and one in three would buy one of the prettily carved wooden replicas he offered for sale. He wondered how many of them missed the views as they walked by, looking in the streams and under boulders for the thing itself. He had looked himself, especially in the first months of his residence in Keswick. Mr Sturgess had done so too, with some application, but his only find had been the stone axe now on display. What a thing that would be, to have the Luck here in a glass case in the centre of the room where the light from the window would make it shine . . . Askew rubbed his hands together again. His museum would be full every day then, and famous, and no one would then compare it with the pitiful collection of minerals Mr Hale had the nerve to call a museum in Kendal. He would rename his annual regatta on the lake the Regatta of the Luck, and the winner each year would receive a little copy of the Luck itself. It could be processed round the town in the morning, or perhaps during the previous evening by torchlight.

Mr Askew turned his round face towards Heaven with a happy sigh, and remained there, building castles till the bell above the door jangled. A lady and gentleman were crossing his threshold. Father and daughter? Foreign? Mr Askew bowed, blessing the sultry weather, since no lady could stand walking for long in such heat. He saw the young woman's eye caught by the picture and reckoned another wooden cross sold, and no doubt tickets to his lakeside entertainment the next day. Bless the dry fog indeed! Though it stank of the Devil it wafted guineas into his pocket like the breath of angels.

I.4

THEIR APPROACH TO Silverside Hall had been looked for, and when Harriet stepped out of the carriage she was at once greeted by a short, rather square woman of perhaps sixty years, who came very close to her on the gravel and shook her hand so heartily Harriet was afraid for her wrist.

'Oh, Mrs Westerman! I am so glad you are come in time

for our party tomorrow! I know you at once, you see. The papers have been so full of talk of your red hair, I swear I would know you in a crowd – and here you are! "The flame-haired widow"! I am delighted, delighted to welcome you to Silverside. I am Mrs Briggs, you know, and here is my home – yes, the view *is* pretty, and here is the Baron behind you, though of course we must address him as Mr Crowther, must we not? Welcome, sir, welcome!'

Harriet managed to smile and nod during this speech enough to satisfy her hostess while taking in some small part of her surroundings. The carriages had come to a halt in front of a noble building somewhat of the age and size of Caveley, though its granite frontage seemed to be built on a slightly grander scale and was of a darker stone. Glancing behind her, she could see beyond the backs of the horses to a steep open lawn edged with woodland that swept down to the lakeshore, complete with jetty and rowboat. The view across the water was indeed impressive, the lake like pewter below them, the wooded islands, then on the far shore a pleasing mix of fields and woodland lapping upwards to the sweep of the mountains beyond.

Having exchanged bows with Crowther, Mrs Briggs had moved on to the occupants descending from the other coach.

'And here is *Master* Westerman! You will be a hero of the seas like your poor, brave father, I imagine, young sir! And this is your tutor – very good, very good. You have the air of a man who could walk the fells all day and eat a good dinner. Is that not so? I am glad to see it. Now, young Mr Westerman, I hope you will run about and make a great deal of noise while you are here. I insist on it. My children are all grown and gone and I hate to have the place so quiet. Remember, lots of noise!

And you may take the rowboat on to the lake whenever you like. I insist on that also. Miriam!'

A young blonde maid bobbed down the steps behind her mistress, smiling broadly. 'My dear, do show Master Westerman — Stephen, is it, my dear? Very good! Yes, yes, Ham, lead the horses round and have the luggage placed. My, what comfortable-looking carriages they are! Now, Miriam, do show this young man and his tutor — your name, sir? Quince? A fine name. I know several men of that name and nothing but good of them! — and Mr Quince to their rooms, and then I am sure Stephen would like to have a run about the place before we dine. Mrs Westerman, I shall show you to your rooms myself. What a pleasure it is to have the house full!'

And so, without having to trouble themselves to utter a word, the party were ushered into the house.

The lobby was a fine bright place — the walls painted cream and the stone flags broken with large carpets of Turkish design. Harriet thought she caught an expression of slight surprise in Crowther's face.

'Yes, my lord. My apologies — Mr Crowther. No doubt much has changed since your day. But when your father built the place, he was not building it for a family like mine. We seem to need a little more light, hence the changes you see. Though the library is still in the same quarter and we have only added to your father's collection. Lor, how many books that gentleman had. We had to cram in ours any old way. Kittie!'

Another maid appeared. 'Show Mr Crowther into the library, dear. There are some refreshments there, and your sister is waiting to meet you.' Harriet discovered by the friendly pressure on her arm that she was not to go to the library with Crowther, but found herself propelled instead towards the elegant sweep of the staircase.

'Now, Mrs Westerman, let me make you comfortable so you and I may have a dish of tea and something in your sitting room and get acquainted, if you will be my host! I wish to hear all about your journey. Lord, I hate to travel! I have scurried about Europe with my husband in our time, but I would not leave Silverside from one year end to the next if I had my way. But then I would never see my daughter and her children if I did not. Have you met Lady Hill in Town? She is my eldest child, though of course she would have mentioned it in one of her letters if she had made *your* acquaintance . . .'

Mrs Briggs's voice died away behind him as Crowther was led into the library. This room was indeed much as he remembered it from his childhood. The last day he had spent here had been the eve of his father's funeral while his elder brother spent that night in Carlisle Prison before being sent for trial at the House of Lords. He had sat here a little while. When he went back to Keswick to complete the business of selling the house and land he had not returned to the house itself but had taken advantage of his lawyer's hospitality in Keswick. He had told himself the arrangement was more convenient, but in truth when he had left the room to see his father buried he had sworn never to come back. Yet here he was – and the room, it seemed, had been waiting for him. Heavy drapes across the windows filtered out the sunlight leaving the space a cavern of shadows in tobacco browns and bottle greens. The old spiral staircase still stood in the middle of the far wall, giving access to the narrow runway that ran round the shelves of the upper level. He realised it was the one part of the house he had missed a little.

What light there was still seemed to fall in the same way — unhurried, as if it entered the library to rest. The considerable floorspace was scattered with armchairs and low tables. In the centre of the room were the promised refreshments. The wine decanter gleamed red; a clean glass stood next to it. There was a movement from one of the armchairs that sat with its back to him, and a thin hand extended, its fingers covered with jewels that echoed the wine sleeping in the decanter, and placed another glass, part-filled, on the table next to the first. There was a rustle of fabric and the lady stood. Crowther saw thin shoulders and hair swept up from the neck and powdered. Then, slowly, she turned.

Crowther would not have known the woman before him as his sister if they had passed on the London streets, yet as he looked at her, around her eyes, in the height of her cheekbones and slimness of her form, he saw something he recognised from the mirrors in his own house, or the reflections he caught in the glass of one of his preserving bottles. She could have been a statue, but the lines around her eyes and mouth were too delicate for any sculptor to have made. He felt her eyes travel slowly over him, and he made his bow. She dressed a little young. Suddenly her shoulders relaxed and she came towards him with her hands extended. Crowther fought the impulse to step backwards.

'Charles!' she said with apparent delight. 'Or rather I shall call you Gabriel. I have so rarely heard either name in my mouth. I can swap them with ease.'

He set down his cane to take her hands. 'Margaret. You look well.'

She gave a shrug. 'Oh, I look old. You missed me at my bloom.'

'I am sorry for that.'

'Are you?' She returned to her seat and perched on it, slightly pouting, and watched him settle himself opposite her. 'I rather doubt it, but I give you credit for saying so.'

Crowther did not reply but poured wine for himself and drank it. It was very good and he remembered vaguely that Mr Briggs had had an interest in the import of liquors.

'So, my lord, what do you think of our childhood home? This room excepted, it is all much changed.' Her tone suggested she did not entirely approve. 'Do you remember how Addie used this space to put on his little plays? When he came up from London I would beg to have a part. Did he ever recruit you?'

'From time to time,' Crowther said, studying her, 'but I fear I was never much of a performer. I found the whole business humiliating.' She gave a knowing smile at that which Crowther found irritating.

'Have you reached that stage of life where one becomes terribly interested in one's own past? Is that why you are here?' she said.

'I came because I was asked,' Crowther replied.

'Is it so simple to conjure you? I had no idea. You mean to say that if I had requested you come to me as a girl in Ireland, or as a young wife in Vienna, I would have had the pleasure of knowing my brother before now?'

Her voice was still light, the babble of the drawing room,

but there was a brittleness there too. Crowther regarded her carefully.

'I have never observed that my acquaintanceship gives much pleasure,' he told her. 'I cannot say, Margaret, if I would have come; the occasion did not arise. But it is possible I would *not* have done so unless the circumstances were extraordinary. We have never known each other; perhaps I would have thought it better to leave it so.'

The Vizegräfin lifted her hand to cover her lips as she drank, blinking rapidly. 'And of course, I have never been able to offer the additional attraction of a mysterious corpse before now. You are honest, at least. I am not surprised. I knew when I was established in Ireland that you wanted nothing to do with any of us.'

'Any of us?'

'I mean my mother, my father, our brother *or* myself.'

Crowther leaned back in his chair. 'Three of the persons you have mentioned were dead. It would have required some great spiritual intervention for me to have any commerce with them.'

She set the glass back a little sharply on the table. The coquette disappeared; her features seemed to sharpen and age. 'They were somehow a great deal more dead to you than they were to me, Gabriel. You would not even do the duty of thinking about them. I did. I felt my losses. You cut them off from you like rotten wood, and myself with them.'

Crowther paused, looking into the air above them as if considering the question for the first time, then replied, 'Yes. That is true.'

He heard his sister take a sharp breath and wondered how

this scene had played in her imagination before he had opened the door. Had she expected him to be ashamed? Had she thought he would approach her on his knees, weeping in self-reproach the moment she put out her hands? If so, he felt a sudden burst of pleasure to have disappointed her. She continued: 'I note you do not come to me in a penitent or sentimental mood. Good. I would not think better of you for it.'

Crowther realised he did not care very much what his sister thought of him. Part of his mind told him he should feel guilt, but he would not. He had made his decisions and would not now revel in feigned regret. 'Do you feel I have wronged you so greatly, Margaret? You have always been well provided for, and as I said, you have never made the attempt to establish any communication with me.'

'I was a child. It was your *duty* to write. And later in life . . . Your pride is in our blood. You were born with it forming the spine of your character, as was I. How could I turn to someone who had so conclusively turned away from me?'

Crowther did not reply directly to this.

'I hope your time with the O'Brien family was not unhappy.'

'They were kind to me.'

'I am glad of it.' They were silent for a while until Crowther asked, 'And your son is well?'

She watched him from under lowered lids. 'You shall meet Felix at dinner. He is young and more idle than is good for him. I wish I had had more children, but I had already remained longer with my husband than I should have. My pride again. I did not wish to admit it to myself, let alone to the world at large, but the marriage was a mistake.'

Crowther dropped his hands to his lap, feeling tired and

somewhat trapped. It was an emotion he knew well and associated strongly with rich women speaking of their disappointments. Why had he come here? If he had not seen his house being pointed out as a curiosity in Hartswood the day the express arrived, perhaps he would have resisted. If his sister had left the room now with a promise never to see him again, he would have been quite happy to let her go. When she spoke again, her voice had resumed the dancing cadence of the drawing room.

'Who is this Mrs Westerman who has dragged you back out into the light again, Gabriel? Who has succeeded where so many before have failed? A Naval wife, is she not? Is she of good family?'

Crowther stood and retrieved his cane.

'Her father had a parish in Norfolk, I believe.' The Vizegräfin snorted into her glass, her eyes a little brighter. He thought women of her age should not wear so many rings. They made their fingers appear more clawlike and scrabbling. 'And her husband was an extremely successful Commander until his murder in eighty-one. She has not your taste for fine jewellery, but if what I understand is correct, his prize money could purchase your husband's estates twice over.' His sister continued to sip her wine without looking at him, smiling. She knew she had needled him, and Crowther felt a surge of irritation that he had showed it.

'I find the journey has wearied me more than I had thought,' he said now. 'We shall meet again at dinner.'

He had thought the conversation concluded and already moved towards the door when the Vizegräfin spoke again.

'You still carry our father's cane with you, Gabriel. Family must mean something to you.'

Crowther's fingers twitched on the latch and he left the room.

'Do you like it, my dear?' Mrs Briggs asked.

Harriet's private sitting room on the first floor in fact delighted her. It was a pretty chamber that managed to be tasteful without unnecessary fuss. The walls were papered and the Chinoiserie designs of peacock, peony and branch made the room light. The furniture was honey-coloured and on the little round table set in the window was a bowl of foxgloves. Mrs Briggs stepped into the room to adjust the fall of the stems. She seemed a little nervous now, for all her volubility on their arrival.

'Quite lovely,' Harriet replied, and Mrs Briggs flushed a little.

'Fairy flowers, my mother always called these. She used to make tea for my father with them when his chest hurt him. All the marigolds in the garden have withered in this strange weather, but these flourish.' She smiled at her guest and took her seat on one of the armchairs by the table. 'But come, Mrs Westerman, take off your gloves and let us be comfortable.'

Harriet was happy to exchange the swaying carriage for the chair indicated, and within ten minutes of taking her place she found that she and her hostess were in the way of coming to a good understanding of each other. No matter how she had talked them into the house, Mrs Briggs was also an attentive and curious listener. Before Harriet could quite take measure of the way her own tongue was running on, she realised Mrs Briggs now knew as much about her home and household as her nearest neighbours, and rather more than they did about her husband's death. The woman offered no homilies, she did not clutch her hand and offer to weep with her, and neither did she retreat into the language of euphemism when speaking of death. Harriet found she spoke with more freedom and feeling because of it. She finished her narration of the events of 1781 and lowered her head, rather shocked by her own openness. Perhaps Caveley had been pressing on her even more than she had imagined.

'Oh, it is a horror and no mistaking it,' Mrs Briggs said, shaking her grey curls. 'I am glad the man who killed your husband died such a death, though I am sure you wish you could have struck the blow with your own hand. So many of our good men die before they see their children grown, while the fat and lazy lie all comfortable in their beds and when they rise cause nothing but trouble.' She spoke with such conviction Harriet wondered if she herself had suffered such a loss, yet she knew Mr Briggs was alive and superintending some of his business interests abroad.

The question must have appeared on her face, for Mrs Briggs explained: 'It was a sweetheart of my youth I lost, Mrs Westerman. And I thought I would never recover from it. He was killed in a brawl in a tavern in Manchester. Such a stupid, pointless death. Yet they all are, however much we try to dress them up.'

'Indeed,' Harriet replied.

'Though of course I was only fifteen then, and recovered from my loss. I would not have such a fine house or fine view if I had married Ambrose Muncaster, apprentice butcher! No, Mr Briggs was only a clerk when I met him, but ambitious — very ambitious. Then came the first store and he began to import, and here we all are.'

Harriet stiffened slightly, expecting remarks on the healing power of time to follow and explanations of the various, secret destinies God has planned for us all. She was rather brutally spared. 'But of course I was a great deal younger than you then, and had not his children before me as constant reminders of what was lost to us both.'

'Is Mr Briggs still ambitious?'

Mrs Briggs threw up her hands. 'Lord, yes! It is his nature and I cannot change it or wish it otherwise. I cannot expect a man to alter his character as soon as I feel I have money enough and want his company at home. Here we are as comfortable as can be, and in such a beautiful situation, good neighbours and good hunting, but he cannot stay here a month together, much as he cares for it and me, before he is as strung and twitchy as a rabbit smelling a fox. "John," I say, when I see him gnawing his nails over the paper or standing up just to sit down again three times in a quarter of an hour, "you are a foolish old man and should learn to keep still, but I cannot change you, so off to Portugal with you. Send me long letters and I shall see you in six months." Then he looks as delighted as a boy let off church, mumbles something about irrigation of the vines in the current season and away he goes.'

Harriet laughed. 'And does he write you long letters?'

'Oh, my dear, he does. So long I wonder he has any time to do his work at all. He is a fine man and I know I am blessed in him.'

Harriet was wondering as she spoke how she would describe Mrs Briggs in the letter to her sister she had half-formed in her head. The woman's movements were birdlike in their quickness but so suffused with a lively good will that 'birdlike' would not quite do. Perhaps a magpie had that glint in its eye. She was still considering when she found Mrs Briggs was asking her a question.

'But you were a traveller, were you not, Mrs Westerman, when you first married? Do you not miss the adventure of it, as my husband does when at home?'

It was the first time in years that anyone had had the perception to ask the question directly, and Harriet answered with immediate honesty. 'Yes, I do. Very much. I think that is why I am here now.'

Mrs Briggs chuckled. 'Indeed, that might well explain why you were so ready to uproot yourself and come charging up to visit us. Though do not mistake me, my dear.' She looked suddenly nervous, her quick eyes searching Harriet's face for any sign of offence. 'I am only too glad to have you here. You seem just the sort of guest I like to have in my home, and the frank and open sort of person it is a pleasure to see every day.' Though Harriet was smiling at her, thinking it impossible to be offended by Mrs Briggs, her hostess still seemed unsettled. 'There I go, running on again and saying all sorts of things one should not say.'

'Mrs Briggs! Why should you not say them? You are only far too kind to me, and I fear I shall disappoint you on further acquaintance.'

She beamed again. 'I am sure you shall not.' Then her face fell. 'But not everyone is of your mind. The Vizegräfin seems to shudder every time I open my mouth. Then I become nervous and make everything worse. She makes me feel like the girl I was, with hardly a clean shawl to keep me decent. I was all charity school and rough hands in my youth, and I think the

Vizegräfin can smell cheap soap on me still. My daughter is married to a Lord, and happily, and my son looks set to only add to the fortune he inherits, as he manages the business with his father now, bless them both – yet ladies like her can make me feel like hanging my head and slinking back to the scullery.' Her shoulders slumped a little.

'I am sorry to hear you say so,' Harriet said, with a slight frown. 'I imagined you and the Vizegräfin must be good friends for her to be staying here. She is not a comfortable person to dine with every day then, if I understand you?'

Mrs Briggs shook her head, her eyes still downcast. 'To be frank with you, Mrs Westerman, I wonder why the woman ever came! Her son seems pleasant enough – I like him, in fact – though he becomes sulky whenever his mother is in the room. My son was the same at one time. But the Vizegräfin never seemed to like us a great deal when we met in Vienna. I invited her to come to Silverside, naturally, when we discovered our connection, but I never thought to hear from her after that. She seemed a little horrified to be associated with us. Then a year later a letter appears done up with as many seals as a quart of brandy – and there it is! She would be very glad to make a long visit if it were convenient and so on, then she followed on so swift after my reply she must have had her bags packed and the horse waiting at the door.'

'You have not asked her about the circumstances?'

'Goodness me, no, Mrs Westerman! But you have not met the lady. If you had done so, you would not ask the question. She can be all twittering and charm when she wishes, but she will put you properly in your corner if you don't bend to her.'

Harriet rested her chin in her right hand, tapping at the

fabric of her dress with her left. 'Her brother is not known for his social graces either, I am afraid, though he inflicts his company on very few. And this body of yours, Mrs Briggs? Was it at the Vizegräfin's suggestion that Crowther be summoned to investigate it, or your own notion?'

Mrs Briggs looked into the air. 'How strange! I suppose it *is* "my body" in my husband's absence. Yes, it was the Vizegräfin. All that we have done this summer is due to her. She decided that a summerhouse on the island was a delightful plan. Then she wished to be present when the tomb was opened, then suggested summoning Mr Crowther and yourself. Perhaps she has become bored with Mr Sturgess, our neighbour, driving her about and playing cards five hours in the day. Still, I wish I had had the idea for a summerhouse of some sort before my son Ambrose grew so old and upright, but perhaps his children shall play there.'

Harriet looked at her. 'You named your son after your first love?'

Mrs Briggs nodded. 'With Mr Briggs's happy consent, my dear. They were friends as children and I think Ambrose would have been glad to see his namesake grown up so strong and well-established in life. We do what we can for the memory of our poor dear dead.'

'And you wish to have the mystery of this extra body in the tomb revealed for the same reason?'

Mrs Briggs spoke slowly. 'Well, I suppose he was someone's son. I believe by the clothing the body is that of a man. I do not know what you might be able to find out. He is a long time gone, poor fellow, but these hills have long memories, the hills and the people. I have been here thirty years and am thought of as an out-comer still.' She clapped her hands on her knees, and became brisk again. 'You will most likely find nothing at all, but I am easier in my mind knowing an attempt will be made. Then we may say some prayers over the poor forgotten thing, and you may enjoy the air and exercise we offer. Now I must go and dress for dinner, and allow you to do the same. Miriam will have your clothes all laid out by now, and will help you if you need her.' She stood and bustled out of the room and Harriet smiled after her, then began, with a grimace, to wonder how she should dress to meet the Vizegräfin, doubting if she had anything sufficient to the occasion.

I.5

STEPHEN HAD RUN HARD up the wooded path to the west of the house and now bent over his knees panting. He was already in love with the lake and the hills, and as he left the house to look at the mountains, he found his mind was teeming so with plans for boating, swimming in the lake and climbing each of the peaks, he had felt a sudden urge to dash about that could not be denied. Mr Quince was already showing himself to be the best sort of tutor for such a trip by remarking as Stephen's plans tumbled out of him that there was no better way to study geography than walking about in it, and he had always thought mathematics best tackled after a long swim.

Around him, oaks and beeches dressed with their summer foliage swung and stretched in the hazy sky. The birdsong was cacophonous: the bark of a chaffinch, the warbling, reaching trill of a yellow-hammer. The calls crossed and cut under each other. The air was full of the smell of dry earth and the competing breaths of wild flowers.

Stephen caught enough of his wind to look up and saw a jackdaw scratching about on the path in front of him. It was smaller than the crows he saw at Caveley and had very bright blue eyes. The feathers on its head were a little grey, giving the impression of a particularly glossy wig.

'Good day, crow,' Stephen said, his general good humour spilling over to the whole animal world.

The jackdaw hopped round in a tight circle before it looked over its shoulder at him.

'Good day,' it replied with the same lilt that Stephen had heard from the servants in the house.

Alarmed, the boy took a step back, caught his heel on a branch and fell heavily on his behind in the track, mouth still open. The bird fluttered away a little, looking offended. Stephen's view was suddenly blocked by a pair of legs in brown wool. A hand was extended to him and he found himself pulled to his feet by a man in labouring clothes. He was the colour of the stained wood floors in the nursery in Caveley, and his beard was whitening in places. It was a round, manly-looking face, and smiling. His hair was curly, and he had a great deal of it.

'You whole there, youngling?' the man said. Stephen nodded, trying to catch sight of the bird again. 'Give you a fright, did he?'

'I was not frightened.'

The man laughed under his breath then whistled, taking something out of his pocket as he did so. The jackdaw fluttered up to his shoulder and allowed the man to scratch his glossy black neck as he ate from his open palm.

'It spoke,' Stephen said at last, suspiciously.

'He does that, he does,' the man replied. 'When he has a mind to. Move slowly and he may let you scratch him as I am doing.' He bent forward, bringing the jackdaw within Stephen's reach. The boy reached up with great care and pushed his fingers in between the feathers. He had thought they would be soft, but they felt like polished wood and strong. The bird took on a slightly dreamy expression and opened its beak a little with a low growling sound.

'What is his name?'

The man tilted his head. 'I can't say as I know in crow language, but I call him Joe and he's willing to answer to that.'

'Joooe,' said the jackdaw, bobbing a little. Stephen took his hand away quickly and offered it to the man.

'My name is Stephen Westerman, and I am very pleased to meet you.'

The man took his hand, giving it a smart downward pull that almost dislocated Stephen's shoulder and set him stumbling again. 'Casper Grace, so please you, sir.' He then sat down on a log that formed a natural bench to the right of the path and took various items from his pockets. The jackdaw remained balanced on his shoulder and for the next few moments boy and bird were united in observing the man as he worked with a knife on a half-whittled piece of wood. Stephen became aware that the forest was full of smaller noises under the calling birds – he could hear leaves brushing together where the wind stirred them like a hand in water; somewhere in the distance, a stream was running; as he moved, the forest floor seemed to shush him. Stephen approached cautiously, keeping one eye on the jackdaw, and sat down carefully at the man's feet.

'What are you making?' he said at last.

Without looking up, Casper reached into his pocket and took something from it which he thrust into Stephen's hand. The boy found himself looking at a neat little carving of a cross that just fitted into his palm. It splayed out towards its four ends and was smooth to the touch, but detailed with an inner line and circle at its centre. The edge was marked out with little dips as if it were decorated with the shadows of something.

'It's beautiful,' he said at last. Casper looked up and sniffed.

'It is a Luck. The Luck of Gutherscale Hall. You may keep it, though don't tell Askew. He sells them at his museum in the town and doesn't like it when I give them away for free. Says I am robbing us both. I made it.'

Stephen turned it over and ran his fingertips along the worked edges. 'I wish I were so clever.'

'Ha! I'd not say I was clever, lad. Not with wood. Herbs, flowers, blessings maybe, but not so as I'd like with wood. Seems as I can only do these carvings of the Luck.' He held up the one he was working on and blew on it. 'I tried to do a portrait of Joe once in wood, but it never came right, did it, Joe?' The bird lifted its wings and clacked its beak. 'Good thing Askew can sell these to the Lakers or I'd have a thousand of them by now.'

'Who are the Lakers, Mr Grace?'

'Call me Casper, youngling. Why, Lakers are people such as yourself who come to see the Lakes hereabout, of course.'

'They are very fine.'

Casper looked at him with bright eyes. 'It *is* fine country, ain't it?' He shot to his feet and grabbed Stephen's hand. 'Come with me.' He raced up the path again, dragging Stephen behind him as the bird fluttered along between perches beside them. Stephen half-stumbled, half-ran along the path, not sure if he was frightened or delighted. Suddenly the trees fell away behind him and he found himself thrust out onto a rough promontory, where the view of the lake made him gasp.

Casper knelt at his side, one arm round his shoulders. He smelled of woodsmoke and tobacco and sweat. Stephen breathed it in deeply. As Casper spoke, he pointed out the hills with his free hand.

'Now that monster there is Skiddaw — you can see ships at sea from there! Then there is Latrigg, sheltering under her like a young lamb by her mother. There is Crosthwaite Church, white and shining as a blessing. There Keswick sits and whistles and is busy, and beyond that rise there are the stones the Druids left to watch us. That forest is Great Wood, and that great rearing is Castlerigg Fell.' He placed both hands on the boy's shoulders a moment to spin him round. 'Now look up! Look up!' Stephen stretched his throat to peer at the slopes above him. 'Causey Pike, and Cragg Hill beyond, and down there, where it all narrows, lie Borrowdale and Rosthwaite. If you are caught there when the snow comes, you must kick your heels till the thaw.'

Stephen tried to repeat the names quietly as they were spoken. 'Have you climbed all these hills, sir?'

The man flashed his teeth in a smile. 'Mostly, mostly. And many times; some plants favour one spot, others another.'

A voice called from the woodland behind them. 'Stephen! Stephen, where are you?'

'That is my tutor, Mr Quince,' the boy offered confidentially. 'We are here, sir!'

Mr Quince had been engrossed in West's guidebook when Stephen took off into the woods, and the heat was making him sweat rather profusely by the time he had caught up. He found his charge standing on the outcrop like a ship's figurehead. A man in working clothes was lying on the rock behind him, enjoying the same view. Stephen turned towards him.

'This is Casper Grace, Mr Quince. He has been telling me all the names of things.'

Mr Quince patted his forehead with his handkerchief then put his hand out to the man. Casper scrambled to his feet and shook it. 'Glad to meet you, Grace.'

'Oh, just Casper. Casper does me fine, sir.'

'Mr Grace knows the names of *all* the mountains,' Stephen said, then looked abashed. 'He told me them, but I fear I have forgotten half already.'

'Do not reproach yourself too much, my boy. They are such a number, and so all on top of each other I have been puzzling to match them to my book.' Quince tapped the little volume in his pocket. 'Perhaps if you have not been too troublesome, Mr Grace will consent to be our guide from time to time during our stay.'

Casper shrugged. 'I'm not in the habit of guiding. Lots of folk do that. I have other business most days, and like to be free to do it.'

'Oh do, please,' Stephen said, going so far as to lay a hand on Casper's arm. 'Then I may see Joe again.' He paused, wondering if this might seem a slight. 'And you too, sir.'

'Who is Joe?' said Mr Quince, looking about him.

The bird provided the answer himself, hopping forward and crooning his name. Mr Quince was taken aback.

'Joe talks,' Stephen said.

'So I see. Remarkable.'

Casper smiled, then mussed the boy's hair and spoke. 'I am not much with company, Master Westerman. I have my days where I must be off and running lonesome.'

'Like a wolf?' Stephen looked up at him.

'Ha! Yes, though my teeth are not so sharp.' Casper rubbed his chin. 'I am out on the hills most of most days, and most of the nights too. Let's say when we meet if I am not too bothered by the witches and weather, I'll show you some places.' He looked down at Stephen again. 'There's a vixen in Great Wood likes to show off her cubs to her friends, and Joe and me are friends of hers. Fancy seeing that one day, youngling?' Stephen nodded. 'We shall then. Good day!'

Before Stephen or Mr Quince were able to draw breath to thank him or make any farewells, Casper had sprung over the edge of the outcrop, and was lost in the woodland below. The bird turned to them and cawed in a familiar sort of way, then fluttered off after him.

Stephen leaned in towards Mr Quince, and his tutor put an arm around his shoulders.

'What do you think he meant about witches and weather, sir?'

Quince pondered a second. 'No doubt it is some saying of the area, my boy. Now all this charging around must have made you hungry. Shall we go and see if there is any food to be had at the Hall?'

Stephen nodded and they made their way more slowly back into the woods. 'Have you heard of the Luck of Gutherscale Hall, sir?' he asked, after they had gone a little way.

'I have read something of it in the guides,' Quince told him. 'The legend says it was originally a gift from the fairy people to the most powerful family hereabouts – the Greta family.'

'I should like to know more of that.' Stephen had realised he was both tired and hungry. It seemed harder going down the hill than running up it had been. 'Do you believe in fairies, Mr Quince?'

The tutor laughed. 'Good lord, no! No doubt the cross was brought over by the Crusaders.'

Stephen looked about him as if searching for a glint among the foliage. 'I would like to find it.'

'You did say you wanted to search for dragons,' Mr Quince reminded him, 'and they are great guardians of treasure in folklore. Perhaps if we find the dragon, we shall find the Luck tucked under its scaly claw.'

The thought was enough to keep Stephen silent the rest of their return down the slope.

I.6

HARRIET FOUND HER way into the drawing room with the help of one of the maids, a little nervous since she was later than she should have been. She had gone first to her son and his tutor's apartments to see them safe and already eating their meal informally in their own rooms. Then she had delayed too long trying to get her curls in order and deciding between a dress of navy with gold trim which she felt rather too grand, and a simpler gown in grey that made her feel a hundred years old. However, when she was shown into the light and spacious room, she found she was among the first of the house's inhabitants to arrive. A young man sprang up from the couch on which he was reclining and bowed, clicking his heels together, then he came forward to take her hand.

Her first impression was of youth. She noted the carelessly arranged and unpowdered hair of the man, and the blue eyes. He was slender and long-limbed and she wondered if Crowther would have looked something like this in his early years.

'Mrs Westerman! I am pleased to see you. I am Felix von Bolsenheim, at your service, ma'am.'

She let him take her hand with a smile. 'I am very glad to make your acquaintance, Mein Herr.'

'Oh please, just call me Felix, Mrs Westerman, rather than mangle your tongue.'

'I would have thought you an Englishman, Felix. Were you at school here?'

He grinned up at her, holding her hand a little longer than necessary and Harriet wondered if the child intended to flirt with her. 'I was indeed. French I learned from my tutors, and my father's native tongue I learned from the servants, on horseback or in gaming hells. I do remarkably well in Vienna as a result.'

He did have some charm. He stood back from her and performed a slow turn.

'Do not keep me in suspense, madam. I have been at such trouble with my appearance this afternoon. What do you think my esteemed uncle will make of me? Knowing him as well as you do, you must be able to give me some hint.'

Harriet had known for a little while of the existence of Crowther's sister and nephew, but until now she had never pictured him as part of a family group. So cut off as Crowther was from the general run of society it seemed impossible to imagine him with the same ties and blood loyalties as other people.

'It would foolish of anyone to claim to know the secrets of another person's mind. Especially Crowther's,' she said. 'In truth, I must tell you I only learned of his given name this morning.'

Felix shook his head at her. 'Yet you travel the country with him and bring murderers to justice by his side! Madam, how remarkable.'

'I am a rich widow, Felix. I may do as I like.'

Harriet at once wished she had not used such a tone. She might be sharing the house with this handsome young man for some weeks to come. Rachel would have put her head in her hands on hearing such a phrase in her sister's mouth. Harriet had wished to sound at ease with herself, but felt she had made herself already not quite respectable.

Harriet had enjoyed an unusual life long before she met Crowther. After her marriage she had travelled the world with her husband and flourished in the variety and challenges such a life entailed. It had made her something of an oddity when motherhood and the need to provide a home for her unmarried sister had forced her into remaining at Caveley. The walls had closed in on her and she found herself continually failing to meet the expectations of country society. She had been thought rather too free in her speech and fixed in her opinions. Then she found herself involved in murder. Those events had given her a degree of fame and she had made some powerful friends, but she could see that for many men and women of her class, her actions had confirmed her as an oddity, rather like the lizard with two heads which the Pulborough apothecary, Gladwell, kept in his parlour. Now here, when the knowledge of the reputation that went before her should make her most circumspect, she was talking like a woman who revelled in her dubious fame. She was angry with herself. Felix, however, was, to all appearances, enchanted.

'Oh, capital! I cannot agree with you more, Mrs Westerman. Always do what you will and leave the Devil standing in your dust.' Harriet opened her mouth in hopes she might somehow smooth out what she had said, but the young man did not give her the chance to speak. 'But please, before my uncle arrives, give me the benefit of your wisdom. What will he think of me? His reputation is rather fearsome, I understand.'

Harriet sighed, and this time considered a little before she spoke. 'Felix, Crowther is not cruel. He will not mock you. But if you wish a serious opinion, it is this. Unless you are dead, or have some interesting remark to make on scientific subjects, I think it likely that Crowther will not notice you at all.' Felix's fire left him and he looked younger than before. Harriet smiled. 'Do not be downcast, sir, but be comforted in this. Crowther will not judge you either. If you do not irritate him, he will probably learn to like you. I have seen him make a number of unlikely alliances in the past, and he should be disposed to think well of you, given your close relation. If he thinks well of you, you could not wish for a better friend. I only mean you should not try to charm him. Be yourself, be frank and do not chatter is my advice.'

Felix smiled lopsidedly. 'You ask the impossible. My mother tells me I chatter far too much, and I am sure I become an irritant to many of my friends, even those as good-willed as yourself. I have had a very expensive education, and know nothing. I have an estate in Mecklenburg and no idea of agriculture. The last two years that I have spent in Vienna, I have been mostly at the card table. I am careless, idle and bored. My uncle will dislike me intensely, I think.'

There was nothing playful in Harriet's frown now. 'How can you say such things of yourself? I understand there is an extensive library here. Perhaps you can use your stay to remedy the defects of your education.'

He laughed – his spirits as suddenly recovered as they were lost. 'Now, dear Mrs Westerman, you sound like one of those dull country parsons. So severe! How could I spend my time in the library with this landscape to explore? And I am sure there are diversions in Keswick too for a man of my age and expectations. Though I do love to read novels. Are there any here? Have you read *The Sorrows of Young Werther*? It is a remarkable book, although I cannot quite believe a man suffering so for love. I have too much English blood in my veins, though every man one meets in Vienna has taken to sighing over some unavailable beauty in imitation of the hero.'

Harriet had read the book when it was translated into her own tongue, and found it rather irritating, so was happy to spend some time mocking it in Felix's company. His tone continued careless, but there was perception in his remarks and Harriet began to think he might be cleverer than he pretended. Once they had entertained themselves in this way for some minutes, the door opened and Crowther appeared. Felix introduced himself and Crowther looked him carefully up and down, said he was glad to meet him, then took a paper from the side-table and sat down to read.

Felix tried to meet Harriet's eye, but she would not engage and instead walked to the window to admire again the view down to the lake. Mrs Briggs arrived, which drew them back together into the island of settees around the empty fire. Though when Mrs Briggs mentioned that she understood there was an acquaintance of Felix's staying in the town, he scowled.

'Would you like to invite them to Silverside for my summer party tomorrow?' she asked uncertainly.

'Do not trouble yourself, madam,' he replied. 'The acquaintance is very slight, and they are not the sort of person to whom my mother would wish to be introduced.' Mrs Briggs was obviously somewhat taken aback, but when Harriet asked about the arrangements for her party, she recovered quickly enough. The ladies discussed the trouble of providing ices for a crowd, and Felix offered his opinion on the arrangements for the archery competition. Crowther did not contribute to their talk, but the others established an easy flow of conversation until the Vizegräfin entered.

She apologised lightly for keeping them from their dinner, and touched the complicated arrangement of her hair by way of explanation. As Harriet stood to make her curtsey, she studied the woman. In her form she was very like Crowther, with the same hooded blue eyes, and high bones in the cheek. She had none of his reserve, however, and as soon as they were seated, began to question Harriet rather thoroughly about her estate, her children and her parents. When she began to make detailed enquiries about the affairs of the family at Thornleigh Hall and the young Lord Sussex, Harriet found she was struggling to answer with any degree of politeness. Twice Mrs Briggs tried to steer the conversation clear of the shoals with some other remark, and twice she was all but ignored by the Vizegräfin. Her eyes were constantly darting between Harriet and Crowther in a way that began to irritate. Felix started to frown and Harriet felt herself examined from all sides; she could sense her fingers tightening on her fan. Having observed the interrogation for some minutes, Crowther sighed audibly, then turned to Mrs Briggs and began to talk to her, listening to her replies with apparent interest.

When the Vizegräfin noticed this, her eyes narrowed and she asked her brother some question. Crowther replied as briefly as possible, hardly looking at her as he did so, then continued to speak to Mrs Briggs.

Harriet's relief when they were summoned to the table was extreme.

At least at dinner the dishes that appeared before them supplied some conversation, and when the subject of the excellence of the carp taken from the lake at Bassenthwaite had been raised, Harriet went so far as to ask the Vizegräfin whether the taste recalled to her her childhood in the area. The Vizegräfin set down her glass on the table and turned towards her, putting her head on one side.

'Perhaps it does, Mrs Westerman. I am beset by all sorts of strange ghosts of my girlhood in this house.' She glanced significantly at Crowther as she spoke, but he showed no sign of noticing it.

'A ghostly fish!' Felix said. 'A strange ghost indeed.' He gave a high-pitched giggle and leaned forward to pull more meat from it, doing so a little messily. His mother looked at him critically.

'I wish you could rid yourself of that foolish laugh,' she snapped. 'It makes you sound like a schoolgirl.'

Felix flushed and looked down at his plate.

When the ladies withdrew, they found a visitor waiting for them by the tea table and Harriet was introduced to Mr Sturgess, the magistrate, who had been one of the party when the tomb was opened. A gentleman who, if not young still appeared vigorous, who dressed elegantly but without ostentation, he stood and made his bows with a steady smile. He wore his clothes well. The chatelaine that bore his watch and seal at his side was gilt and white enamel, but managed to seem at home against the dull sage of his waistcoat, whereas the more gaudy version Felix sported seemed to wheedle for attention. Harriet felt him study her and was glad she had decided on the blue. The Vizegräfin all but skipped to his side.

'Mr Sturgess, what a delight to see you! You have come to look at Mrs Westerman, I suppose.'

Mr Sturgess smiled at her and bowed, though it seemed the remark surprised him a little, then he turned to Harriet. 'I have come in hopes of meeting Mrs Westerman and Mr Crowther, naturally. It is an honour for us all to have them among us. I am glad there is such a comfortable home as Silverside to welcome them.'

Mrs Briggs and Harriet were perhaps happier with this statement than the Vizegräfin.

Harriet took her seat with her usual, open smile, saying, 'You are the magistrate here, I believe, Mr Sturgess. Have you discovered anything about this strange body in the tomb as yet? Are you here to tell us Crowther and I are no longer required?'

He took his tea from Mrs Briggs and shook his head. 'I am indeed magistrate here, though the people are well-behaved enough and seldom trouble me, so my official duties are light. Of the body I can tell you nothing. I had the news spread and bills put up in town, but no one has come forward with any information as yet.'

'A true mystery, then. Perhaps he is indeed an ancient or was a stranger here,' Harriet said. She noticed Sturgess had grey eyes and a square jaw. There was something of the military in his bearing for all his ease of manner. She thought she might like him.

'Perhaps so, Mrs Westerman, but just because no one has come to me, it does not mean that they know nothing. The people here are a close-knit and close-mouthed lot. I learn what business of the town I know only when something comes to blows in the public street. Perhaps that is how it should be. It might have been different with a magistrate born in the area, but I am only five years into my life here, so am regarded of very little consequence – unless you need a licence for a new ale-house.'

Harriet was about to ask more about Mr Sturgess's history, but he forestalled her, getting to his feet and approaching her chair while the others watched.

'However, I do have *something* here for you.' He reached into his pocket and produced a snuff barrel, putting it into her hand before sitting down again. It fitted snugly into Harriet's palm. As she turned it over with a frown he continued, 'There was a fight in Portinscale outside the Black Pig last night, and it turns out that that snuffbox was at the heart of it.' He turned to Mrs Briggs. 'I am sorry to say, it seems that the two men your steward hired were less than honest. Apparently the snuffbox fell from the clothing of the body as it was moved, and they snatched it up behind your man's back. The fight was over the division of the spoils.'

'Thieves! How dreadful!' said the Vizegräfin.

The magistrate shook his head sadly, but continued speaking to Mrs Briggs. 'Madam, I hope that as the property is now returned to you, we need proceed no further in the case. You could have them both transported should you wish to prosecute, but though they are difficult men, I do not think them irredeemable.'

Mrs Briggs patted his sleeve. 'Quite right, quite right. I am of the same mind. We shall not have them on our property again, but you may tell them I shall carry the matter no further.'

'Wrongdoers should be punished,' said the Vizegräfin stiffly.

'A little mercy, Vizegräfin,' Sturgess murmured.

Mrs Briggs cleared her throat. 'Let your investigations commence then, Mrs Westerman! I am sure I think you so clever I expect you to give me all the details of the matter from this one object.'

Harriet turned the snuffbox over in her hands. Ivory and mahogany, she thought. The hinge was in the form of a silver butterfly and on its lid bloomed a single rose in the same metal. She lifted her eyebrows.

'Your poor wretch was a Jacobite, then, Mrs Briggs.'

The woman almost spilled her tea. 'Good Lord, Mrs Westerman! I spoke in jest! How can you say so?'

Harriet shrugged, and felt rather than saw the Vizegräfin

stiffen in her chair. She held the box towards her host. 'When I was a child there was an old gentleman in my father's parish whom we used to visit. My father felt it was his duty, as there was no Catholic priest in the area to tend to him. He was a Jacobite, still convinced the true King lived on the continent rather than in the Palace, and his home was full of items with these sorts of designs. I mean the rose and the butterfly, madam, and the use of ivory in the construction as well, I imagine, since white was the colour of the cause.'

Mr Sturgess was looking at her steadily. 'Bravo, Mrs Westerman.' Harriet almost blushed.

Mrs Briggs sipped her tea. 'I *do* remember, my dear. I am quite old enough to remember the colours being worn. Of course, the rose. How clever of you to see it so quickly! And of course the last Lord Greta was such a Jacobite. Perhaps you have solved the mystery at a stroke, Mrs Westerman. Herbert's Island was part of the Greta estate before it was bought by Lord Keswick, and then by ourselves. No doubt this was one of his followers who suffered some injury and was carelessly buried in the heat of the times.'

'I would not call the burial careless, Mrs Briggs, would you?' Harriet said, leaning back and taking up her fan. The heat was still oppressive. 'But perhaps you are right. We shall know more when we examine the body in the morning.'

The Vizegräfin swung her head round to face Harriet. 'You assist my brother in these examinations, Mrs Westerman? How horrible.'

Harriet fluttered the fan. Her sister had painted it the previous year for her, and it had been one of her successes; it showed a wooded glade where a figure of Pan played pipes to an audience of a fox, a crow and a pair of small children whom Rachel had modelled on her nephew and niece.

'I am sorry to say, madam, I have not the skills to "assist" in any practical way. Perhaps you think I am too delicate? I have acted as a nurse in my husband's commands when it was required. I assure you it is a far more delicate procedure to examine a corpse than hold down a young man while his leg is removed. I take no active part in the autopsies Crowther performs. I am merely present and offer what conjectures I may, suggested by the evidence he discovers.'

Sturgess looked serious. 'I am sure your contributions are invaluable, Mrs Westerman. Mr Crowther is lucky to have you.' The Vizegräfin sniffed, and Harriet was relieved to see Mrs Briggs looking rather amused.

Before anything further could be said, Crowther and his nephew came into the room. Harriet noticed that Crowther was looking bored, and Felix rather deflated. She suspected he had ignored her advice and chattered over his wine. It seemed unlikely they would bring any great cheer to the group so she was pleased when they were almost immediately joined by Stephen and his tutor, summoned from their own amusements to spend a little of the evening with the company. After the various introductions and explanations required by the gathering of the party, Mr Quince took a chair a little removed from the rest of them, produced his guidebook from his pocket and began to read. Stephen, however, began at once to tell them of his adventures in the wood and the talking jackdaw. He turned to Crowther.

'Can all birds speak, sir? Do they have throats as we do? Mr Quince said he did not know.'

Crowther looked steadily at him and brought his fingertips together. 'What do you think, Stephen?' The boy bit his lip. It was also a habit Harriet had when she was thinking. Crowther wondered if her son had mimicked her, as one generation of birds mimics the songs of its forebears.

'I think if all birds *could* talk, I should have met one before now. And the crows near our house sound a little like people at times, do they not? So perhaps they are more like us than sparrows or jays.'

Crowther nodded. 'That seems a sensible speculation, though of course you would have to make careful experiment to support your theory.'

A look of wary concern crossed Stephen's face. 'But not on Joe, sir? He is a nice bird and I would not like to see him hurt.'

'We shall not steal and cut up someone's pet, Stephen.' Crowther lifted his chin to look across at Mr Quince. 'I can recommend a book or two about the anatomy of the throat to your tutor, if it would interest you. And I believe there are some interesting works on birds in the library here. My own experiments in anatomy began with the study of the canaries of a neighbour here – my father's solicitor, then my own – a Mr Leathes.'

Mrs Briggs clasped her hands. 'He looked after all our business at Silverside until he passed the practice to his son. He has his aviary still.'

As the conversation continued, touching the various persons still living on the lake shores that Crowther and his sister had known in their youth, Felix seemed to sink further into his chair, and Harriet thought she saw a jealous glint in his eye. She suspected Crowther had not offered to lend him any books.

Stephen smiled and reached into his pocket. 'I am glad you shan't cut up poor Joe. It would seem unfair when all he has done is learn to say "good day". Mr Grace gave me this too.' He produced the carving of the Luck and handed it to Crowther.

'Very pretty,' he said simply, and passed it to Mrs Briggs.

'Oh yes. These are the ones that Mr Askew sells in his museum.' She looked up at Harriet. 'The Lost Luck. Well, Luck left the Gretas certainly. The last Lord Greta lived out his life in exile, and his younger brother was taken in 1745 and executed for treason the following year. An unfortunate family. These hills are so magnificent, but we have made all sorts of bloody histories between them.' She suddenly remembered her audience and looked up very pink. The Vizegräfin was staring at her with horror; even Mr Sturgess looked uncertain.

'Very true, madam,' Crowther said.

No one seemed quite sure how to continue the conversation, but Stephen spoke, unaware of the strained silence in the room. He had picked up the snuffbox and was examining the inside of the lid with his eyes screwed tight. 'What little writing!'

Harriet turned to him. 'Where, Stephen? What does it say?'

'*Semper fideles. Greta,*' he said slowly as he read. 'That means always loyal, does it not?'

Mrs Briggs put her hand to her mouth. 'Why, Mrs Westerman — it is much as we thought! A follower of Lord Greta's from 1715 — this proves it. How *interesting!*'

'There is a date here, too, Mama.' Stephen held it out to his mother. 'It says 1742.'

Harriet took the box from him and turned it over in her hand. The writing was indeed tiny. She wondered if her eyes were growing old. 'So we have not quite solved the mystery as yet, Mrs Briggs. Tell me, Crowther, who owned Saint Herbert's Island in the forties?'

Crowther cleared his throat and put his fingertips together. 'In 1742? The island was owned at that time by my father, Sir William Penhaligon, later made First Baron Keswick. He made a number of purchases after Lord Greta's lands were forfeited. He bought Saint Herbert's at the same time as he bought the land on which to rebuild this house and create the gardens — 1720 or thereabouts.'

Mrs Briggs looked surprised. 'Perhaps the dead man was a follower of Lord Greta's brother then, who came over in 1745. But Lord Greta's brother was taken at Preston — not near here. What would one of the family's followers be doing in these parts at that time?'

For the moment, no one had any reply to offer her.

From the collection of Mr Askew, Keswick Museum

From the *English Post*, 12 July 1712

Some remarks on the Luck of Gutherscale Hall

Sir,

On a recent journey to the North of England, I had the honour of being received in the ancient and beautiful seat of Edmund de Beaufoy, 7th Earl of Greta, namely Gutherscale Hall on the shores of Keswick Lake. The Hall is based round the ancient pele tower which offers a delightful prospect over his wild lands, so long held and defended by this noble family, though in the current Lord's father's time the Hall was much extended to create a number of generously-sized apartments befitting the standing of the Greta name. At that time, and through the kindness of my host, I had the pleasure of seeing there the fabled Luck of Gutherscale Hall. I made some notes as to the folklore surrounding this remarkable item and its appearance which I am happy now to share with my fellow readers of your excellent magazine, should you find room to print them.

The Luck is kept in the Hall in a strongbox made on purpose and to which only Lord Greta owns the key. On viewing it, one can readily see why such a precaution is necessary. The Luck is a cross roughly the size of a grown man's hand spread wide, and fashioned of gold. Its surface is studded with a number of fine

83

gemstones, including a large ruby in its centre, four considerable diamonds inter alia, and its edges are studded with good quality pearls. Though one hesitates to assert a definitive opinion I would hazard it is Byzantine in origin. When I offered this opinion to Lord Greta he was happy to inform me that the local legend claims that the cross was presented to an ancestor of the Greta family by none other than the fair-folk when he disturbed their celebrations in the local stone circle! Legend further informs us he was warned that, if the Luck ever left the ownership of the family, disaster would follow. The current Lord does not seem of a superstitious character, though he laughingly told your correspondent that many of the local people still regard the cross with great reverence as a gift of the fairies, given to celebrate their acceptance of Christ as their Lord, and he means to keep it under close guard rather than earn their wrath.

Yours &c M.C.

PART II

II.1

Wednesday, 16 July 1783

EVER SINCE HER HUSBAND had died Harriet had woken early; it was no different here. For a while she tried to climb back into her dreams but they were lost to her. The house was still. She rose, finished her letter to Rachel, then decided to walk. The mention of the ancient family of Greta the previous evening had intrigued her, so she dressed as simply as she could and leaving Silverside still sleeping behind her, set out along the path that she thought would lead her towards their ancestral home, Gutherscale Hall.

The carriage road that had once run along the hillside above Silverside Hall, then fallen past Gutherscale Hall before more sedately following the lakeshore towards Grange and the jaws of Borrowdale, had become impassable within ten years of Lord Greta's exile in 1716. Where a road was not in regular use, the weather and winds would soon shake it from carriageway to bridleway to path within a few years. The footpath which Harriet took led more directly from the lawns of Silverside and followed the line of the lake through a cool woodland of birch and beech. Derwent Water appeared through the trees to her left, silken and dark grey, and on her right the ground rose, the moss and leafmould-covered ground studded with holly.

The morning had brought no freshening of the air with it but Harriet was soothed by the water and wood around her. Mrs Briggs had told her that although Crowther's father had sold the timber on his land, she and her husband had been less inclined to clear, and since they had bought the land the hillsides had redressed themselves in rowan and ash.

She was glad to be alone. It was a luxury to take in the morning without the pressing awareness of orders to be given, letters written or visitors to be endured. The scents of the woodland reminded her of the copse on the edge of her lawns at Caveley, though it was subtly different here. Other bird cries, a variety in the grasses; the change in the soil and shape of the land from Sussex was expressed in such ways and it gave her pleasure to note them. Such pleasure, in fact, that when she came upon the ruins of Gutherscale Hall it was with surprise. She had been examining the flowering mosses at her feet and wondering if Mrs Briggs might know their names, when she looked up and found herself standing before the ghost of the great building. They must have been a very influential family in their time, to judge by the height of the remaining walls, but now nature was busily undoing their works. It was remarkable how it was so reduced in only, Harriet bit her lip, sixty years. There had to have been a fire. She had seen a great house burn in the summer of 1780 and knew how quick and thorough flames could be. That house, Thornleigh Hall, had since been rebuilt and reborn; here, weather and plant growth had completed what fire had begun, if it had been fire. She began to look for signs of it and saw some dark scarring on the stones. She would ask Crowther.

It seemed the oldest parts of the building had survived longest. The square pele tower, though broken in places and breeding saplings in its mortar, looked almost intact. To one side of it, a flight of stone stairs made a shallow ascent to where the more modern parts of the mansion house stood. She climbed the flight cautiously. Surely the trees surrounding her were more than thirty years old. Perhaps Sir William had left a ring of old wood around this place, the better to hide from the lake the signs of its former master. She stepped in through the open mouth of the main entrance and looked about her.

The floors and ceilings were long gone. At intervals halfway up the height of the walls were the hollows of fireplaces. She rebuilt the place in her mind, saw Lady Greta in the fashions of seventy years before sitting by the upper fire with her sewing on her lap and a greyhound at her feet, then smiled at her imaginings.

There was a sudden beating of wings, and the rough shouts from a murder of crows echoed about the ruined walls. She turned and saw them lifting from the ground where once Lord Greta and his men had drunk and eaten before the main fireplace, and fly into the surrounding trees. Through a break in the wall at the opposite side of the Hall she saw Felix appear, his bow slung over his shoulder and his arrows at his side.

He lifted his hat and bowed to her. 'Good morning, Mrs

Westerman. You are like myself. I can never lie in bed and wait for my hot chocolate unless I have been at cards till dawn.'

She was sorry to lose the peace of the place and the pleasures of her fancy, but smiled warmly enough as he walked towards her.

'The crows do not like you, Felix. They did not trouble themselves to fly away as I entered.'

He shrugged. 'I am afraid they know me. I brought down a couple in our first week here and since then they have had an eye out for me.'

'Remarkable.'

'The crows' ability to recognise me, or my ability to bring one down with a bow and arrow?'

Harriet laughed. 'Both, I suppose. You must be quite the expert. Were the birds in flight, or was it a surprise attack?'

He looked a little angry. 'I would not be so unsporting as to take them on the ground. Though, as you see, they give me no credit for it!' He looked at where the birds now hunched in the branches above them and Harriet waited for him to speak again. 'You see I failed to take your advice last night, and now my uncle does not like me,' he said at last.

'Does that matter to you?'

He frowned. 'More than I had thought it might. My own father prefers the brats of his mistress. Perhaps I thought my uncle would like me better. It is a dangerous thing, to feel oneself unloved, Mrs Westerman. One begins to seek affection in unsuitable places.'

Harriet lifted her eyebrows. 'Stop being so tragic, Felix. You are too young to carry it off effectively.'

He gave a tight smile, then said with forced brightness,

'Have you investigated the pele tower as yet? That was built to last by someone who knew their business. The stairs are a little uneven in places, but it is still possible to climb, if you would like to see it. The platform is intact, though the floors below are gone.'

Harriet nodded. 'I should like to. Let us go together. Do you know anything of the history of the building?'

He ushered her through the low stone arch at the base of the tower; it was immediately cooler in the column of old stone. 'Your son's tutor would be a better historian,' he said, his voice following behind her as she climbed the shallow spiral stairs. 'He had his nose in the guidebook all evening. But I believe this place was built in the fourteenth century as defence from the Scots' raiding parties, then when the Greta family grew in importance the building was extended. That would have been in the life of the First Earl, the one whose tomb bred an extra corpse.'

Harriet's fingers traced the old stones as she climbed; there was no sign of fire damage here and the steps were smooth, if rather uneven. From time to time an arch appeared. She leaned forward and saw it gave out onto nothing but air shrouded and clouded like a well. The interior walls were spotted in places with ferns of violent green searching for the splashes of sunlight that crawled around the walls as the world turned. She stepped back a little quickly and felt Felix's hand under her elbow.

'Careful, Mrs Westerman.'

She nodded and carried on climbing, then, when her heart had steadied a little said, 'You did not seem pleased to hear that friends of yours have arrived in the area, Felix.'

'I hope I was not rude to Mrs Briggs,' he said after a long

pause. Their voices were low; something in the age of the stone made it natural to speak quietly.

'No, I think only that she was a little disappointed. She wished to please you.'

Felix sighed. 'I spotted them in town, and they are not acquaintances likely to win me any credit. A cardsharp and his daughter. I lost money to him in Vienna last year.'

'How strange they should appear here.'

'Yes.'

'Still, I suppose that the beauty of the region is known across Europe.'

'As you say.'

It was clear that Felix wished to say no more, so Harriet fell silent in her turn and saved her breath for the climb. Where the staircase broke into daylight at the top, the world seemed white with light. As she reached it, she hesitated, wondering how far to trust the stone flags at her feet. She looked back at Felix behind her in the gloom. He smiled up at her encouragingly from the shadows.

'It is safe enough near the door, Mrs Westerman. Only avoid the western corner.'

She edged out. The world seemed to sway somewhat around her, and she put a hand behind her back to steady herself. From either side of the door through which she had emerged extended a lower crenellated wall. At intervals along each was set the sculpted seal of Lord Greta's house: a pair of arms raised as if growing from the stone, the elbows crooked outwards, and the hands holding between them a fat-faced sun with a bloom of carved, petal-like rays and a beatific smile. The effect was rather disturbing. It looked as if the stone wardens had lifted their beaming heads free from their shoulders. At the western corner of the tower their regular pattern became broken and unsure, and the gap told the story of one watcher fallen, crashing down through the flags. Felix was observing her.

'It fell all the way to the bottom of the tower. I found it there on my first exploration of this place. The arms are broken, but the sun face is still there.'

Harriet nodded.

'You are nervous of heights, Mrs Westerman?' He had come through the doorway and was now leaning casually on one of the merlons.

'It varies, Felix. Sometimes I am bold, at others my balance appears to fail me.'

He stared down gloomily over the wall. Harriet gripped the stone behind her.

'You don't feel the temptation to throw yourself into the void then?' he said, without looking at her.

'No, I do not,' she said as firmly as she could. 'Only a little weakness.' With great effort she turned herself to look at the view. A falling run of trees, a glimmer of lake and the crags beyond. She felt her knees shake and her hands were white on the stonework.

'A little weakness . . .' His voice was soft. 'What do you conclude from the snuffbox, Mrs Westerman? Do you think my grandfather was involved in the disposal of the body? What do you think you will learn from that poor mangled corpse?'

She looked round quickly and the world lurched a little. He was gazing directly at her.

'It is impossible to say. I think that is a matter best discussed with Crowther, Felix. When he is ready to tell you something, he shall. Or he will inform your mother and you shall hear of it through her.' He crossed easily towards her and stood rather close; she felt him examining her and the effect the height was having on her. 'The view is charming,' she said, 'but this weakness has me today. Will you give me your arm, and help me down, Felix?'

His eyes were resting on her white fingers. 'Do you think you have found new mysteries, Mrs Westerman? Are you and my uncle going to bring some new scandal to light, to taint our family name still further? It seems hardly fair that you should know so much of our business before my mother and I. One day I shall be Lord Keswick, you know.' He was very close to her now, and his gaze moved slowly over her face and form. 'Unless my uncle marries a woman who could bear him a son. Then I should be lost. It would be dreadful to be lost.'

Harriet gritted her teeth, released her grip on the stonework and forced herself to take a step forward, making him move out of her way.

'If you shall not give me your arm, I shall walk unaided.' She stepped towards the doorway, hoping the trembling that seemed to run up and down her limbs was invisible to him. As her hand touched the stone doorframe she heard him laugh. He took hold of her elbow again and spoke in his usual easy tone.

'No, I shall certainly be your staff and rod, Mrs Westerman. I am sure my uncle will tell us all in due course.'

She hesitated, but looking into the gloom of the staircase allowed him to take her arm, and with one hand on the central column began to walk down at his side. Going down was far more uncomfortable than climbing, but Felix began to chatter happily about his hunting in a boastful, boyish manner. The memory of his closeness on the roof began to seem less threatening as they descended, but she kept the memory of his words, and turned them over like coloured stones in her mind as he rattled on.

Breakfast at Silverside was an informal meal. The household helped themselves from the warming platters to local bacon and good coffee from the tall silver pot. Mrs Briggs did no more than greet her guests before disappearing into the house to review the arrangements for her garden party. The Vizegräfin took her breakfast in her rooms, and Crowther retreated into his newspaper. Stephen and Mr Quince competed in their enthusiasm to be off and exploring. Harriet ate with an appetite that surprised her, and by the time the household had gone their separate ways, the crows and her feeling of weakness on the rooftop seemed more part of her dreams than her reality.

Hetty Briggs was writing at the desk in her bedroom when she heard the door below her open and close, and looked out to see Mrs Westerman and Crowther step into the morning air. She liked Mrs Westerman for herself, but also had a sense of fellow-feeling with her. It had taken many years for Mrs Briggs to lose the notion of being an impostor in her own home. She looked at the comfortable and elegant establishment of which she was mistress, and would think of the bare and cold cottage in which she had been raised. People saw her as a curiosity too. She knew the polish she had acquired over the years sometimes came as a shock to those who knew her background and were meeting her for the first time. It made them uneasy, as if their own maid had just married a duke. They expected her to sound like her cook and have the manners of a street-hawker. They would watch her suspiciously, waiting for some sign of her birth to make itself apparent – just as, she supposed, they were always examining Harriet's cuffs for old bloodstains.

Knowing Mrs Westerman and Crowther were about to begin their examination of the body, she sighed and wished luck to their retreating backs. When the body was found in the tomb on St Herbert's Island it seemed only right to Mrs Briggs that it should be brought to Silverside Hall, and that when Mr Sturgess and the Vizegräfin had been returned to the shore, she should remain to accompany the bones back across the lake herself. Her boatman returned with linens to lift the fragile remains clear of the tomb, and as she watched her workmen shift the body onto the cloth from its cold dry home, she had felt herself start like an anxious mother. She tried to remember if she had heard the snuffbox fall. It must have been worked loose in the tomb itself as the sheet was passed under the body. She thought of it, the flesh of a man returning to earth under the steady gaze of Falcon Crag, becoming less and less a man, more and more at one with the rotting leaves that lapped about the stone flags, the broken reeds.

There had been a peace to their return across the water. Her boatman at the oars, herself in the prow, the body decently wrapped and laid on a plank in the middle of the boat. She watched Catbells rear up to greet them in the dusk, the haze above it touched blood-red and purple, the lake gathering and shifting the colours into slate and gold as the boat glided away from the Island of Bones. The boatman had asked her what was to be done further, and she thought at once of the old brewery. Her house had no chapel of its own, but this outhouse had the calm and high windows she felt somehow the corpse must have become accustomed to on St Herbert's Island. She had closed the door and locked it with her own hands, and promised the body a place in Crosthwaite Church in due course, and wondered what words she would ask to be carved, to mark where it lay. They came to her out of the silence as if spoken by the hills themselves.

' "For the Son of Man is come to save that which was lost", ' she said aloud, and the curlew cried out in reply on the fell above her.

She had returned to her house, and as she entered the hall, she smiled at the familiar furnishings, the bright grin of her maid as she took her shawl. She shook the sadness off her shoulders like rainwater, and went to her library to begin her express to Mr Crowther. Let him and his friend see if they could bring this lost man home.

Now she continued her letter to her husband who would be fussing over his vines in the heat of the Portuguese summer. To her description of her new guests, and their thoughts on the snuffbox, she added a description of Harriet's fan.

My love, the image made me think of nothing so much as dear Casper Grace, though he is no musician, of course. And if Casper wanted he could sleep in a warm bed every night and feast all day. He has the Black Pig, and I know he is well paid for the services he gives to the people, yet he wanders the hills in plain cloth and takes Mr Askew's pennies for his carvings. I mention it because I have heard rumours that our good Mr Sturgess has had some piece of bad business and that his housekeeper hardly dares ask for further credit from the butcher. Mr Postlethwaite told me even this

*morning that he has sent both housekeeper and maid away to save
on their wages. Do you think we might be able to offer him some
assistance without causing him embarrassment? He has been a good
neighbour to us since he arrived. How strange to think a smart
gentleman like him rides about on his own horses without the money
to buy good meat, while a man who might buy his own house and
furnish it sleeps in the old charcoalburners' lean-tos like a beggar.
Do tell me what you think, my dear, in your next. For the moment
I shall continue to invite him to our table as often as I can. Now
there is Mr Gribben coming up the path to ask me any number
of questions on the arrangement of the tables, and Miriam I know
has a dozen questions from Cook.*

II.2

THEY HAD LEFT THE breakfast room together, and as they
stepped out of the house, Harriet thought she felt Crowther
flinch at her side. She could see nothing to alarm them, only
the broad sweep of the landscape rearing up on the far side of
the lake, and the lawn being prepared for the party. A number
of trestle tables were being set out, and the large man Harriet
recognised as the coachman of Silverside was setting up an
archery target by the lake. 'What is it, Crowther?'

'Nothing,' he said with a frown, but then lifted his cane to
point towards a place on the flank of the far hills. 'Only, when
I was a boy there were woods there. Great oaks. There were
more at the head of the lake in Crow Park. When I was very
young the village boys could cross from one side to the other
without touching the ground. My father sold the timber shortly

after he purchased it. It was strange, but for a moment I expected the woods to be there again.'

'Did you play there with your brother?'

He lowered the cane to the gravel path in front of them with a snort. 'No, madam. I do not remember ever playing with Addie. Though once or twice he forced me to act in some nonsense play. I refused once, and he tore up some drawings of mine of which I had been very proud. Luckily I was no actor, so he did not ask again. We did not ever have a close bond, even at that time.'

'You were a solitary child.'

'I cannot believe that surprises you, Mrs Westerman. The events of 1750 did not change me. They simply confirmed in me what I was.' He looked down at her with a slight smile. 'I hope you have not been imagining all this time I was the sort of creature my nephew appears to be, until my father's murder and my brother's execution drove me into my current reclusive character. You are not so foolishly romantic.'

Harriet almost blushed. 'No. But having heard you say that . . . Crowther, was there a sense of freedom when you sold the estate and sent off your sister to Ireland? Were you relieved? Did you ever have any love of this place at all?'

The haze in the atmosphere seemed to soften the light, though the heat of the day was already building. It gave even Crowther's face a glow, and he closed his eyes for a moment as if to drink it into himself.

'Addie was always the favourite with my parents. Then they doted on Margaret as the youngest child. I had some friends of a sort here, and there are places of which I was once fond, but my wish was always to escape. I became myself when I could leave Cumberland, so perhaps yes, I sold the estate in both anger and relief. There was even a certain pleasure at throwing it all to the winds. I never thought I would return.'

He began to walk towards the old brewery again, and Harriet followed him, deep in thought. Crowther might believe that returning to this house, meeting his nephew for the first time, and his sister after thirty years meant little to him, but he had never said so much to her before about his upbringing and the relations within his family.

They were met at the entrance to the old brew house by Miriam, the fair-haired and cheerful-looking maid Harriet had met the previous day. She dropped them a quick curtsey and a broad smile. Her face was rather red.

'The range in there is well built up now, Mr Crowther, as you asked, and the coppers bubbling away. They took some finding today!' She began to flap a breeze into her face with the corner of her apron. 'My, but that is warm work on a day like today. It's like Hell itself up by the fire. Though of course they say that is coming to us all now, the sun being all shorn and the meat spoiling on the day it's butchered, my lord.' Here she covered her mouth with her hand. 'I'm sorry, I mean to say, Mr Crowther, sir.'

Harriet looked down and smiled. Crowther said, 'I prefer the name Crowther, if you would be so kind, Miriam. What was that you said of the sun?'

'Shorn, sir. Does it not look to you as if its beams have been cut off?' They all three turned towards the east. Harriet found she could stare straight at the sun without pain. It was dull red, like the last embers of wood in a winter fire.

'It does,' Crowther agreed. 'But the world will not end today, Miriam.'

'I am glad to hear you say that, sir. For it would be a shame to spoil Mrs Briggs's party. Nor tomorrow?'

'Not for at least a hundred years. I have it on the best authority.'

Miriam looked considerably cheered and there was a skip in her step as she headed back to her duties in the main house.

'You were kind to that girl, Crowther.'

'I am practising better manners with my servants. I cannot stand firm under Mrs Heathcote's stern stares any longer. Who can say? Perhaps I shall become a civilised old man after all.'

Harriet cast a look at the heavens and pushed open the door to the old brew house.

It was a large structure with few signs as to the business that used to be done there, other than its name. She supposed that Mrs Briggs had her beer brought in from the village now. She did the same, and at Caveley too there was an outbuilding that had once been full of the yeasty smells of the weekly brewing for the table. The interior walls were roughly plastered and the earthen floor was beaten into an uneven but solid surface by years of use. At the back of the room, a simple stone fireplace had been well stacked with fuel, and there was a healthy fire under it. Harriet was about to ask why Crowther had requested it on such an oppressive day when, as her eyes adjusted to the relative gloom, she noticed an open coffin on the long table on the westerly wall. It was made of unpolished planks. A utilitarian object. The sight of it chilled her. She was at once back in the house where her husband had died, watching him being laid into his own coffin and the lid nailed down. The hammers had seemed unnaturally loud.

If Crowther noticed anything in her reaction, he chose to ignore it, simply walking over to the rough box and looking inside. She saw him raise a corner of the corpse's covering and sniff.

'Interesting. The remains seem to have been partially mummified; the tomb obviously provided an efficient seal. We must lower this to the floor, then lift its occupant out onto the table in his winding sheet. I can do nothing, leaning into his coffin.' Crowther set his cane against the wall. 'Shall I ask for one of the servants of the house to assist me, Mrs Westerman?'

Harriet shook out the apron she carried over her arm and started to tie it about her. 'They are much occupied with the preparations for the garden party. Do you doubt my strength or my stomach, Crowther?'

'Neither,' he replied. 'The body is highly desiccated – it should weigh very little.'

Harriet put her hands on to the coffin. It was indeed very light – the planks were thin. They placed it on the floor between them, Harriet cursing softly under her breath when a splinter caught a thread on her cuffs. She imagined explaining the damage to her housekeeper and grinned as she wondered what Mrs Heathcote's expression would be. Next they reached forward to grasp the sheet. As she adjusted her grip, Harriet felt the slight weight of the body shift in its shroud and a shiver ran through her.

'Mrs Westerman, I need only call—'

'Enough, Crowther. Let us lift him.' She was glad enough though when it was done, glad to release her grip as Crowther folded back the rough linen in which the body was wrapped.

100

It seemed hardly human — a leathery, twisted form. Unpleasant, unnatural, shocking even at first glance, but she did not turn away — instead, allowed herself to become accustomed to the sight. As she looked, her mind began to understand its contours as those of a human form, and it became under her eyes a corpse rather than a mass of leafmould and rotted clothing. There was the head, and that perhaps was hair framing it. Not a face, a skull wrapped in hessian and ashy paste. It was curled up on itself like a sleeping child. The head though was angled upwards, and the mouth was wide open as though the figure were screaming at someone above it. The head was a deep grey, only holes where the eyes had been. The teeth were visible though, apparently bared by the shrinking flesh around them. For a moment, as if watching from within, Harriet saw the heavy lid of the sarcophagus being shifted into place, the light disappearing with the grinding sound of stone on stone.

'Crowther, is there any chance this person was buried alive?'

He looked up from his own examination of the body then lifted the matted cloth of the cloak and folded it back to expose the hands. They lay one atop the other in front of the dead man's chest, shrunk into thin claws.

'I think not. Come here.'

Harriet crouched down to examine the dead fingers by his side. 'His nails are still intact,' she said, and reached out to touch them.

'Take care, Mrs Westerman. The body is delicate.'

'I am being careful. The nails are unbroken.'

He watched her as she touched the body, lost in concentration, her smooth cheek so close to the skeletal hands that if one finger had straightened it might have brushed her hair from her face. 'I think we can assume that if he were buried alive, he would have broken them in his struggles for release,' he said.

'Indeed,' she replied, then straightened up and smiled, apparently herself again. 'So in what manner *did* he die?'

'It is often impossible to answer that question when the body is still warm, madam. I have seen deaths recorded as a result of rage, or grief. On some occasions, all we can say is that a man or woman died because they ceased to live.' Harriet recognised the rebuke and removed herself a step, her hands crossed in front of her and looking as meek as she might without being suspected of satire. Crowther continued, 'The position of the mouth, I think we can assume, is a result of natural processes. This man had no one to close his jaw in death.' Harriet's mind clouded for a moment with the memory of her husband's body, but she thrust the thought from her.

Crowther stood back from the corpse and ran his eyes over it, noting the coloration, the flesh withered rather than rotted away as one might expect in a grave in the earth. Then the degree of degradation of the clothes, which were in a better state than they first appeared. If they were cleaned, the cloak and boots might still be almost wearable, if rather old-fashioned.

'It is remarkable what happens to us after death,' he said eventually. 'It would be of interest to document the process. Of course, most human bodies are too valuable for dissection to allow us the luxury of watching them rot, but it might be possible to conduct a useful experiment with pigs.'

This was too much for Harriet's meekness. 'You will be the patron saint of our butcher – though he might resent seeing good meat rot, as might anyone hungry in the village. But is there any way you can say how long this body was in the tomb?'

Crowther shook his head. 'We must make those experiments. Of course, it is easier to estimate when a body is relatively fresh. Now we can only say that the process of decay is more or less complete.'

'We have seen the date of the snuffbox, but that only suggests he could not have been so unceremoniously interred before 1742. Though I suppose it is possible he was placed in the tomb a hundred years ago and the snuffbox was dropped in there at some later date.'

'And tucked into his pocket by the opposite of a grave-robber? Unlikely. I do not think I can offer any definitive statement. It was more than ten years ago, I would hazard. I do not think these effects could have occurred in a lesser period.' Crowther sighed. 'There is much to be discovered in the area. I wonder if Sir Stephen would be interested in assisting me?'

Sir Stephen was an acquaintance of theirs in Pulborough who had an all-consuming interest in the insect world. Harriet was confused by his sudden appearance in the conversation.

'I have noted how some insects appear in the flesh at various stages of decomposition,' Crowther continued comfortably. 'If Sir Stephen would be interested in making a systematic study . . .'

'I have no doubt he would, but you are neither of you in the first flush of youth. You might have to bequeath your work to others before your experiments were complete.'

The thought did not seem to concern Crowther unduly. 'From what I have seen of my nephew, it would give me some satisfaction to leave him a field of rotting pigs.'

Harriet smiled. 'You do not like Felix. I thought him rather intelligent.'

'Did you? He reminds me of my brother at that age, so I suspect his temper. No, I do not like him.'

Harriet turned away from the body. 'I like him less today. I met him this morning in the ruins of Gutherscale Hall. I think he meant to frighten me.' She hesitated. 'He seems to fear I might be a threat to his inheritance.'

There was a silence. 'I shall horsewhip him myself.'

She shook her head. 'You shall do no such thing, Crowther. I believe he regretted saying such things as soon as they were spoken.'

'Are you quite sure, Mrs Westerman?' Crowther asked, opening his eyes a little wider. 'I have had the urge to horsewhip him ever since I saw the manner in which he ties his cravat.'

Harriet shook her head again and tried not to laugh.

Stephen had bolted his breakfast and was outside as soon as he could persuade his tutor away from the bacon. Mr Quince was pleased to oblige and proposed a walk through the village of Portinscale and into Keswick. 'Mr West informs me,' he said, tapping his guidebook, 'that the best views of the lake are from a point on the other shore. Shall we test him?'

Stephen was happy to try it, and ran to and fro along the path like a young dog. 'I was asking Miriam about Casper, sir,' he said when his first flush of energy was run off and he found himself back at Mr Quince's side.

'Were you? And what did Miriam have to say?'

'That he lives in the hills almost all year round and sleeps in the charcoalburners' huts or the woodcutters' old camps, though he is quite rich.' Mr Quince looked down at the boy. He obviously saw something to admire in Casper's sleeping arrangements. 'And also that he knows all about bogles and dobies and the fair-folk and witches, and comes and visits people when they are sick. He is a cunning-man. They say he has healing powers, but the boggarts pull his hair sometimes and make him strange. But only sometimes.'

'And what are bogles? Or dobies, for that matter.'

Stephen looked proud. 'There, now I can tell *you* something, sir. Dobies are often helpful. Bogles are bad luck and look like dead people. They say Casper's father saw one once, and that was when the small-pox came upon him.'

'You are very thoroughly informed! How long did you keep that girl from her work?'

'She did not mind.' He kicked a stone in the path and it skittered across the road, startling a pheasant into flight. They paused to watch it retreat clumsily into the field, clucking in outraged magnificence.

'Do you believe in ghosts, Stephen?'

'I do not think so. But perhaps I would if they pulled my hair.'

Quince breathed the air in deeply. 'I do not think even Mr Crowther could fault your logic on that point, my lad. Now let us not dawdle. I hope we may join one of the boats that leave from Keswick to show the lake, and perhaps visit the museum in the town. They have a picture of the Luck there, and we can compare it to your carving.'

Distracted by the body itself, Harriet only now remembered to ask Crowther about the fire and the pans steaming above it.

'I intend to boil this gentleman's bones.'

Harriet was aware he was watching her for a reaction. 'Why?' she managed at last, faintly.

'This body is far too old for me to make use of my usual methods, madam. What little flesh remains is mummified.' Harriet nodded. It looked like rotted wood to her, as if a touch would turn it to dust in places. In others it was leathery and black. 'It is very unlikely to tell us a great deal. However, the bones may. To remove the remaining flesh by slow boiling will reveal anything they have to say to us without damaging them further.'

She frowned at him. 'You know the body is to be buried in a few days? I understand the vicar has found room in the graveyard at Crosthwaite for him. Mrs Briggs has even picked the verse for the tombstone. Do you think it will please the reverend gentleman to know you have been making soup of the corpse?'

A smile glimmered across Crowther's face. 'We can spare the vicar's feelings by sealing the coffin before he takes charge of the remains. And by not giving him too many details of the manner of our investigation.'

No one else would have thought Crowther looked in any way excited, but Harriet could tell he was delighted at the thought of cleaning the bones. She watched him with amused resignation. 'I am glad the cook has not lent you her best pans.'

A shadow crossed the edge of their vision, and they looked up to see they were observed from the doorway by Mr Sturgess and another gentleman. He was an oddly dwarfish little man, though powerfully built, purple-faced with very full lips, and was blinking rapidly at them.

Mr Sturgess advanced when he saw they had been noticed. 'Good morning, Mrs Westerman, Mr Crowther. Mrs Briggs told us where you were and I am afraid we could not resist disturbing you briefly. I wished to introduce you to Mr Askew.' The other man shuffled in. 'He owns our new museum in Keswick.'

'Delighted,' Harriet murmured and dropped a curtsey. It was peculiar to find herself acting as if she were in a drawing room with the corpse lying exposed between them, but she was unsure what the *Lady's Magazine* would advise in the circumstances.

Mr Askew bowed in return and continued to inch towards them. 'This is the poor fellow then? How horrible.' His eyes bulged a little. 'We put a notice in the window of the museum, you know, but no information has been offered.'

He craned his neck upwards and stared down at the corpse's open mouth, his lips opening a little as if he were mimicking the expression of the body. Harriet glanced at Crowther, who was looking at the museum owner very coolly, then she turned to the magistrate.

'Any more ill-gotten treasures for us, Mr Sturgess?'

He shook his head, but before he could put his reply into words Mr Askew had turned his shining eyes towards Harriet.

'Mr Sturgess mentioned you were in possession of a snuffbox that was found on the body. May I see it?'

Harriet hesitated, then reached into the pockets of her skirts and handed it to Mr Askew over the remains of its former owner. He licked his lips and turned it over in his hands. Harriet felt the sting of his sweat in her nostrils. 'Oh, that is very pretty! I hope Mrs Briggs might be persuaded to donate it to the museum in due course. It is just the sort of thing that grabs the interest, you know. Do you not agree, Mr Sturgess?'

Sturgess stepped forward to view the body. 'Undoubtedly,' he said as he examined the corpse's face, then almost to himself, 'how these little objects mock us. It so solid and this man . . . Alas, poor Yorick . . .' He stepped back again. 'Forgive us, we are keeping you from your work. We came to invite you to Mr Askew's entertainment on the shores of the lake this evening.'

'Indeed,' Askew said with a beam. 'After the gathering here at Silverside we are to have fireworks launched from Vicar's Island at the north end of the lake. I hope all of the party at Silverside will grace us with their presence. I have left tickets, with my compliments. There will be punch, and I expect quite a squeeze. The town is full of visitors at the moment.' He handed the snuffbox back to Harriet. 'And all of the neighbouring gentry will be in attendance. I had it also in my mind to mention to Herr von Bolsenheim that I chanced upon an acquaintance of his from Vienna in town, visiting with his daughter, but I understand he has left to spend the morning in Cockermouth.'

Harriet put the box back into her pocket. 'I think he is already aware. Mrs Briggs mentioned to us there was some such person in town, but I do not think they are closely acquainted.'

Sturgess seemed ready to take his leave, but Mr Askew was not yet done with them.

'I was also wondering if I might persuade Lord Keswick . . .' he bowed towards Crowther, 'to address a small meeting at the museum on the unusual atmosphere of this summer at some time during your stay. We should like to take advantage of having such an esteemed Fellow of the Royal Society in our midst.'

'I must decline,' Crowther said shortly. 'I have no specialist knowledge in the area.'

Askew looked a little deflated, making Harriet pity him, however much she wished him away.

'This part of the country has spent much of its history largely cut off from the world,' said Sturgess. His voice was rich and light. Too conscious though, Harriet thought, too aware of itself. 'Many people in the villages are ready to blame witches and bogles, and light needful fires to try and drive off this haze. Will you not help to educate them?'

'Would such people attend a meeting at the museum?' Crowther asked.

Sturgess paused, then said frankly, 'No, I cannot pretend they would.'

'Well then.'

'But perhaps the vicar will attend, then he can share the information with his flock,' Mr Askew said, in a hopeful tone.

'You cannot persuade a population out of superstition so easily,' Crowther said, his tone dismissive. 'The people here will believe in witches and lucks and any parcel of nonsense till it suits them to think otherwise. Neither the vicar nor myself will convince them.'

'You think the local legends nonsense?' Sturgess said.

'I do,' Crowther replied, meeting the other man's eye.

Harriet did not like the tone of the exchange, and gave as warm a smile as she could muster to the two gentlemen, saying, 'Crowther believes that the Italian earthquakes may be in some way to blame for the dry fog, but he is like all natural philosophers, in that he devotes himself to one problem at a time, and for the moment that problem is this poor wretch. I hope you will excuse us.'

Mr Askew seemed comforted and Harriet could see him planning to offer up this opinion around the village even as the words were leaving her mouth. Mr Sturgess bowed to her again and they returned to the sunlight. Harriet was only relieved that neither of them had thought to ask about the fire.

'You need not trouble yourself to explain me away, madam.' Crowther's mouth was firm set. 'And I am quite capable of dealing with several trains of thought at one time.'

Harriet folded her arms. 'I am aware of that, Crowther. But I do not think you need to be so uncivil to strangers. Oh, and as I seem to be scolding you, I shall add that whatever his behaviour this morning, I pitied your nephew last night.'

Crowther looked genuinely surprised at that. 'Did you? Why?'

'I do not think you were kind to him.'

'He has no head for wine. He talked a great deal of nonsense to me at the dinner table after you had withdrawn, including his reflections on the fairer sex, none of which made me think well of him. Then he asked me for money.'

'Poor Felix. I take it you did not give him any.'

'No, I did not.'

'He is handsome – perhaps he will marry money if he cannot afford to wait until he inherits your field of rotting pigs.'

Crowther did not reply but placed his scalpel at the corpse's neck and began to test the resistance the mummified flesh gave to his blade. His mind had obviously turned back to their late visitors. 'I do not understand why people feel the necessity of quoting Shakespeare at every turn. Have they no words of their own?'

'You have few enough, sir,' Harriet replied as she watched his delicate movements. 'I admire a talent for quotation.'

'Parroting great writers is no substitute for understanding them.' Crowther bent low over the body and sighed. 'A being of above average height. I suspect we will learn nothing further until the flesh is removed, and even then we may discover nothing. This is not good for my vanity, Mrs Westerman. All we may ever know about this man may be learned by the snuffbox that fell from his pocket and your son's sharp eyes. Let us remove the clothing.'

To mock his own pride, however gently, was as near to an apology for his irritability as Harriet was ever likely to receive from Crowther. She went to the feet of the corpse and, taking another of Crowther's knives in her own hand, began to cut free the man's boots. The leather was tough. When she had split it from the calf to the foot she pulled it, very gently, free and set it down on the table to her side, then did the same to the other. There was a moment as she was pulling the second one free that she was afraid she was in danger of separating the man's joints.

'Mrs Westerman, I think we must turn the body.'

'Very well.' She stepped next to Crowther and they placed their hands along the man's side and pulled him towards them. The limbs were awkward, but they managed to turn the body without damage. It was an intimacy with the dead that Harriet did not savour. She moved away and washed her hands as Crowther cut and pulled free the remaining cloth. By the time she turned round again, he had managed to untangle the remains of the cloak, and remove the coat. He was building a small pile of buttons and fastenings to one side.

'This cloak was once fine quality cloth,' he said.

'The boots are also well made.'

He nodded, lifting the coat into the air. 'A traveller.' Something fell through the rotted material on to the earthen floor. Harriet bent down to pick it up – a leather purse with a drawstring on it.

Crowther watched as she shook the contents out onto the table. There were a number of shillings and two sovereigns. 'The motive for this murder was not robbery then,' he said.

Harriet looked up from the collection of dark coins; she was examining the dates stamped on each. There was one from 1720, three from the 1730s and the youngest of the collection was from 1743. 'We know so little, and yet you are ready to call it murder?'

'Why else would the body be concealed?'

She frowned. 'There might be several reasons. Crowther, have you formulated a theory already about this death? That is unlike you.'

He hesitated. 'My brother was often in Cumberland in the forties, avoiding his creditors or trying to persuade more money out of our parents. A man who in the end murdered his father for the bills in his pocket might well have killed another to escape a debt. It would be like Adair to kill, and then in his panic forget to search his victim's pockets for coin.'

Harriet stared at him as he turned again to his instrument case. His voice was utterly cool.

II.3

THE VIEWS FROM THE Duke of Portland's launch were impressive even in the haze. Mr Quince was content for Stephen to enjoy them without comment and let his own mind wander. His eye fell on the profile of a young woman seated in the stern, apparently unaccompanied. She was perhaps a little younger than himself, scarcely twenty, yet she held herself very upright. Quince did not see pride in the straightness of her spine, however, only the habit of strict self-control. It interested him and he was inclined to look at her longer than perhaps he should have done. She felt his eyes on her and turned towards him. Her eyes were almost black and set large in a heart-shaped face. Quince was embarrassed to have been caught staring. The wild beauty of the landscape was making him romantic. He turned his attention to where Stephen was engaged in helping the loading of a small cannon on the prow.

Quince thought his charge a sensitive and intelligent boy, but was most impressed by his ability to make friends with whomever came in his way. Even Mr Crowther, who could barely conceal his disdain for his own sister and nephew, was apparently fond of Stephen. It was natural then that in the few minutes that had passed since they began their cruise, Stephen would have become a trusted member of the crew. He was thrusting the charge into the little cannon now under the encouraging eye of one of the oarsmen. Quince was watching him with a smile when he felt a light touch on his sleeve and turned to find the black-eyed beauty leaning towards him.

'Excuse me, sir.' Her voice had a heavy German accent

which gave her English an oddly precise tone. 'What are we shooting at?'

He felt a sudden pride at being so accosted, quite out of proportion with the honour, and became a little pink. After all, the only other pleasure-seekers in the boat this early in the day were a young couple who sat so close together, and were so involved in each other's thoughts and exclamations at the scenery, Quince could only assume they were on their marriage tour. He cleared his throat.

'We will not shoot at anyone, I am glad to say, madam. I understand the gun is to be fired to test the echoes in the valley. They are said to be remarkable. Every shot is heard a number of times around the lake.'

This answer seemed to satisfy the lady and she began to turn from him again. Quince felt a strong desire to prevent her attention slipping away from him.

'Do you like the scenery, madam?' he enquired.

She looked about her as if noticing it for the first time. 'It is very pretty,' she said in a rather dull voice, and while Quince was struggling for some further remark, his attention was called by Stephen. He had a slow match ready and, once he was sure Mr Quince was watching, he set it to the charge.

The powder in the pan fizzed yellow and red a moment, then the cannon gave a sharp crack and the smell of gunpowder enveloped them. The launch trembled. The crack was followed by answering roars from the hills on each side, as if it had awoken a tribe of giants on the fells. Quince counted seven distinct reports before the sound folded into a low thunderous growl and died away. The men on the boat looked pleased.

'Peter, mark this spot,' one said to the other, with a wink. 'I've never heard it go off as well!'

Stephen seemed to take this as a compliment to himself and beamed at the company. The female of the young couple had given a little yelp as the cannon fired. From the German woman there came no sound at all; she only closed her magnificent eyes briefly and Quince saw her fingers tighten on the bench on which she sat.

Preparing the body for the pots was grisly work. Now and again, Harriet would become aware of what she was about and shudder. She wondered about Crowther's idea that this man was a creditor of his brother's. It was to a degree plausible. If his brother had been capable of patricide, might he not have committed another murder? Surely that was more likely than two beings who were capable of killing, existing in such a small community as this. But the dates on the coins that pointed so closely to the 1745 rebellion, and the apparent sympathies of the murdered man, troubled her. Could a man marked out for his loyalty to the exiled Lord Greta be also a creditor of Lucius Adair? Wasn't it more likely that the man had returned to the region because of some business of his master's, and wouldn't that business more likely be with Crowther's father rather than his brother?

She shook her head as if she could in that way settle the questions into some sort of order, then continued with her task. Crowther, she noticed, looked quite cheerful at his work. She thought uncharitably of cannibals. When the pots were cooking at the intensity Crowther thought correct, Harriet found herself keen to leave the building. The odour had become unpleasant almost at once. The moment he pronounced himself satisfied, the pots stewing gently, she removed her apron and walked into the hazy sunshine, breathing deeply. Crowther followed her with a basin of clean water and a towel over his arm like a valet. He set it down on a bench by the door and with a look, invited her to make use of it.

'It will take some hours before the bones are clean enough for me to examine,' he said. 'But the fire is low and may do its work unsupervised.' She nodded and put her hands in the water, only stepping aside when her skin was pink with scrubbing. She watched him take her place.

'Crowther, have you ever wondered how different your life might have been had you offered your sister a home with you?'

'No,' he said shortly, but as he moved his hands through the water he thought of what a check on his studies and travels taking charge of a young girl would have been. He thought of the lecture rooms of Europe where he had gained his knowledge of anatomy while his sister had learned French and country dances. For ten years his clothing had carried the continual scent of preserving liquid and he doubted she would have liked the smell. The places where he had studied and the things he had learned would have been lost to him, and all for the dubious pleasures of driving fortune-hunters away from his unsympathetic sister. Then something reminded him that Mrs Westerman had given up her own life of travel to provide a home for her orphaned sister. He told himself she also had a son to care for, so the circumstances could not be compared, but as he dried his hands, he said: 'At least, I had not considered it until now. And I do not think I shall do so again.'

Harriet turned towards the lake. 'I suppose we must prepare

for the afternoon's entertainment. Let us lock the door and pray no one thinks to enquire what is happening in the brew house while they are enjoying their ices and watching the archery competition.' She was suddenly startled by the sound of a gunshot, and looked about her as the hills seemed to grow alive with the harsh coughs of repeated explosions. Crowther came up to her and pointed towards a small boat in the centre of the lake. A little grey plume, darker than the general haze, hung over it.

'They are testing the echoes, Mrs Westerman. No need to be alarmed.'

Stephen was still very pleased with his success with the cannon when they reached the shore again, and chattered away as they disembarked. He distracted Quince to the extent that his tutor hardly knew he had turned to offer his hand to the German beauty and was helping her onto the jetty. He tried to think of a way to introduce himself to her in a gentlemanlike manner, but was pre-empted by the boy, who had already put out his hand to the lady, and was looking up at her with a friendly smile.

'Good morning! Were not the echoes fine? I am Stephen Westerman, of Caveley in Hartswood, Sussex.'

The woman shook his hand. 'Then you find yourself far from home, but not as far as I. I am Sophia – Sophia Hurst from Vienna. They were good echoes.'

'You are German!' Stephen said.

'Austrian,' she corrected him gently.

Quince cleared his throat. 'Are you walking up into town, madam? May we accompany you?'

She nodded, and as they walked away from the jetty, she was treated to a monologue from Stephen of all he knew of Austria. Quince wondered if he should check the boy, but Fräulein Hurst seemed happy to hear the history of her nation retold to her. Just as he was beginning to think Stephen's account might be becoming tiresome to even the most forgiving listener, he heard a whistle from the woods along the track and saw the boy's face break into a smile.

'Mr Casper!' Stephen shouted. 'Did you hear the echoes? Is Joe with you?'

Their strange friend sauntered out of the woods to meet them, a pair of dead rabbits slung over his shoulder. Quince had never seen a man move with such careless ease and watched with admiration. Quince always suspected he was in danger of making himself ridiculous, or had just done so. He was reasonably sure such thoughts had never entered the head of Casper Grace, and envied him. Casper nodded, then pointed into the woods behind him where the jackdaw was visible on the path. The bird was turning rotten leaves over with the same air of sceptical interest that Quince saw on Crowther's face when he was reading; the jackdaw's bright blue eye and silver flash on the top of his head made the resemblance only stronger. Casper put his hand in his pocket and took out a fistful of corn.

'Go offer him that, youngling, and he may speak to you.'

Stephen took the corn from him and stepped forward carefully, intent. Apparently Casper only now became aware of the lady and he hesitated. Quince took charge.

'Fräulein Hurst, this is Casper Grace.' Casper looked at her for a long moment and Quince thought he saw an expression of concern cross the man's face. Then Casper seemed to feel that he had looked too long and, blushing, began to stow the rabbits in his shoulder pouch.

'I am glad to meet you, Casper,' the lady said in her precise way. He looked pleased and scratched the back of his neck.

'Saw you, Mr Quince, and the young one on the boat. Thought I'd come and meet you. Wondered if you'd like to go up and see the stones, as if you've a mind to be guided, I've time.'

Now Mr Quince's eyes seemed to shine. 'The Druidic stones? Oh yes, I should like that very much indeed. I had hoped to see them as we came into town yesterday, but I missed them, I fear. We were thinking of visiting the museum, but no doubt we may do that on the morrow.'

Sophia tilted her head to one side. 'Druidic? I do not know this word.'

Quince thought her frown delightful. 'Of the Druids,' he explained. 'The ancient religion of the area.'

She nodded. 'Of course, foolish of me. We have the same word in my language.'

Casper addressed her. 'You would be welcome to come too, miss. They can be a comfort and help, the stones. Men have spoken there of serious things since time began, and they keep the wisdom, I reckon. If I have a thought needs cracking, it's where I go.'

Quince turned to her with a formal bow. 'If you are at liberty, Fräulein, we would be very glad of your company.'

She paused before making her decision, but when she did, she smiled. 'I thank you. My father, with whom I am travelling, today has business elsewhere. I should be happy to come.' She took his arm, and Quince wished some of his acquaintance might observe him dressed as a gentleman, with this beautiful woman at his side: they might mistake him for a man of consequence. Stephen approached them again, with Joe perched on his shoulder.

'I am glad you are coming, Fräulein,' he said, then tugged on Casper's sleeve. 'May I have Joe on my shoulder as we go, Mr Casper?'

'You may,' he replied, turning on to the track again, 'though the lazy beggar could just flap his wings.'

Quince glanced at the Fräulein's profile, though he saw only in her face a slight glimmer of amusement that gleamed in her eyes like reflections in polished marble.

It was further than Quince had guessed; the path was steep and they went slowly in the heat. The tutor estimated they must have walked some two miles from the lakeshore when Casper let them into a cornfield off the Penrith road and he saw the Druidic stones for the first time. He held his breath. They were arranged in a slightly elongated circle some thirty yards in diameter, perhaps fifty hulks of grey granite of varying size. Casper led them between two individuals which seemed to form a sort of gate and into the centre, then watched them as they took in the sight. The ground where the stones had been set was on the top of a smooth rise, and the field around them gently curved like the backbone of a cat that wishes to be stroked. The lake itself was hidden from them; instead they seemed to be at the centre of a wide amphitheatre of hills that hid the horizon like piles of crumpled linen. There were fields and farms visible at their bases, then they climbed and tumbled over each other till they disappeared into the haze of the sky. Behind them Skiddaw slept, softer seen from here. Mr Quince thought of ancient peoples gathering in this place, and wondered if they had lit grand fires between the stones, and what was consumed in their flames, what prayers made, what bargains struck with their gods and each other.

Stephen was not as bloodthirsty as many boys of his age, no matter how much he liked to re-enact the naval battles of his father on the lawns of Caveley Park. His first question, however, was still about whether human sacrifice had taken place there.

'Maybe, maybe, Master Stephen,' Casper replied. 'They say there was a time the cunning-men used to burn maidens here for their gods till one day, such was the love the son of the tribe's leader had for the girl to be burned, the skies opened up in mercy and the rains put out the fires. So they let her live and no other girls were killed thereafter.'

Mr Quince smiled. 'Do you believe that, Mr Grace?'

Casper shrugged. 'There are many stories about the stones, and I am sure they have some power in them, though I hope it was not bought with blood. That was an old story, and here's a fresh one. I know that one time a year or two back, when that Mr Sturgess wished to excavate this place with gunpowder, there was such a storm on the day he came up here! Such lightning and rain to make this year's weather look like a summer shower, and it seemed to fall right here.'

'The excavations were halted then?'

'They were. And he was told there'd be no more. So I reckon the stones and sky do talk.'

'I have met Mr Sturgess at Silverside,' Quince said, frowning.

'He came with a passion to know of old things and old ways,' Casper said. 'Though perhaps he just likes to dig like a badger. He carved out a cave on his own land and had it lined with seashells.'

'How charming!' Quince said at the thought, then saw something in Casper's look that made him blush and drop his eyes.

'Still, he found some stone axe heads for Mr Askew's museum, before the rain drove him off and his workers' pay was stopped,' Casper finished.

Quince turned to see if Fräulein Hurst was listening. He could not say, since she seemed lost in contemplation of the hills surrounding them.

Stephen spoke. 'Are *you* a cunning-man, sir? Miriam at Silverside Hall says you are.'

Casper scratched the back of his neck and Mr Quince began to fear he was finding them wearisome. 'She may call me what she will. There are some who come to me. Hope I have some influence with them when their animals get sick, or they have a pain in their belly.'

'And what do you do? Are there really witches still? Can they change shape? Was Joe a witch once – is that why he can talk?'

Quince stepped forward to put a warning hand on Stephen's shoulder, but Casper sank down on his haunches and looked the boy in the eye.

'Joe was always what he is. I found him fallen from the nest when he was but a bit of a thing, and he learned his speech from me. I know something of the calendar and of healing, maybe enough of flowers and roots to be thought cunning.

Witches there are. Though I think 'em for the most part like that lightning rod stuck up on Crosthwaite Church. There are people that just suck up the magic in the air whether they will it or not, and it can flash out of them. Some know it though, and learn its ways. Some use it to help and heal, some to curse and trouble – and magic does to them as they do to others. Most people carry a bit of rowan with them, stop it flashing at them and theirs. You have yours now in that cross I gave you. Have you kept it?' Stephen nodded, and Quince noticed the lad's fist clenching in his coat-pocket. He wondered what his employer would think of her son learning a philosophy of witchcraft when under his care. 'There, that's rowan, so you'll have nothing to fear.'

Quince cleared his throat. 'Stephen, it is said to be impossible to count the stones twice and get the same number. Will you try it?'

Stephen looked a little surly for a moment, as if he might resist so obvious an attempt to separate him from Casper, but the challenge was an interesting one, so he walked to the edge of the circle and patted one of the blocks, then moved onto the next, allowing his elders to return to a contemplation of the view.

'I think you have no belief in witches then, sir?' Casper said to the tutor.

'No,' Quince replied, 'but if I had lived my life among these hills and alongside these stones, I might.'

'Vicar tries to beat it out of us,' Casper shrugged, 'but his God seems like a child to me at times.'

Quince found his mind's eye filling with ancient fires again. He noticed Casper's hands, callused working hands, then looked at his own, white and clumsy. The two men watched Stephen on the other side of the circle pause for a moment, then continue in his count. Fräulein Hurst was turned away towards the road, deep in thought. Quince fumbled for his watch and cleared his throat.

'Fascinating. I fear the hour is more advanced than I thought, Mrs Briggs is having her summer party at Silverside this afternoon, so we should return.'

This seemed to wake Miss Hurst. 'You are staying at Silverside?'

'We are, madam. Perhaps we shall see you among the guests?' She shook her head. 'Or perhaps at the fireworks display in the evening?'

'I hope so,' she said, and lowered her eyes.

'Will you be coming to see the display, Mr Grace?'

Stephen was near enough to hear this exchange, and was caught mid-count by the mention of fireworks.

'Oh, I had forgotten the fireworks!' He then turned back to the stones and put his hand to his head. 'Oh Lord, I have lost count.'

Casper was squinting into the haze. 'No. Joe and I don't like the bangs and crashes so much. I'll head down into Borrowdale till they're done.'

As the little party passed into Keswick, Casper bowed to them awkwardly then turned to head back out of the town. Then he hesitated and returned to them with a swift step and pulled another of his carvings of the Luck out of his pocket. Taking the Fräulein's hand, he pressed it into her palm.

'Here you are, ma'am. A little Luck for you.' Then he began to move away again with his shoulders hunched.

Quince smiled, tutting a little. 'Mr Askew will be angry with him for giving away his wares again.'

A look of sudden realisation crossed Stephen's face and he trotted up the track after Casper, ignoring the tutor's exasperated sigh.

'What is it, youngling?' Casper asked as the boy came panting up to him. He looked fierce, and Stephen was suddenly afraid of him, and backed off a step.

'I only wanted to say you have no need to worry about Mr Askew because I have asked my mama, and I am to buy a cross from the museum for my Aunt Rachel, and for my little sister Anne too, so you gave one away, but sold two, do you see?'

Casper's face lightened and he dropped his hand on Stephen's shoulder. 'That's a kindness to me, and one to your aunt, and one to your sister. So there's one kindness become three. How old is your sister?'

'Three and a half, Mr Casper. So I think it safe to give it to her. She has stopped chewing things so much, though she is not careful with her toys.'

'I had a sister once, used to say the same of me.'

'What happened to her?'

Casper blinked rapidly a few times. 'She was always walking, and one day she walked away. She wished me luck, and said she was sorry to leave me, but the valley had drawn tight and felt to throttle her. Well, bless her wherever she might be. Sure she says the same to me. So there's more kindness for the pile.' He sniffed and settled his bag across his shoulder again. 'I've got to go, youngling. There is smoke in the air, and whispering, and I've a mind to be ownsome.'

Stephen stepped aside and Casper set off up the path again, murmuring under his breath. He turned to see Fräulein Hurst and Mr Quince still bent over the little carving. Sophia was smiling at it.

'Oh, that is kind. I asked my father to buy me one at the museum, but he would not.'

'How much better to have it as a gift, then, from its maker,' Quince said.

As Stephen approached Sophia asked him, 'So do you think Mr Casper is a cunning-man, Master Westerman?'

Stephen considered. 'I am not sure what he is, Miss Hurst. But I think he is very clever.'

She looked again at the cross in her hand. 'Yes, I think he is too.' She drew in her breath and turned to Mr Quince. 'Sir, I wonder if you could do me a great kindness.'

II.4

MRS BRIGGS'S GARDEN PARTY was always an event. But this year's in particular provided much conversation for the gentry of Cumberland in the months that followed. It was the lost Lord Keswick, Mr Gabriel Crowther, who attracted most attention during the party itself, though Mrs Westerman was also narrowly observed by each matron and frankly admired by many of the younger men. Mrs Briggs was as pleasant as ever, the Vizegräfin considered to be rather high-handed, and Felix, until the unfortunate events of the latter part of the afternoon unfolded, was said to have set the hearts of many a young woman beating at an unnatural pace.

Mrs Briggs was acknowledged an excellent hostess by her friends and neighbours, and it was agreed she had surpassed herself this afternoon. Shades had been set out at convenient intervals all about the lawns so as to provide some shelter from the heat. Ices were served on the upper parts of the lawn, and by the lake her guests could watch the gentlemen who were so inclined shoot arrows across the width of the grass, then compete for a silver arrow that had been commissioned in London for the occasion.

Harriet allowed herself to be handed about by her hostess for as long as she could bear it, and paused to watch the archery competition. There were a surprising number of competitors and she was impressed by the quality of the shooting. The prize was taken by a lawyer's son visiting relatives in Ambleside. He was delighted, but several gentlemen had cause to be sorry at his success. The betting had heavily favoured Felix after the practice sessions, but when the competition was opened he seemed to have been cursed, since his shots were barely competent. He was heard to complain, and the gentlemen were embarrassed at having put any faith in him.

Harriet continued to shake hands, but after the fifth time she had heard herself referred to as 'original', she pleaded exhaustion in the heat and retreated to the most shaded part of the lawn, from where she hoped to see Crowther being pursued by the curious for a change, and watch him swat them away like biting flies.

As soon as she seated herself, however, she found she was not to be alone after all. There was a stir in the shadows and a woman appeared, of early middle age and dressed neatly in grey with a bonnet that cast a further shadow over her face, so that her features were almost invisible to Harriet's heated eyes.

'Mrs Westerman!' The lady offered her hand. 'I am Katherine Scales. My father is the vicar of Crosthwaite. I am delighted to meet you.'

Harriet took the hand offered and gathered her strength for the proper niceties.

'Now please, Mrs Westerman, I saw the expression on your face as you sat down. You are worn out with meeting people, I am sure. Do make yourself comfortable and we shall watch the party together. Or rather I shall chatter, and you need do no more than pretend to listen.' Harriet thanked her. 'I would be a monster to say anything else, but I *am* glad to meet you, Mrs Westerman! It is like becoming acquainted with a character from a novel. My father loves to hear me read in the evenings, and sometimes encourages me to read from the newspapers as well as from Mr Clarke's *Sermons*, so we have heard all about your cleverness and bravery.'

Such speeches normally made Harriet nervous, but it was all spoken with such comfortable warmth she could not help thinking the lady sincere.

'They write a great deal of nonsense,' she replied politely, 'but if they have managed to create a good opinion of me, I shall hold my tongue.' Her eyes were now adapting themselves to the relative gloom, and she saw she had been correct in thinking Miss Scales was some years over forty. In her figure and features there was much to admire, but the skin on her face and hands was badly marked with the pitted scars of small-pox, and one of her eye-sockets was apparently empty, judging by the way the lid fell over it. She reminded Harriet of a statue of some ancient god found among the rubble of its former temple. The disease had chipped away at her and left her face a ruined memory of itself.

'Now let me take advantage of meeting a stranger to say all sorts of cutting things about my neighbours, Mrs Westerman.' Miss Scales folded her hands in her lap. 'As the daughter of a clergyman I have to be terribly understanding about everybody most of the time, so it would be a great release to me.'

Miss Scales was an amusing guide to Mrs Briggs's neighbours, but even having claimed the freedom to say what she wished, she said little that was not generous in spirit and humour. Miss Scales had apparently not been driven into solitude by her disfigurement. It became clear while she chattered and Harriet rested that she kept house for her father, went among his parishioners every day, seemed quite happy in the company she found and was confident of her usefulness.

Harriet was still listening to Miss Scales when her son approached and silently climbed into her lap. He was bored, she supposed, or had been eating too many ices. Mr Quince had been shooting arrows with the other men, and she had no doubt that, unsupervised, Stephen would have charmed more rich food than was good for him out of the servants. After a few moments Harriet realised he was staring at the scars on Miss Scales's hands and hoped the lady did not mark it. Having finished her description of last year's regatta, however, Miss Scales turned to the boy at her side.

'You are looking at my hands, Mr Stephen. And so you might, for they are funny-looking things, are they not?'

Stephen nodded. 'Why are they like that, ma'am?'

'I had small-pox when I was a young girl.' She pointed to her dead eye. 'It cost me this too, you see. But I am thankful. I lived, and whatever other sin I commit, at least I shall never be vain. Think of all those ladies who must suffer so when

129

they lose their looks with age. I shall never be any uglier than I am now, even if I live to be ninety! But I lost far more than what you see. My mother and sister were taken to God by the illness, and I miss them still every day.'

Stephen looked up at her with his clear blue eyes. 'I think you look kind. And you must be very strong, ma'am, to have lived.'

Harriet saw a flush touch Miss Scales's face and was proud of her child.

'I like you almost as much as I do your mother. She has let me clear out my lungs for the last ten minutes and had the courtesy to look amused the whole time. I was saved, my boy.'

'You are not sad then, ma'am?'

'No, bless you. Well, perhaps a little when I see a lady as pretty as your mama, but I have the love of my father and my friends, and of God Himself so I am thankful for every day.'

'Did Mr Casper come and see you when you were sick? He visits sick people, does he not?' Stephen asked.

'Casper was very young himself at that time. It was his father, Ruben Grace, who was the cunning-man in those days, though Ruben did service as a steward in this house for many years too, and owned the Black Pig Inn in Portinscale in later times.' She frowned and lifted her hand to her face. 'I think I do remember them coming to see me though, Casper and Ruben. Must have been a hard way for the lad to learn his father's trade. They visited every house where the sickness was, bless them for their kindness, and there were many that year, but I was so ill I hardly know what I saw and what I dreamed.'

Harriet shifted to face them. 'He brought his son with him?

I cannot imagine taking Stephen into a house where the sickness was.'

Miss Scales smiled sadly. 'They were stuck close together, Mrs Westerman. Ruben had lost his wife some years before and clung to the boy, though he had sent his daughter to live with her aunt. Now what *was* her name? She was thought of as a troublemaker in the village, though I'm sure she was just injured by the way her father cast her off, and the aunt was never a kind woman . . .' She lifted her hand to the sky, then gave it a sudden flourish. 'Jocasta! That was it — married a man called Bligh over in Kendal, then we all lost sight of her.'

Harriet smiled widely. 'Jocasta Bligh! We know her! She lives in London now. I had every intention of making enquiries after her family, but the matter slipped my mind until now. So *she* is the sister of the famous Casper Grace.'

Miss Scales tilted her head to Harriet. 'You know her? How remarkable! How came you to be acquainted?'

Harriet's face clouded. 'It was in eighty-one.' She then continued after a moment of silence, 'As it happens, I hope to hear from her shortly — and Stephen, would you not like to give your new friend news of his sister?'

'I am sure he would like that. I can tell him of her patchwork skirts and her dog, and Sam.' Stephen scratched his leg, and when Harriet put her hand over his, he looked a little guilty.

'Why was she thought of as a troublemaker, Miss Scales?' Harriet asked. 'She seemed a good enough woman to me.'

Miss Scales tried to recall. 'She had some trouble in our little school, I think. Ruben was a reading man, had to be, to rise to the position of steward to Silverside, but Jocasta never got the way of it, and was beaten for it. How does she manage now?'

'She reads fortunes,' Stephen declared, never happier than when instructing someone, 'and helps catch spies.'

Harriet was afraid this might lead to more questions than she cared to answer, so decided to steer the conversation another way.

'What does your father think of such traditions, Miss Scales? Here is Stephen, brimful with tales of witches and cunning, men.'

Miss Scales grinned. 'There are enough such stories to fill us all up! Have you heard that the last Lord Greta is said to walk the hills in hard times? And you will find a dozen households that put out bowls of milk and oats for the dobbies, and there are stories of bogles and devils in every village. I ask the people why they believe, and they say the butter is churning and the milk is gone in the morning, so why should they not believe the dobbie has had his feed and blessed them with his aid? For myself, I think butter churning is all in the wrist, and it's foxes and hedgehogs that drink the milk. As to my father, he tries at least once a month to tell them there are no such things as witches, and he and his parishioners all walk away from the church, each thinking the other foolish and hoping for their enlightenment. Then all agree to say no more about it and carry on just as before. I say let them hear the word of Christ and love Him, and I'm sure the Lord will forgive a few shreds of the pagan hanging on the souls of such good Christian people. And they *are* good people here. Certainly there are some that take more than they give, but my father says he is blessed by his flock and I agree with him.'

Harriet was surprised. It seemed entirely foreign to her that in her own country there should still be so many who clung to the old ways. She wondered if there was something unusual about this place, or if her own father's parishioners had held similar beliefs. Her father had been blessed with a firm faith, but he had seen lively debate on matters theological as part of his Christian duty. He confessed his own doubts and confusions honestly and sought through conversation with his wife and daughters and his own careful reading to understand and overcome them. He had felt his efforts to come to a deeper understanding of the Christian message to be part of the same project for the enlightenment of the nation that the natural philosophers continued in their laboratories, or the anatomists in their lecture theatres. Harriet's father, Mr Trench had believed there was no danger in knowledge, and all enquiry could only lead in the end to a deeper love of God and His works. Harriet could not recall, however, a single occasion where the subject of witchcraft had been mentioned in their home, other than as an historical oddity. Yet here such things blossomed like moss on her lawns at Caveley, and not all the raking and seeding of Church and State could pull it out. However far we come, she found herself thinking, we are at times still all animals huddled round the firelight fearing what moves in the dark.

Stephen was asking Miss Scales about Casper.

'Whenever I see a picture of the Green Man, I think of Casper,' she said. 'It is his beard, I suppose, but also he has that light in his eyes and that thirst for the spaces and hills. He seems part of them to me.'

'Witches talk to him, Miriam told me,' Stephen said.

'Certainly someone does,' Katherine said a little sadly. 'I have seen it. He'll look fierce, or sometimes you are speaking to him and suddenly it appears he can hardly hear you.

Sometimes they are kind and sometimes cruel to him, I think. There have been periods when he has disappeared into the hills for weeks on end, and come back very weak. I am sure it is they that drive him to distraction at those times. It leaves him a little strange, but he is a good man and I think he knows what can harm and heal in these hills.'

'When did they begin to talk to him?' Harriet shifted her son's weight, and hoped her dress would not become too badly crushed.

'Soon after his father died, I believe. It was 1754. Ruben was taken in the same illness that took my mother and sister and left me as you see me now. Poor Casper was still very young.'

Stephen looked concerned. 'I hope they shall not start talking to me.'

Harriet wondered what she might say to reassure him, but Miss Scales was already patting his hand. 'Do not trouble yourself, young man. Not every boy who loses a father is haunted in such a way.' Miss Scales lifted her face and Harriet followed her gaze to where Crowther was standing on the lawn with Mr Askew. He looked severe.

It was at that same moment that Harriet became aware of a disturbance coming from where the lower lawns reached the lakeshore. She saw heads turning, the ladies covering their mouths then huddling together. Gently shifting Stephen from her lap, she stood. At the foot of the little wooden jetty she saw Felix, shoulders hunched, standing with an older man she did not recognise. He appeared to be shouting at Felix. To their left, a pair of younger men were helping a third man, soaked to the skin, out of the water. The third man was Mr Quince.

'Stephen, stay here with Miss Scales, please.' And when he looked as if he might be about to protest, she repeated, 'Stay here,' and before he could argue she began to walk briskly between the groups of staring guests, reaching the little group just as her son's tutor managed to set foot on shore again.

Mr Quince was in a sorry state. He had lost one of his shoes, his hair was flattened to his pink face, and his pale coat was dirty, and clinging to him. He was gasping a little and his chin wobbled. He sat down on the bank and began to shiver, wrapping his arms around his thick waist and keeping his back to the staring crowd.

Harriet came to a halt by him. 'Are you injured, Mr Quince?'

He looked up quickly and saw her. 'No, I thank you, Mrs Westerman.'

'What happened here?' she asked.

An older gentleman stepped forward and pointed at Felix.

'He pushed him in!' He spoke with emphasis and passion enough to fill a theatre. 'I saw it all. That gentleman,' he indicated the unfortunate Mr Quince, 'joined him on the jetty. They exchanged a few words. He bowed and turned away, then this damned boy pushed him in — just like that! I have never seen such a thing.'

The head-shaking and murmuring that followed this statement flowed up the lawn in ripples. The fierce gentleman's words were being repeated and exclaimed at, all the way to the house.

Harriet glanced down at her shivering employee. He looked utterly miserable and she felt her palms itching to slap Felix's face. 'Felix?'

Before he could lift his eyes, they were interrupted by the trill of the Vizegräfin as she came down towards them almost at a run. Mrs Briggs followed behind her with a towel over her arm.

'It was an accident! A silly accident. No doubt Mr Quince slipped. A narrow jetty for a big man.'

The witnesses' looks were speaking. Mrs Briggs said nothing, but laid the towel around Mr Quince's shoulders and helped him to his feet. He turned his blotched red face towards Felix with a look of loathing. 'I did not slip.'

'Wasn't it, Felix, dear? An accident?' The Vizegräfin put her hand on her son's arm and smiled at the world in general, but Harriet noticed her fingers tightening round his wrist. Felix seemed to shake himself awake.

'Naturally. I am so terribly sorry. It was I that lost my footing and stumbled against him. Please accept my apologies, Mr Quince. Unforgivably clumsy of me.'

He stepped forward and put out his hand. Mr Quince looked at it but made no move. Harriet was keenly aware of the total silence around them and the fixed attention of Mrs Briggs's guests.

'Mr Quince?' she said, very softly and not moving her head. Mr Quince took Felix's hand and shook it without a word. 'Thank you,' she said. Quince glanced at her, water still dripping from his hair onto the towel round his shoulders, then allowed himself to be shepherded by Mrs Briggs up the slope. The groups of people made way for him as he hobbled past, and stared, then as he passed began to whisper.

Felix watched his progress up the lawn, a slight smile on his lips, then turned to Harriet. 'I am sorry your son's tutor got a drenching, Mrs Westerman. These larger fellows can be rather unsteady on their feet.'

The Vizegräfin fluttered her eyelashes. 'True, Felix, very true.'

Harriet moved away from them both without a word and followed Mr Quince up the lawn. Had Crowther renewed his offer to horsewhip Felix at this moment, she would have taken him up on it with delight.

II.5

CASPER GRACE DID not travel as far from the lake as he had intended. He heard word as he left Keswick that one of the farmers between that village and Naddle Bridge had been asking for him, so he retraced his steps past the Druidic circle to call on him. The farmer, Kerrick, was a tall man with thick knuckles and the grave demeanour of a man who trusted neither his luck nor his land not to play a trick on him. He consulted Casper in a regular way, so Casper was welcomed into his kitchen with respectful friendliness. While Mistress Kerrick served them with house cheese, oatcakes and beer, her husband told Casper slowly that he was thinking on the purchase of a piece of land on the edges of what he already owned. Casper listened to the terms and when the beer was done, walked the ground with him. Casper thought it a fair price and he said so. He was ready to make his way off again, his eye on the progress of the red disk of the fogged sun, when Kerrick put a hand on his arm.

'There's also the matter of our lass, Mr Grace.'

The man had three daughters. The two younger ones were still infants, and if it were a matter of fever or shakes, Kerrick would have said so at their first words.

'Agnes?'

Kerrick nodded and studied his thick boots. 'There's something in her manner these last weeks. She's off and away in her head half the time, been out late in the evenings when she's no right to be, and there's a twitch to her. The livestock are nervous of her.'

Casper heard the rising whisperings of the witches in the still air. No wonder that Kerrick looked so wary. Casper liked Agnes. He had watched her grow from a stumbling toddler to a fine dark-haired girl of sixteen wearing the shape of a woman like a new dress. She had a certain wit and manner and had been quick to learn from him whatever he had thought to tell her. She was a wanderer in the wild places, like himself. He had seen her as he walked up to the stones with the boy from the Hall and his friends, and had thought the genteel company had made her shy when she did not come to meet them. Now he wondered if she had been shy of *him*.

'Is she in the house now?' he asked. Kerrick nodded. 'Send her out to me then.'

Kerrick went back to his cottage, his shoulders hunched and his footsteps heavy. Casper sniffed. Then took a seat on the mossy turf, pulled his carvings from his pocket and began to work his knife.

As the evening started to darken, Mrs Briggs's guests began to make their way around the head of the lake towards Crow Park for the next stage of their day's entertainment. There, in a roped-off area where the park's low swell sank gently again to the shore, they found their numbers augmented by the local yeoman farmers and tradesmen and their families who could afford the shillings necessary to watch the fireworks from a comfortable seat and with a glass of punch in their hands, but were not eligible to be invited into the grounds of Silverside Hall.

As they surveyed the ground and assessed the quality of the refreshments, the continual topic was the dousing of Mr Quince. There was much speculation as to whether any of the party resident in Silverside would attend the fireworks at all. Some maintained that Mr Quince would stay away, too humiliated to show his face; others vigorously disagreed and said rather it was Felix who should remain at the Hall. Others still agreed he most certainly should, but reminded their friends that von Bolsenheim was a foreigner by birth, for all the advantages of his heritage and education, so his behaviour would be unpredictable. He had proved himself to be no gentleman by pushing Mr Quince in the lake. He might now do so again by inflicting himself on the company. A certain amount of money changed hands. Several women also remarked they thought Felix's good looks had been over-rated, and Mr Quince was of a much more English mode. All the men claimed to have spoken to the tutor and thought him a promising young man of great good sense. They also muttered darkly that some 'foreign manners' seemed to have rubbed off on the Vizegräfin.

While these opinions were being rehearsed and refined in Crow Park, Mr Quince was sitting in the little room next to his own bedroom which served as a temporary study for Stephen and himself. He was no longer wet, but was perhaps still a little damp around the edges. He had changed his clothing, but still felt the lakewater on his skin.

Harriet sat opposite him.

'I do think you should come to the fireworks, Mr Quince.' He did not reply. 'Please do, for my sake.'

He shifted in his seat and sneezed, then having buried himself briefly in his pocket handkerchief said: 'I do not wish to be stared at and talked about, Mrs Westerman.'

'You have my sympathies,' she replied dryly and when he looked up at her, she saw a glimmer of reluctant amusement in his eyes.

'Mrs Westerman, I appreciate you have insight into being discussed by a crowd, but nothing you have done has rendered you *ridiculous*.' He twitched as he said the word. Harriet wondered if it was difficult for this young, educated man to have an employer like herself. She had never really considered the matter or the man, beyond his abilities to educate her son. She realised that she knew nothing of his ambitions and tried to recall if she had mentioned to him that she intended to send Stephen to school in a year or so.

'You have not made yourself ridiculous, Mr Quince. He did push you, I suppose?'

'Oh, yes.' Quince hung his head again. 'It was quite deliberate. Though I must count myself lucky he claimed it was an accident and apologised as he did. I should have had to call him out otherwise, and then probably would have ended up dead as well as wet. I have no doubt he is an expert shot. Men such as he always are.'

'I don't suppose you would be willing to tell me what passed between you?'

He shook his head, which made the flesh under his chin wobble. 'It was a private matter, but there was nothing offensive in it to my knowledge. I have never been so surprised in my life as when I found myself spitting up lakewater.'

Harriet laughed softly and saw a smile twitch again on Quince's face.

'I am beginning to consider Felix a rather foul young man,' she said. 'If he continues like this, Crowther will find some way to cut off his inheritance, I think.'

'But he is very handsome,' the tutor said sadly.

Mr Quince would never be handsome, but Harriet hoped very much he would someday find a woman who would make him believe he was, at least from time to time.

'I would rather have a man like you in the circle of my acquaintance, Mr Quince, than a dozen Felixes,' she said firmly. 'Now will you come to the fireworks? Crowther, I know, intends to spend his evening among the boiled bones of the wretch from the island.' She caught Quince's look of surprise and lifted her hand. 'Please, do not ask, Mr Quince. But I would like to go with Stephen. May I take your arm as we walk? Then we may be talked about together, as it were.'

Mr Quince held his head on one side. 'Does the Vizegräfin intend to go?'

'Her son will drive her in the phaeton. You and Stephen will travel in the carriage with Mrs Briggs and myself.'

'I should go. I know it.' He put his hand to his head and smoothed his hair, then straightened his back and met her eyes. 'Very well, Mrs Westerman.'

'I shall see you downstairs in a quarter of an hour then, Mr Quince.' She stood and made her way to the door.

'Thank you,' he said quietly, and she let herself out of the room.

Casper heard the girl approach but continued to carve, listening to the chatter of the witches and spirits arguing with each other, advising, cursing or cajoling him until her shadow fell softly over his work. The black witch, loudest and most vicious of them all in his head, spat and growled.

'Sit down, Agnes,' he said without looking up. She did so, just opposite him on the grass with her legs tucked under her and leaning on her arm. He lifted his eyes to her face and the black witch howled. She was a good-looking girl. Thick dark hair hung round her shoulders in a sheet; grey eyes with a sharp edge to them. She was paler than she should be, and her lips had a whiteness to them. He knew then.

'Well?' he demanded. Her chin started to tremble and she put her arms around her knees. Casper continued to carve. 'Who began it?'

'*She* did.'

'What occurred? Steal your beau, did she?'

The girl had started to rock a little. 'I thought she was my friend, but then at the Greeup wedding in May she wouldn't leave him alone. She's not even pretty.'

Casper sniffed and wiped his nose on the back of his hand. 'Such things occur, girly. No reason to start playing games you shouldn't. You know those games have a price. Tell me what you did.'

The girl pushed back her hair from her face and lifted her eyes towards the horizon. 'I made a poppet.'

Casper felt the air chill around him and was afraid. 'You fed it?'

'Blood and rue.'

'How do you know such things?'

She looked uncomfortable. 'They are spoken of.'

His knife ceased work for a moment. 'So this girl we are

speaking of is Stella Giles, who broke her ankle in June?' The black witch was already howling as he asked.

'Yes.' She looked at him, mumbled, 'I didn't mean it to be so bad, but she *deserved* it.'

He leaned forward and pointed at her chest with his knife so that she flinched back. 'And what do *you* deserve now, Agnes? This is hateful work. You get snubbed by some lad, then young Stella isn't able to work for a month. I should have known there was something in it, her taking so long to heal. You might have killed her.' He spat on the ground. 'You'll have to pay it back, my girl, or it'll go rotten on you — on you and in you.' He paused, picking up the threads of talk from the arguing voices in his head. 'Such matters are black. Tonight, no fireworks. Dig up the doll and take it up Swineside. Wash it in running water, and wash it well. Gather rowan and hazel enough to pack round it tight, tight — and bury it. Then you sit and you pray over it for forgiveness and think on what you have done. Never let me hear tell of you playing with such things again. Till dawn, mind no creeping off. We'll find a way for you to pay what you owe to Stella too, but first the lines must be straightened out.'

He got to his feet in one fluid movement and walked quickly away without waiting for an answer, carrying off his anger before it spilled all over her.

The reception of the party from Silverside was all but passionate. Harriet and Mr Quince found friends on all sides and were ushered to their seats like royalty. Harriet tried to ignore the sight of money changing hands between some of the men, and simply enjoy the warmth. Every word Mr Quince managed to utter was treated as gospel and his occasional attempts at a witticism were greeted with such gales of refined laughter one expected to see a duke in the centre of all this attention rather than a humble tutor. Mrs Briggs and Harriet shone contentedly in his reflected glory and found themselves feted as his supporters and friends.

In spite of the assiduity of their welcome, Harriet was still able to see enough of the reception Felix and the Vizegräfin received to note it contrasted most markedly with their own. It seemed that the populace of Keswick were suddenly overcome with a terrible clumsiness whenever they came close to Felix. His elbow was jogged repeatedly. He received apologies ranging from the curt to the satirically effusive. Harriet noted his smile becoming rather tight. The Vizegräfin was finding that men and women who a few hours before had found her fascinating were now passing her by with hardly a nod, and those that were forced by the press of people into conversation with her, seemed to be continually finding something far more interesting to look at over her shoulder. Harriet was glad to see them seated at last, and relieved that Felix made his way back from the refreshment table with glasses for himself and his mother only a little lessened by one or two unfortunate spillages.

Harriet had found herself in crowds that seemed to disapprove of her too often to take great pleasure in this treatment of the Vizegräfin and her son, but she did take a certain pride in the way her countrymen adopted so wholeheartedly the cause of the underdog. She was not surprised to find that, by the time the crowd's attention was drawn to the north shore of Vicar's Island where the fireworks were to be let off, the seats of the Vizegräfin and her son were empty.

Mr Askew, having made sure the more popular members of the Silverside party were comfortable, looked around him with satisfaction. It was a profitable arrangement for him, and he hoped an easy one for his guests. A great number of tables and chairs, rented from every inn in Keswick, had been placed in the area and he had sat at each one to make sure they would provide a noble view of Vicar's Island. He had paced that shore a dozen times with the gentleman who was providing the fireworks to check that all was well, and was assured it was a perfect spot. He had supervised the placing of the torches and seen them stamped firmly into the ground. Mr Askew had also arranged for a collection of passable musicians, hired from Cockermouth, to provide an accompaniment to the display. As the party from Silverside arrived they were already sawing away at old Handel with all of the delicacy and less of the artistry than the fellers of the oaks of Crow Park had displayed some forty years before. However, the gentry Mr Askew had gathered together seemed to be happy enough with the performance and he found, in the moments he had between greeting newcomers and shooing away local boys from the supper table, great pleasure in composing in his mind a description of the scene for the *Westmorland Paquet*.

Stephen, having spent over a year with only his country neighbours for society, was as pleased by the company as he could have been at Versailles. He realised everyone was being kind to Mr Quince, and enjoyed the fact that the good humour spilled over onto himself. He was perhaps patted on the head too often, but two men had already given him shillings and for that, he felt, they could pet him like a toy poodle if they wished. He saw beautiful powdered women about him, and men in tight coats, decorated with enamelled fobs and jewels. It seemed to him a scene of splendour.

Harriet, her memories of polished London society rather more accurate, saw in the company the simple manners and dress of a provincial crowd, but was pleased to be among them. She had found the brittle brilliance of the capital trying when she was last in Town, though that might have been an effect of her preoccupations whilst there. Here, by the still darkening shores of the lake, she was disposed to see in every face honesty and prosperity earned, rather than inherited. She knew she was surrounded by a few minor nobility, but the bulk of the crowd behind Mr Askew's velvet ropes were professional men and their families, traders and farm owners. She felt, as the wife of a self-made man, that she knew them and their concerns, and was at ease, particularly after Crowther's sister and nephew removed themselves. It must be bitter for them, so used to ballrooms crammed with ducal crowns, to be snubbed by lawyers and shopkeepers.

She smiled and let her eyes pick out one character from the crowd, then another: the man with the large wig must be a lawyer, the lady who watched from behind her fan and frowned as he refilled his glass at the punch bowl again, his wife. It was possible she had been introduced to them at Silverside. The red-faced man with large hands who shifted awkwardly from foot to foot was a farmer and surely only one generation away from earth floors, so still not sure in his blood of how to conduct himself at this level of society. She was pondering the fine distinctions made in her country and the silk-like strength of polite conventions when she noticed Mr Quince stiffen at her side, and turned to see what had caught his attention. There was a very beautiful dark-haired girl standing just beyond the ropes — looking, it seemed from her attitude, for someone in the crowd.

'Do you know that lady, Mr Quince?'

'Stephen and I met her today. She accompanied us to the Druidic stones,' he said, still watching her.

'She seems to be looking for someone, don't you think? Please, do go and offer your assistance. I am quite content here.'

Mr Quince stood at once and bowed to her before making his way through the throng to the place where the lady was. Harriet watched as he addressed her. The woman's first look was of recognition, then as Mr Quince spoke, her face darkened. After a moment of silence Harriet saw her ask Quince something. He bowed and crossed to where Mr Askew was standing. Again a question was asked, Mr Askew shook his head, then Quince went back to the woman. For Harriet it was like watching a dumbshow and she found it quite entertaining. The lady's eyes as he approached were again hopeful, then when he spoke, downcast once more. Quince said something further — he seemed to be inviting the young lady to join him. She shook her head and in the same moment turned away from the ropes, and Harriet found Mr Quince returning to her side with a frown on his face. She realised she had not been alone in observing him. Mrs Briggs was taking a seat to Harriet's right, and as Quince came up to them, she opened her mouth to speak.

'Who is that handsome lady, Mr Quince? She is not a native of this place, I think. Will she not join us?'

'Her name is Fräulein Hurst,' Quince replied. 'Stephen and I met her today during our explorations of the town. She mentioned that she might attend this evening, but tells me she came here in search of her father. He did not return to their lodgings when expected. Mr Askew informs me that, although he bought tickets for the entertainment, Herr Hurst has not been seen here. I asked her to join our party, but she said she would rather return to her lodgings, and insisted on doing so alone.'

'She will be quite safe,' said Mrs Briggs, and patted the tutor's arm. 'The lakeside people make far too many guineas out of these visitors to allow any harm to come to them, young man. Her father has probably found his way into one of the inns of Borrowdale and will spend the night under their roof.' She added more quietly, 'They brew very strong down there.'

'No doubt,' Quince replied, then drew his watch from his pocket. 'I believe the fireworks will commence shortly. May I fetch any refreshment for you, ladies?'

The ladies wished for nothing, and all turned their chairs in the direction of the lake and waited.

Crowther's work that evening was delicate. It required concentration and care, and he was glad of it. He was content to do this sort of work alone. It made him grateful his intellectual interests had not turned towards pure scholarship; here in his temporary laboratory, he looked as much a butcher or cook as a baron. He wrestled answers, or more questions, from flesh rather from the immateriality of his own brain, and he took pleasure in the physicality of his work. As he looked into the cooling coppers he thought of his brother, and wondered again with a revulsion that his work never normally engendered, if he were looking at Addie's first victim. Then he found his thoughts straying to his family and his own youth. His father had been an exacting parent, and Crowther remembered being sent away from the family group in disgrace if he had appeared unscrubbed or with the chemical signatures of his early experiments on his sleeves. What would Sir William think now, to see his son bend over old coppers in the semi-darkness?

Crowther realised he had become still with thought, and returned to the practicalities before him. The last of the body's flesh had melted away in the water and heat. Now it was his intention to remake the form of the man. In the silence of the old brew house, in the pools of fluttering light shed by the lanterns, he lifted each bone from the warm water and on the old work-bench, remade the skeleton.

Time passed.

When the bones were laid out before him, Crowther removed his apron and dried his hands, then began to examine them in detail. The body was that of a mature male. He had guessed as much from the probable height of the corpse and the clothing, but the bones of the pelvis confirmed it. *Ilium, ischium* and *pubis* all fully fused; the pubic arch showed the steep incline typical of the male of the species. Next he lifted the skull, letting his fingers travel across it like a blind man trying to trace the features of a friend, then, settling it on his fingertips, he brought it towards himself in the lamplight until he stared into the empty sockets, turning it from left to right. There was no sign of damage, or of damage healed.

'What would you tell us, friend?' he murmured under his breath, and for a moment touched his free hand to his own thin face. 'Alas, poor Yorick indeed . . .' As he set the skull down at the head of the table he was momentarily startled by the sound of explosions from the lake and saw the darkness outside the window stained suddenly red and yellow. The fireworks hissed and flashed, their light enough, even at this distance, to colour the pale bones below him. Something cracked in the air and a white phosphorescence fell across the bones, making a new shadow across the ribs.

Crowther knelt and brought the lamp as close as he dared to the flattened cage. On the underside of the third rib, on the left side, there was something not quite right. He traced his finger along its falling edge and found a nick in the bone, such as might be made by a blade driven into the chest. The mark was suggestive, not conclusive. Crowther was sure the damage was not a result of his own treatment of the relics. He had handled each bone as a craftsman handles gold leaf.

Moving away from the remains to the pile of clothing remnants, he gently teased the waistcoat flat, then straightened and placed his fingers on his own chest, counting down his own ribs until he reached that which matched the damaged bone on the skeleton. It would be on the left, far enough clear of the button-holes. The shirt was too ragged to be of any use, but the material of the waistcoat had been thicker.

He bent low, inhaling the gravesmoke that hung around the clothes. Perhaps. The threads here were cut rather than thinned with age, but the blade, if blade it was, must have been very narrow. He lifted the waistcoat to his eye and shifted to let as much light fall on it as it might. Baron, butcher, now he seemed a tailor. A hole indeed, and another, possibly, to match on the back panel of cloth. There was no particular staining he could see, but the fabric was dark. He teased it with his fingertip.

There was another flash outside, a sound like heavy rain, and the light in the room shifted into the deep reds of blood in darkness.

Stephen flinched when the explosions began. The man Mr Askew had hired provided a brave show. Stephen could see the workers moving along the shore, shadows in front of the blaze of light they controlled, like minions at work in Vulcan's forge. He would ask Mr Quince tomorrow about gunpowder. For a moment his ambition to be a ship's Captain like his father wavered, as he thought of himself grinding powders to make all these rainbows of noise and light. He glanced towards where his mother was sitting, her face bathed white, red and green, and he could see the red of her hair light up as if the glowing sparks had fallen on her and were burning coldly among her curls.

There was a pause and the crowd began to applaud, then Stephen saw another shadow, moving towards the centre of the wooden platform from whence the fireworks flew, torch in hand. The crowd saw him too and the applause fell away. Suddenly a breath of white fire ran up from the place where the man had touched his torch, drawing the outline of a cross on the darkness behind it. Catherine wheels caught all round its edges, spewing white sparks in tight circles. Then within the shape, fires of other colours caught till it seemed alive with angry jewels of red and green. The crowd gasped, and Stephen closed his hand round the little rowan Luck in his pocket.

Crowther put out the lantern that swung above the skeleton and, content that the place was secure, he left the brewery and locked the door behind him before beginning to climb up the steep lawn to the main house. It was still so warm he barely needed the coat that hung over his shoulders, and the moon was bright enough that he could have made his way along the gravel path without the light he carried. He looked up at the house above him, showing palely against the wooded hillside. Most of the windows in the upper storeys were dark, but the one that gave onto what had been his mother's room had a candle showing on the sill. He caught a movement in the shadow above it. His sister, watching him, he presumed, as he so often had been used to watch his neighbours from his house in Hartswood. She must have returned early from the fireworks. He guessed the reason. He would have to speak to her in the morning and ask her what she could remember of Addie's visits home, but not until he had allowed Mrs Westerman to pick through his thoughts. Margaret seemed to have survived the disgrace of their youth. Had she loved their father? Had she found something in the baron he had not, or seen something?

Crowther had left home in 1741 first for a repellent boarding school for sons of rich men in Lincolnshire, then for Cambridge, returning rarely and reluctantly. His mother he had been glad to see in Town, but although she at times made some effort to understand her second son in the years before her death, she reached across a gulf that could not be spanned, and he remained a mystery to her, so cold and inward. His intellectual pursuits meant nothing to her. She seemed always to be surrounded by light and noise, even in her isolated home in Silverside. Lady Keswick had been a joyful, rather impulsive character always ready to be amused. She teased Sir William, and her dour husband had seemed to dote on her as a result;

Addie had always made her laugh, and Margaret she could dress up in costumes that were copies of her own and parade with her as some women did with little black slave boys in a parody of exotic dress. She had loved him too, he supposed, but his strongest memory of her was the sound of her laughter coming from some other room in the house, from some place where he was not.

Casper made for the woodsmen's cabins above Silverside, flinching as the fireworks rattled behind him. He was satisfied that the night in the open would be punishment enough for Agnes, but he still felt angry, and the explosions on the lakeside made the witches shriek till he could hardly follow the thread of his own thoughts. He wondered where she had got the idea of the poppet from. It was a strong notion – he could feel the tang of magic on it. Agnes was a clever girl, but she'd become a dangerous one if she got into the habit of such tricks.

Casper had only once in the last twenty years named a witch in these hills. She was an old woman, Blanche Grice, grown powerful and used to her power while he was still gaining and measuring the strength of his own. When she cursed a young woman in Portiscale one winter and made her miscarry, he had gone up against her at last. It had been a bitter thing, but much as she played the innocent, he knew he had been right. She was spurned on his word so left her home, setting out on the Kendal Road, and had not been seen since. Some said she had changed herself into a hare and now stayed that way most of the time. Casper knew better. She had crawled into the old mines on the flank of Ullock Moss and let her body die there, ready instead to live in Casper's mind, chattering at him and cursing. He found her body in the spring and buried it himself, but though he had red threads tied round his wrists, she still crawled into his skull somehow and had been there ever since. She was loud now, yelling delightedly at the explosions from the lakeside, trying to twitch him round so she could see them through his eyes. He was striving to quiet her as he approached the clearing where his cabin waited, so did not mark the nervous twittings and cawing from Joe — and the blow that felled him came like thunder from a clear sky.

The applause for the fireworks and their glorious finale was still rippling around a beaming Mr Askew when the first fat drops fell. Harriet looked up, then hissed as something stung her arm. She turned towards Mr Quince, who looked as bemused as she did herself, then with a crack something fell into Harriet's glass of punch on the table between them and splashed the liquor onto the tablecloth. Mr Quince picked up the glass and looked into it.

'My goodness! Hail!' he said, then sneezed.

The air seemed to chill around them with such rapidity Harriet felt as if she had fallen out of a glasshouse and into an ice cellar. All around them, the crowd had begun to move. Mrs Briggs yelped as a hailstone the size of Stephen's fist landed on their table and rolled to the ground.

'Mr Quince, if you will give Mrs Briggs your arm, perhaps we should return to the carriage. Stephen! Come here, please.' As the boy hurried towards her there was a crack and roar that made Harriet start and turn to the lake. A blast of lightning coated the water in white light that made her eyes hurt and she froze, stupefied by the image of the lakes and hills so suddenly revealed in all their folded outlines, then hidden again. She felt Stephen's hand slip into her own and squeeze it. The touch woke her and she turned to hurry after Mrs Briggs and Mr Quince.

The hailstones were falling faster now, and as she went towards the carriage as quickly as she could manage in her long skirts, Harriet could hear them rattling the crockery through the exclamations of the crowd. The coachman, Ham, was waiting for them, and managed to get them onto the road before the great press of people clogged it solid. Harriet turned and in repeated flashes of light saw, like a series of engravings, scenes of the breaking-up of the party: the musicians struggling to protect their instruments, the men and women scattering to the protection of the trees, chairs and tables overturned. As the carriage drew them out of sight, the hard rattle of the hail on the roof ceased and for a moment there was silence from the sky. Then the rain began to thunder down, slapping its palms on the roof like judgement, and lightning cracked the sky wide open again. Stephen pressed himself to his mother's side, watching the world appear and disappear beyond the window.

Mr Quince was shivering when they returned to the Hall and was sent to bed just as firmly as Stephen was, though he was encouraged to take a large glass of brandy with him. Harriet said goodnight to her hostess, and with her mind still flashing with gunpowder, made her way upstairs.

She entered her sitting room just as another sheet of lightning rattled the glass – and in the sudden whitening she saw Crowther seated in one of the armchairs facing her. She started and put her hand to her chest.

'Good God! That was like something from *The Castle of Otranto*,' she said. 'I shall expect to be kidnapped by faceless monks at any moment.'

The rain beat steadily at the windows and she saw Crowther smile in the candlelight. He was holding a single sheet of paper in his hands.

'I am sorry to alarm you, Mrs Westerman. It was an unfortunately timed strike.'

'Not at all.' She took her seat opposite him. 'I would not miss the excitement for all the world. I need fear no bogle or ghost if I can stand the sight of you revealed by lightning without a scream.'

He frowned a little, which amused Harriet, and passed her the note he held. He had his pride, this strange friend of hers, and it pleased her to tease him from time to time. She unfolded the piece of paper and her smile faded quickly.

Master Charles,

The man came looking for something and found your father. I saw them leave together for the Island of Bones. The man never came back. I grieve that you find more blood in your history.

Charlotte Tyers

'Who, Crowther, is Charlotte Tyers?'

Crowther tented his fingers together. 'The housekeeper here in my father's time. She must be in her eighties now, and has a cottage in Portinscale.'

'And do you understand this note?'

He shook his head. 'No, other than "Island of Bones", which is how many of the local people refer to Saint Herbert's Island because of the tombs in the old chapel. But I am sure you have guessed this for yourself. I think we should pay Mrs Tyers a visit tomorrow, don't you agree?' A gust of wind threw another handful of rain against the window. 'Unless we have all been swept to the bottom of the lake by then. The man was stabbed through the heart, I believe.'

'And this note suggests it was your father, not your brother, who struck the blow.'

He was silent for a moment. 'Indeed it does, Mrs Westerman. It is curious, I have remembered . . .' The thunder rolled round the house again, and he stood up. 'But no more gothic tales tonight. Even my imagination may be enlivened to a dangerous degree. I will see you in the morning, Mrs Westerman.' And with that he disappeared into the darkness again.

From the collection of Mr Askew, Keswick Museum

Letter to *The Gentleman's Magazine*, July 1752

Mr Urban,

As one of your correspondents expressed themselves curious as to the life and character of the late Sir William Penhaligon, 1st Baron of Keswick, and as none of his remaining family has come forward to furnish those details, I send to you these notes and observations on the history of this unfortunate gentleman, and while one may not presume to probe the secrets of another mind, they may be relied on as the witness of a near neighbour of many years' acquaintance.

Sir William was born in 1683, the only surviving son of a baronet who had more pride in his position in society, and a greater love of show than his property could bear. I have heard Sir William remark more than once, that the very spoons and knives in his father's house were found to be mortgaged on his parent's death. There was little that could be saved from the estate, but what remained included a small house on the banks of Derwent Water called Silverside, perhaps preserved because Sir William's father had all but forgotten it. Sir William took up residence there in 1712, and for some time busied himself with a study of the minerals of the area, and made an attempt to repair his fortunes by severe retrenchment. This gentlemanly scholarship became the

159

well-spring of all Sir William's fortunes. He was often out on the hills, and told his neighbours he witnessed in 1715 the last Lord Greta make his preparations to ride out from Gutherscale Hall to rebellion, ignominy and exile. Some little while after Greta and his family left these shores for ever, Sir William was able after years of stringent economy to buy from the government a small piece of land on which he discovered the last copper deposits in the area. His cottage was rebuilt as Silverside Hall and was ready to receive his bride, the Honourable Julia O'Brien, in 1724. His charming wife was an ornament to the area, he was made a proud father two years later, and all his enterprises seemed blessed.

How unlucky, however, is the man who outlives his most successful and happy years! In '44 Sir William purchased the land on which stood Gutherscale Hall itself, and convinced he was now the true inheritor of the lands of the ancient Greta line, declared he would take his family to that ancient Hall and make it their own. However, the tragic fire of '45 which rendered that great house a ruin, intervened, and Sir William's frustration was extreme. Not even the title of Lord Keswick could mitigate his disappointment. Nor were his family able to lighten his burden. His eldest son began to develop an unsavoury reputation as a gamer and libertine, and his younger brother was thought of as an awkward and eccentric child. His lovely wife, Lady Julia, began to spend more time in Town, and after her death, Lord Keswick became a complete recluse, his solitude alleviated only by the presence of his young daughter till she too left his once-happy home for her schooling. His death at the hand of his eldest and favourite son made a tragic finale to his history. One can only hope that in his last moments he was ignorant of whose hand had dealt the fatal blow. His second

160

son sold the estate entire to a Mr Briggs and now is thought to travel incognito on the continent. His daughter has made a home with her mother's relatives in Ireland. Thus we see that though ambition can make a man, it can also poison our happiness with frustration at the last.

Yours &c W. L.

PART III

III.1

Thursday, 17 July 1783

AT SOME POINT IN the night the storm ceased as abruptly as it had started. When Harriet awoke to the light rap of the maid on her door she felt a lightness, expecting that the storm must have broken the heat of the weather, and the day would content itself now with a more pleasant temperature.

'Good morning, Miriam,' she said, pulling herself up onto her elbow. 'You have learned I am an early riser then.'

The maid set a cup of tea by Harriet's bed and began to tidy the room. 'That didn't take long, madam. I shan't go to any of the others for a while yet, but I thought I might take the chance you were wakeful. It's still hot and close, madam. The lawns are steaming.' She folded Harriet's stockings over her arm and smoothed them. 'I did glance in at poor Mr Quince. He's sleeping, but I didn't like the look of him.'

Harriet sat up and put her hand to her forehead. 'I shall

163

look in on him directly. I should not have encouraged him to go to the fireworks after that soaking.'

Miriam shrugged, and unhooking Harriet's dressing gown from the back of the closet door, she brought it over to her. 'You weren't to know, madam.'

Harriet slipped it over her shoulders, enjoying the brief coolness of the fabric. 'Did the storm cause much damage?'

'Not to us. Hail broke a couple of panes of glass in town, and the butcher's boy had a job of it to make it up to us this morning, the path was so covered in branches torn down. Though, he had such a story!' The girl paused, looking at Harriet uncertainly.

'Do tell me, Miriam.'

The maid perched briefly on the edge of the bed. 'Seems the Black Pig was broken into last evening. Looks like mischief mostly. Tom and his wife were shut into their room, but that's where they keep the money, under their bed, so there's luck, but furniture was thrown about, and all the pewter from the mantel chucked to the floor. Lucky for them the storm was so lively, or Tom would have heard them and been down there with his cudgel! They didn't know a thing of it until daybreak and they found their door jammed. Tom had to climb out of the back window.' She suddenly became conscious of her seat on Harriet's bed, and stood quickly. 'But I must be off, Mrs Westerman.'

'One moment, Miriam.' Harriet held up her hand. 'How many servants are there at Silverside?'

The maid paused at the door. 'Nine in the house, madam. But if you are wondering who put that note under Mr Crowther's door yesterday, it was me. Charlotte Tyers is my godmother. She placed the paper in my hand and asked me to get it to the baron quietly, and so I did. Do you need any help to dress?' Harriet shook her head. 'Then I'll wish you good morning, madam.'

Crowther was not, by inclination, an early riser. From his youth he had felt most comfortable in the hours of darkness, letting his mind wander undisturbed among its own peculiar pathways of experience and observation, with no other guide than the silence of his work room and the flutter of candlelight. It was a habit his few friends knew well. One evening earlier in the year Crowther had been walking with Mrs Westerman in the walled garden behind her house at Caveley. He had been explaining to her some detail of his work as the evening began to fold around them, when he had noticed her smiling in the gloom. Suspecting her attention had wandered away from the topic under discussion he had asked her, rather sharply, what she was grinning at.

She had plucked a fragile-looking bloom from a pale-green climbing plant on the wall behind her and handed it to him. Around a yellow eye its white petals were open like a pinwheel and its scent was delicate.

'Night-flowering Jasmine, Crowther,' she said. 'I happened to notice it while you were speaking. During the day it is tight closed, then when it grows dark it begins to bloom, as you do.' She moved on along the gravel. 'As far as you are able.'

Crowther had made no reply, but placed the flower in his waistcoat pocket and the conversation had drifted on its own way. Later that night though, as he prepared his work back in the shades of his own establishment, he had found the flower again, and placed it in the drawer of his desk amongst his papers before he opened his notebook and picked up his pen.

He was prepared therefore for Mrs Westerman's surprise when, on the morning after the firework display, he ventured into the gardens to find her before breakfast. Harriet was sitting on a low wrought-iron bench which offered a fine prospect over the lake, reading a letter. The tables and chairs from the entertainment had been cleared away to leave the view uninterrupted once more. As Crowther's footsteps shifted the gravel, she looked over to him, and after raising her eyebrows and rather pointedly consulting her pocket-watch as he approached, her smile faded and a look of concern crossed her face. He realised he probably looked as tired and sick of his own thoughts as he felt. He took a seat beside her and for a moment watched the flat mirror of the lake, the cultivated shore opposite and the fierce crags of stone rising above them, holding the water and people below it in their appointed places. It was a view his father had spent many hours admiring, contemplating the land he had made his own, the land Crowther had sold as quickly as he might.

Crowther had never been fond of his father. From his childhood Sir William Penhaligon had appeared a dangerous, unpredictable being, best avoided. Crowther had never learned how to please him, realised his father thought him a strange, alien being in his home. They shared no interests, and it seemed at times they hardly shared the same language. Crowther recognised that his father must have had some abilities; after all, Sir William had been born a baronet with nothing but debt to polish his title with, but died a rich man and Lord Keswick. That indicated he had both political and financial skills; however, to Crowther he had appeared nothing but a bully.

When Crowther was much of the age of Stephen Westerman, his father had decided over breakfast that he would teach his younger son to swim. Crowther had tried to run away, but was not quick enough for his father or his father's servant Ruben Grace. He had been carried to the lake struggling and biting, then bundled into the rowing boat kept tied up at the landing-stage on the edge of the water. Sir William had pulled on the oars till they were some thirty yards from the shore, then ordered his servant to throw his son into the water. Crowther could still remember his own protests, the sense of powerlessness then the grasping cold as he was cast into the lake. The shock of it had stopped his tears at once.

Looking down from their comfortable seat at the wooded islands of Derwent Water more than forty years later, Crowther could see quite clearly the image of the two men in the rowboat. His father's face red and fleshy, his white full-bottomed wig, the splay of his coat-tails, and Ruben, his thick shoulders, his brown hands. They were watching him, implacable as effigies as he spat out the icy lake and trod water.

Crowther had known well enough how to keep his head above the surface. And now instead of the chill of the lake, he felt angry. His fear had left him. His father had slapped his fat thigh.

'Good, Charles. Keep your head and you'll live through most things. Now swim to me and we shall take you in again.' Crowther could still taste the mix of lakewater, rage and disgust, could still see the hooded eyes of his father as he stretched out a hand.

Crowther had not swum towards him, but rather turned in the water and struck out for the bank at the north edge of his father's property, certain he would rather drown than get back in the boat. He did not hear the squeak and clunk of the oars in the rowlocks as Sir William and Ruben had given up observing him and instead headed back for the landing stage.

Crowther had stayed away from the house as long as the cold would let him, then returned by the kitchen door. The housekeeper, Lottie Tyers, who was kinder to him than most, had sat him in front of her fire and fed him, sending a maid to Lady Penhaligon to assure her she still had two sons, but said nothing to him. Crowther had watched the flames in the range until his pale skin began to warm in silence. The incident was never mentioned again.

Crowther realised that Harriet was still watching him quietly.

'My thoughts are as gothic this morning as they were in the storm, I fear. There were indications on the bones of a blade strike near the heart. There is a corresponding hole in the waistcoat of the corpse.' Crowther placed his cane on the gravel in front of them, and folded his hands over it.

'You said as much last night. There is something more?'

He nodded. 'When I first inherited this cane from my father, it was a swordstick. The blade was broken.' He felt rather than heard Harriet's reaction. 'I do not know what, if anything, we might find on the Island of Bones after so many years, Mrs Westerman, but I should be glad to go and examine the place at once if you are willing. Then later I shall pay a call on Lottie Tyers.'

She was quiet a moment before speaking. 'I see. Thank you for not waving the broken blade at me during the thunderstorm.'

'I would have done, were it still in my possession. You will accompany me to the Island then?'

'Naturally, but first another matter. Mr Quince is ill. He was shivering as he went to his bed last night and this morning is feverish. I have asked that the local physician be consulted. Do you though have any advice?'

He smiled slightly. 'You know my subjects are dead, as a rule.'

'Nevertheless . . .'

'Do not let the physician bleed him. It is as superstitious a practice as witchcraft, and often, I believe, more harmful. Mrs Briggs seems a sensible woman. I would trust in her and her people. What of your son?'

She stood; she was wearing her riding dress of dark green, and smoothed its folds around her. 'He has disappeared into the hills as his tutor is ill. I understand he intends to hunt for treasure. He shall be safe, don't you think?'

'Tell him to avoid the old mines. These hills are honeycombed with them, and they can be dangerous.'

'They sound just the place for treasure.'

Crowther let his eyes drift towards the wooded banks above him. 'Mention I have said they are also just the place for bogles.'

Harriet smiled. 'I shall tell him so.' They heard the crunch of gravel under wheels, and she turned to see a man in a black suit with an old-fashioned wig emerge from the carriage. 'Let us see what the physician has to say. I would be glad if you can attend and look severe when he examines Mr Quince. Then I am at your disposal.'

III.2

HAVING TOLD HIS mother of his plans while she dressed, Stephen stole into his tutor's room for a moment and found Mr Quince still asleep, though not at peace. The boy watched with concern as he tossed his head on his pillow a little, and beads of perspiration shone on his pink forehead. Stephen filled the water glass by his tutor's bed, then sat and watched the young man's heavy face rocking from side to side as if the whole house were moving with the regular swell of waves on the ocean after a storm. He knew the medical man from town had been called, but he had no more faith in doctors than Mr Crowther. Stephen moved the water glass a little, hoping to place it exactly where Mr Quince might reach. He liked Mr Quince and had been shamed and sorry when Felix pushed him into the lake. He thought of his conversations with the servants and Casper of the day before, and came to a decision. Treasure could wait a little while yet.

He stood, then bent forward to Mr Quince and whispered to him, 'Do not worry, sir. I shall fetch Casper and he shall mend you,' then with a sense of purpose that made his steps firm again, he headed out of the room, just remembering not to let the door clap too sharply behind him.

Only when he reached the bottom of the main stairs did he pause to think that he had no idea where Casper might be found. Their meetings so far had been accidental. Luckily Stephen was not a boy to be put off from his purpose as easily as that, and so rather than heading out onto the shores of the lake at once, he instead found his way into the kitchen and scared Cook by appearing out of the thin air at her side like a sudden spirit, shining with zeal.

The physician having been sent away before he could unpack his bleeding bowl, Harriet left Mr Quince to Miriam's care and set out for the Island with Crowther. Isaiah, one of the Silverside gardeners who offered his services as a boatman, rowed with practised ease and sang softly to himself as they went. Harriet let her mind wander, and found her thoughts turned as ever to the husband she had lost. James would have enjoyed seeing this country, and the regret that he would not, filled up her mind like the water in the lake. She knew she was no longer the broken creature she had been when she had first buried him, and the worst of her grief was, she fervently hoped, behind her – but she still saw him in her mind's eye every other hour. Sometimes she remembered to be grateful for having met and married him; sometimes she cursed herself for ever having been happy, since it made the current darkness only deeper. Still, she could feel that the change of air was some help, or perhaps it was her interest in the strange body. She could only hope when their business was complete in the north and she returned home, that the darkness would not press so heavily on her.

Only the gentle knock of the prow against the shore woke her to the present. She followed Crowther out of the boat neatly enough to earn a look of commendation from Isaiah, and she drew over her face the mask of a woman not grieving as deliberately as she had buttoned on her gloves in the lobby of Silverside Hall.

'I'll wait here for you then,' Isaiah said, and settled himself

171

on a flat rock near his boat on the little bit of beach. Harriet nodded, and the man produced pipe and tobacco from his pockets while Crowther leaned on his cane and looked about him, saying nothing.

The little chapel was found up an easy path. It was in a sadly dilapidated state.

'This was the home of a hermit, was it not?' Harriet asked as the trees closed off their views of the lake.

'The Island was, yes, many centuries ago. Saint Herbert, friend of Cuthbert, lived here. This chapel is of a much later date, of course. I believe the family of Greta had an establishment here while King Henry was at Agincourt, and the chapel was a part of that construction. Saint Herbert's original residence has long ago returned to dust.'

Harriet pushed the branches clear of her way and emerged into the clearing. They must, she imagined, be in the very centre of the little island now. Much of the chapel was still intact; its grey walls, however, were heavy with greenery and there was no trace of the doors and windows that must once have completed it. She thought of the skeleton. Here was the same story in stone. The summer home of the ancient Gretas must have stood to the right. One proud wall still tried to raise itself upright from the rubble around it.

'Mrs Briggs told me that Mr Askew suggested she build new ruins here, rather than a summerhouse. He offered to hire a hermit to live among them for the delight of the pleasure-seekers in town.' Crowther made no comment and she turned to see him standing in a square of sunlight that had struggled down through the trees. 'I told her she need only provide you with a place to experiment and they might have a hermit at no charge.'

'How did she take to that proposal?'

'She did not know you at that point, so presumed I was only funning.'

Stephen found the nest of woodcutters' cabins on the far edge of Overside Wood. Beyond it, a crop of new timber reached up the hillside, but he had climbed through old fat oaks to find it, then walked along the edge as Cook had instructed. He had a parcel of cold meats and cheese under his arm, an offering from the servants in the kitchen.

There were three cabins, grouped round a number of large stones that had been arranged to serve as benches and fireplace for those who sheltered here. It was simple to see which was the most regularly occupied. Of the three cabins, only one looked neat and solid, and the other two had fallen into disrepair so between them they laid open the manner of their construction. It was like looking at the pictures in some of Mr Crowther's books where on one page was a picture of an animal whole, then next to it, Figure 2 showed the animal in the same attitude, but with its skin removed, and next to that, the skeleton alone. The hut to the west of the camp was the skeleton. It was no more than several long poles set in a circle, but tilted inwards so their tops met and were tied together in a bundle. Some thinner branches remained weaving through the struts. The second still preserved, laid over these thin branches like slates, shallow strips of turf, though it was fallen in places showing the basketweave below. The third, however, still had its skin whole and complete.

There was something wrong. The hurdle gate of the complete cabin was lying some feet off. Still, Stephen would never have thought to enter the cabin if Joe had not been dancing and cawing in front of it.

Stephen approached cautiously. He could hear no sounds from within.

'Casper?'

A groan, and an arm appeared in the narrow hoop of light in the entrance to the cabin. Stephen sucked in his breath and stepped back.

'Here, youngling.' It was Casper's voice but dry and faint as fog. Stephen moved forward again and crouched in the entrance. Casper was a low shape in the darkness. The sleeve on the arm that lay in the light was torn, and there were bruises blooming on the wrists.

'Water.' The arm lifted slightly off the ground, and in the darkness Stephen made out the shape of a pitcher lying on its side on the earth floor. He scuttled past the prone body and picked it up, then holding it to his chest ran out of the clearing and down the path to the place where it was crossed by a brook, then washed and filled the jug, his heart thumping uncertainly. He returned as quickly as he could without letting any of the water splash free.

As he approached the clearing, he slowed. Casper had dragged himself out of the cabin and was now sitting with his back to Stephen, his legs straight out before him, and his head low on his chest. Stephen stepped beside him and crouched down. The brown hands reached up rather blindly. Stephen guided them around the jug. As Casper lifted it to his mouth and tilted his head back, Stephen gasped. The left side of his face was red and scraped. His left eye was purple and swollen shut. The right gleamed, however, as Stephen drew in his breath.

Casper drank deeply and the corner of his mouth twitched. 'Pretty, am I?'

Stephen swallowed. 'What happened, Mr Casper?'

Casper drank again, then upended the jug over the top of his head. The water beaded on his dark hair, ran over his face like tears and made his shirt cling to him. His nose had bled, crusting his mouth and chin, and there were dark spots all over his shirt. The blood on his mouth began to run in the water, dripping from the corners of his lips.

'More,' he said, lifting the jug.

Stephen ran off again, this time with Joe bobbing along beside him, rattling and whistling as if trying to give a full narrative and a fund of good advice.

'Shush, Joe,' Stephen said. Then, as he put the water next to Casper and watched him drink again, he felt guilty for slighting the bird, and as Casper panted and drank, he fed the jackdaw crumbs from his pocket.

'Beaten,' Casper said at last, as if there had been no interval between Stephen's question and his answer. 'Last night before the storm. Knocked me flat, turned everything I own over, then did the damage you see.'

'Are you badly hurt?'

'I ain't dead, so I guess I'll have to live,' Casper said, after considering a while. 'They stole my rabbits though.'

Stephen remembered the parcel from Silverside and set it down by Casper, who undid the string and nodded appreciatively; he broke off a piece of cheese and ate some, feeding the scraps to Joe. 'From Cook,' Stephen said. 'She sends her best greetings. Who beat you, sir?'

'Just told you it was dark, haven't I? Though I have a

thought.' Casper began very carefully to roll up his shirt and try to squint down at his side. Then he placed one hand on his flank and winced. 'There's a rib gone.' He let the shirt go and looked at his hands, flexing and curling them and frowning as he did so. 'Two men. There might have been another in the shadows.'

Joe jumped up onto his master's thigh and began to work his way slowly up Casper's leg, his head down and his wings very slightly open, making a low noise in his throat. Casper extended a hand and scratched the back of his black head. 'Shhh. I've said I'll live, haven't I? You daft bugger.'

'What can I do, sir?'

Casper squinted at him as if he had forgotten he was there for a moment. 'Can you make a fire?'

'Yes.'

'Get one going then, and see if you can find my kettle and set it to boil. I'll brew myself something that'll help me mend, though I might need you to go foraging for me. You not expected back at the house?'

Stephen shook his head. 'Mr Quince is ill, so I am free. Should I not get help?'

'You are help.'

Stephen set to work.

The tomb had been left open, and its proper occupants removed to their new resting-place in Crosthwaite Church. Their effigies would follow them there shortly. For the present they still leaned against one of the far walls, watching them. The base of the tomb was carved with biblical scenes, though between the Ark and Jonah's whale Harriet noticed a number of other faces, local grotesques, ghosts and witches the carvers had formed from life. Harriet walked up to it and ran her gloved hand over the stonework.

'I presume this place had been abandoned before you were born, Crowther. Did you ever come here as a child?'

'Long before, Mrs Westerman. I came here from time to time. I think my brother used it as a place to meet whatever girl in the town he had managed to seduce. I came only during the day. He came and went by night.'

He began to turn his cane between his hands, staring at the ground as the tip dug itself into the rotted leaf matter which was scattered over the floor. 'I do not know why I wished to come here.'

'A little peace perhaps.' She ran her hand over the strange stone faces. 'You have found yourself caught amongst all your old family ties like a fish in a net. You must talk to an old woman who knows the misery of your childhood, you must discuss with your estranged sister the possibility that your father was a murderer. I think that was the implication of the note, and your remarks about your father's swordstick. You must also contemplate the possibility that all your riches will be spent after your death on the card tables of Europe by your nephew.' She looked up at Crowther. He was studying the pattern of shade on the floor of the chancel. 'I am only surprised, Crowther, that you have made this temporary escape. I half-expected you to leave Silverside this morning.'

She waited.

'Ha!' he said. She felt her jaw tense, thinking she had over-stepped the limits of their friendship in speaking so frankly, then realised he was not speaking to her at all. Instead, he thrust his cane towards her and, with the air of a pointer spotting game, fell to his knees then produced a knife from his pocket and began to work at a gap between two flagstones some feet in front of her.

'I need my tweezers. I should have brought my instruments with me.'

He rocked back, frowning. Harriet set down his cane and reached into her red hair. She pulled something loose and handed it to him. A silver hairclip, on a steel base, hinged and sprung, tapering to a fine point. He tried it; the two fine points closed neatly and firmly.

'Excellent,' he said, and bent forward again. The ornament did its work, the flat points coming together with a satisfying click, and he pulled something free. He dropped it into his palm, handing the clip to Mrs Westerman, and as she wiped it on her glove then with practised fingers worked it back into her hair, he examined his find in the thin light that fell across them from the high overgrown windows, turning it in the whispering shadows of the vines. She knew better than to ask what he was about, instead watching patiently till he turned towards her and lifted his palm. Across it lay an ugly shard of metal roughly the length of Harriet's thumb. One side worked, the other was rough.

'Is that the sword tip? How on earth did you find it?'

He stood and brushed the dirt from his knees. 'Luck, largely, I am grieved to say. If the man had been killed anywhere other than in this church, then it would be as simple to roll his body into the lake. If the shard survived here through forty years, it most likely must have worked its way between the flagstones. Then as you were speaking, the shadows moved and the shape caught my eye.'

'Lucky indeed.'

'I had the advantage of knowing exactly what I was looking for.'

'You seem well content for a man who has just proved his father guilty of murder,' she said.

'I have done no such thing, Mrs Westerman,' he said impatiently. 'I have shown that the man in the tomb was most likely killed with a thin blade. I have also shown that my father's swordstick was broken here. That is all. It may still be this man was a victim of Adair.'

'But Mrs Tyers's note, Crowther! And why should a man pursuing Adair for debt be carrying a snuffbox — a gift from Lord Greta — as he did so?'

'My brother was always in want of money. Suppose he knew something of my father's business and thought he could sell the information to the former owner of these lands, or his agents.'

'You normally accuse *me* of wild supposition.'

'The habit must be catching.'

'Could your brother have stolen the cane, then?'

Crowther hesitated. 'It is unlikely. The cane rarely left my father's side, Mrs Westerman. It was a wedding present from my mother, and he valued it above all things.'

She turned to look at it. The silver bundle of foliage at the head of the cane glowed in the weak and creeping light like an icon placed for the believers to worship. Her mouth was a little dry. His only inheritance; for all these years, Crowther had been leaning his slight weight on an instrument of murder.

'We must speak to the Vizegräfin,' she said at last.

III.3

CASPER GAVE STEPHEN very precise instructions on the various herbs he was to gather, and the boy returned to the clearing slowly turning the leaves over in his hands to be sure he had the right ones. His search had taken him higher up Swinside, so he approached the clearing through the trees above it. He was only a few feet from the camp when he heard a woman's voice, and dropped to his knees.

'You are hurt, Mr Grace,' it said, soft and precise. It was the Austrian lady. He hesitated, suddenly shy of joining them, of being a child between adults again.

'What was that?' the woman said.

He heard Casper sigh. 'No creature that will do you harm, I reckon. And I will live through my hurt. Rest for a moment, miss.'

Stephen wondered if he should retreat up the hillside again, but he would not know how long to wait and was impatient to give Casper the herbs he had gathered. Perhaps she would not stay long. He could just make them out through the holly branches. Casper and Miss Hurst were sitting opposite each other on a pair of the low stones by the outside fireplace. The lady was drinking thirstily from a wooden cup. When she was finished, she wiped her mouth with her handkerchief and held the cup out to Casper. He took it from her, looking serious but kind. She smiled at him, but seeing his expression flushed and looked down again.

'You should not walk so fast in your condition, lady, so very early in the day. You must have had more than an hour in the heat already, and you ladies never dress for walking,' Casper said, so quietly Stephen had to strain to hear him. Sophia drew in her breath sharply and then began to cry. Stephen frowned, wanting to comfort her, but at the same time wishing she would leave. She wept very quietly, with her head still low.

'I had thought no one might know it yet,' she said at last.

Casper drew his bit of wood from his pocket and his knife from his belt and began work before replying. 'Not many would, from looking at you. It was half a guess. Though you taking sick when you found me says it loud.'

'You are wise then, in these matters.'

'There are women in the village better able to tend to you than I.'

'I heard you spoken of as the cunning-man in these parts. That little boy Stephen said . . .'

The mention of his name made Stephen feel suddenly guilty, though he could not say why. He drew up his knees and rested his cheek against them.

'I do no scrying.' Casper worked his knife hard into the wood, with his brows drawn together. 'I shall not look into the water and tell you about your life to come.'

'But they say you know herbs. There are herbs for what ails me.'

Casper's knife stopped suddenly. 'There are. Tansy, Pennyroyal if you know what to do with them, but lady, do not ask me. There might be a thing I'll do for a sick woman with five little ones to feed already, but I shall not do them for you. It's playing dice with the Devil and can kill you or take you to Hell first. You are young. And if it is the shame you are thinking of, here you are away from the world, you know.'

Miss Hurst shook her head.

'There's life there,' Casper continued deliberately. His bruises made him look very fierce. 'And it wants to be. Go to Kendal, call yourself a widow then go back home saying you have picked up an English orphan.'

'It is not possible! You say it as if it were simple, but it is not.'

Casper took up his carving again. 'It *is* simple. Man lies with woman then there comes children and the caring of them.'

'I am married.'

Casper shrugged. 'Then you are respectable and all is well.'

'My husband will not acknowledge me. He says my father tricked him.'

Casper looked up at her. 'You have proof of the wedding?' She nodded slowly. 'And the baby is his? He has lain with you?' She looked up, her mouth open in shock, and Casper laughed gently. 'No one tricked him into *that*. Go to the magistrate then where your husband is, or send your father.'

She started to cry again, and Stephen felt suddenly angry with her. Casper was hurt, and Mr Quince sick, and all she could do was cry. Casper watched her for a while, his knife forgotten in his hand, then patted her awkwardly on her knee. 'Matter of love, is it? A handsome man. You wish him to come running home from care of you, not fearing the law? If you are free of the child, you think that more like to happen?'

She took out her handkerchief and wiped her eyes. 'You think I am foolish.'

'Foolish as any woman touched by love. And that is a *fine* fool.'

She picked up one of the half-burned sticks from the old fireplace and began to draw circles in the earth. 'I was happy. I was only two months out of the convent. I thought my wedding night . . . I thought I would be free . . .' She started to draw long vicious lines through the circles. 'He owed my father money. I think he thought the ceremony a – how do you say it – a "lark".' Her voice was bitter. 'But my father is clever. It was legal. My husband found he was trapped in the morning and left, cursing us both. I want to explain I had no wish to trick him.'

'Where is your da now?'

'He says he has business, but he did not come home last night and the landlord says there is money owing. Perhaps he has left me too. I hope he will be at the inn when I return. I want him to take me away from here, but he laughs at me.' She looked up at Casper, her lip trembling again. 'I could work! I learned music and languages at the convent – I could teach. I should like to. But I have no money now, and with the child . . .'

Casper sniffed. 'How old are you, lady?'

There was a long pause. 'Seventeen.'

Casper sighed. 'Speak no more of herbs, but I shall help you if I can. Where is this man, your husband?'

She opened her mouth, then closed it again, before getting up and saying quickly, 'Oh, I should not have come. You will not help me!'

'Sit down, lass. And tell me who this man is and where he bides.'

'No, I cannot.' She shook her head. 'I shall return to the inn, and if my father is not there . . . what shall I do? I must get away somehow. If he cannot help me, perhaps someone else might. I need only a little money.'

'You have an offer of help here, my girl.'

'Perhaps my father has got hold of some money – I could steal it. And if my father is gone then *he* must see me . . .'

Casper was frowning. 'These are wild words, girl. The heat is pressing you. Be calm now.'

'Goodbye, Mr Grace. I thank you for your words, but it is not your help I need.'

Crowther and Harriet rejoined their oarsman on the lakeside in silence and settled into separate contemplation of the movement of the water. Harriet knew Crowther well enough not to interrogate him. Her own thoughts she allowed to empty until the song the oarsman was singing curled round some corner of her mind and tugged on it.

'What are you singing, Isaiah?'

'Sorry, madam. It is a habit I fall into when I row.'

She smiled at him. 'If you would be happy to sing out, I should be glad to give you audience.'

The man nodded and cleared his throat, then in a deep bass that seemed to sing in the wood of the boat, began:

> *'And when James came back to his country*
> *And Greta answered his call*
> *The light folk fancied the German King*
> *And must have set their standard for him*
> *For the Luck left Greta's Castle then*
> *And fortune abandoned them all.'*

184

It was a merry tune for such dark matter. Other verses followed detailing Lord Greta's escape, and there was a coda that covered his brother's execution in 1746, but at the conclusion Harriet was still frowning over the first verse. She smiled and patted her hands together as the man finished. He nodded shyly and looked to his oars.

'So the Luck is lost then?' she said.

'Some say Lord Greta dropped it in the lake when he was crossing to meet his men in Keswick, though I don't believe that. Reckon some bright spark thought that story up so he could get pleasure-seekers leaning out of his boat to look for gleams in the muck.'

'Why don't you believe it?'

The man paused in his rowing to point behind him, south along the shore from Silverside Hall. 'He would ride from there, where the Hall was. Why trouble to cross the lake if you had horse and baggage with you? He'd have just ridden round the top through Portinscale, same as they do every day since from Silverside.'

Harriet leaned forward and put her chin in her hand. 'Did you ever meet anyone who claimed to have seen the Luck, Isaiah?'

'Oh aye, madam. There was a woman used to care for me when I was a bairn who served in Gutherscale Hall. She'd seen it – rubbed it clean, she said. Used to love talking on that, she did, and on the love Lord Greta had for his land. Must have tore him up to leave it so.'

Harriet searched in the woodland opposite for any sign of the Hall. Isaiah saw what she was about. 'Have you seen the ruins yet, madam?'

She nodded. 'I visited yesterday morning. There is not much of Lord Greta's home left.'

'It was all cleaned out by the Crown in the year 1716, then when Lord Keswick, Sir William he was then, bought it we thought he'd be in there, but after the fire he let it rot. Daft to rebuild when he had a house. Careful with his money, he was.' As he mentioned the 1st Baron his eyes flicked carefully towards Crowther, but the latter gave no sign he had heard his father named.

'I thought I saw some signs of fire there.'

'Aye, that was the winter of forty-five. Lit up the sky, it did. You'd remember that, my lord?'

'I was not at home,' Crowther said, then fell into silence again.

'How did it happen, Isaiah?'

'It was a cold evening, some fool lit a fire there, I suppose to sleep by, and got more warmth than he wished for.'

'Thank you,' Harriet said, letting her mind drift again.

'Glad to oblige, madam,' he replied, and pulled on the oars with new vigour. Crowther kept his eyes on the haze-clouded hills and did not speak again.

When Fräulein Hurst had left the clearing, Casper called Stephen down to join him without turning his head.

'How did you know I was there?' Stephen asked, as he slid down the last of the slope.

'Joe was sitting on that holly and staring down at you the whole time.'

Stephen turned and saw the grey-headed bird sunning himself just where he had emerged from the undergrowth.

'He didn't say anything.'

'He's a wise bird.' Casper examined the herbs that Stephen had gathered then began nipping the buds from some and dropping them into the kettle over his fire. 'My thanks for this, youngling.'

'Mr Quince is ill. Will you help him? Mr Crowther sent the physician away.'

Casper looked at him. 'Your tutor is a young fellow – he might be better for not being meddled with. Nature weaves its ways. What manner of sick is he?'

'He fell into the lake yesterday. That is, Felix pushed him. He was shivering last night and this morning he is all hot and sweaty and rolls his head about.'

Casper began to pick through the herbs Stephen had gathered again. 'Have you a handkerchief, lad? A clean one, mind.'

Stephen nodded and produced it, then watched as Casper laid it flat on the ground and began to drop buds and leaves from the various plants onto the linen.

'You'll take this to Miriam. Tell her to steep it in hot water, not boiling, a pint or so, and give him a glass of it.' As he spoke he folded the corners of the handkerchief together, then tied them to make a neat package.

Stephen put his hand out to take it, but Casper twitched it away from him. 'Most people pay for my services, youngling. Far as I can see, the food was from Cook. What do *you* have for me?'

The boy looked at the ground. His store of coins, such as it was, he had already spent in his mind on little crosses from the museum. Suddenly his face brightened.

'Your sister, Jocasta Bligh, lives near St Martin's Lane in

London. In her own room. She tells fortunes with cards, has patchwork skirts with lots of colours. She has a little dog called Boyo, and takes care of a boy called Sam. I am sorry I did not say so before – I forgot. And I only knew she was your sister yesterday.'

Casper's eye became bright and a slow smile opened his face. 'Now there's payment that binds me to you and yours, youngling.' He dropped the package into Stephen's hands, then rested one fist on the boy's shoulder. 'There's payment, indeed. Now tell me every word you can of her while I let this brew work on me.'

III.4

WHEN THE LITTLE boat had deposited them once again on the lawns of Silverside, Harriet and Crowther climbed the gentle rise together, but instead of re-entering the house returned to the gravel walk to its south and took a seat in the shade.

'Will you not speak to Mrs Tyers before you talk to your sister, Crowther? Find out how she knows of your father going to the Island with a stranger?'

Crowther spun his cane in the gravel in front of them. 'I have not been a good brother, Mrs Westerman. I perhaps do not regret that as I should, but I do acknowledge it. I think it is my duty to inform Margaret of the note and what we have found before I go to discuss such matters with our former servants.'

Harriet was about to say something more when there was a

rattle at the garden gate and Stephen was dashing up the path towards them with his face pink.

'Mama! I have been to see Casper! He was so happy to hear of Mrs Bligh. He has given me some herbs for Miriam to make tea with for Mr Quince. I had to gather them myself because some men attacked him last night and he is injured, but I got all the right ones.'

This all came in such a rush, Harriet found herself struggling to take in the information offered. 'Mr Grace was hurt? Did he know the men? Will he speak to Mr Sturgess?'

Stephen came to stand before her and let her take his hands between her own, shaking his head. 'I asked. He said it would be a poor thing if a cunning-man had to go to a magistrate.'

Crowther put out his hand. 'What are these herbs?' Stephen handed the handkerchief to him, looking a little suspicious. Crowther carefully untied it and picked through what was there before retying the corners and handing it back to the boy.

'Well?' Harriet asked.

'I can see nothing in there that will do him any harm, and I have no doubt it will do him more good than anything that physician from the town can provide. I begin to have a respect for Mr Grace and his skills.'

Stephen made for the kitchens before Crowther could withdraw this rather limited assent. As his steps faded, Harriet asked, 'Crowther, do you think your father capable of murder?'

Crowther pictured Sir William in his study puffed up like a toad and roaring at one of his tenants.

'I think any man capable, though I never saw him washing blood from his hands. Yes, I think it possible. But I wish to know if my sister remembers something that I do not. I must tell her what we have found and see what memories are stirred.'

'Did you know Ruben Grace then, Crowther? What sort of man was he? Did you know him as a cunning-man? Stephen is very taken with his son, and we know his daughter to be a woman of talents.'

At the mention of Jocasta Bligh, Crowther began to spin his cane in his hands. 'I wonder why she never mentioned who her father was when we met in London. Perhaps she was waiting for me to question her further. I should have done. I simply let her tell me her story and watched Sam feed the dog scraps. Yes, I did know Ruben. My father trusted him and I was surprised when I heard from my mother that he was no longer steward at Silverside and had become owner of the Black Pig. My father and he were allies in the household in my youth. The housekeeper, Lottie Tyers, though she served my father before his marriage, was more of my mother's party.'

They both fell silent for a while. Stephen had re-emerged and was playing a few feet away from them. It seemed he had fashioned an area of the gravel into a battlefield, and now an army of slate splinters were ranged against granite enemies. He was singing softly under his breath the same song they had heard from the boatman during the morning. *'When James came back to his country . . .'*

Harriet put her elbows on her knees and cupped her chin in her palm. 'How might we continue, Crowther? If we can put a name to this man by whatever means, this body in the tomb, then all well and good – at least his grave may be marked. But if you remain convinced your father was his murderer, what further steps can we take? Will you read a proclamation in the town square condemning him?' Crowther said nothing. 'Whatever happened, it happened long ago – and nothing now will be helped or hurt by our exposing these secrets to the air.'

Crowther listened to Stephen's song and wondered again why he had come here. A hot wind stirred the lake below them, and there was an answering sigh in the wooded slopes above the garden. If his father were a murderer, there could be no trial. Might the victim still have children living? Could the truth not help seal some wound left long open? More likely it would only expose the rot to the air.

Harriet spoke again. 'Perhaps we should let the dead bury the dead.'

He raised an eyebrow. 'That is not your usual attitude in these matters. What of your reputation as a "warrior for truth and justice"?'

'These are not usual circumstances. But perhaps there are those now living who should know the truth.'

It still surprised him how often Mrs Westerman's thoughts formed the mirror of his own, but if any further reply occurred to Crowther, he had no opportunity to make it as the gravel on the path announced another footstep. There were two, in fact, since the Vizegräfin was walking arm-in-arm with her son. She was holding him very close to her side and speaking rapidly to him. From the expression on his face, the topic of conversation was not a pleasant one. Her normally fine features were distorted by anger and Felix's head was downcast, his dark hair falling over his face as if he were trying to hide from her words. The Vizegräfin was speaking to him in rapid French, so Harriet could make out none of the matter, but she was transfixed by the vicious expression on the woman's face. She stood therefore, to make their presence known, slightly later than she should have done. Becoming aware of them, the Vizegräfin turned and aimed at Crowther and Harriet the same look of angry contempt she had just fixed on her son.

Harriet made a curtsey and wished the pair good morning as though she had seen nothing, and heard Crowther get to his feet beside her.

It was Felix who recovered first. Gently detaching himself from his mother's grip, he bowed to them both.

'I am glad to see you,' he said. I am sure of that, Harriet thought to herself. 'Mrs Westerman, after my poor show at the competition I am planning to spend the morning practising with my longbow in the lower gardens.' Without turning round, Harriet knew that the little group around her now had her son's complete attention. 'I was wondering if Stephen might wish to join me. I understand Mr Quince is indisposed. I am sorry my carelessness deprived your son of his guardianship. Perhaps I might supply . . .' Harriet was pleased to see him blush over these last words.

There was a flurry of movement and Stephen appeared at her side, eyes wide with appeal.

'Oh, may I, Mama? There are targets and everything! I was not allowed to yesterday and I watched very carefully. Oh, please, may I?'

Harriet looked down at her son and felt her heart jump. It was a terrible thing to be a tyrant, a dictator – even a kind one. The responsibility made her afraid every time she looked at the boy. Hers was all the power, all the freedom. Again the loss of her husband stung her. 'You may, Stephen. Thank you, Felix.'

The young man smiled and Harriet again saw something of the charm of the boy. The Vizegräfin looked more herself again, bored rather than angry. Harriet wondered if it were possible the other woman had ever felt for her son what she felt for Stephen, if it were possible she herself would ever whisper into Stephen's ear with such an expression of poisonous disgust.

There was another herb that Casper wished to make use of, but he knew it grew most powerfully in a place he was unwilling to send the boy, so when he felt he had strength enough, he stripped a length of ash for support and began the trek towards the hollowed slopes of the old mine-working up Swineside from Ullock, with Joe flapping behind him. Almost at once, the black witch started laughing.

'All beat up, Casper? Coming to see me, are you? Coming to gather my flowers? You useless dog. No help to that girl, were you? And they call you cunning! I'd have helped her, but you are blind and stupid and there's all there is to it.'

Casper concentrated on placing one foot in front of the other. His ribs were sore enough to drive the breath from him every other step.

'Poor Casper! Felt the fists, have you? Worm, you deserve it. Oh, I love to see you aching and pining. Wish they'd have killed you. You, all respected by the scum of the village, you fraud, you monster. You murderer.'

He was used to it. Ever since he had buried her, Mother Grice chattered and scratched at him. It was like a wound that never quite healed. She grew stronger and happier when he approached the place where her bones rotted, up the track to the old mines where few people ever went, though the path was good. Her bones must have tainted the air and made it taste evil, even to those who didn't know whose bitterness it was they felt on their lips. The yellow blooms of St John's Wort flourished there, and though he could gather the leaves and flowers in other spots, they did not seem to have the same potency as these. He was sure she breathed on them specially to bring him back to the place where he had found her little body. This was high-days and holidays for her now, him all bruised and hurting and coming to her weak.

'*Your bitch sister still lives then? Maybe she should come home. Maybe you could call* her *a witch and have* her *die in the cold.*'

'Whisht, will you!' he said, and Joe lifted his beak and cawed unhappily. She laughed like the Devil with a fresh soul. Nothing made her happier than drawing him in to speak. He gritted his teeth and climbed the last few yards to the shade of the old mine and the pool of yellow blooms outside it, then came to a sudden halt. There was something wrong about the opening. Stones had been moved – he could see the scars of them in the soil – and the old logs and fallen branches that usually lay about the place were missing. He stepped to the mouth of the mine. There was a wooden barrier a few yards inside, but in front of it was a pile of what had been missing outside – a rough heap of stones and branches. He approached carefully and bent down, hissing as he did so from the pain in his side, then lifted a rock from the pile and set it aside, then the next. Then became still. For a moment even the witch was silent. Another grave. A man, his head turned to one side and his eyes open. Casper reached forward and touched the skin. Cold.

Grice had got her breath back. '*Another one of yours, Casper?*' she crowed. '*Can't say, can you? What if it was him who beat you?*

194

All went a bit dark then, didn't it? What if you killed him and brought him here? Who is it, Casper? Was he a witch?'

Ignoring the voice Casper continued to remove the stones and branches.

Within minutes of the invitation being made, Stephen found himself standing on the low lawns of the park with Felix bending over him, showing him how to attach a soft leather bracer to his arm. He was beginning to think the incident at the lake was an accident, after all. He reached for the long yew bow.

'A moment, Stephen,' Felix said, holding it out of his reach. 'Remember that an arrow can be as deadly as a musket if used properly. I would not put a gun in your hands without making sure you knew its use first.'

'I fired a cannon yesterday.'

Felix grinned. 'Watch what I do. Then you may try.'

He turned sideways to the target, a brave painted cloth on a bound straw backing some thirty feet away. He had removed his jacket in the heat and Stephen could see the muscles of his shoulders bunch as he drew the string of the bow back to his cheek between two fingers of his right hand. The arrow's shaft was pale as buttermilk, its metal tip resting on the circle of his thumb where Felix's hand held the shaft of the bow. It looked to Stephen like an animal coiled and ready to escape into the woods, and he remembered suddenly the excitement he had felt running up the steep paths behind Silverside before he had met Casper. Felix's gaze was fixed on the target at the far end of the lawn. He released the arrow, the string sang a low clear note and Stephen heard the point sigh through the air as if it were tearing the haze apart like frayed silk. With a dull thump the arrow buried itself in the centre of the target.

'Shot!' Stephen cried. Felix made a slight bow then bent towards him with a confidential smile.

'I have hunted boar in the forests near my father's home. They are dangerous animals when wounded. One must be accurate and deadly with the first shot.'

Stephen's mind was suddenly full of forests, and he imagined himself riding next to Felix and shooting off arrows at wild animals.

'Was it frightening?'

Felix considered. 'Yes, but it is an exhilarating sport. I dislike being bored and such hunts are never boring. Maybe I shall take you some day. But first let us teach you what to do.'

Stephen took the slim body of the bow in his hands. It was very smooth. 'Why did you not win yesterday, sir?'

He frowned. 'I was distracted. No, stand more straight, bend the elbow a little or you will be flayed alive.'

Mrs Briggs was still enjoying her breakfast when they went back into the house. She marvelled aloud at their energy, having been to St Herbert's so early, given all the activity of the previous day. The Vizegräfin looked up sharply.

'You have been to the Island of Bones? Why?'

'I understood you were eager to see it yourself,' Crowther said evenly. 'And to watch the tomb being opened.'

She looked back down to her coffee. 'Our father used to sit in the library and stare at it, particularly after Mama died. I always wondered what he saw in it, as he never made any effort to improve the place.'

Crowther could almost feel Harriet's thoughts on that casual speech. He watched his sister drink her coffee and eventually drive Mrs Briggs away from the table with acid remarks about the superiority of a Viennese firework display to those she had observed from her window the previous evening. He hoped that as their hostess left, he might be able to begin with his sister the discussion of the body in the tomb and his suspicions, but Mrs Westerman seemed to feel differently.

'Perhaps, madam, you missed the sight of the legendary Luck from your window?' she was saying to Margaret. 'It was most impressive from the seat we had in Crow Park.'

The Vizegräfin made no answer. Harriet turned in her chair a little to look out of the window to her left and took a delicate sip from her coffee cup. 'Your father came here while Lord Greta was still master of much of these lands, did he not? Do you know why Lord Greta turned rebellious?'

The Vizegräfin's gaze flickered up from the table-top and she examined Mrs Westerman. 'Indeed, I understand my father was acquainted with Lord Greta, though he was a far poorer man at that time. I believe that Lord Greta was a friend of the Pretender during his childhood in France. Greta was also a Catholic, so when he received word that the Rebellion was being planned, he chose to support his friend and his faith.'

'And he rode from his home at Derwent Water, Gutherscale Hall?'

'He did. He never returned here again.'

'What happened exactly?'

The Vizegräfin found, as many had before, that Mrs Westerman could be a persistent questioner. There was no dignified way to remove herself from the conversation, and perhaps thinking of the wrongs of men sixty years ago was more pleasant than thinking of her son's behaviour and its effect on their reputation in Keswick, so she continued, 'When the Rebellion failed, he was taken to London to stand trial in Westminster Hall. Most thought the King would spare his life, but when it became clear that his wife and friends' appeals were not softening the King's resolve to have him executed, Lady Greta managed to smuggle him out of the Tower. He reached his friends and his younger brother in Paris.'

'That is a romantic tale.'

The Vizegräfin smiled, and for the first time Harriet saw something more than coquettishness in her eyes. She saw intelligence, and amusement shimmer briefly there, like quartz lost in a cloudy pool.

'The trouble with our human lives is they do not conclude neatly where a dramatist would leave off. Is that not so, Mrs Westerman?'

Harriet turned gracefully and set down her coffee cup.

'I have often thought so,' she replied. 'So Lord Greta's later life was less romantic?'

The Vizegräfin nodded slowly. 'He had a child in the forties, then found himself called to the Young Pretender's side in forty-five. His wife reminded him of his debt to her, and for her sake and that of the child he did not go, but instead trusted his brother with his money and the power of his name. Of course, as you know, the second Rebellion went no better in the end than the first. His brother was taken and did not escape the executioner's axe. It was said the guilt and grief made Lord Greta bitter to his family and he drank them all into poverty.'

Harriet nodded, then tilting her head to one side asked, 'So how did your father come to own so much of Lord Greta's former estate?'

The Vizegräfin's face became set again and she straightened her back. 'The estates were forfeit to the Crown after Lord Greta's trial in sixteen. My father was in a position to make a number of purchases over the years from those estates. He bought the last of the land in forty-seven when he became Lord Keswick.'

Harriet was still wearing her most engaging smile, and despite the sudden chill in the air was inclined to continue her enquiries; however, just as she opened her mouth to speak again, the door was opened and Miss Scales was announced. They hardly had time to greet each other, when the hall bell clanged again, and there was another voice in the house.

The words were not clear but the voice suggested distress. The door to the breakfast parlour sprang open and Harriet saw in the doorway the beautiful Austrian lady who had been looking for her father the previous evening. She was pale and her hair very loosely arranged. She looked at the company and flushed.

'Oh, he is not here! I must see him!'

Harriet got to her feet and stepped round the table to take her arm. The young woman's weight fell into her side almost at once.

'Fräulein Hurst? I am Harriet Westerman — my son's tutor told me your name. Is it he you have come to seek? Dear girl, what on earth is the matter?'

Harriet looked into her face; she was quite lovely even with her eyes reddened. Miss Hurst shook her head and tried to hold herself more upright.

'My father has not returned to the Royal Oak. I went walking early, and was sure I would meet him at breakfast, but the servants say his bed was not slept in. I am most concerned. I must speak to von Bolsenheim.'

'To Felix?' Harriet said.

The Vizegräfin's chair scraped back. 'As you see, Fräulein, my son is not here, and I do not know in what manner you think he might assist you if he were.'

'You are the Vizegräfin von Bolsenheim?'

'My dear girl,' said Harriet, trying to steer her to a chair, 'you can barely stand. Do sit down!'

She resisted. 'Then I shall leave him a note.'

Crowther, apparently unalarmed by the sudden drama, fetched quill and paper from one of the side-tables and set them in front of the young woman – then watched her curiously.

'*Danke, Mein Herr,*' she said under her breath, then sat and began to write. Miss Scales was examining her pocket-watch and frowning.

'I am surprised no message has been sent to you as yet, Miss Hurst. The morning is almost gone indeed. Is your father a great walker? Might he have become lost on the fells during the storm?'

The girl shook her head without looking up from her hurried writing. 'He is not fond of walking.' She folded her note then looked about her as if in hopes of finding some way to seal it. The Vizegräfin put out her jewelled hand.

'Fräulein, if you wish to leave a note for my son, you may leave it unsealed. He has no secrets from me.'

The girl's dark eyes flashed, and staring into the Vizegräfin's face she ripped the note in two and pushed the scraps into her pockets. 'But *I* may, I think. I must find my father. Will no one help me?'

Miss Scales put her arm around the young woman's shoulders. 'Dear girl, of course we shall help you.'

The Vizegräfin said something in German, and the Fräulein flinched. Crowther had heard the word before, but only in the darkest and dirtiest alleyways of Wittenberg. He turned to his sister.

'Margaret!'

The Vizegräfin swept from the room. Harriet stared at Crowther, who merely tightened his lips in reply.

The departure of the Vizegräfin had put new breath into the Fraulein's body. 'I must go and look for my father! He must be searched for, but I have no money and the landlord says I must leave if the bill cannot be paid today.'

Miss Scales's hands fluttered into the air. 'Now dear, do not despair,' she said, letting one hand fall on the young girl's shoulder. 'You shall come to my father's house – he is the vicar here, you know – and we shall arrange everything from there. Mrs Westerman will tell Mr Felix you called for him, I am sure. Now do you think you might come back to the vicarage with me? I am sure Mrs Briggs would press you to stay, were she here . . .'

Harriet interrupted her. 'Mrs Briggs has just taken the carriage into Keswick. I do believe, Miss Scales, she meant to call on you as she returned.'

'We said we would speak today about the burial of your poor ghost, though I thought we had arranged to meet here. My mistake, I am sure. Well, his grave is almost ready and may he rest more comfortably there. I should have remembered, but then I would have missed the pleasure of a jog along the lake.'

Miss Hurst stood up a little shakily.

'Oh my dear, do come back to the vicarage with me. Then you shall be closer to the village when news of your father arrives, and we may rouse up some fellows to go and search for him.'

Crowther reached into his pocket and Harriet heard the thin crinkle of paper. 'I shall speak to my nephew, Fräulein.' He crossed the room and placed something in Miss Scales's free hand. 'If you would be so kind, Miss Scales, perhaps you could have that conveyed to the landlord at the Oak and tell him should any other payment be required, he may address himself to me.'

Miss Scales glanced at what he had given her and went a little pink. 'Yes, of course, Mr Crowther. Now my dear, you saw my little trap outside as you came in? Let us gather you into it and you may spend the last of the morning with me, for I am sure we shall find your father before it is fully passed.'

Miss Scales carried off the young woman very swiftly, leaving Harriet and Crowther to stare at one another over the coffee cups.

'What did your sister call that young woman, Crowther?'

'A whore,' he replied shortly, and examined his fingernails.

Harriet considered. 'She did not look like a whore to me. And I rather liked her spirit, tearing up that note.' She could not help noticing that Crowther winced slightly when she said the word. 'Do you think she looked like a whore, Crowther?'

He frowned at her and she smiled, a reasonably convincing simulacrum of innocence. 'I could not possibly judge, madam,' he said, then hurried on as she opened her mouth again to continue the topic. 'However, the relations of my sister and nephew with this young woman are no concern of mine.'

'You made it your concern when you handed over that money. For a man who seems to despise his fellow creatures, at times you can be oddly generous.'

'More often than not I find money a convenient way of buying peace. Now will you come and speak to Margaret with me, and when we have taxed her memory perhaps we can consult Mrs Tyers.'

It was Harriet's turn to frown. 'You wish me to be present while you speak to her, Crowther? I would have thought, given the delicacy of the matter, you would have preferred to speak to her alone.'

'You presumed wrongly, madam. If you have finished your coffee . . .'

Harriet put the cup to her lips again, then wrinkled her nose. 'Quite cold!'

The Vizegräfin was surprised to see them enter the library and walk towards her with such firm steps. At first she ignored Harriet and turned to Crowther.

'You have no intention of lecturing me, I hope, Brother?'

Harriet squinted up at the bookshelves on the upper levels and walked behind the Vizegräfin's chair.

'You are right to be concerned, madam,' she said. 'He has lectured me any number of times, and as you see, it does me no good. However, I have yet to call a lady a whore at the breakfast-table.'

The Vizegräfin reflected on her jewelled hands lying in her lap. 'Your grasp of the German vernacular is impressive, Mrs Westerman. Did your sailor husband teach you the word?'

'No, I speak only a little German. Though I think Miss

Scales understood the word, or at least its import, by her expression when you spoke. What a great many books! I was proud of my library at Caveley till I came here. Were you bookish as a child?'

'I learned what was befitting to my role.'

'Enough,' Crowther said. 'I neither know nor care what your association is with that young woman . . .'

The Vizegräfin clasped her hands together so her rings clicked. '*I* have no association with Fräulein Hurst. I believe her father knew my son a little in Vienna. They are not the sort of people with whom *I* would associate.'

Crowther tapped his cane firmly enough on the carpet to make both ladies start. 'Margaret, I wish you to tell me something of my father. Can you manage to do that without making yourself ridiculous?'

The Vizegräfin shot out of her seat. '*I* make myself ridiculous! You dare say such a thing to me, *Gabriel*, when every paper in Europe has written of your exploits in the company of this woman! Why did you not remain in hiding? Stay under your rock with your knives and your little experiments? My father made you rich, and you sold everything he had worked for before his body was cold, and slunk away. I can tell you this of my father: he was a better man than you shall ever be.'

Crowther looked at her very steadily. 'I am no murderer.'

The Vizegräfin froze and Harriet thought of them as twinned dragons facing across a family shield. They had the same eyes, the same trick of holding themselves absolutely rigid when angry.

When the Vizegräfin spoke it was as if she had licked each

word with something bitter before letting it leave her mouth. 'No, Gabriel, you only pick amongst the *leavings* of murderers like a butcher's dog. My father never murdered any man. Rupert de Beaufoy died at the hands of the law as a traitor to his King. My father did his duty.'

She crossed the room and left the library, her skirts hissing and crackling over the floor. Harriet sank into the chair that she had vacated. 'We might have managed that better. Your poor sister will soon run out of rooms to leave in high dudgeon.' She folded her hands. 'Who might Rupert de Beaufoy be?'

Crowther sighed and sat down opposite her. 'He was the brother of the last Lord Greta, whom my sister mentioned to you a little while ago. The one who was caught in the Second Rebellion and executed in forty-six.'

Harriet stared hard into the carpet in front of her, her fingers tapping at the fabric of her dress. She could feel the thoughts and questions plaiting into a braid in her mind like rope in the chandler's shop.

'Crowther, when was your father awarded his peerage?'

III.5

STEPHEN HAD PULLED Felix's arrows free from the straw bed of the target and was now wrestling his own from the slight rise in the lawn either side of the painted roundel. He was just fastening his fingers round the second of these when he felt a hand on his shoulder.

'Careful there!' Felix said. 'Those arrows are delicate things. Free them gently at the angle they went into the ground, or you will weaken them.' Stephen adjusted his grip, and slid rather than yanked the shaft free from the grass. 'That's better. A weak arrow can split under the strain of the string, you know.' He showed Stephen his palm. In its centre was a faint puckered scarring. Stephen touched it with his finger.

'Did it hurt?'

'What do you think? Treat these things with respect, Mr Westerman.'

Stephen squinted up at him. Felix did not seem a man who treated many things with respect. Last evening in the drawing room he had seen him pick up and twirl on his fingertips a tiny porcelain dish of Mrs Briggs's that he himself would have feared to breathe on in case his lungs might shatter it.

'Tell me more about hunting boar, sir,' Stephen said. 'You must be very brave.'

Felix shrugged, resting the tip of his bow on the ground in front of his feet. 'I suppose I was. My heart was thudding, certainly. I was mostly excited though. It is one of those times that you are too engaged with the task at hand to think of anything else. The world becomes small and all your worries disappear. No bills, no thoughts of your own future. Just you and what is in front of you. It makes one feel free.'

Stephen was confused. To be a man *was* to be free, surely? Out of the schoolroom, no longer having to ask permission for anything. He tried to say so, and Felix shook his head.

'I am sorry, Stephen. We are never free. It is simply as we grow older, the negotiations become more complex.'

As they walked back towards the firing line Stephen watched Felix grow serious; his eyes were clouding and he handed the bow to him without comment or further instruction. Stephen felt his companion's sudden gloom fall on his shoulders. He thought of his mother, the way she could be so bright at times and quick, then of the number of occasions over the last year when he had found her curled up in her chair in the drawing room looking so still she might have been carved. He knew she was thinking about his father then, and seeing her so sad with her memories meant he did not speak of Captain Westerman as often as he would like. He would lie in his bed trying as hard as he could to remember how it felt to be lifted in his father's arms and have the air pressed out of him. He would wriggle as if he wanted to get away, but laughing and only in truth trying to get closer to the man, his scent of salt and sweat, the rough stubble of his face.

'Do you have a father, sir?' he said suddenly.

The question shook Felix out of his thoughts and he looked down at Stephen with eyebrows raised. 'I do. Everyone does, you know.'

Stephen lifted the bow, but found he could not see the target very clearly. He felt Felix's hand on his shoulder, slightly correcting his posture. 'I do not,' he whispered to the feathers of the arrow's flight and then released the string. The arrow fell short and skidded through the grass. Felix said something swiftly in German under his breath.

'Damn stupid thing to say. Sorry, Stephen. I know your father was a fine man. My mother is right – I am an idiot not fit to be let out.'

Stephen let the bow drop to his side. 'It does not matter. You are being kind to me.'

Felix shook his head. 'Do not trust me, Stephen. I have bad blood.' He looked up, distracted by some movement at the edge of the garden, and his expression changed from curiosity to sudden shock. 'Good God!' Stephen turned to see where he was looking and saw Casper emerging onto the upper lawn from the path into the woods. He was leaning heavily on a stick. Slung around his shoulders was a thick rope, and with it he was dragging something that looked like a sledge. There was a body on it.

Felix set off up the hill at a run with Stephen at his heels. When Casper saw them heading towards him he came to a stop and waited, breathing deeply. One of the gardeners who had been working on the beds outside the front door turned, then dropping his trowel, raced into the house. Felix arrived by Casper's side, and as he looked at the body, went completely white. He turned at once to Casper.

'What happened? Where? You are injured! Did you have some sort of fight with this man? Did you kill him?' Casper looked at him coolly but said nothing. Felix flushed. 'I said, what happened? Answer me!'

Stephen moved away from him and closer to Casper, who put his hand on the boy's shoulder but still said nothing. The door to Silverside Hall burst open again and Harriet and Crowther appeared, the Vizegräfin following behind them.

Casper leaned over to Stephen. 'Is the lady with the red hair your mother?'

Stephen nodded. 'And the man with her is Mr Crowther.'

'Him I know, I think. Don't be frightened, lad.'

Harriet was in the lead of the little group from the house. As she reached them and saw the body on the sledge, she slowed her steps, then put out her hand.

'I think you must be Casper Grace,' she said.

Casper took her hand and shook it. 'I am, and glad to know you.'

'I am sorry to see you have been hurt. Stephen told us.'

'I shall mend, madam.'

Crowther had crouched down beside the body and having touched the neck for a moment, stood again. 'And who was this gentleman?'

Casper lifted the ropes from around his shoulders, wincing as he did so, and dropped them to the ground. 'I cannot tell you that, my lord. Though by his looks, I'd say this man,' he nodded towards Felix, 'knows what name he went by.'

Stephen watched as Crowther turned his cold blue eyes on his nephew. Felix put his hand briefly towards his throat before replying.

'Hurst, his name is Hurst. I knew him in Vienna.'

Stephen started. 'Casper! He is Sophia's father!'

Casper squeezed his shoulder, but continued to speak to Crowther. 'I found him in the old mine on the flank of Swineside. You know the place?' Crowther nodded. 'He was hidden beneath rocks and branches, just in the lip of the workings. If I had not had business there, he might have lain a year.'

'Hidden?' Harriet repeated, looking intently into Casper's face.

'Yes, ma'am. Someone had aimed for him to stay there.' He sniffed, and settled his satchel under his arm. 'Good morning to you,' he said, and with another squeeze of Stephen's shoulder he was gone. Stephen looked at the body. It was a man about the age and size of Ham, the coachman. Old, but not as old as Crowther. He had black hair, curled over his ears and very shiny like his daughter's. Mr Hurst was wearing a buff jacket with gold buttons, and a high, pale waistcoat, a little dusty. There was a twig sticking out from under his collar. His face looked very grey, and his lips were a strange pale purple. The only corpse that Stephen had seen before now was that of his father. James Westerman had looked in the first minutes after death as if he were sleeping, his eyes closed. Mr Hurst's eyes were still wide open and his mouth a little agape. He lay in the sledge as a man might in a hammock with his ankles together and his arms by his side. His shoes had gold buckles on them and the skin on his face looked very smooth. Stephen could see no blood.

'Why has he left?' the Vizegräfin asked, suddenly shrill. 'What are we supposed to do with the body?'

She was ignored. Stephen felt a pressure on his arm. His mother had crouched down until she could look him in the eye, and was turning him away from the body. 'Stephen, would you go and find Isaiah and Ham for me?' she asked, and looked up at Crowther. 'We shall carry Mr Hurst into the brewery . . .' She seemed to be asking Mr Crowther something. He nodded and she stood again. 'Quick as you can, young man.'

Stephen shook himself, and set out for the house.

Only someone who knew Harriet as intimately as Crowther did would have noticed the set of her mouth, and slight paleness in her cheeks. To anyone else she would seem almost unnaturally calm in the circumstances. She turned to Felix.

'This man's daughter was here only half an hour ago, Felix, asking for you and concerned about her father. Miss Scales took her to the vicarage. Perhaps you should go and give her the news that his body has been found, since you know the young woman.'

Felix put his hand to his face; he was still staring at the body. 'She was here? I did not kn—'

His mother interrupted. 'There is no reason my son should be sent to talk to the girl! Let one of the servants carry a note. And why should the body be left here? Let it be taken away.'

Crowther listened to the rising notes of her voice, and once again thanked the fates that Mrs Westerman was not inclined to be hysterical.

'Felix, perhaps you should take your mother into the house. Mrs Westerman, I suggest once the body is secured, that we send a note to Mr Sturgess. He is the magistrate, and the coroner must be summoned. Perhaps then *we* may go to the vicarage and speak to Fräulein Hurst and Miss Scales.' He looked again at his nephew. He was waiting, perhaps even hoping that the boy would insist on accompanying them. Felix, however, only took his mother's arm and Crowther felt his lip curl.

When they were out of earshot he turned to Harriet. She had crouched down next to the body, and lifted the head between her palms, turning it carefully to left and right. 'I can see no signs of injury, Crowther. The skull seems intact.' She gently lowered the head. 'Our skeletal friend is safely boxed then, I take it?' She took hold of the far shoulder of the corpse and attempted to roll it towards her.

Crowther knelt by her side and assisted her until they could gain sight of Mr Hurst's back. The limbs were rigid. His tight jacket appeared unmarked, only dusty, as his waistcoat. They let the body rock onto its back again.

'Nothing,' Harriet said. 'But the body is quite dry. His daughter was concerned for him before the fireworks last night.'

'We can assume he was in his hiding-place before the storm of yesterday evening then,' Crowther said softly. As they stood again, the two servants of the Hall came trotting out towards them. Both exclaimed at the corpse. Harriet was surprised to see Ham pull one of Casper's rowan crosses from his pocket and kiss it. Crowther gave them their orders and they picked the rough sled up like a stretcher and headed towards the old brewery. As they followed a few steps behind, Crowther leaned towards Harriet. 'Let us delay sending to Mr Sturgess half an hour.'

Harriet said nothing, but nodded.

Having delivered his message in the house, Stephen hesitated on the steps a moment then turned and ran off in pursuit of Casper. He was haring down the track he thought most likely when he heard a whistle and Joe's rough call and turned. Casper was sitting among the shadows a little higher than the path. His clothes and skin so matched the colours around him, Stephen would have run straight past him unless he had been summoned.

'Are you feeling better, Casper?'

The man looked up. His left eye was still almost completely shut, and the bruising on his face had already moved from raw red to purple and yellow, spotted with black and blood blisters. Stephen's eyes widened, and Casper smiled.

'You're better than a looking-glass, lad.'

Stephen looked away, embarrassed. 'I told Miriam you had been hurt, and she wanted me to give you this.' He reached into his satchel and produced a half loaf, a cheese and a hunk of sausage that was greasy between his fingers.

'I'll have eaten all of Mrs Briggs's store cupboard in a day if those women have their way. The food is welcome. Set it out then, and I'll go about my business all the easier with a full stomach. Pulling that man free and down the slope took all the food in my belly.'

Stephen set his treasures down on a flat stone at his feet, then sat beside it cross-legged and began to carve the cheese and bread into pieces with his penknife.

'What business?' he said at last. 'Are you going to tell the magistrate about you getting beaten, after all, or finding Mr Hurst? Or about the Black Pig?'

Casper looked at him. 'What of the Black Pig? Think on, youngling. I've seen no one but yourself, that poor lass and her da today. And he had no news.'

Stephen stuttered a little. 'Miriam said, Miriam said someone had been in during the storm and knocked it all about! Knocked over the plates and jugs and dragged things about. The man who owns it didn't hear because of the storm.'

'You're speaking to the man who owns it. But it's indoor work, so Tom and Issy run the place in my stead. How is your tutor?'

'A little better. Cook is giving him the tea.'

Casper drew a clay pipe from his waistcoat, and a little tobacco pouch, and set about filling the bowl.

'I have some things to think on, youngling. Can you stay quiet an hour while I walk them about in my head? Then if you are willing to keep me company, I might have need of you in a little while.'

Stephen settled himself and nodded. 'Why did you bring the body to Silverside?'

'For good or bad, that is where it belongs. And I thought Lord Keswick might want to see it.'

'You mean Mr Crowther.'

'He may call himself what he will elsewhere, but when he walks this land he is Lord Keswick whether he likes it or no. No more talking now.'

He lit his pipe and began to draw on it, his eyebrows bunched together and his bruised face cloudy with thought.

'He looks as if he was killed by witchcraft.'

Crowther looked up at Mrs Westerman. She was standing at the head of the table gazing down into the dead man's eyes.

'In that case, so do most men,' he said dryly.

'But not many men are found with their pockets stuffed with mistletoe.'

They had found the plant bundled into the man's pockets within moments of being left alone with the body, along with some money and an elaborate pocket-watch. Harriet had liked the look of Casper Grace, but nevertheless, as soon as she saw the tear-drop leaves she had thought of him and wondered. 'I suppose Casper might have done that on finding the body, as a mark of respect to the dead.'

'Then I wonder he did not close the man's eyes.'

Harriet nodded. 'Do you think he might have killed him? Why then bring the body to us?'

'Mrs Westerman, do stop asking me impossible questions.' Crowther's sudden snap of irritation took him by surprise. There had been something in his nephew's face as he looked at the body that chilled him, something in his refusal to be the bearer of the news to Miss Hurst that had disgusted him. He felt angry in front of the body, harried by questions from the past and present. He thought of a man he had seen in a hospital in Padua. His leg had become black with gangrene, and in the damp heat of the summer he was tormented by flies buzzing and settling on his stump. They had all been grateful when he died. He had a sense of fellow feeling with that patient now which troubled him.

'My apologies.'

She did not look directly at him. 'We only have a little time, Crowther. You are right, I may speculate as much as I like – later. For the moment let us only observe.'

Crowther removed his coat and began to fold up his sleeves, trying to discover his usual calm. 'The body may conceal any number of hurts within it, Mrs Westerman. If a man falls down dead and another says before he did so he clutched his chest, I would suspect his heart and look for signs of disease there. If our putative witness says his speech became slurred and his movements awkward I would look first for signs of bleeding in the brain.'

'And where there is no witness?'

'I examine all the organs and see what they can tell me. I have told you before, sometimes people simply die, they are dead because they ceased to live. That is not witchcraft, just the usual fate of man. Will you help me remove his coat?' She did so. He was grateful she had let his spasm of bad temper pass without comment.

Much of Crowther's work meant he dealt with small samples, animals or parts of the human body transported to his desk by colleagues interested in his opinion. They came packed in straw and ice or pale and floating in preserving solutions. It still astonished his animal mind how heavy a body becomes when the life has left it, how awkward and unwieldy a thing. It was lucky the coat was not overly tight and could be pulled free of the body without cutting it. He suspected that the rigor was just beginning to pass, and began to speculate on what that might tell him of when the man died. Mrs Westerman held the coat up, then frowned.

'Crowther!'

She approached, her finger on the collar of the coat. The buff material was stained. It was a small patch, he could have covered it with his thumb, but it was there. Crowther wet the end of his finger and rubbed it into the stain, then put the finger to his mouth for a moment. He nodded then turned round to spit onto the floor.

'Blood.'

Harriet gathered the coat in her hands and lifted it towards the light. 'There is so little of it.'

Crowther had turned back to the body.

She laid the coat on one of the benches and joined him. The corpse was still lying on its front. Crowther took the head between his hands and gently shifted it, moving it further onto its face so the chin was tucked into the chest.

The black hair of Mr Hurst was as thick as his daughter's. Crowther placed his fingers at the place where the spine and skull touched; it was matted and slightly gritty under his touch.

'There is a wound there?' Harriet asked.

He went to his roll of instruments on the table and withdrew one of his scalpels – it sighed out of the leather. 'There is more blood in his hair. I think there is a wound. I wish the man had worn his hair shorter. I hate to blunt my knife. Will you hold his head steady for me, Mrs Westerman?'

She put her hands either side of the man's head again without flinching. She had the pale skin common to most red-heads. The black of her mourning ring stood out against it like coal in snow. Crowther cut away the bloodied clump of hair, gradually uncovering a two-inch square of skin. At its centre was a bloody spot the size of a shilling. He placed his little finger on it, then began to work the tip into the wound. The head shifted and he looked up; Mrs Westerman had turned her head away. He returned his attention to the wound; his finger met no significant resistance. He nodded to himself, then carefully freed his finger before wiping it on his handkerchief.

Harriet released her grip and he saw her bend over the wound with a look of deep concentration. She then reached behind her neck and touched the same spot on her own skin where the skull hinges on the spine. He thought of all the injuries she must have seen serving with her husband, or those she had seen in his company. It would be unusual indeed if she had ever seen anything so neat.

'Could such a thing have killed him?' she asked.

Crowther examined his finger and decided it was as clean as he might make it. 'The wound appears deep. It could very easily have proved fatal at once.'

'This is not a knife wound.'

'No. Something long and thin. An awl, such as Casper must use for his carving?'

'Or an arrow,' Harriet said quickly, then looked up at him, her lips slightly parted.

He closed his eyes briefly. An arrow would indeed produce such a wound. 'If I am to examine him more fully, we shall need more time than we have at our disposal now, Mrs Westerman. It is time to write to Sturgess, and visit Miss Hurst.'

'I am a little surprised you do not suggest I do so alone, and allow you to continue.'

'I might have done so, had I not been so unreasonably rude to you a few moments ago. Now I feel I have not the credit to send you on such duties alone.'

III.6

AS THE CARRIAGE RATTLED down the slope Harriet bit her lip and stared out of the window.

'Speak, Mrs Westerman,' Crowther said at last.

'What possible motive could Casper Grace have for killing this man? A stranger, a foreigner . . .'

'Perhaps the witches told him to do it.'

'I have spoken to Mrs Briggs and Miss Scales about Casper Grace. He does believe that witches and spirits speak to him, and they are sometimes cruel, but he has been hearing them for over twenty years! They began soon after his father's death. Why should he do this now? There have been foreigners and strangers enough to provide sacrifice pouring through Keswick every summer.'

Crowther turned to the view from his side of the phaeton. It did not inspire him. 'The season is unusual. Perhaps he believes the hills demand a sacrifice to carry off this dry fog. I read in the news-sheet that only last week, the magistrate in Kendal put a man in the stocks who claimed that the end of days was upon us. When the magistrate arrested him, he had already gathered a crowd of acolytes around him.'

She shook her head. 'Lucky Kendal to have such a magistrate. But Casper does not seem a fool or a zealot.'

'We do not know the story of his beating. Perhaps this was an act of revenge. To bring the body out of the woods would be an unusual act for a murderer, I concede. However, Casper is eccentric, and the act of killing may fracture a mind already weakened with the chatter of witches. Did not Stephen say that Grace believed that rainstorms protected the stones from the archaeological fervour of Mr Sturgess?'

'He was repeating a story for their entertainment. And he told Stephen that same day that the traditions of blood sacrifice were long over . . .' She let her sentence trail away.

Crowther cleared his throat. 'Mrs Westerman, I know you are not simply thinking of Casper Grace. Let it be said.' She did not answer him. 'You are wondering if Felix had anything to do with this death. He knew the man. He described him as a cardsharp. Presumably my nephew owed him money. The death was not accidental. Judging by his pocket-watch, Mr Hurst was not robbed, so it is likely his murder was a personal affair. We are aware of only one person in the area who knew him, other than his daughter. And that is Felix.'

'Perhaps his daughter killed him,' she said, almost sulkily.

'If so, that was quite a piece of theatrics she gave us this morning.'

'Many women are accomplished actresses, Crowther. It is a useful skill. Naturally I am wondering about Felix, but I find

I cannot speculate freely about these deaths that crowd your family history. How can I say to your face with my usual carelessness that your father or nephew may have murdered?'

'You need not be so careful on my account, Mrs Westerman.'

She snorted. 'Nonsense! Your father's murder and your brother's execution have haunted you thirty years. We should never have come here. I thought only of escaping my role in Hartswood as the local tragedy for a while. I think you thought only of the same. Now we are caught between old mysteries and new horrors. I cannot build castles of speculation in the air, and expect you to find the evidence to give them foundation here. It is all too close.'

Crowther lowered his chin as he let the truth of what she had said filter through his mind. 'Perhaps it is time I faced my demons. In their way, they pursue me just as Casper's do him. I have become too old to outrun them.'

He was speaking almost to himself He felt her hesitate, then she put her hand into her pocket and produced a letter. 'It is interesting you use that phrase. I received this today. It is Jocasta Bligh's account of what she saw on the day of your father's murder.'

'I have heard it.'

'I know, Crowther. But I think you should hear it again.'

It was a long hour. But eventually Casper put his pipe back in his pocket and cleared his throat. 'News will have lapped up all over by now,' he said.

'Of the body?' Stephen asked.

'Of the body, of my hurts and the Black Pig. Time to take a place in the story.' He stood carefully with the help of his ash staff. It made Stephen think of Crowther's polished cane, though he hardly ever saw Crowther put any weight on his stick, and Casper was leaning heavily on his.

'It is a serious hurt,' Casper said after a few minutes of silent walking.

'Your injuries, you mean, Mr Casper?' Stephen said.

Casper shook his head. 'They are bad enough. But a man must have a powerful reason to take to robbing or beating me.' It was said without pride, but rather a concerned curiosity, a serious man thinking through serious matters.

'Because people are afraid of you?'

Casper smiled, which made him wince. 'They respect me, just as they respected my father. So they should.'

'What did they take?'

Casper sniffed. 'Nothing. But they were looking for something.'

'But what . . . ?'

'Whisht, lad, we're nearing Portinscale. From here on you say nothing. Walk a few paces behind now, keep silent and keep an eye out. Watch.'

'What am I watching for?'

'You're watching for whatever you see. Now quiet yourself.'

There was something dream-like about the next hour as Casper, with Stephen trailing respectfully behind, made his way through Portinscale, along the road to Keswick and up the hill through the marketplace.

Women began to emerge from their cottages and kitchens, or stopped fussing over their animals or weeding their patches to turn and watch him come. They looked somehow both scared, and happy to see him. Small children joined them from the fields and ran ahead of them like dolphins dancing through the bow wave of a great ship. As they turned into Portinscale, a woman hurried to Stephen's side and put a cloth wrapped round something that smelled of warm ovens into his hands. Stephen slipped the package into his bag, and smiled at her. She only nodded to him in return, her face serious, then stepped away. When Stephen had walked through the village with Casper the day before, he had seen people smile and raise their hands, give Casper their greetings and turn at once back to their work again. It was not so today. Where the fields ripened between Crosthwaite Church and the town, men laid down their tools and approached the roadside, then, as Casper came close, took off their caps and held them in front of them with their eyes down. It was as if he were a walking church.

The children must have carried the news of their coming in front of them. Before they reached Keswick itself, Stephen had begun to feel as if he were following a parade. The doors of the cottages opened. Fires and animals were abandoned for a little while as men and women emerged to respectfully observe Casper pass. Stephen's eyes darted about, trying to catch each expression as he passed. Another woman trotted up to him; the flesh of her face was heavy and her hair was thin and greasy. She gave him a narrow package of paper and string. He smelled the tang of hard cheese, nodded his thanks and put it with the loaf.

In Keswick his bag became so heavy the strap was starting to cut into his shoulder. At the bottom of the village he looked up to see Mr Askew in his smart waistcoat emerge from the museum and watch them approach from the top of his neatly swept steps. As they drew level, he ran lightly down them.

Like the others he did not approach Casper, but fell into step with Stephen. For a moment he looked as if he might want to say something, but in the end he silently removed from his jacket-pocket a silver flask. It made a little sloshing noise as he tucked it into Stephen's swollen satchel. He then stepped back to the side of the road and waited for them to pass. At the Royal Oak the landlord came out and stood quietly at the door.

Casper did not pause, or stop to lean on his stick. He kept his eyes on the road in front of him and at the same steady pace led Stephen, and a couple of younger children who seemed to have joined them, up the hill in the shadow of Latrigg. Stephen had guessed where they were going now. His back was aching and he wondered how Casper was managing it, but aware of his duties he kept watching the people who came to see them pass. At last Casper turned off the road and unlatched the gate to the field where the stone circle stood. Stephen glanced about him and followed. The other children hung around the gateway, punching each other on the shoulder, or murmuring as Casper crossed the cropped turf and entered the circle.

Stephen hovered between the gateway stones until Casper had reached the centre of the circle and slowly knelt down. Something stopped the boy from following. Instead he circled round, and slipped between the two stones to the south where there seemed to be a smaller inner oblong of slabs, like a sanctuary within the church. Without taking his eyes off Casper he settled himself on the ground between them and, gratefully, lifted the strap of the satchel over his shoulder.

After some time the children dispersed at the gateway, and

Stephen was startled out of his contemplation of the falling ranks of hills around them by Casper's voice.

'Come then.'

He took the satchel in his arms, and jogged over, keeping low and quiet as if he were in some holy place. Casper gave him time to settle, then said: 'Well?'

Stephen drew the flask that Mr Askew had handed him from his pocket and passed it to Casper, who raised his eyebrows at it, then smiled slowly, uncapped it and drank.

'Everyone looked very grave,' Stephen said.

'So they might.'

'The third cottage on the left in Portinscale . . .'

Casper nodded. 'Thin man in back. Woman at the gate.'

'He didn't look up as you went by, just kept turning the muck.'

'And the woman?'

'Eyes all over, kept glancing back at him, and her hands were twitching.'

Casper smiled, creasing the sunset of his bruises, then took another swig from the flask. 'You have sharp eyes. Get them from your mother, did you?'

Stephen hugged his knees and looked at the turf in front of him. 'Her eyes are green. Mine are blue, like my papa's.'

Casper pulled at the flask again. 'As may be, but I reckon you got your manner of seeing with them from her. What else?'

'There was a man in his stable yard at the Oak kept his back turned.'

Casper was looking north at the curve of Latrigg and the upward swell of Skiddaw. He upended the flask into his mouth and shook the last of the liquor out of it, then screwed the little silver top back on and handed it back to Stephen.

'Time for you to go now, Master Westerman. Take that food back to my cabin if you would, and untie Joe.'

Stephen looked around him. 'Are you going to ask the fair-folk for their help? Will they tell you who beat you, or who killed that man?'

Casper gave him a lopsided grin. 'I've already learned what I intended, youngling. I shall sit here for a while longer though.' Stephen looked very confused, opened his mouth and shut it again. 'My business is more with people than magic. Herbs, yes. Seeing how people are, knowing them and protecting our faith.' He frowned suddenly. Stephen followed the direction of his eyes and saw a thin, older man at the entrance to the field. 'Take the flask back to Mr Askew, and thank him,' Casper continued. 'Don't go in. Just stand at the steps till he comes out. For the rest, say no word and keep your eyes low. And that man by the gate is Mr Kerrick. Tell him he may come to me.'

'Can I come and see you later, Casper?'

He nodded. 'Do that. I may have need of you, fool that I am.'

On enquiring at the vicarage, Harriet and Crowther were told that Miss Scales and her guest were taking a turn in the church grounds, so Ham turned the horses down the slope to deliver them to the church gates. The situation of Crosthwaite Church was a splendid one, nestled as it was under the curving arm of Skiddaw. Around the wooded churchyard, fields of well-grown oats rolled down to the main road and the edge of the lake. The church itself was a good-sized building, with a square, crenellated tower and white-washed. Thus it provided both a place of worship for its community, and an appropriate point of interest for Lakers sketching from their rowboats on the water.

Crowther handed Harriet down from the carriage and they left Ham and the horses to enjoy the scenery as they liked while they went in search of Miss Scales and Miss Hurst. Before they could enter the churchyard, however, they heard themselves hailed from the road and turned to see Mr Sturgess just dismounting from a rather showy-looking roan horse, and making his way towards them, leading it by its halter.

'You let him just walk away?' Mr Sturgess said at once.

Neither Harriet nor Crowther replied until he was within a pace or two of them.

'To whom do you refer?' Crowther said, with a slight drawl.

'That charlatan, Casper Grace, of course!' The magistrate was rather red in the face. 'It is obvious to a child he must have killed this German in the same brawl where he was injured. He brought the body to you and you let him go.'

Crowther shook his head very slightly. 'The man was Austrian. He did not *look* guilty, Mr Sturgess.'

'Look? *Look*! I have no objection to you and Mrs Westerman amusing yourselves with guessing games over some skeleton, but a murder here and now does great injury to the town. Grace must be taken at once and held in Carlisle till the quarter sessions.'

'On what evidence?' Harriet asked.

'How could it be anyone else? The man is known to be half-crazed, and he delivered himself into your hands. It is nothing but plain sense. Though I do not know why I speak to *you* of that. Mr Grace is at the Druidic circle. I know this why? Because

I saw him from my window processing through the village with your son at his heels, moments before I received your note.'

Harriet would have given a great deal not to appear surprised, but she feared by the satisfied smile on Mr Sturgess's face that it must have been clear she had known nothing of this. Guiltily, she realised she had not even thought of her son after the moment she sent him into the house for Ham and Isaiah.

'I am shocked, madam!' Sturgess said, drawing himself very straight. 'What would your husband say if he were to know you allowed your son to run around with a person of that type?'

It would have been better for Mr Sturgess if he had simply enjoyed her discomfort and left the matter there. He had now invoked her husband, and that made her angry. Somewhere behind the white light of fury in her mind she was aware that Crowther had very slightly edged away from her.

'Did you know my husband, sir?' she demanded. Mr Sturgess began to look a little less sure of himself. 'Did you serve with him? Were you acquainted in any way? You did not — yet you presume to tell me what he would think of my behaviour! It is the same arrogance which is sending you after Mr Grace, and in my experience, arrogance is seldom rewarded!'

'Mrs Westerman, a cunning-man with your son . . .'

Harriet smiled at him. 'Get back on your horse, Mr Sturgess. My husband was once cured by a witch-doctor on one of the Polynesia Islands. He would have the greatest respect for Casper Grace.'

Mr Sturgess still managed to retain some of his air of outraged righteousness, but he did as he was ordered and climbed back onto his mount, then with a savage pull at the animal's mouth, turned it out onto the road again.

'Was that true, Mrs Westerman?' Crowther murmured as they watched him retreat.

'About James? No, though it happened to a friend of his. No, Crowther, I am afraid James would be as shocked as Mr Sturgess that I did not know what Stephen was about. But he was my husband; that would be his right. Mr Sturgess does not have it. I shall speak to Stephen later.'

Crowther offered her his arm and she took it, telling him, 'I notice Mr Sturgess had no interest in finding Miss Hurst.'

'He has his suspect, he has no need for the girl. Let us find her ourselves.'

The ladies were among the shade in the walks behind the church itself, hoping to find some relief from the heat. In the heavy stillness of the air it was difficult to imagine the sudden shout of rain the previous evening. Harriet saw the two women arm-in-arm and paused, and with that strange instinct humans have of sensing when they are watched, the women turned and waited for them to approach. Harriet expected to see some sign of either dread or hope on Miss Hurst's face when she noticed them. She gave no mark of either, however; it was Miss Scales whose ruined face flitted with hope or concern.

'Miss Hurst,' Harriet said as she reached them. 'This morning a man called Casper Grace brought a body to Silverside from the hills. Mr von Bolsenheim recognised it as that of your father. He is dead, I am afraid.'

The girl lowered her head and sighed, murmuring something in her own tongue that Harriet could not catch.

'Some accident?' Miss Scales said, clinging tightly onto her companion's arm.

'That seems unlikely,' Crowther replied.

Miss Hurst looked up quickly. 'When?'

Crowther rested his cane on the ground between them. 'Some time yesterday before the storm, I believe.'

Miss Hurst watched Crowther for a moment, then said precisely, 'Thank you, Mr Crowther. I also thank you for your actions this morning. You have been kind to a stranger. Heaven sees what you do.' She turned to Miss Scales who was trembling on her arm. 'I should like to return to my lodgings now, Miss Scales.'

'My dear, there is no question of you returning to the Oak. You shall stay at the vicarage with my father and myself as our guest. But what are you saying, my lord? That Mr Hurst was attacked? Can there be some doubt, some mistake?'

'I am afraid there is no mistake, Miss Scales.'

'Oh, how very terrible. How shall we manage?'

For a moment Harriet thought that Miss Hurst was going to refuse the invitation to the vicarage, but as Miss Scales pulled a little on her arm, she yielded. Miss Scales looked very distressed, and Harriet thought she saw the younger woman pat her arm. They turned towards the back way to the vicarage. Harriet watched them go with a confused frown.

'Miss Hurst seemed a great deal more distressed this morning when her father was only missing,' she said. 'Is it some trick of the national character? No screaming, no fainting, no tears. I have never seen such news being taken in a like manner. Shall we follow on, Crowther? I feel a great curiosity to know more of her father. What did she say?'

'Indeed.'

Harriet turned towards him and saw he was looking at a

granite monument before which Miss Scales and Miss Hurst had been standing. She followed his gaze and read the engraving. *Julia Penhaligon, wife of William Penhaligon, Baron Keswick, died 5th January 1750 aged 41 years.*

'Your mother's grave. I am sorry, Crowther.'

He looked at her down his long nose. 'Why, Mrs Westerman? I do not think she hears us.' He sighed then continued a little more easily, 'I think we must speak to the Fräulein. I thought she looked worried rather than grieved. As to what she said, she spoke in her own language but I recognise the quotation. It was a favourite of one of my tutors in Wittenberg, from the Book of Isaiah: *For My thoughts are not your thoughts, neither are your ways My ways, saith the Lord.*'

Harriet's eyes lifted to the stirring leaves above them. 'What might she have had in mind at that, do you suppose?'

'I cannot say, only that the professor of whom I spoke used the phrase to remind us that God's works were not readily understandable by men.'

'So perhaps she finds God's hand in this . . .'

Crowther looked weary. 'There are those, Mrs Westerman, eager to see God in everything that passes before them. I look at that wound and I see a man with a weapon in his hand and nothing holy in his mind. Shall we follow them?'

Harriet did not move. 'Let us give them a few moments. Perhaps you might look instead at the letter from Jocasta.'

She saw Crowther frown and hurried on. 'I wrote to her before I left Caveley and asked her to tell me what she remembered of her time here.' She flushed faintly. 'I did not mention it till now, as I did not know how those events might be related to the body on Saint Herbert's Island, and I had no wish to speak of them until I thought they might be of significance.'

Crowther said coldly, 'Mrs Bligh claims she saw a man who was not my brother standing over my father's body and that he wore a green coat. I also told you I believe that she simply saw the first discoverer of the murder.'

'But she did not recognise the man! Who was it that first discovered Lord Keswick?'

Crowther was silent for a moment. 'As I recall, it was the coachman from Silverside.'

'She would know *him*, surely. She must have seen him every day in the village. Had he been in service with your family long?'

'Yes, but seeing a body might confuse any person. Certainly a young girl. Often people are wrong about what they have seen. I do not understand what you mean to accomplish by having me hear her account again.'

'Please just let me read it, Crowther.'

He moved sharply away from her. 'Mrs Westerman, my brother confessed! Confessed in front of the servants and the Vicar of Crosthwaite in his room at Silverside within an hour of the body being discovered. He came suddenly from London with his debts pursuing him. He had assaulted one of his most pressing creditors in the street only days before. He arranged to see my father and within hours Lord Keswick was dead. My brother was found weeping in his room with a knife in his hands, and only the actions of the servants prevented him ending his own life on the spot! He slashed Mrs Tyers's face when she attempted to disarm him. Are those the actions of an innocent man? Your perversity is remarkable. The whole world knows my brother murdered his father, so you must believe he did not. Whatever the crimes of my father, he did not murder himself. And what has any of this to do with the body on Saint Herbert's Island? Explain that to me! You are spinning fictions out of the air and trying to build roads between them!'

Harriet kept her eyes lowered while he spoke. She heard his breathing, and looked up to see him with his back to her, his head lowered and staring across the churchyard into the meadows between Derwent Water and Bassenthwaite. 'Crowther,' she said very quietly, 'let me speak.' He did not move, so wetting her lips she smoothed out the paper in her hand and began to read.

Dear Mrs Westerman,

I am well thank you as is Sam, who asks to be remembered to you. We continue just as we were though Boyo does not like the heat of the season. Morgan found me with your note yesterday evening and read it to me. I had the night to think on it and so now will answer you. You ask me to tell you everything I remember about the death of Lord Keswick, and so I shall, though I don't think Mr Crowther will want to hear it again. Thinking on it seems to stir up all his devils, and he spends half his energy trying to sit on them. Maybe you will have better luck than I at getting him to face them and knock them down.

Harriet glanced up at Crowther's profile. He remained entirely still, but she could see he was listening. She found her place in the letter again and continued:

I was just thirteen when the Baron died and living with my aunt in Portinscale. She was a hard woman, and not over fond of me so I kept away from her and spent all the hours I could out wandering and listening to the winds talking. On the day Lord Keswick died it was foul enough weather to keep most folks in, so I was surprised to see a gentleman at the edge of the woods. I was on the far side of the field by the lake, some twenty yards away, but I'll answer for it: there was a man there in a dark green coat. It was the colour made me curious. I thought it might be one of the new footmen the Baron had just lately hired, because he was a burly type like them, but they all wore red like soldiers do, not green. I was told later I might have seen Mr Adair, because he wore green that day, but he was as thin and tall a man as Mr Crowther is now. The magistrate wanted me to say about the man in the green coat that it was Mr Adair, but when I swore it wasn't, he told me I was a stupid girl. They all thought me stupid since I could never get my eyes round written words. Then he called me a liar and said so to my aunt too. I ran away a while after. But they couldn't shake that picture from my head. There was a big man in a green coat bent over a man on the ground. I couldn't see it was Lord Keswick then, but I saw there was something evil in it and let out a yelp. The big man turned round, but I don't reckon he saw me. I dressed in brown and grey like all the village in them days, so I'd disappear into the woods like water into a stream, but I was scared so I ran away and hid up on Catbells till the cold drove me home.

If you chance to meet with my brother Casper Grace while you are at Silverside, can I ask you for the friendship we have, to give him my greetings and tell him I am well, and if he is in want I would think it most kind if you would put a guinea in his hand from his fond sister who thinks of him still, and I shall certainly send it back to you as soon as you wish it, for I am busy and have it to give. Any note you might send me to tell me how he goes will be held and looked for here at the chophouse in St Martin's Lane if you put my name on it, and thankfully received by your respectful servant, and Mr Crowther's too, of course,

Jocasta Bligh

Written by Thomas Ripley as Mrs Bligh spoke it on this day 9 July 1783 and despatched with his best wishes the same day.

Crowther had not moved at all, and still looking into the distance said in a dull and tired voice, 'It is just as she described it to myself, Mrs Westerman. I am at a loss to understand why you find the narrative so significant, though it reminds us we must write and tell her of what has befallen her brother today. If Mr Sturgess captures Casper and takes him to Carlisle, he will have need of friends.'

'That will be a pleasant letter to write. "Dear Jocasta, your brother is considered a madman and hunted through the fells for murder by the local magistrate".' Harriet bit her lip and said more gently, 'There is one thing here though, Crowther, that you have not spoken of to me before. Who are these "burly footmen" your father had lately hired?'

Crowther looked round at her, abandoning for the first time the view over the fields. 'I cannot say. Mrs Tyers did mention when I arrived that some of the casual servants had been given a month's wages in lieu of notice. My father became somewhat eccentric after my mother's death, withdrew from local society, and his former friends tell me they were turned away at the door.'

'Crowther, do you see yet what I am trying to suggest? A man refuses company and hires new servants notable for their size. Do you think that after your mother's death, Lord Keswick might have become aware of some threat on his life, and this withdrawal from society, the presence of these men, might have been an attempt to protect himself? Do you think he feared Adair?'

Crowther shook his head. 'No. Adair he loved. He was angry with him over his debts, over his debauchery with his friends, but I never saw him go in fear of him.'

'It seems to me he feared *something* in those months before his death, Crowther. You thought that Adair was responsible for the skeleton on the island. Now the point that came from your father's swordstick and the letter of Mrs Tyers about the stranger with the snuffbox seem to suggest that your father might have been guilty of that murder. What if Adair *were* innocent of patricide? What if your father were killed by someone who knew he was responsible for the death of the Jacobite on the island?'

'And the betrayal of Rupert de Beaufoy.'

Harriet remained very still. Crowther had told her he had attended his brother's trial and execution. She knew he had always considered his guilt beyond doubt, but wondered if that faith in his brother's venality had begun to be questioned. To give up a certainty, even when it is a cruel one, is painful. We do not know how firmly we have bound our truths into our lives till we try and rip one free.

'You are a remarkable woman, Mrs Westerman, to talk to a man of such things as you stand on his mother's grave.'

Harriet met the coldness of his eyes steadily. 'You said, Crowther, that she did not hear us.'

For a moment she was afraid she had made him very angry, then he sighed. 'So I did. Very well. I think we must go our separate ways this afternoon, after all. Today's events need your attention. Those of some years ago are still demanding mine. I shall look over Jocasta's letter again, then visit Lottie Tyers and ask her to explain her note. After that a visit to the museum, I think. We shall meet back at Silverside and pick over whatever, if anything, we have learned.'

Harriet felt the relief touch her skin like a breeze. 'You go to see Mr Askew?'

Crowther smoothed the silver ball at the head of his cane with his right hand. 'You are right in one way I fear, Mrs Westerman, you and Jocasta. I must continue the battle with the old demons, having begun, and that means discovering more of my own history. For a little while I shall make Mr Askew the Virgil to my Dante.'

The thought of Mr Askew in the habit of an Ancient Roman made Harriet grin, as she was sure was the intention. She began to follow the other ladies slowly out of the graveyard, then before she had reached the angle of the church, she turned round again. Crowther had leaned his cane against his mother's headstone, and rested his elbow on the same. He was reading Jocasta's letter again. Harriet continued on her way.

III.7

'HAM, I AM TO pay a visit at the vicarage before we return to Silverside,' Harriet said. 'I shall take the path, but will you come and find me there?'

She was distracted from his answer by the sight of a portly gentleman lumbering along the road from Keswick towards them. He was waving something in his hand.

'Who is that gentleman, Ham? Do you think he wishes to speak to me?'

Ham glanced up the road and nodded. 'That's Postlethwaite, madam. Landlord of the Royal Oak. Looks like he does.'

She stepped away from the carriage and walked a few steps to meet him. He was rather red in the face and puffing in the heat. He did not have the figure of a man used to stirring much outside his own house, and though he raised his hand towards her, at first he had only breath to bow and touch his forehead with a rather stained-looking handkerchief.

'Apologies, madam,' he wheezed after a minute or so. 'A man must fight to get air into his lungs in this weather. The news of Mr Hurst has charged about the village like a mad bull. Are you looking into the matter? I hear Mr Sturgess is after Casper. I thought perhaps I should go to him, but I have heard such things about you and Mr Crowther, and Walter my pot boy said he saw the carriage here . . .' He ran out of his store of breath at this point and was forced to break off to replenish it.

'Indeed, sir, I understand you are the landlord of the Royal Oak?'

'I am, I am. Might I have a moment of your time? I did not know who best to consult. Mr Sturgess walks the other way every time I see him anyway, in case I might ask him to settle his account, though truth be told, as long as he holds the rights to license my house, he has no fear of me. Might we just sit down a moment, madam? I walked faster than I should have done . . .'

Harriet accompanied him to a little bench by the church gate that offered some shade and let him recover himself; however, before he had breath quite enough to speak again, he pulled from under his arm a folded newspaper and put it into her hands, then jabbed at an advertisement in the middle of the page with a fat finger. Harriet began to read.

To Herr Hurst, thought to be travelling in the Northern Counties. Our attempts to contact you in Cockermouth having come to naught, we wish to let it be known the information mentioned is indeed of great interest and humbly request you communicate with us again. Please apply to the firm of Hudson & White in Church Street, Cockermouth, who have power to act for us in this matter. Your grateful friend.

Harriet shook her head. 'This is today's paper, Mr Postlethwaite! What on earth can this mean?'

'Just what I thought myself. "Postlethwaite, what can this mean?"' He dabbed his forehead. 'Then I thought, "Whatever it means, it means something, that's certain", and then Walter came in and said his piece, so I thought, "Well, maybe that's where I should go then", and set off while I still had my coat half on, and have trotted all the way for fear of missing you.'

'I am happy indeed that you did, Mr Postlethwaite.'

The landlord spread his fingers over his knees and wagged them. 'I am glad, I am glad. It was no accident then? Oh, it's a tragedy for our little town! Skeletons are interesting – attractions, even, if it's a good story – but fresh bodies? Of a travelling man? Who will come look at our hills if they think they might end up buried between them . . .'

'Do you think it likely Casper murdered him?'

The fingers began to waggle quite ferociously. 'I can't think it, but then he was seen talking to the young lady, and handing her something, and he is a man. He is a man, a cunning-man and a man of parts, but still a man and men do as they do.'

Harriet decided it might be best to pick over the philosophy of this statement at a later date.

'What was his business with the lady?'

The landlord gave the back of his head a ferocious scratch, then lifted his hands to the height of his shoulder.

'I saw Casper, your young lad and his tutor in company with her yesterday, then early in the day heard her asking Walter where Casper might be found. Hardly day at all it was, but off she set, even though the roads were still thick and dirty from the storm, and her a delicate-looking bird.'

Harriet nodded over the information and read the advertisement again. 'Can you shed any light on this business, Mr Postlethwaite? Anything you saw in Herr Hurst's behaviour that might relate . . . ?'

He lifted his hands and patted his cheeks as he thought then, as if he had massaged the memories out of them, dropped them again. 'Well, I might or might not. I shall tell you and you may tell me if I give light or shadow to the business. He was a nosy beggar, I'll say that. Most ask after the paths and the museum and where they might hire a boat and a man to wield the oars, but his questions were all "Who lives here, and who stays there, and who are these folks?" That might be character, of course. Character. Ha!' He stared ahead in silence for a moment, then started off again like a rabbit crossing between hedgerows. 'I know he sent a letter. An express. Only

239

a day or so after he came. On account. Always on account, that fella. And now Mr Crowther has swept his slate clean – well, well. Then Sunday evening he wants a horse ready for the morning and I say he's welcome to one, but no more of this "on account, on account" until the bill he's already run up is run off, if you take my meaning.' Harriet smiled to show the meaning was taken. 'So he gets himself all "of all the things", and "shocked, shocked", and announces he's off to take one from the Queen's Head instead if that's the case, thank you very much. And I say to myself, "Well, fine and dandy to him". So he takes himself off, then comes back late and full of strong drink and he has no need of a horse at all, thank you.'

'Did you see him yesterday morning?'

'Aye. Saw him send off his girl and tell her he had business to do. He spoke awful sharp to that child. Then she's off and he's off and he don't come back for dinner or breakfast. Then the news he's dead comes, and while I'm still catching my breath from that, I see the advertisement.'

Harriet frowned. 'Let me see if I have this correct, Mr Postlethwaite.' He grinned at her, bunching and flexing his fingers. 'Some time ago, soon after his arrival, Mr Hurst sends a letter. Then on Sunday evening he says he will need a horse the following day, but as far as you are aware, does not take one. Tuesday he waits at the inn. Yesterday he goes out, and does not come back. This morning the advertisement. Is that correct?'

'Quite so, quite so. I like the look of your boy, madam. Nice lad. Is he to be a sailor like his da?'

Harriet hardly heard him. 'Yes, yes . . . that is his intention.

Did any message reach Mr Hurst while he was waiting at the inn? What was his demeanour?'

Mr Postlethwaite seemed to have recovered. He lifted his chin and sniffed the air. 'None through my hands, but there's many a way of getting word to someone. I'd say he was happy on Sunday and Monday, grim on Tuesday though he went to bed cheerful, then a peacock on Wednesday as he headed out. Well, ma'am, I have done what I set out to do. If I have been of help, then I'm glad of it. If not, then I am sorry to waste your time and thank you for being so civil.'

They stood and Harriet held out her hand. 'Thank you, Mr Postlethwaite. You are invaluable. May I keep the newspaper?'

He bowed slightly over her hand. 'Indeed, indeed. With the compliments of the Royal Oak, Mrs Westerman. With our compliments.'

Some time later, having folded the letter into his pocket, Crowther thought of the last occasion he had stood in this place, which had also been the last time he had seen Casper's father, Ruben Grace. It was a fleeting encounter; he had looked up from the graveside as his mother's coffin was lowered into the ground and seen Ruben hovering on the far side of the drystone perimeter of Crosthwaite churchyard. It was winter and the man was bundled up against the damp chill of the valley, standing in the shade of a skeletal oak, one hand on its dragon-scale bark, the other round the shoulders of a girl. It must have been his first sight of Jocasta, as well as his last of Ruben. Crowther remembered her as a thin shadow. He had never had friends among the village children, nor thought to enquire about the families of the servants in the house. Strange to think that that young girl, her grey shawl shrouding her face, had become the remarkable Mrs Bligh, who strode through London in gypsy-coloured skirts with her dog at her heels; who could not read, yet who was brave and intelligent enough to help her King, and to assist Harriet and Crowther discover and destroy a criminal conspiracy that had threatened their country. Had she got that bravery, that intelligence from her father? What *was* a cunning-man? A person who knew the fears of the people, guided them through them, offered them spells and symbols to make sense of the space around them. Such, it appeared, Ruben had been even while he had added up the columns in Sir William's accounting books; such now was his son, defending his neighbours from witches; such was his daughter, turning her cards in her London room, offering comfort to the shop-girls and servants, advice to fools.

Crowther was no believer in witches, cards, Lucks or the rest – but he had the grace to wonder if some of those who called themselves his colleagues in science and medicine had anything more valuable to offer than rowan twigs. And Ruben and his son knew herbs. He thought of Ruben standing in the shade of that tree. He had seemed as much a part of the landscape as the stones and water. Where that man had decided to set his foot he would not be moved, whatever blustering winds ripped round him. There must have been bad blood between Ruben and Sir William by that point, or he would have come into the churchyard to pay his respects to Crowther's mother.

Crowther seemed to feel the thrum of the rain by the grave again, his hands cramping with cold, his own sense of being cut off from everything around him. He could even hear his sister weeping damply into the housekeeper's cloak as the vicar let the words of Scripture fall from his lips and into the slippery grave. He blinked, and found himself with the grave grown over under his feet and the gasping sun on his back. He picked up his cane and readied himself for the walk to the cottage of Lottie Tyers.

As Kerrick crossed the field towards the stones, the black witch started to chatter at Casper.

'You know in your bones, what he has to say. He's come to say Agnes is not home. Sent her out in the storm, girl like that, and nice and close to where you took your beating.'

Casper had clenched his teeth, but Grice continued spitting at him. *'Maybe she saw you kill that man. Like you, that would be — murder a man in your madness then lecture his daughter about life the next morning! Oh, that makes me laugh! Maybe you killed Agnes too, and buried her better.'*

Casper could remember very clearly when the first voice had begun to speak to him. It had been just after the funeral of his father. Funerals had been poor affairs in '54, the village had seen so many of them, but his aunt had baked the funeral bread and every household in the village was represented by the graveside. Ruben had died helping them through the pox. Then, as they walked away from the church, a young man had touched him on the arm and asked if he might call on him the following day. He wished to marry his girl and wanted to learn the day to do it. He was three years older than Casper, and Casper had always looked on him from the place of a child as they grew. He realised then that the title of cunning-man had fallen over him at his father's death like a cloak, and could not be given up.

He mumbled some agreement, then went to his aunt's house to sleep. He could not. He knew something of finding days of fortune in the calendar, but not enough. His father had not planned on leaving him so soon and he was kept awake by the knowledge of his own poor learning. So Casper had risen from his bed and taken his inheritance in his hands, then made his way to the circle of stones. There he had stared into the dark, seeing again the blistered faces of his father and his neighbours till the silence seemed alive with the sounds of their suffering, and under it all he heard the first of the voices. It was a whisper at first, like hearing a conversation through a wall at night. It was soft and friendly, a woman's voice. It seemed a shape dressed in white; though he could not see it, had come to sit by his side in the darkness and was trying to make itself heard. As the cold night drew on, the voice had become clearer and the shape became a woman dressed in a white gown. She told him he knew all he needed to, and that she would speak to him and guide him when he was in doubt. So she had, through the next day and the ones that followed, and Casper grew to trust her.

There was a price to be paid for her help. The lady had opened some door in his mind and other voices had used to clamber inside: these were the cruel, mocking voices of the bogles and dark witches that liked to tell him when he was foolish or wrong and laughed at him. Then came the affair of Blanche Grice, her death and burying, and she had ruled loudest in his mind for twenty years now. The white lady was still there, but it was hard to catch her whispers. Grice was crowing and flapping her arms now. The young man who had come to find Casper on the day of his father's funeral was

Kerrick himself. Casper watched him now, lumbering across the field to join him.

'Hast thou seen her, Casper?' Casper shook his head as he got to his feet. Kerrick gathered up his shirt in handfuls in front of him. 'She was quiet when you had left, and kissed her mother, then said she had duty to do and set out at dusk.'

Casper put his hand on Kerrick's shoulder. 'I'll find her. Stay close to your place today, in case she makes her own way back.'

Kerrick nodded. Gasped, 'There was a man killed.'

'There was. Trust me, old friend.'

Kerrick managed to nod again, then put out his hand and Casper took it, then he turned away and set off back towards Keswick.

'Trust you? Trust you, when you most like killed the pair of them? Find her? Find where you've buried her in your madness, and bring her back all muddy?' The witch laughed; he could hear her stamp her feet.

Casper came to a stop in the middle of the path and spoke very softly. 'I shall find her. If she is hurt, I shall punish them that have hurt her. If that were me, I shall drown myself off the Island of Bones, and that'll be you done with too, hag.'

That stilled her.

III.8

THE DOOR TO THE cottage had been opened by a flustered middle-aged woman, who became all the more flustered when she discovered Mr Crowther outside. She tried to curtsey and tidy her hair and brush the flour from her dress all at the same moment. Crowther, unnecessarily, gave his name and asked to see Mrs Tyers. The tongue-tied woman nodded, then beckoned Crowther through the rough earth corridor that divided the living chambers from the down-house and into the rear courtyard. There in the shade, with a rolling view of meadows and the glimmer of Bassenthwaite in the haze, he found an old woman at her spinning wheel. She was dressed in black, and had shrunk with age. Crowther felt he could have placed her into his pocket and walked off with her into the hills.

'You got my note then, Master Charles?' she said, glancing up. Crowther felt his memories swirl round him like leaves in a sudden gust. He saw in the old lady the stern housekeeper of his childhood, saw her walking the corridors of Silverside with a set of keys on her belt, a notebook and that tiny black pencil with which she used to jab the maids if she felt they needed encouragement in their work. She had a thin scar running across her face from the corner of her eye-socket to her jaw. Crowther had thought that age would have hidden it, but it was bright on her tanned skin and ran against the natural lines of her face. 'Fetch a stool for the man, Nancy,' she continued, nodding to the woman who had opened the door. 'There's a good girl.'

Crowther cleared his throat. 'I did get your note, Mrs Tyers. I am glad to see you in health.'

'Surprised, I should think!' She laughed to herself and then continued more softly, 'Eighty-seven summers I've seen now, and I hoped I'd lived through all the excitement I needed to. Dare say you didn't think when you settled ten pounds a year on me for life you'd be paying out so long?' She looked up from the wheel with a proud glint in her eye. The eyes were the same, as sharp and seeing as they had ever been.

'I am happy to pay it, Mrs Tyers.'

Nancy emerged from the house, wrestling a large carved oak chair with her. Crowther helped her place it and she fluttered back into the house again, only to emerge red and sweating with a pint-pot which she handed confusedly to Crowther, then dashed back into the dark once more.

Crowther sat down and drank, painfully aware he had eaten nothing since breakfast and the dinner-hour was probably already passed. Mrs Tyers sucked on her gums.

'You may call me Lottie still, as you did in your father's time, my lord.' She shook her head. 'I said a stool! Daft lass that, but good-hearted. Married my nephew and has bred him three good sons. They'll all marry on what I've saved from your money. Maybe that's why she thought your backside too good for anything but that monster, Master Charles. No doubt she'll treat it as a holy relic now.'

Crowther smiled slightly. 'I go by the name of Gabriel Crowther these days, Lottie.'

'That's your choice,' said the old lady, raising her eyebrows and nodding at her wheel, 'but my note was to Mr Charles. It was Mr Charles who stole Cook's knives for his investigations, Mr Charles I clouted round the ear for it, and it is Mr Charles I shall talk to now, thank you.'

Crowther wondered if she had not so much cheated death, as given it a firm talking-to. He recognised an immovable object when he saw it though, and decided to let her call him what she would.

'Lottie, this note of yours . . .' The old woman turned back to the wheel and began to work the pedal. 'Who was this man?'

'That I cannot say, Master Charles.' Each time she spoke his old name, Crowther felt it push against his chest. 'I heard tell of the snuffbox, and I remember clear as day seeing one like it. Striped, is it? With a rose on the lid?' He felt her sharp eye on him again and nodded. 'Was the day after the fire destroyed Gutherscale and your father's hopes of living there. The year was forty-five, just as we got news of the Young Pretender beginning his games. You and Master Adair were away at school, Margaret just a tiny child. A man in travelling clothes arrives at the Hall. My age he was, and a strong-looking devil. I opened the door to him, and there he was taking a pinch from that box, and such a look on him. Fierce. Angry. He had bitter eyes.' She chuckled. 'Not much left of his looks now, I'll bet.'

'Did he give his name?'

'Not one I trusted.'

'What was it?'

'Percival. He wanted speech with your father. Sir William went out and they had words on the lawn.'

Crowther considered. Percival. The name of the knight that went searching for the Grail. 'What else, Lottie? Did you hear their conversation?'

She was silent for a long time, and Crowther heard nothing but the clack of the wheel. 'Full of threats and flounce, he was. But you shouldn't threaten a man's children, no matter what you're looking for. Your father took him off to the Island of Bones and I sent Ruben after them. Lord, I ran to him where he was stamping out the embers at Gutherscale.' The spinning wheel paused for a moment and she stared in front of her. 'I had served your father from the day I was twelve years old, Master Charles, and I feared for him that day. So I ran to Ruben and set him running to his boat. I thought they'd paid him off. That's what Ruben said that night when I asked. That the man was paid.'

'We think he might have been a follower of Lord Greta, over here with Greta's brother Rupert de Beaufoy.'

She continued to work the pedal on the spinning wheel, and Crowther watched a while as the wool was twisted out from between her fingers.

'Maybe.' She glanced up at him. 'Lord Greta loved Gutherscale, Master Charles. It was the home of his father, and his father's fathers. Think he'd want to see another man set up house there?'

Crowther felt suddenly cold. 'Lottie, are you saying this man put the torch to Gutherscale on Greta's orders?' he said slowly. 'What did my father tell you?'

'Your father was not the sort to confide, Master Charles, you know that. And your ma knew to keep clear and quiet when he was feeling dark. And they were dark days. But there was this man, you say he was Greta's man and there the day after the fire.' She sighed. 'Your father was not the same man after Gutherscale burned. He carried the embers in him.'

Crowther drank again from his pint-pot and leaned back a little, listening to the wheel clicking and turning.

'Adair was not at home at the time?'

'I just told you he was away.'

'Did my father have his cane with him?'

He saw her glance at it, leaning up against the wall of her nephew's home. 'He always had it. That is like asking me if he had both hands attached, Master Charles.'

He watched the meadows frothing out below them in wedding finery, all white clover and dog-roses, though this year there were not the poppies he remembered from his youth or the sparkle of cornflowers. He wondered if it were the effect of the strange weather that the fields were weeded of them.

'I wanted to believe that Adair killed that man.'

'I know you did, Master Charles.'

Crowther put his hand to his forehead for a moment. 'Lottie, do you recall Ruben's daughter, Jocasta?'

The spinning stopped and Lottie looked up with a smile. 'I do. Wilful lass, but I always liked the ones with a bit of fight in them. Any news of her?'

'She tells fortunes in London, and is well.'

'I'm glad. She was wise to go.'

Crowther set his tankard on the ground and felt his weariness rise through him. 'She made mention of my father having hired some extra footmen – burly types – in his last months. Is that true? Do you know why he did such a thing?'

Lottie shifted her hands to knead the raw fleece while she spoke. 'Good for the joints, raw wool. I reckon spinning has saved me from rheumatism.' She reminded Crowther of the housekeeper's cat in Caveley, pulsing its claws on the kitchen stool. 'Master Charles, some say grief can make a man do odd things. Lord Keswick shut the doors on Silverside a while after the mistress died, then they came to keep it shut. All business to be done by letter and they let anyone know who came to call that the Master was not receiving.'

'You think that was a symptom of grief, Lottie?'

She lifted a finger. '*Some* might say that, Master Charles. I think it was the letter.'

'What letter?'

She shook her head. ' "What letter?" he says, as if I read my lord's papers through of an evening. What letter indeed? All I know is with the letters of condolence came one that shook him up. I put it into his hand and saw him freeze solid as he read it. An hour later I saw him stow away something like it in that little hidden safe in the office, and the same day I was told to find two or three more men for the house, men who looked like they could land or take a blow, he said. And I was to arrange to send your sister away for schooling. There was no mention of her leaving Silverside till that day.'

'I knew nothing of such a safe.'

'It wasn't often used, nothing of value in it by then,' she said vaguely. 'Nasty brutes those men were, and he paid handsomely for their company. Much good they did. I suppose they did not think to protect him from his own son. I sent them on their way quick.'

Crowther looked up at her. Her eyes were clouded, looking out at the view, seeing something else.

'You do believe it was my brother who murdered Lord Keswick then?'

The pedal started up again, briskly. 'Course I do. I found him, didn't I? In his room, his hands all bloody, weeping and cursing himself. Though he didn't *mean* to cut me, Master Charles. Not sure if he meant to cut himself either, just the knife was in his hands and he was so wild. I should not have got so close, but we'd just found Lord Keswick and all of us were a little mad. Poor stupid boy. The coachman got the knife off him, we turned the key and he was still raving when the vicar and the magistrate arrived. But you know that. Told you myself.' She stopped spinning again, but this time did not look up. 'He apologised to me, you know. That I didn't tell you. Yelled it out while they were taking him off to Carlisle – said he was sorry and it wasn't his fault.' She shook her head. 'Nothing was ever his fault though, was it? Wheedling little bully since the day he was born, but I never thought he'd kill the master. I am only glad your mother was dead. Died younger than she merited, but at least it saved her from dying of grief.'

Harriet found Fräulein Hurst in the upper parlour. She was in the windowseat, and so lost in her reading that she did not hear Harriet enter. Mrs Westerman took the opportunity to study her for a moment. She seemed very calm. Harriet found it difficult to stay still even now; at Miss Hurst's age she would have been out of doors at all hours. Had she herself ever looked so young? She could not believe it. The lines around her eyes had become so familiar in the mirror she could not imagine they had once not been there at all. She sighed, and the Fräulein turned quickly. Harriet thought she saw in her face hope – happiness, even – then it fell away into disappointment. As she set down her book she seemed suddenly more distressed than at the moment she had heard of her father's death.

'Mrs Westerman?' Harriet crossed to a sofa in the centre of the room and took a seat, patting the fabric next to her. Sophia obediently crossed to join her and placed her hands together in her lap, her eyes lowered. 'Mr Scales has so many fine books.

I have not had the chance to read very much since I left the convent.'

'Forgive me for interrupting you, Fräulein Hurst.'

She flinched as her name was spoken. 'Please, call me Sophia, madam.'

Harriet watched the soft profile. 'Sophia then. I asked to speak to you alone for a few moments. I hope you do not mind.' A slight shake of the head. 'Sophia, my dear, I wish to find out why your father was murdered.'

The girl looked up quickly, then back to her folded hands. 'You are certain he was murdered, then? How was he killed?'

Harriet wondered how to respond; then, thinking of all the times she had heard facts frustratingly glossed over with half-truths and euphemism, said simply, 'It appears that he was stabbed from behind, in the neck.' Sophia accepted the information calmly. Harriet watched her face with a frown. 'The blow went up into the brain. There was very little blood. He would have died on the instant.'

Sophia asked nothing further.

'Did anyone want to harm your father, Sophia? Did he have enemies here?' The girl shook her head, but it was not clear if she was refusing to answer, or answering in the negative. A tear ran down her cheek. Harriet wished she had learned the trick of weeping so neatly. Whenever she cried for James, she snuffled and sobbed and bit her pillow, leaving her face blotched and her eyes red as demons.

'Can you tell me something of him, of your father?'

Sophia swallowed and produced a handkerchief from her sleeve, wiped her face and blew her nose in a businesslike fashion.

'I have little to say of him, Mrs Westerman.' Harriet did not normally enjoy the sound of an Austrian accent, but in this young woman's voice it gave her words a frost⁄like clarity. 'I only met him six months ago. I was a boarder at a convent school from the time my mother died. That was when I was four years old, and her relatives paid to have me educated. They did not approve of her marriage, but they felt they had a duty not to see me starve. The nuns taught me to write to my father twice every year. I never had any reply. Then, just after my seventeenth birthday, a letter arrived from Vienna. My father wanted me to live with him in his house there. Within a week I had left the only home I had ever had.'

'And what did you find in Vienna?'

Sophia stood up and went to the window, looking out at the view across the gardens to the lake and the hills beyond. 'Why do you ask me these questions?'

Harriet watched her with her head on one side. 'Mr Sturgess thinks it was Casper Grace who killed your father and will track him down and have him hanged if he can. I think he is being rash.'

'Casper? What reason would Casper have?'

'That is my question. I have just learned that your father had some kind of dealings in Cockermouth.'

The young woman shrugged her shoulders. 'I know nothing of Cockermouth.'

'I am sorry if you find my questions discourteous, but I would find out what I can to make sure the wrong man is not punished.'

'I do not know this word "discourteous".'

Harriet extended one arm along the back of the sofa. 'Rude.'

Sophia gave a short laugh. 'You are not as discourteous as *meine gnädige* Frau von Bolsenheim.'

Harriet lifted her arm from the sofa and examined her fingernails. Good Lord, I am becoming Crowther, she thought, and let the arm drop again. 'I thought you handled that lady rather well.'

Sophia turned away with a toss of the head. 'I understand she called you a whore,' Harriet continued. Sophia crossed the room and picked up a romantic little porcelain model of a shepherd and shepherdess from the mantelpiece.

'Why must *you* ask questions?' she said crossly. 'Why not this Mr Sturgess or the vicar? He does not ask questions, only offers to pray with me for my father. I find I cannot.'

'There are longer answers, but I shall give you the shorter one. I ask questions because I wish to know the truth. Mr Sturgess does not. The vicar is busy enough with the truths of his parish. Do you not sometimes wish to do what you want to, Sophia?'

The girl's grip tightened on the figurine. 'I wish to smash this ugly, lying thing. I wish to dance on its splinters.' Her breathing slowed and she placed the model back in its place. 'But I shall not. First because it belongs to Miss Scales and she might be fond of it. Secondly because a good young lady does not do such things. Does not do what she wishes. A whore *would* smash it.'

Harriet watched her straight spine. She was too thin. Harriet could count the vertebrae of her bare neck and thought of the space on her father's neck where the blow had been struck.

'It is my understanding that whores are often expected to do what they are told to, Sophia.' Sophia turned round and stared at her. 'My dear, I mean only to say that sometimes, we ladies are not so distant from those poor creatures as we like to think.'

Harriet was not sure what reaction to expect at this, but she did not think the girl would collapse to her knees. She stood very quickly and crossed to her. Sophia was crying again, but more after Harriet's fashion than the single poetic tear she had shed for her father. Harriet crouched down beside her, her skirts blooming about her, and gathered the dark head onto her shoulder.

'My dear! Do tell me what has happened. I am so sorry. All will be well, I promise you.' It was such an easy promise to make. She had made it to her sister years ago, she had made it to her husband and to her son a thousand times. Sometimes it had been a false promise, she knew that. So they sat for a few moments while the birds sang about their business outside and Harriet's dress developed creases for the maids to despair over.

When Sophia had begun to calm herself and made use of the handkerchief again, she spoke.

'I was happy to be summoned to my father. I had seen so little in my life. When the carriage entered the city I could not help laughing. All those people. All those fine clothes.' Harriet stroked her shoulder and was suddenly very glad she was no longer young. 'The house where the carriage stopped looked so fine, and there was a footman to help me with my trunk. I was afraid, but happy. I wanted my father to love me. He showed me into the parlour. It was pretty. Yellow paint on the walls, and the furniture all new. I was so pleased to arrive at such a house.' She wiped her eyes. 'He did not own any of it. It was all hired by the week. When he is in funds the house looks like that, then a few days later men would come to the door and hammer away, then take all of it. There was a little desk in my room. He told me it was mine, but it was a lie. They took that too.'

Harriet said nothing, but continued to stroke the girl's back, just as she did to calm her son when he was ill.

'When my father came in, I thought he looked so handsome. He had me stand up and make my curtsey, then walked around me as if I were a horse for sale. He spoke to me in French, then English, and nodded and smiled at me. I was so glad. I thought I had done well for him. Then he opened the doors to the other room. They were great doors that fold back between rooms, to make two rooms into one . . .'

Harriet nodded. 'I know the sort you mean, my dear.'

'It was darker in that room. There were men there, sat round a card table. Bottles everywhere and cards. Their waistcoats were all undone and the floor was filthy where they had dropped their meat. The pisspot was standing on the side. They must have been at play all night.'

She sighed. 'I did not like the way they looked at me. They whistled and clapped as if I was at the theatre. My father pushed me forward and one of them tried to put his hand on me. I stepped away, and they all laughed. I looked at my father. He was laughing too.' Harriet closed her eyes, while the voice continued, rather flat, like a child reciting a lesson learned. 'They said, "Lucky Christoph! You have a *Jungfrau* for a daughter".'

'Virgin,' said Harriet automatically.

'They said, "A pretty virgin. You will get a thousand Florins for her". I ran away then. I did not understand, but I knew it frightened me.'

'My dear girl . . .'

Sophia looked up into her face with her clear dark eyes. 'You must not ask questions, if you do not like the answers, Mrs Westerman.' Harriet looked away. 'My father kept me in my room. Every evening I was brought down and made to stand in the doorway and they would stare at me and talk as if I was stupid and could understand nothing. Then, ten days after I arrived, my father came into my room and told me I need not come down that night. That instead I was to wait in my room, and a friend of his would come and see me, and I must be nice to this man and do whatever he said.' The voice seemed remorseless now. Harriet could feel it pressing into her skull, leaving some trace there. 'I fought. I bit him. He went away shouting.'

'And your father?'

Sophia dropped her chin. 'He beat me. Then he left me alone for a while. Then he came to tell me he was sorry for hurting me. When the bruises were healed he took me walking in the park. It was there I first met Herr von Bolsenheim. My father bought me a dress. These people we met outside were more polite. At night I was locked into my room.'

Harriet looked at her hands. Her own history seemed to her nothing but a series of lucky chances. A family that fed and cared for her, a husband who loved her and was lucky and talented enough to become rich, and now, even if some regarded her as an oddity, even if her actions raised the sculpted eyebrows of the *haut ton* from time to time, she was swaddled and shielded by the money he had earned.

Sophia suddenly put her hand on Harriet's, and Harriet realised with shame that she was being comforted by the sufferer. 'No one is unhappy all the time, Mrs Westerman,' she said. 'Though I was afraid. I thought maybe he was showing me off again, that before long there would be another "friend" . . .'

'But how came you from that life in Vienna to Keswick of all places?' Harriet asked gently. 'Did your father rethink his ways? Was this trip an attempt to atone?'

A look of disgust crossed Sophia's face. She got up rather hurriedly and went towards the window, her long white hand resting on the frame. Harriet began to clamber to her feet and attempt to straighten her gown.

'Who is that?' Harriet saw that Sophia was standing very still and straight. She joined her at the window and looked out into the road. She recognised the figure just turning into the gateway of the vicarage.

'That is Mr Sturgess, the magistrate whom we have mentioned,' Harriet said, and pulled at her sleeves. 'I am sorry, my dear, but he will most likely have questions for you, after all.'

Sophia turned to her. 'I cannot answer anything else today. I am unwell. Tell him I shall not see him.' She crossed towards the door very swiftly.

Harriet held out her hand. 'Sophia, you have not yet told me . . .' the door closed behind the fleeing woman '. . . how you came to be in Keswick,' she finished to the empty room.

She sighed and thought of the party at Silverside, then pulled her watch into her hand. They had dined at five the day of their arrival, and it wanted only half an hour to that now. She had left poor Mrs Briggs with another corpse in her outhouse and only information of the servants to let her know what had passed. She would have to follow Miss Hurst's story another time. The most pressing thing was to try and smooth over any offence she had caused at Silverside, and speak carefully to her son.

She met Mr Sturgess and Miss Scales in the hallway. On hearing that Fräulein Hurst wished to be left alone the rest of the day, Miss Scales was nothing but understanding. Mr Sturgess, however, seemed annoyed. His reply, though apparently polite, made it quite clear to Harriet that he was marking this inconvenience up as the first result of her meddling.

'I am surprised you wish to speak to the girl, Mr Sturgess,' Harriet said flatly. 'You are so convinced that Casper is the guilty man. Have you taken him into custody?' She heard Miss Scales draw in her breath. Mr Sturgess smoothed a hand over his forehead.

'Casper was no longer at the stone circle when I arrived. The Constable is conducting a search. He will be found. I came here because I wished to express my condolences.'

Miss Scales replied in slightly clipped tones, 'I shall carry them this evening to Sophia with her supper tray, Mr Sturgess.'

He was forced to bow and depart unsatisfied at that. As soon as the hall was free of him, Miss Scales turned to Harriet. Her face was a little pink, which made her scars look all the more angry.

'Casper kill a man? Nonsense!'

Harriet replied mildly, 'Perhaps Casper believed that Hurst attacked him?'

Miss Scales looked as if she were in danger of stamping her foot. 'Why on earth should he think such a thing? In any case, Casper has dealt with that business in his own way, as you may have heard. And I know for a fact that you would never allow Stephen to keep company with Casper unless you were absolutely certain he had no part in this.'

Harriet blushed a little. 'Miss Scales, I did not know that Stephen had gone to Casper again after he delivered the body to us.' There was a pause.

'I see.' Her voice had become suddenly colder.

'I hope, for Stephen's sake, you do not think Casper might be guilty,' Harriet said.

'I cannot think it. I pray he is not — for the sake of our town, as well as for your son. The people trust in him and his abilities; he is part of the fabric of this place. There are other cunning-men and women in the area, but few use their influence with the care that Casper does. We have been friends of a sort since I was a child.' Miss Scales put her hand out to touch the wallflowers cut and arranged on the side-table of the hall, and Harriet caught a breath of their fragrance.

'Miss Scales, this walk through town to the Druid circle. What did Casper mean to achieve?'

Miss Scales continued to examine the flower blossoms for a moment before she replied. 'He is playing Hamlet, Mrs Westerman. As the Prince with the play, so Casper with his march to the stone circle. He will have watched the reactions of the village, and he will have frightened those who hurt him into thinking the fair-folk will be after them for insulting their friend. Such is the power of a cunning-man.' She tapped her foot. 'Those men must have had a powerful motive for doing so bold-faced a thing. Most of all, I am distressed by Mr Sturgess's hypocrisy in this matter.'

Harriet frowned. 'You think Mr Sturgess a hypocrite?'

Miss Scales glanced over towards her father's study rather guiltily. 'I should make no such charge, but it *burns* me a little. When Sturgess first arrived in Keswick he sought Casper out! He was in the grips of his fascination with the local history even then, and spoke most respectfully to him in order to find out what he could. That was before he tried to excavate at the stone circle, of course. I believe that when he found he could not ride roughshod over the people in such a matter, it decided him to buy his way into the role of magistrate. Then when he became magistrate and found the people were still as likely to go to Casper as to him for redress against their neighbours he cast himself as a warrior of reason and has sought to condemn him at every turn. Pride. The people of these villages are as good or bad as any, but their respect must be earned. Mr Sturgess seems to think that respect should be his by rights.'

'So you *do* believe Casper is innocent of this killing?'

'Yes,' Miss Scales said simply.

Harriet hesitated. 'There was mistletoe in the man's pockets.'

'No doubt Casper put it there, to protect the man's spirit and stop it wandering.'

Harriet shook her head. 'This mix of pagan and Christian confuses me, Miss Scales. I cannot understand it.'

'Dear Mrs Westerman, do not even try! Just know this: belief in these old ways, braided as they are with Christian teachings, lie deep in these hills. And belief makes things powerful, very powerful, and we would all do well to respect that. Do not understand it. Respect it. That is all.'

It didn't take Casper long to find the place where Agnes had reburied the poppet. There was a spot between the roots of a rowan where the earth had been turned. He scraped the loose stuff away until he could see the pale straw figure wrapped in rowan leaves and berries. He lifted it out. It was neatly made. Agnes had set harebells in its face as eyes, the same blue as Stella's. Clumps of raw dark wool had been worked into the straw for hair and it was wearing a folded blue handkerchief as a dress. It had been washed as he instructed, and he could see no trace of blood on it now. He pulled the handkerchief loose and a handful of leaves fell from it. Henbane and rue. He could feel the power on it. He would burn it on his own fire among healing herbs. Agnes would need guiding, but she would be powerful indeed in time.

Blanche Grice was eavesdropping in his mind. *'Shame she's lost then, isn't it? Shame you most likely went and dropped her in a hole.'*

He ignored her, and looked about him. The sudden rain of last night had caused a dozen little riverlets to run, but the earth in which the poppet had been buried was still dust dry, so she had been here before the waters came. He tried to think about the beating. He was sure that the storm had come while they were still at work on him. Yes, it had scared them. There had been a pause, a consultation with another man, then they had dropped him and gone into his cabin. He looked about him again. He had told Agnes to wait here till dawn. Where would she have hidden when the rain came? He turned round slowly. Perhaps she had gone higher first to try and get sight of the fireworks, though missing them was supposed to be part of her penance. He walked up the slope away from the trees then looked towards the lake, then back down the way he had come. He could see the three cabins that made up his summer home.

Blanche Grice had started to sing. She made Joe sound like an angel, but Casper smiled. She did that when she wanted to stop him thinking on something. He went back into his memory of the night before, felt the blow to his ribs, the taste of his own blood in his mouth. In the rain, when they seemed to have it in mind to start in on him again, a shape had come through the woods. He had heard a call, then another blow across his head had made him stupid. The next memory he could find was the heat of morning and Stephen's voice calling him.

'I did her no harm,' he said aloud. 'She came to my aid.'

The witch gave up singing now that the memory had come back to him. *'Where is she then?'* she said, sulky and slippery.

'I shall find her.'

He turned back towards his camp, his fire and his duties.

Mrs Briggs was nothing but welcoming when Harriet arrived in the drawing room finally dressed for dinner, full of apologies and half an hour late.

'No, Mrs Westerman, you have done quite the right thing.' She said this with a significant glance at the Vizegräfin and Harriet realised that the town's display of displeasure with Mrs Briggs's uncomfortable guests had given her courage. 'You and I shall speak of all these matters after we have dined, I hope. In the meantime I shall say only I am glad that you are here to aid us in these difficult times. Cook is quite happy to hold dinner for such an *insignificant* time when you are doing so much for us.'

Harriet thought briefly how pleasant the world would be, were more people in it like Mrs Briggs, and they went into dinner.

'How did Miss Hurst take the news?' Felix asked, after they had been seated some time.

'Calmly,' Harriet replied. The thought of the girl being insulted and turned away by the Vizegräfin, then Felix's refusal to deliver word to Sophia himself made her angry. Felix deserved no news about her. She thought of the flat empty voice in which Miss Hurst had told her of her past; it made her hate all men and Felix in particular.

'Did you know, Felix, that Miss Hurst left the convent in which she had spent most of her life only six months ago, since when her father tried to prostitute her to the men he had gulled into playing cards with him?' She put some of the game pie onto her plate. 'She had to fight, and was beaten for her resistance.'

Harriet felt the movement of one of the footmen behind her, and her glass was filled. She cursed inwardly. She had, in her anger, forgotten about the presence of the servants, and here was Mrs Briggs's footman in the most subtle of ways reminding her of it himself.

'I did not,' Felix said. For a moment he sounded almost like Crowther.

Mrs Briggs began to talk about the danger of chills with a certain determination, and went on to say how glad she was Stephen had fetched a brew from Casper.

The Vizegräfin was largely silent, till waving away the joint that Mrs Briggs was offering her, she looked at Harriet and demanded, 'Where is my brother? Is he cutting up the Austrian?'

Harriet wet her lips slightly. 'He wished to visit your old housekeeper, then I believe it was his intention to call on Mr Askew.'

'What – Lottie Tyers?' The Vizegräfin shuddered. 'I can't believe that old woman is still living; she seemed ancient when I was a child.'

Mrs Briggs put down the joint. 'I told you of her on the first day you arrived, Vizegräfin,' she said very precisely. 'I thought you might wish to see a woman so intimately associated with your childhood.'

The Vizegräfin shrugged. 'She was a servant.'

The rest of the meal passed in silence.

Mr Askew was never absolutely punctual about the hour his museum closed. He lived in fear of shutting his door just as some member of the quality, whose name could add further lustre to his visitors' book, might be pondering a visit. At around a quarter to the hour advertised of five o'clock he would generally appear in the square, looking up and down the street for any ladies or gentlemen who seemed to be at leisure to let them know his museum was still at their disposal, and in their absence he mourned the looks of his town. He could not help feeling that most of the houses which surrounded his museum looked hunched and low. He wished he could white-wash the whole settlement. The same thought came into his mind every night as the clock-chimes faded, regular as the bells. Only some minutes after the hour had struck would he, with a last look about him and a sigh, confess that he had had all the custom likely in the day, and return to his front door with slow steps and draw it closed. Such were his actions now.

He had his hand on the door when he saw a movement in the shadows of the alley opposite and saw Mr Crowther emerging from the gloom. He started. The man unnerved him at the best of times, and he had seen nothing in Crowther's behaviour to suggest to him they were likely to become friendly. His manners were cold to the point of incivility. Mrs Westerman seemed a pleasant enough woman; she had praised his fireworks. He had mentioned the fact in his paragraph about the event for the London papers, hoping that the mention of her name and the account of the storm might make the gentlemen in the capital think it worthwhile to set his letter in type. Mr Askew paid her the compliment in his mind of being certain that she would never of her own volition become involved with the sordid business of murder, and was privately convinced Crowther must have some dark power over her to force her to aid him in his investigations. If she had appeared on his doorstep in this way, he would have known what to say, and how to say it. With Mr Crowther before him, Mr Askew felt his tongue stick in his mouth.

'May I see your museum, Mr Askew?' Crowther said. Askew opened the door and bowed him in, though the skin on the back of his neck prickled and, given the choice, he would rather have welcomed a devil into his living room. He turned the key in the door behind them, then turned to watch Crowther as he examined the displays. He felt his usual enthusiasm for his little establishment wither like cut grass. He watched Crowther move his gaze from the case of minerals, to the examples of stuffed birds, to the portrait of the Luck, and saw only shabby, provincial attempts at science, at art. He dropped his gaze to the floor, and the dusty toes of his own boots, unwilling any more to see his museum suffer under that cold regard.

'Mr Askew?'

He looked up like a schoolboy in front of a headmaster.

'Yes, my lord?'

'Where are the materials relating to my father's murder?'

It seemed to Mr Askew that he had tied his cravat with too much enthusiasm this morning, though he had not noticed the pressure on his throat before now.

'Materials?'

Crowther pointed his stick to the alcove where an unfortunate stuffed fox mouldered.

'There. I see the engravings and notes you have assembled on the unfortunate history of Lord Greta. If I were in your trade I would relate the misery of his successor to these lands about there. Instead I see areas where I can tell by the brightness of the paint that certain items have been removed, and an example of *vulpes vulpes* that does no credit to the museum, the art of the taxidermist, or the works of nature herself. So I ask again, where are the materials relating to my father's murder?'

Mr Askew swallowed. 'Small display, merely the facts, my lord, tasteful . . . Taken down at your sister's request.'

'You have them here, however?' Mr Askew nodded and pointed mutely in the direction of his office. 'May I examine them, Mr Askew, if that would not inconvenience you?'

The civility of the question brightened Mr Askew considerably. He bustled towards the office door and unlocked it with his usual buoyant stride and then invited Mr Crowther to sit in his own chair, at his own table, before leaning into the press and dragging out a packing case in which any number of papers seemed to have been crammed in haste. It occurred to him that the murder of Mr Hurst might not do as much damage to his trade as he had feared. If Mr Crowther and Mrs Westerman happened to discover the killer, perhaps the loss of Mr Hurst would not be much of a loss at all, especially if they found that some mysterious foreigner had been responsible. That would be an excellent outcome. Their names would be even more closely linked with the area, and he was in a perfect position to describe events for the press. Perhaps even write a little book on their investigation, to be sold exclusively in the museum. He was aware that people enjoyed reading about such things.

'As you see, sir,' he said, pulling a framed engraving free, 'here is our portrait of your father, and one of your brother. It was their marks you noticed on the wall.' He placed them on the blotter in front of Crowther, and was about to place his other papers over them when Crowther held up his hand. He was staring at the two portraits with steady concentration.

After a significant pause, Crowther let his hand drop. 'They are faithful likenesses,' he said, then looking up again added, 'What else have you there, Mr Askew?' Askew put down the volume that was in his hand delicately on top of the 1st Baron's portrait. Crowther examined the first page. *A collection of the most remarkable and interesting trials with the defence and behaviour of the criminals before and after condemnation.* Mr Askew coughed slightly, then turned the pages till he reached the relevant section. The words swam rather in front of Crowther's eyes. Mr Askew, however, was beginning to brighten. Mr Crowther had not come to insult him, or his museum. Indeed, he seemed to be seeking his help. Mr Askew was glad to offer it. Mr Askew only wished he could do more. Mr Askew began to say so.

'I think it vital that little establishments such as my own gather together materials relating to the history, the geography and the personalities in a place such as this. I am sure many guineas have been spread around this town because of our humble display on the Luck of Gutherscale Hall, for instance, which perhaps you noticed; and to those whose interest is more scholarly, we may offer materials to aid them in their own researches. Again I mention our display on the Luck. Mr Sturgess is an enthusiast for the legends of this area and has read every reference I could gather on the fall of Lord Greta.'

'Indeed?'

'Oh yes. For an out-comer he has gathered a quantity of information. Indeed, I hope his business will allow him to visit me soon, as I have just taken possession of a rather good likeness of the last Lord Greta, superior to that already in my museum and am keen to share it with him.' He delved back into the press and emerged with a neatly rolled paper which he unravelled and held aloft.

Crowther glanced up briefly. 'Very fine.'

'I am *so* glad you agree, sir. Yes, this likeness was taken in Lord Greta's last years in exile in France. They say he was quite poor by that time, though of course the artist has still discovered that aristocratic nature which remained to the last. A fine eye for detail is what an artist requires . . . How very strange!'

'What is strange?' Crowther asked, without looking up.

'Oh, nothing – nothing at all,' Askew said hurriedly. 'Have you found anything of interest in the volume, my lord?'

Crowther lifted it by one corner. 'May I take it away with me, Mr Askew? I shall return it tomorrow.' Mr Askew bowed his consent and Crowther slipped the book into his coat-pocket and stood. Mr Askew watched him; he was staring again at the portraits of his father and brother, but Askew could see no sign of great emotion on his face, only those of quiet study. Then Crowther nodded once, as if to his own thoughts, and with a final bow left the room and the museum to its proprietor's sole care.

She had been too late to see Stephen before dinner. The extent of Harriet's information came from Miriam. Her son had been at home for the greater part of the afternoon and had been working at whatever tasks Mr Quince had been fit enough to give him. She had sent word that she looked forward to seeing him in the evening, but by the time she had said all she thought proper to Mrs Briggs, the sky had finally grown dark. She approached her son's room on tiptoe. His papers were arranged neatly on the desk of the little room between Mr Quince's closet and his own. She looked at them idly, grateful for the peace. There were phrases in Latin on one sheet, in Greek on another, and rows of calculations on the next. Her own education had been a patchwork of occasional tutors and she had been encouraged to spend more time on needlework than mathematics. She sighed now, thinking of it; she would have made fewer mistakes in her first seasons at Caveley if the rows of figures in the account books had not been such a mystery at first, but at least she had not disgraced herself at the country dances. No doubt the local gentry would have been happier if she had limited herself to quadrilles. There was money enough to hire a steward now, but she had grown to enjoy feeling the condition of her home and lands through those estate books, and they had become almost friends in the months of her widowhood. Another eccentricity for her neighbours to puzzle over. Though she would never be able to keep her papers as neat as her son did. It was the habit of a sailor's son.

The door to his room was slightly ajar; she crossed to it and pushed it open gently so the light of her candle spilled over Stephen's bed. He lay very still, and for a few moments she did no more than watch him. His face was turned away, but she could see the gentle rise and fall of his breath under the sheets. She bit her lip, and told herself now was not the time to talk to him of serious matters. They would keep until morning, but if she turned away for her own sake or his she could not say. She did not know that Stephen's eyes were wide open in the dark.

Crowther began his walk back to Silverside Hall thinking of the portraits. He knew the original paintings. His sister had taken them from the house, and still had them, he supposed, in her possession. He had seen neither face since 1751. They looked better men in the pictures than in his memory. It was only with great effort that he could conjure any image of his brother other than in the cell in the Tower the night before his execution. With a painful clarity he could see Adair on his knees and weeping. He tried to think calmly of the body on the Island and consider Harriet's suggestions. Had his father been afraid of something before he died? Had the dead Jacobite come to haunt him in some way?

Slowly, the story his brother had told him began to seem plausible, when before it had seemed ridiculous. The man paying him for a moment alone with his father. Adair arranging to talk to his father away from the house, then sending the other man in his stead. Becoming concerned when his father did not return. Discovering his body, pulling out the knife and stumbling back to Silverside half-mad with guilt and grief.

Crowther could see nothing but Addie's face, the terror of his approaching death consuming him. Crowther began to feel the memory of that evening in the cell creeping towards him like a living thing. He had spent the greater part of his life refusing to think of it; now he could not turn away. The memory suddenly took him, and as if he were living the hours once more, it flooded over him: the smell of the fire in the damp cell, the sound of Addie's retching, the glint of the coins Crowther left him for the hangman, his own words as he promised he would forgive his elder brother if he could, the snap of the rope.

When he managed to open his eyes once more, the light had bled from the day and the scents in the air had shifted to juniper and evening-rose, gorse, meadow-sweet. It was very quiet. The lake had taken on the colours of the moon and the high mountains had shifted to dark green silhouettes. A gull crossed the field of his vision in search of moths. He let his father's cane fall onto the path beside him.

'Oh God, Addie! Who is there to forgive me?'

Harriet had retired to the library to wait for Crowther. She sat watching the darkness outside the window and wondered where Casper Grace might be hiding himself. She had no doubt that he could avoid detection if he wished it, but feared that in his innocence, he might approach the village and be taken before he could be warned that he was being hunted. Perhaps his friends among the people would find their ways to let him know of Sturgess's intentions. She thought of the conversation she had had with Mr Scales as she left the vicarage. She had noticed how two or three of the low doors in the village bore signs of a cross only hours old. One was made of rowan twigs, tied and nailed. The other two showed light, since they had been carved there – an outline that recalled the elegant shape of the Luck. She mentioned it to Mr Scales as he saw her to the carriage.

'News of this unfortunate gentleman's demise has spread, Mrs Westerman. The people look to guard themselves.'

She had smiled. 'You must be glad to see them turn to Christ at such moments.' The old vicar opened the gate for her to pass through.

'I am not so naive, madam. They look to the Luck, and as it is lost they draw its shadow on the walls and hope that the memory of it will guard them. It is the fair-folk they ask for protection, though they use the cross to call them. It was the same when the small-pox struck us in fifty-four.'

'It is a foul disease.'

'One episode in our history Mr Askew has seen fit to ignore. It cost me my wife and one of my daughters, and my faith.'

Harriet came to a sudden halt. 'Mr Scales?'

The old vicar smiled at her. 'I pray every day for its return, and I am grateful that my daughter remains devout. But I can understand why the local people prefer their spirits wilful and cruel; it suggests a better understanding of the way the world treats us. Do not tell the bishop if you meet him, my dear. It would disturb his digestion.'

He had patted her on the arm and nodded to Ham, then turned back up the path.

As Crowther entered the room Harriet stirred and looked up at him enquiringly. He did not speak, but instead placed the volume detailing his brother's trial in front of her and settled into one of the leather armchairs. She took it up and began to read. At some point, Miriam came into the room and placed wine on the table beside Crowther. The night gathered closely about them. Crowther continued to watch the air, and the only sound to be heard was the occasional flick of paper as Harriet turned a page. The moon had dragged itself up and peered in at them across the lake before she set the book down. He finally shifted his head and looked at her. Then without waiting for her to speak, offered up the substance of his conversation with Lottie Tyers.

Harriet put her chin in her hands. 'You did not know of this strongbox?'

'No, or at least I knew nothing of it when I sold Silverside and its lands. All papers relating to my father's property and possessions were to hand, his personal correspondence was in his desk in the study, my mother's jewels in the strongbox in the wine cellar. There was nothing else to look for. But I did receive a letter from the solicitor in Keswick some years ago informing me that a strongbox had been found, that Mr Briggs believed to be the property of my father.'

'And?' Harriet said.

'I told them to force it, see there was nothing significant in it and then destroy it,' he said, staring at the high ceiling above them.

'Crowther! I wish you had not.'

'I was not aware it might contain evidence to implicate my father in murder,' he said. 'If I had known, I would naturally have asked them to preserve it.' The room was silent for a while at that, then Crowther continued, 'However, I suspect if my solicitor is anything like his father, he probably did not destroy it.' Harriet felt herself brighten and tried to hide it, but suspected she was unsuccessful, judging by the slight lifting of the corner of Crowther's thin mouth. She looked back down at her lap and the book.

'So your brother protested his innocence to the last?' she said.

'He did.' Crowther's smile had disappeared and his skin seemed to have become a little more grey in the candlelight.

'And you were with him the night before his execution?'

'I was.'

Harriet tried to imagine it for a moment, then shook the thought from her head. 'Did no one believe him? Not even your sister?'

'She was only a child at the time, but yes, at first she believed him and we did make enquiries about this mysterious man. But it was such a fantastic story. I had never heard of Jocasta's testimony, of course. I am sure that I would have dismissed it even if I had, even as I did in eighty-one when I spoke to her of it in London. I cannot blame the magistrate whom she says called her a liar. She had been a bored and difficult pupil at the parish school, and it was held against her. There was Adair shut into his room with blood on his hands, and scarring Lottie Tyers in his madness.'

Harriet picked at the lace on her sleeves, making the silver threads catch and drop the light. 'I do not believe you *did* entirely dismiss Jocasta's testimony when you heard it for yourself, Crowther. I think we are here in part because of what she told you. Even if the body had not been found on Saint Herbert's Island I still think you would have found your way here eventually.'

He smiled, slightly. 'Perhaps you are right, Mrs Westerman. Though, as always, I have needed you to goad me into doing what needs to be done.'

She shrugged. 'I am so crowded and confused at this moment, I am not sure if I could say *what* I think needs to be done. If we manage by some miracle to prove your brother innocent . . .'

The thought was left to turn in the candlelight, till Crowther seemed to pluck it from the air between his long fingers and turn it over in his hands.

'I do not believe in spirits, Mrs Westerman. Neither Addie nor my father have visited me to claim justice or confess, and I have been too long in this world to expect it to reward virtue. The world does not care who lives or dies, or why, but I still think we may search for truth, that such a thing exists. That may be the only right thing to do. What follows, we cannot hope to know.'

Harriet watched the yellow flame on the candle. The air was so still it never wavered. 'Let me ask you this then. Do you still believe that your brother killed your father?'

He slowly shook his head. 'No, Mrs Westerman. My family have been guilty of many crimes, but I am very afraid now that Addie was innocent. But he could not convince us, and half London saw him hanged.'

'I am sorry, Crowther.'

'That my father was a murderer? Or that my brother was not? That my nephew might be?'

'For all of it.'

His face remained calm, but Harriet could guess what saying those words had cost him. The story on which his life had been founded, unpleasant as it was, he now suspected a fiction. So here they found themselves, in the darkness of the old fells, and the lies had built and climbed one upon the back of the other like the ranges of hills that struggled upwards to the unseeing sky and the pewter moon.

'Are you tired, Crowther?'

He turned towards her and looked up from under his hooded eyes. 'I am always somewhat tired, Mrs Westerman. What have you in mind?'

'I am thinking on the dedication in the snuffbox, and your sister's immediate idea we were suggesting your father was instrumental in the betrayal of Lord Greta's brother in forty-five. If the body in the tomb *was* the reason your father was murdered, then we must learn more than Mrs Tyers has told you and general gossip. Was he indeed Greta's man? What business had he at Silverside so pressing he would risk his neck by knocking on your father's door the day after setting light to Gutherscale? What became of Greta and his family? Whom did they blame for the taking of Rupert de Beaufoy? I am wondering if we might have among our friends in London a gentleman likely to know a great deal about the enemies of the King domestic and foreign, and who has a talent for coming by information he does not have immediately to hand.'

Crowther pressed his fingertips together and smiled. 'I think

I know whom you have in mind. Our friend Mr Palmer probably does have more chance of knowing such things than any other man living.'

'Then write to him, Crowther.'

'While I do so, perhaps you can tell me of your investigations into the death of Mr Hurst.' He paused, looking at her. 'What is it, Mrs Westerman?'

'I have found nothing but a little misery and many more questions. And I fear we may have to have more dealings with other lawyers in the morning.'

Crowther sighed as he prepared his pen. 'Explain, if you please.'

From the collection of Mr Askew, Keswick Museum

Letter to *The Gentleman's Magazine*, June 1746

Concerning the fire at Gutherscale Hall, last November

Mr Urban,

Though the pages of your worthy periodical have been heavy with reflection on the late Rebellion against our King, now the storm is passed it seems fitting to give you some account of the terrible fire of Gutherscale Hall. The destruction of this mighty house acted as a harbinger of the fates of the family that once dwelled between its walls, as within only a sennight of its being consumed by flames, Rupert de Beaufoy, younger brother of the last Lord Greta who now languishes in exile, was taken on his way to join the Rebellion. It seems his location was betrayed by one of his followers, a man much trusted by the Greta family.

All loyal subjects to the King have, however, suffered a great loss in this fire which consumed a home noble for many generations in the space of a single night. How the fatal conflagration began, none can say, for there was no sign of lightning on the night in question. One must suppose some vagrant managed to start a fire there for his warmth, but a spark spread and consumed the whole. The smoke was first noted by labourers ending their day's work on the opposite side of the lake, and word and assistance was rushed

281

at once to Silverside Hall, residence of Sir William Penhaligon, current owner of these lands and Gutherscale itself. The loss of this fine house is all the more bitter as, having survived its master's exile and the forfeiture of his lands for thirty years, it had just been purchased from the state by Sir William, who had declared his intention to refurbish this ancient house and make it his own. Alas, it was not to be!

Sir William was at Silverside when word arrived, and at once raced to the scene to do what he could to halt the flames, but it was already beyond the efforts of any man to save it. Sir William's distress was extreme, and only the appeals of his young daughter clutching at his coat and begging him not to risk his life prevented him from plunging into the fire as if he could extinguish it with his own hands.

At dawn the ancestral home of the Greta family had been reduced to ashes. Would that the Young Pretender had seen this for the omen it proved to be and removed himself at once again to the court of his father in peace, rather than suffer his followers to feel the mighty wrath through Cumberland of the true King of this country.

Yours &c W.L.

PART IV

IV.1

HARRIET EVENTUALLY FOUND her son by the lake. He was seated on the jetty watching the ruffled silk of the waters, and though he glanced up as he heard her approach he did not come to her until she called. When they had settled on a wrought-iron bench at the edge of the woodland, Harriet realised she was not entirely clear in her own mind what she wanted to say to him. She felt she should prohibit any contact with Casper, but could not bring herself to say the words. Instead she found herself twisting the thin black band of her mourning ring.

In the end it was Stephen who spoke first. 'Miriam says Mr Sturgess is after Casper for killing Mr Hurst.'

'He is.'

'Are you going to tell me to stay away from Casper, Mama?'

Harriet drew breath, then shook her head. 'I do not know what to tell you, Stephen.'

'He needs my help.'

Harriet put her arm around his shoulder and pulled him to

her. 'I want to keep you safe, but I do not know how.' She felt his small hand reach up to take her own, and they looked out across the lawn together. There was a cough behind them: Harriet started and turned. Casper appeared from the shadows as if speech of him had summoned his form out of the woods. Joe sat on his shoulder, his wings lifted slightly.

'Mr Grace!' Harriet said.

'Didn't mean to alarm you, Mrs Westerman,' Casper said, 'but I'd be glad of some speech with you.'

'Morning, Casper.'

'Good day, youngling.'

Harriet took her arm from round her son. Casper's bruises were rainbows of purple and yellow, and his features more drawn than when she had seen him standing by Mr Hurst's body. 'You are welcome to sit with us. You look weary.'

He shook his head. 'Best I'm not seen from the house. Let me tell you a thing or two and then I'll go about my business.' Harriet waited, and he watched her for a moment before apparently coming to some decision in his own mind. 'There's a girl gone missing from the village. Agnes Kerrick is her name. I think she was taken by the men that beat me, since she came upon it. I mean to find them, and her.'

'Do you know who they were?'

Casper nodded. 'I've got an idea of two of them. I had a prowl around last night and they ain't sleeping in their own beds no more, but I think I can rattle some words out of the mother.'

'Do you think they have harmed this girl, then? Can you tell me their names?'

'If they have, I shall know it. As to naming them, I'll keep that to myself for now. I know these folk, and have my ways. I must ask your trust.'

Harriet sighed, but eventually nodded and said quietly, 'Do you think the attack on you is connected with the murder of Mr Hurst?'

'Can't make sense of that,' Casper said, scratching hard at the back of his neck. 'The placing of that body is a pebble in my shoe. It was done by someone who knew it as a secret place, but did not know it as a place of mine. The people here know I have reason to go there often enough. The men I have my eye on for my beating know that as well as anyone.'

'So who . . . ?'

'Gentry.'

Harriet was quiet for a while.

Casper sniffed. 'I'm sure the men that beat on me made all the ruckus at the Black Pig too.'

'From what Miriam said, it sounded as if they were looking for something,' Harriet told him. 'But what? Did they mean to steal money from you?'

Casper looked out on the lake. 'How is Miss Hurst bearing up?'

Harriet told him what she could of the interview with her son listening, and of the notice in the paper. 'Can you see any join here, Casper?'

'Can't say I do. Can't say it, unless this season has made all men mad and there's blood boiling all over. If I learn anything that touches on him, I'll get word to you. But I've got to find Agnes. That's my first thought. You look for traces of her where you go, and I'll stretch my ears to the wind for any word of your business.' He made to leave but Harriet put out her hand and rested it on his arm. He flinched as she did so, and she felt the tight strength of his muscles under her white fingers.

'The Island of Bones, Casper – the skeleton. What do you know of that? Did your father ever mention—'

'Nothing. But this I'll say. In forty-six, Sir William set my da up with enough money to buy the Black Pig. And he was not a man who parted with his money easily.'

Harriet released him and bit her lip.

'What can I do, Casper?' Stephen said. 'Shall I come with you?'

Harriet felt Casper's eyes flick to her and back to her son.

'Not now. Come to the cabin in an hour, and we may have words.' He pulled something from his satchel. 'And here's fresh for your Mr Quince. How is he?'

'A little better,' Stephen said quietly.

Casper ruffled the boy's hair. 'Mind your ma, lad.' Then he touched his forehead to Harriet and was gone. The trees swallowed him like light.

Harriet realised her son was looking at her. 'Just please be careful, Stephen,' she said softly.

Crowther was examining the third of the dozen arrows in his nephew's quiver when he heard the door open and saw Felix in front of him. For a second they simply stared at each other, then Crowther placed the arrow on the baize of the billiard table to his right and picked up the next.

'May I ask what you are doing, sir?'

'I am examining your arrows, Felix, for any sign of the blood or brain matter of Mr Hurst. I would have done so last night, but feared there would be insufficient light.'

Felix made a harsh noise in his throat, somewhere between a gasp and a laugh. 'You are being humorous, dear uncle.'

Crowther set the fourth arrow next to the third, and plucked another from the quiver. 'I never make jokes, Felix. And if I were to do so, I should make better ones.'

Felix stepped forward to the billiard table as Crowther continued. He leaned on it in an attempt to appear at ease, but as Crowther glanced up he could see the young man's fingers were shaking.

'May I ask then why you think this necessary?'

'I wish to spare Mrs Westerman the task. You knew Mr Hurst indeed, as far as we are aware you are the only person here who did know him. Did you owe him a great deal of money?' He looked up again, but Felix did not reply. 'Is that why your mother dragged you across Europe to visit poor out-of-the-way Mrs Briggs whom she neither likes nor respects? And where there is one creditor, I have no doubt there are others.' Again he gently placed the arrow down and picked up the next, bringing the point close to his light blue eyes and turning it slowly. 'It must have been a considerable amount, for Mr Hurst to pursue you so far.' He paused and looked more closely at the arrow's tip, then laid it down. 'Only dirt.'

'Do you enjoy seeing members of your family hanged?'

Crowther lifted another arrow. 'Have you ever seen a man hanged, Felix? From close to, I mean, not from the distant seats where it is reduced to a puppet show.' Felix did not move. 'I have, on those occasions when I was sent to claim the body for dissection. A horrible death: a foul sound, how the breath struggles in the throat against the rope, the jerking of the legs, the eyes distended . . . Most soil themselves. No, I take no pleasure in seeing any man hanged.'

'I did not kill Hurst. You are right, I did owe him money still. But he had debts and enemies of his own.'

Crowther turned to him. 'If you *did* kill him, may I suggest you flee at once? You may have lived a life protected from the consequences of your actions up to this point, but I am afraid, Felix, our crimes catch up with us in the end, one way or another.' He thought of his father, of himself, then he set down the last arrow. 'No trace that I can see. Though that proves nothing.' He tried to read his nephew's expression, humiliation and fear badly masked. 'If I remember correctly, you claim to be quite a shot. Perhaps as you are in such need of money, I should be careful when I am out walking.'

He stepped towards Felix, then waited for him to move aside and give him passage out of the room.

'Perhaps you should.' The skin around his lips was white. Crowther smiled slightly and raised his eyebrows and Felix moved aside. Crowther walked past him but, as his hand touched the door, Felix spoke again.

'I did not kill him. I have been foolish, but I am not a murderer.'

Crowther turned back towards him. 'You remind me so much of Lucius Adair, Felix,' he said, and with no further explanation, left the room.

Agnes woke suddenly in the darkness and cried out, then looked about her, waiting for her heart to slow. Her hands were bound in front and her fingers were cramped and uncomfortable, but she could still grapple for the bottle at her side, and she got the neck of it to her lips without spilling any. She drank, then rested her aching head against the damp earth behind her. There was something different in the air. The indecipherable darkness that had met her at her last time of waking had given way a little and there was a scent of something other than earth. She began to shuffle forward and got to her knees. Yes, there. She had been sleeping in the blanket in some kind of deep alcove in the wall. Some old passing place of the workers perhaps, and as she crept out of it she began to see forms around her, or shadows of forms. Her eyes strained to make sense of it. She felt forward towards the place the air seemed a little brighter, keeping her shoulder to the wall.

There was a sudden sharp turn which almost made her stumble – and there *was* light. It was a weak, hazy sort of light, but it seeped around the edge of the tunnel, like a silver lining on a thundercloud. She managed to get up onto her feet and shuffled towards it. Maybe they had only wanted to keep her out of the way for a day. She knew what sort of place this was now. A child had been lost in one of the ancient mines when she was an infant, and after that the townspeople had arranged for all the tunnels to be boarded up. Her own father had blocked up many of them. She must be behind one of those barriers. They had carried her through, then, no doubt, just propped it up again, knowing she'd free herself when she came to. Maybe they hadn't even been beating on Casper after all. With the dark and the rain, how could she be sure? It had been nothing, a lark gone a bit far. As she got nearer to the light she felt a laugh bubble up inside her, and she was ready to shake her head at Swithun and box his ears and tell him all was forgiven. She reached the barrier and kicked at a likely-looking space near the base, expecting it to fall back and show her the sky and the hills and all the light. It did not move. She kicked harder, then again and again. It would not give. The laugh left her.

'Damn you, let me out!' she yelled at the wood. Then something caught her eye and she looked up to where the boards rested against the joists that framed the entrance to the mine. It was the end of a nail, clean and sharp. There were others. Fresh, rust-free. She dropped to her knees, trying to fight back down the panic that rose in her, but she could not. The rope cut into the flesh of her wrists. She remembered something from those first hours of pain and half-understood darkness. The sound of hammers. She wrapped her arms around her knees and tried to stop herself trembling.

The bell rang so brightly as Harriet and Crowther entered that the clerk, high and hunched on a stool by a desk in the shadows, almost fell from his perch and dropped his pen across his page. Crowther waited for him to recover himself as he looked about the room. It had not changed in its essentials since he visited it last some thirty years before. A dark wood floor, panelled walls and a smell of ink and dust in the air. It was here he had made the arrangements for the disposal of the estate and maintenance of his sister. Throughout his subsequent travels on the continent he had felt no need to change his representation, and it was through this office that he had heard of his sister's marriage, the birth of her son and her separation. The oak panelling had absorbed it all.

There were a number of etchings hung about the walls, discreet and inoffensive as the firm which had handled his affairs for so long. Under them, along one wall was a long ottoman, upholstered in green leather, where a client might wait for the portals of the law to be opened to him. It was an impressive office for a solicitor in such a small and out-of-the-way place. Crowther supposed that the dealings with Silverside over the years had enriched it considerably, and his own fortune, ignored by himself, probably gave them business enough to employ a boy and an upholsterer.

The clerk had managed to recover his pen and his composure, and made a little bobbing bow. He was probably still well under twenty, and had the air of a boy caught out playing in his father's office.

'Mr Crowther, my lord? I am Dent, sir. Would you be wishing to see Mr Mark Leathes, sir? Let me just slip in and say you are here, and he will be with you directly.' The youth paused and flushed, feeling perhaps he had mismanaged his speech. Then, deciding too much in way of respectful address was better than too little, he added an extra 'sir', looking at his shoes.

Crowther recognised the name. At some point the signatures that appeared on his business correspondence had changed from Thomas Leathes to Mark Leathes. He had been a little sorry that the old gentleman was not handling his concerns any longer and had turned away from his knives long enough to write and express his thanks for many years of service before putting the matter from his mind. His affairs continued to be managed efficiently, and the new Mr Leathes did not trouble him with too much correspondence.

Crowther agreed that he and Mrs Westerman would be glad of a moment of Mr Leathes' time, and the lad was about to escape into the inner offices, when he turned and with another blush asked if either himself or Mrs Westerman were in need of any refreshment. Harriet smiled at him, and Crowther was surprised, as he often was, at how wide and open her smile could be. He wondered if her frank good humour was as genuine as it had been when he first met her. Perhaps. Just as he remained in his fifties the awkward, bookish boy he had once been, perhaps she too was still at her core the open-hearted, if wilful girl who had first made her husband love her by listening to his tales of adventure on the seas with that same delighted grin.

'We have no need of anything at the moment, Mr Dent,' she said, then as the boy slipped into the shadows, she turned from the engravings, saying, 'Would it not be a delight, Crowther, to arrive in the offices of a lawyer and find his walls decorated with great oils of the Muses decked out in pink drapery?'

He raised his eyebrows. 'Diverting perhaps, though I would not wish to trust such a lawyer with my business.'

She laughed softly, continuing to admire, or at least scrutinise, an engraving of *The Royal Courts of London*. 'Because of the extravagance of the oils, or their subject?'

'Both. Though I am glad to see *these* here, and they are not typical of a lawyer's office, I think.'

She crossed to look at the engravings by which Crowther stood. They seemed to be technical drawings of various machines. Harriet saw in them a confusion of gears and wheels. They were pleasant enough compositions, but she could understand little of them.

'The gentleman here has regularly invested my money in a

number of manufacturing schemes in the northern counties. From their accounts he seems to have done so wisely. Indeed, I sometimes fear my money has managed to do more to grow the stock of knowledge and expertise in this country than I have done myself.'

'Are you fearfully rich, Crowther?'

'Fearfully. Quite rich enough to make murdering me for my money seem a risk worth taking.'

Harriet recalled what she had been told of Crowther's interview with Felix that morning and grimaced. She would never succeed in puzzling out Crowther's character. The thought of his nephew trying to murder him for his fortune seemed to have rather amused him.

The young Dent slid back into the room and behind his desk again, and Crowther noticed him glance at Harriet as he did so. He had taken the opportunity to smooth his hair. He was followed out in a very few moments by his master, a gentleman of roughly Harriet's age with a long face and bags under his eyes, very respectably turned out and with an air of intelligent good humour. He was glad to welcome them and led them back into his own office with the minimum of chatter. Harriet wondered if he had learned enough of Crowther through their business correspondence to know this was by far the best way to deal with him.

He showed them into an office with a large window on one side that overlooked a neat flower-garden behind the house. Harriet had noticed on entering the offices of professional men in general, that if their rooms offered such a view they usually set their desks so they had their back to it, as if underlining their own seriousness with their refusal to enjoy such frippery things as the open air. Mr Leathes, however, had set up his desk the other way, at right angles to the window, so that, as he worked on his papers he might look up from time to time and watch the seasons change. Harriet was ready to like him for that, but before she could take her seat she was distracted by a fluttering in the garden, and going to the glass, saw that part of the little lawn was taken up with an aviary. She tilted her head to listen and realised that the air which struggled warmly through the open window was freshened with birdsong.

Mr Leathes noticed her attention and joined her at the window. 'My canaries. An inclination I inherited from my father. Even we lawyers must have something cheerful about us, Mrs Westerman.'

'You do not think it cruel to shut away these creatures, Mr Leathes?'

He shook his head. 'It is a good-sized aviary, designed for their convenience. My little daughter told me once that she thought the wrens and sparrows all hoped when they died they would be transported into my aviary as if to heaven. There they are safe from buzzards, well-fed, and I have even means to warm the air in the winter.'

'You sound as if you envy them a little yourself,' she said, putting her hand to the glass.

'Perhaps I do,' he replied, returning to his chair, 'on days where there is unpleasant business to be done, and unpleasant things to say. I hope today will not be such a one.' Harriet was in the midst of framing a gentle smile for him, when she was surprised to hear him continue: 'But I fear it must be.'

'Indeed, Mr Leathes?' Crowther said. 'Are you about to tell me the new factories are all burned up and I am a pauper?'

The man shook his head. 'No, my lord. You continue to do very well. It would take a great many fires to consume your fortune, and should any such event occur, I would not wait until you happened to visit me to tell you of it.' The birds in the garden piped and whistled as he spoke, and Harriet found herself thinking of children at play. 'I was in the process of writing you a note when Dent came in to tell me you were here. I wished to speak to you about your nephew.'

'What of him?' said Crowther calmly, and Harriet watched Leathes' eyes flick up to his client then back down to the tooled leather of his desk.

'He came to see me some days ago – why, I am afraid I could not quite be sure. It was an awkward sort of interview, but I gained the impression he wished to learn the extent of your fortune and his own expectations.'

'And how did you answer him?'

'That I could be of no assistance to him, naturally, and if he wanted any information on the subject he should apply to you directly.'

The two men watched each other carefully for a moment, then appearing satisfied, Crowther nodded. 'I apologise on my nephew's behalf if the interview was uncomfortable, Mr Leathes.'

The lawyer smiled. 'My impression was it was a great deal more uncomfortable for Mr von Bolsenheim. I fear he finds himself at the end of his resources. He asked me in passing as he left if I knew a reputable place, not in the immediate area, where he might get a fair price for his watch. He seemed rather distracted. I was considering suggesting to you it might be wise to make some proper enquiry into the extent of his debts, and perhaps settle some amount on him for the promise of future good behaviour.'

Crowther sighed, crossed his legs and sat back in his chair.

'Not today, Mr Leathes. Though I shall consider what you say. Some years ago, Mr Briggs found a strongbox at Silverside, and brought it to you, believing it was the property of my father.'

Mr Leathes looked a little wary. 'Indeed. I wrote to you regarding it.'

'And I requested that you force the lock, ascertain if there was anything significant contained within and destroy the contents if there was not.'

The canaries chirrupped in the heat. Mr Leathes turned towards the window and leaned back a little in his chair. 'I believe the phrase you employed, sir, was "dispose of the materials".'

'Was it indeed?' Crowther continued to observe Mr Leathes from under his half-closed eyes. 'And how did you choose to interpret that phrase?'

Harriet was glad to see that the scrutiny did not appear to discomfort Mr Leathes. Instead, he reached into his pocket and produced a small brass key with which he unlocked the bottom drawer of his desk, and bent to retrieve something from it. Then, with an effort, he placed a small iron strongbox on his desk-top.

It was perhaps twenty inches in length, and rectangular, bound with metal bands and riveted. It looked to Harriet like the relic of a much earlier age. They examined it together a moment before Mr Leathes chose to answer Crowther's question.

'I am not sure if you recall, my lord, the circumstances of its discovery. Mr Briggs found during his last renovations of your father's office in Silverside a concealed hiding place behind the panelling and this within it. He at once had it brought to me, and I wrote to you for instruction.'

'A safe box within a hiding place? What could require such security?' Harriet asked. The box was very dirty and there were marks around the hinges.

Mr Leathes sighed. 'I cannot say, madam. The lock on this box had already been forced, though I did not discover that until I had received Lord Keswick's note and tried to open it.' If he noticed the slight tic in Crowther's face when he used his title, he gave no sign of it. 'We lawyers must develop at times an ability to read blindly. I opened the box, and although I saw there were no bonds or papers material to the estate within, I did not feel easy about destroying the box or the contents. I chose instead to interpret your phrase according to my own conscience and stored it in our archives.'

Crowther gave no sign of either annoyance or gratitude, but raised one eyebrow.

'In your *archives*, Mr Leathes? Yet now when we arrive at your office without warning, we find that you have the box with you. You will forgive me for remarking that this seems rather convenient.'

It seemed Mr Leathes was beginning now to find his seat a little uncomfortable. He shifted in his chair and cleared his throat. 'I said we lawyers read blindly, but perhaps I might have gained some *impression* of the contents, and when I heard you were coming to investigate the discovery of the skeleton on the Island of Bones . . .' He tailed off.

Harriet smiled to herself. 'You had the box brought to you. And Felix's visit provided you with the necessary pretext to ask Crowther here,' she said. 'On his coming to you, you thought no doubt to introduce the subject of the strongbox. But we have pre-empted you.'

Mr Leathes looked a little sheepish and he held up his hands. 'You have discovered me, Mrs Westerman.'

Crowther lifted the lid, saying briskly, 'You have done very well, I think, Mr Leathes, to be so nice in your interpretation.' The solicitor closed his eyes and breathed out slowly through his mouth as Crowther put his hand into the box and pulled out a single sheet, much yellowed with age. He unfolded it and then handed it to Harriet. 'Mrs Westerman, would you be so kind. Your eyes are so much sharper than mine.'

Harriet knew very well that Crowther's eyesight was at least as good as her own, but took the paper without demur and studied it. It was a short letter, and reading it, she breathed in sharply.

After a moment or two Crowther's voice broke in on her. 'Mrs Westerman?'

'Yes, yes. It is dated fifteenth May 1750, which places it a few months after your mother's death, does it not?'

'Yes, Mrs Westerman, but if you would be so kind . . .'

Harriet brushed a curl from her cheek and started to read.

'*My Lord,*

Much as I do not want to add worry to your grief over the loss of my dear aunt, I cannot, in honour to her memory, see how I can fail to communicate with you a disturbing rumour that has recently reached my ears. Some, who out of love of my aunt have hitherto kept silent have, at her death begun to speak, and powerful suspicions have been raised against you. I speak of '45. I say the name de Beaufoy. I say that those who once believed themselves betrayed by a trusted servant begin to question their intelligence. I hope you may be able to communicate to me any proofs you may have of your innocence in that matter. I shall undertake that they will reach the interested parties. If not, may I ask you make arrangements for the security of yourself and your home.

With my sincere regards,
Robert O'Brien, Killarney House.'

The birds outside seemed to sense some change in the air and whistled even more stridently than before.

'Who is Robert O'Brien, Crowther?' Harriet said at last.

He closed his eyes and put his long fingertips to his forehead. 'My mother's nephew through her older brother's marriage. My mother came from a Catholic family in Ireland.'

'Jacobites?' Harriet asked.

'It is possible they had such sympathies,' Crowther replied after a pause. 'It was O'Brien who provided a family for my sister after my father was murdered. She was sent to Ireland direct from her boarding school.'

Mr Leathes watched them. Mr Crowther had his fingertips together and was examining them closely. Mrs Westerman was tapping her foot on the Turkish rug.

'So it seems my father had reason to fear, and Lottie was right,' Crowther said slowly. 'I wonder why he kept the letter about him?'

'Perhaps he had a thought that if anything did occur . . .' Harriet said, then saw Crowther flinch and hurried on, 'Our friend in London might well be able to put some flesh on these bones, though we cannot hear from him for several days.' She looked at the solicitor again, who was trying, not unsuccessfully, to give the impression of having been struck suddenly deaf. 'Mr Leathes, is there anything you can tell us about Sir William's affairs in the forties? Or what his behaviour was in the period before his death? You must have records of those times.'

If Mr Leathes thought it strange this question came from Harriet rather than Crowther himself, he was too well-mannered to show it.

'We do, of course, Mrs Westerman, have in our archives copies of all communications between this office and Silverside from the time Sir William first settled here in my grandfather's time until the present day. But perhaps, if you wish it, I may take you to a better, living oracle. My father Thomas dealt with Lord Keswick for many years. He retired from practice some ten years ago, but his memory is still sharp.' Mr Leathes consulted his pocket-watch. 'If you are at liberty, I should be very glad to invite you to pay a morning call at my home and meet him. The box Mr Dent can take to Silverside, and it will be there for you to examine at your leisure.'

Crowther actually smiled at the other man. 'I would be glad to see your father again.'

'He will be happy to see you too, sir. He speaks fondly of you still.'

Neither gentleman noticed Harriet raise her eyebrows at that.

IV.2

CASPER WAS QUITE confident he could avoid any hireling of Mr Sturgess as long as he chose, but he came the back way into Portinscale and let himself into the yard of Mrs Fowler's place quietly nevertheless. The Fowler family had always been a weariness to their neighbours. The grandfather of the family had drunk away any reputation the family had had, and they had been a charge on the parish ever since. Casper could remember the grandfather from his youth, a foul-tempered old man who would beg on market days and say he was too sick to work the rest. His wife carried ill humour with her the way other women carried their baskets. Her children she made work the little piece of land they had until they were old enough to dodge her blows and flee. There was always someone in the village soft enough to feed her offspring, but as soon as they had their fill they went back to their wild and vindictive games. A sheep went straying, and the Fowlers would be eating mutton; a trader found his take short or a laker their pocket empty and the Fowlers would be drunk. But they were just smart enough to make sure their crimes were not easily discoverable and their victims without the resources to prosecute. They were loud about their enemies and in their own righteous defence, and continual in their complaints.

The grandfather had one son who stayed in the village, Isaac and who was just like himself – then the old devil slunk into his grave. Isaac had found a simple-minded woman to marry, and soon mocked and bullied her into a sullen and bitter drudge. Swithun was their only surviving child, and at nineteen, looked to follow his father and grandfather in his ways, but Casper would have thought both Isaac and Swithun too much a pair of cowards to try and rob *him*. Petty thieving, certainly, but to attack the cunning-man? Still, it was Swithun who was in the field looking away when Casper passed, his mother who had her eyes all over, and Isaac earned the occasional shilling in the stables of the Royal Oak.

Casper ducked under the lintel of the back door and walked into the cottage. Swithun's mother was sat, bent over the fire – Casper could smell rabbit cooking. She twisted round as he entered and her face went from a grin to a flat mask in the moment of seeing him.

'Mother Fowler. Where's your boy and your husband?'

The woman rocked back from her pot and wrapped her hands in the brown wool of her skirts. She shook her head. Casper took a solid step forward and she hissed, 'Don't know, Casper, swear it.'

Her eyes flinched all around the room, and her face was red and sweating. Joe stretched his wings and gave a low caw like a pipe drone when the bag is old. Her eyes became wide.

'They didn't do it! They wouldn't! They didn't tell me!' The last came up almost as a shriek. 'They's gone.'

The black witch was enjoying herself. Fear always fed her and made her loud. She badgered at Casper to hurt the woman, kick the stool out from under her and see her head smack against the cobbles. Mrs Fowler must have seen some of it in Casper's eyes, for she whimpered again and looked as if she would clamber up the wide chimney if she could.

'Swithun came back first though, didn't he?' Casper said in a low growl. 'Came back, as if he could tend to the pig and do his chores and no bill to pay? Gave you my rabbits to turn to sludge in your pot? And your man shovelling shit in the Royal Oak. Then they ran when they saw me going up to the circle.'

'Their clothes were wet through! They had to come home,' she yelped. Joe cawed again and she could hardly speak fast enough. 'I sent them away when I seen youse.'

'Where are they? Give them here.'

She looked about her as if she thought the devils might come and take her for the fires at once. 'Who, what, Casper?'

'The clothes, woman!'

She scuttled away from the fire, keeping so low she was almost on all fours, and snatched up a couple of shirts and two pairs of breeches from the drying rack and thrust them at him.

Casper turned them slowly in his hands, lifted up the fabric to his face and breathed. Fowler was no better as a laundress than a cook: there were stains on the shirt, fresh on the sleeves.

He felt a touch on his leg, and looked down to see the woman crouching on the flags at his feet. 'Don't hurt him, Casper – not Swithun. Swithun's my only boy. He'll pay you back, he'll do penance.'

The black witch was talking so loud behind his ears he could hardly hear the begging. *Kick her, kick her in the belly, you bastard, while she's there and begging for it.*

'What good has penance ever done you and yours? Time and time over?' He had to shout over the voice of the black witch. The Fowler woman covered her head with her hands.

'He got in a fight with his da at the Pig, then they said they had to go out. He came back unhappy – he didn't mean it! Nothing like this, please Casper, he's my boy, he's my boy! Don't curse him!'

Joe flapped and stamped on Casper's shoulder and the witch shouted and carolled. Casper couldn't take the noise of it any more. He threw the clothes to the floor and walked out the way he came with the crying and pleading shaking the air behind him.

Mr Leathes' home was only a few minutes' stroll from his office and seemed just as neat and pleasant as his place of work. A modern villa of comfortable size set back from the road towards Crosthwaite Church, it had high hedges that defended his garden both from the winds of the valley, and the stares of his neighbours. He ushered them in through the wrought-iron gates, then found himself rather hampered in leading them further by the sudden embraces of two young children who came dashing down the path to meet him.

'Yes, Tom, yes, Sally! I am glad to see you both. Now tell me, is your grandpa out reading in the garden?' Somewhere in the burble of talk, the children confirmed it. 'Thank you! Now away with you and tell your mother to bring us tea in the summerhouse. We have guests here, you little savages.'

The children noticed Harriet and Crowther for the first time and became still. They were sturdy-looking children, both of them, with a high colour in their cheeks and matched straw-coloured hair. 'Go, go,' their father chided them and they turned to race back into the house. Mr Leathes led his guests towards the side of the house where the garden ran long from neat beds into a little sort of wilderness that crouched below the greater wildness of ever-present Skiddaw. There was indeed a summerhouse there, and in it a man sat reading. He was dressed in dark brown and his shock of white hair looked like snow on a mountain top.

Harriet watched as the man looked up at them from his book and raised a hand in greeting, then stood and began to walk towards them. His steps were a little slow perhaps, but Harriet had been expecting a decrepit relic of extreme old age, swaddled in blankets and helpless as an infant. This man looked no more than sixty.

Mr Leathes perhaps noticed her amazement. 'My father is eighty-five, Mrs Westerman. There is something in the air of this valley that preserves those who love it.'

Harriet looked between the faces of the old lawyer and Crowther as they came together. She saw her friend smile as he bowed and watched the old man pause, open his eyes wider, then step forward with renewed vigour and his hand outstretched.

'Charles! My Lord! How many years has it been since I saw you last? You were a young man then. I knew of course that you were at Silverside, but did not know if I'd have the pleasure of meeting you.'

'Mr Leathes, I am sure you know exactly how long it is since I and you last had sight of each other,' Crowther said, and took the lawyer's hand in his own. It was the first time Harriet had seen Crowther show any sign of warmth to those he had known in his youth. Old Mr Leathes chuckled into his neat cravat.

'It is thirty-two years, three months and some odd days, I believe.'

Crowther turned to Harriet. 'Mr Leathes, may I present Harriet Westerman?'

The old man bent over her hand in courtly style then looked at his son. 'Are we to have tea, Mark? So these young people may keep their mouths from drying out while I tell them old stories?' His son nodded. 'Good, good. But first, my dear . . .' old Leathes continued as he drew Harriet's arm under his own, 'let me show you my birds. Lord Keswick must allow me to bore him with my experiments in their rearing and breeding at some other time, but I cannot let you sit down until you have had a chance to tell me how pretty they all are, and hear how charmingly they sing.'

Other men might have found that such an appeal to Harriet's presumed female interests would be met with a cool response, but she had decided to be charmed by the old man so let him guide her steps with pleasure.

The aviary attached to the villa was more extensive than the one at the solicitor's office. It was built out from the side of the house and half-formed of glass, with a number of walls constructed of a thin brass mesh. The floor was a mix of gravel and turf, studded with low bushes and tree branches. It was the sort of construction that Harriet might have expected to see in the grounds of one of the great country houses; to see it here was astonishing. The old man smiled and patted her hand.

'We must all feed our souls as well as our bodies, I believe, Mrs Westerman. I have spent a great deal of money on these little singers in my years, but never regretted a penny of it.' He opened a door to his right and led her into the aviary itself, took corn from his pocket and whistled. A gold and red canary fluttered down from the branches above them and settled on his finger. 'Ah! She is a bold lady, this one. Most of the others are too timid to join me, you see, when there is a stranger by, but this creature's fear is always outweighed by her curiosity.'

Without being quite sure what she expected, or hoped for, Harriet removed the glove from her right hand and lifted it close to where the bird perched on Mr Leathes' finger. It put its head on one side and examined her for a moment, then hopped across onto her finger. She felt its thin claws like pin scratches on her skin; the lowest feathers on its belly brushed her as it puffed itself out and shook itself then trilled at her, holding its beak open as it did so, like an opera singer.

'I think she recognises a fellow spirit, Mrs Westerman,' the lawyer said, then he glanced over his shoulder. 'Ah! My daughter-in-law is bringing out the tea. I must leave my darlings for now. How is Charles?' Harriet started at the question and realised Crowther and Mark Leathes had already turned back towards the summerhouse. Alarmed by her movement, the canary retreated onto one of the perches elsewhere in the aviary.

'I have known him three years, Mr Leathes, yet still do not know how to answer the question.'

The old man laughed very softly. 'Then I may assume he is not much altered.'

'You knew him as a boy, sir?'

'I did, and a strange and lonely child he was. But he would come and watch my birds with me, and when age or disease took one we would open up the body together. Is it not strange, madam, that here are creatures so unlike us, yet they have lungs to sing with, a heart to drive the blood through themselves and a brain much like our own, though what thoughts they have are a mystery. But then I suppose so are the thoughts of our fellow man.'

Mrs Leathes left them, pleading her domestic duties as soon as the tea was poured, and taking care to shepherd her children to a more distant part of the garden for their play, returned to the house. In the brief pause while they watched her cross the lawn, the sound of the canaries filled the air. Harriet had seldom heard such a range of song since her time in the Indies. Indeed, the weather reminded her of those regions as well as the birds, since the air was as close as ever, with the sun like a pewter disk through the haze.

Old Mr Leathes looked between Harriet and Crowther, and having taken a mouthful of tea, produced a long clay pipe from his pocket and began to fill it from his tobacco pouch.

'Perhaps it is the lawyer in me,' he said as he did so, 'but I think you have come to make me talk about the past rather than hear about my birds. Now I have heard singing in the village about this body found on Saint Herbert's Island. Do I assume too much in thinking your visit here is connected?'

'You are correct, sir,' Crowther replied.

'Then with Mrs Westerman's permission, I shall light my pipe,' Leathes said, settling into his chair, 'for you shall make me talk, and I talk better with a smoke to cool my lungs.'

Mrs Westerman's permission was given and the pipe lit. Harriet could not help noticing the way that old Leathes gave his attention to them, quietly and with the air of a man prepared to wait them out. He wondered if Crowther realised how much he had benefited from his acquaintance with the lawyer.

'I believe my father may have murdered the man we found on Saint Herbert's Island. I do not know why he might have done so – though we suspect the murdered man might have set the fire at Gutherscale Hall in forty-five. Why he then chose to visit my father the following day is a mystery.' Old Mr Leathes merely raised his eyebrows and waited for Crowther to continue. His son coughed into his cup, but following his father's lead, said nothing. 'I was wondering, sir, if you can remember anything of my father's concerns in the forties that might guide us.'

The old man smiled slowly. 'You have not lost your habit of plain speaking, Charles.' His voice was kind. 'Have you been as frank with your sister?'

Crowther frowned at his cuffs. 'To a degree. She misunderstood my meaning, however, and only stated that our father had no part in the death of Rupert de Beaufoy. It is possible my father discovered de Beaufoy's location from the man he killed, then made use of that information.'

The lawyer nodded and sighed. 'Charles, as you know, I was your father's adviser in legal matters for many years, but I never believed I was in his confidence. What your sister meant by that remark I cannot say with any certainty, but I suspect you wish me to speculate.'

'I do.'

'Your father was elevated from baronet to baron in forty-seven. De Beaufoy's location was betrayed to the government in forty-five.'

Harriet spoke. 'Do you think it was Sir William who gave them the information that led to de Beaufoy's arrest, Mr Leathes? And the title was his reward?'

'I cannot say, Mrs Westerman. It was rumoured de Beaufoy was betrayed by one of his servants. There was an interval, which would have been only proper, but remember also that Sir William had been growing in importance and stature in the area for many years by that point. After Greta's lands were forfeited to the Crown in 1716, Sir William purchased a number of parcels of land from the government. He managed his business affairs well, and was already a rich man by the forty-five Rebellion. He was proud of the fact, and I am sure he had been campaigning for recognition well before then. His elevation was a reward indeed, but it might have been for his influence in this part of the country and his loyalty to the government of the time, rather than a direct result of a simple piece of treachery.'

Harriet glanced at Crowther, but he seemed unwilling to speak and kept his eyes on his cuffs. She felt the burden of the questioning pass to her as clearly as if Crowther had spoken out loud. 'Sir William did not arrive here a rich man, did he, Mr Leathes? Was there some moment where his fortunes began to improve?'

Leathes nodded. 'I see, Mrs Westerman, why your alliance with Charles has proved useful to you both. Yes, there was. It was in the spring of 1718. Sir William came to see me, to ask me to assist in the purchase of a parcel of land that belonged to the Crown on the western shore. I remember he arrived in the middle of a rainstorm and asked to speak to my father, William, but finding him engaged was content to speak to me. Remember, we were both young men at that time. I think he had found my father a little precise, a little slow in his manner of conducting business. I was keen to prove myself in the practice and in the area as a coming man, so was glad of the chance to do well, whatever piece of business he might have in mind. He paced my floor with his coat dripping – I can see him as clearly as I do you young people now. I could swear there was such energy and urgency radiating from him, he seemed almost to steam in front of me. He told me he had hopes of mineral deposits untapped on the land he hoped to buy, and was ready to stretch his resources to the limits in order to exploit them. He asked me to find the price and see what the likelihood of the purchase was.'

'And so you did?' Harriet asked.

'I did, and quickly enough to earn his praise, impatient as he was. Though when I gave him the news he was not pleased.'

'Why?'

The lawyer shrugged and devoted a moment or two to his pipe before replying, 'He could not afford it. He had calculated what money he could raise and found that his resources were still not sufficient. He might be able, by extending himself and borrowing whatever money he could lay his hands on, to buy the land, but he would need more capital to mine there. There was no room to negotiate the price down any further. The figure given to me was already generously low.'

'Why did he not take a partner, then?' Harriet asked.

The old lawyer's eyes flicked up towards Crowther and it was his dry voice that replied.

'My father would never have become involved in such an enterprise, if he did not have complete control.'

The lawyer nodded his agreement. 'He would not. I went up to Silverside – it was hardly more than a cottage in those days – to give him the news the moment the express arrived from London. His frustration was extreme. He strode about in front of the fire as I spoke, and as he heard the price he kicked the logs in the fire so hard the sparks showered all around us. It was lucky the floors were stone, or Silverside might have found itself such a ruin as the old palace of the Gretas appears now.'

Harriet found herself confused. 'But you told us, sir, that this period marked the beginning of the *improvement* in Sir William's fortunes?'

'So I did. Three days later, having left the Hall thinking the business lost entirely, I was visited by Ruben Grace with a letter from his master telling me to proceed with the purchase and a banker's draft, drawn on a private bank in Cockermouth, for the total sum. I helped with the documentation necessary to mortgage what property he then held in order to fund the works, but that was a simple task once the land itself was purchased. The mine proved fruitful and laid the foundation of the fortune that Sir William then accrued in land and other speculations for the next thirty years.'

'How did he come by such a large amount of money?'

'Mrs Westerman, I cannot say. Perhaps if he himself had visited my offices with the banker's draft I would have asked him. As it was Ruben who came with my instructions, I did not. I can add only two things that might interest you. Firstly, I thought Ruben did not like his task. He and I knew each other from childhood in a passing sort of way, and I thought he looked . . . angry. Secondly, I dined with the manager of that bank some months later, and he mentioned to me – I am afraid he was rather in his cups – that he had never seen such a pile of greasy banknotes as were deposited in his hands by Sir William the day he began banking with them and asked for the draft to be prepared.'

'Who were the bankers?'
'The same as your own, Charles. Botts in Cockermouth.'

IV.3

WHEN CASPER FOUND himself again, he was on the high ground. Below him, Great Wood tumbled down towards the lake, and off to the south he could see the narrowing and folding of Borrowdale. He rolled his shoulders and hissed as his bruises stung him. Only when he opened his eyes a second time did he notice Stephen sitting on the thin turf a little way away from him playing with Joe. They seemed to have made themselves some game together. Stephen would place a few stones, one atop the other, then Joe would knock them flat again and caw.

Stephen looked round and smiled, a little nervously.

'How long you been there, youngling?' Casper said at last. Sounded like the black witch had shouted herself hoarse. There was no sign of her voice in his mind.

'A while,' the boy replied with a shrug. 'I could not find you at your cabin, so went to see the museum and saw you passing. Then I followed you. Mr Sturgess almost saw you in the Square, but someone ran up to him and started telling him you had gone to Rosthwaite.'

Casper considered the earth in front of him. The black witch had her ways of tricking and fighting with him. Times were, she would get to yelling so hard that he could not say where or what he was for a time. Not often. But it happened.

'And you followed me all this way?'

'You go *very* fast! But you did not seem well, so I thought I might . . .'

'How do I seem now, Master Stephen?'

'Better.'

Casper lay back on the heather for a moment and looked up into the heat and haze. 'There is a girl lost somewhere in these hills. She isn't at home with her people, which means she's either dead or she's trapped. If dead, I must carry her home. If breathing, then she must be found before hunger or thirst take her. She's smart and she's strong, but that's not always enough.'

'You like her, don't you, Mr Casper? Mr Askew told me she is thought of as your apprentice. Are you going to teach her about bogles, and witches, and how to fight them?'

'I might at that.' He had never thought of it so clearly before, but the girl did have a power, and someone had to take on the job when he died. The thought pleased him before his mind caught the tone of the question.

'Lad, my learning is not for you. We cannot choose the world and ways into which we are born. You are gentry. I'll take your help now and thank you for it, but this is not your calling. It might be Agnes's though, if we can find her.' Stephen still looked miserable. 'A mouse might wish to be a king, and times are, I reckon, when a king might wish himself a mouse. But there's that and there's the other, and there's done.'

'Where might she be?' Stephen said with a sigh. Joe cawed at him, and he began piling the stones for him again.

Casper hugged his knees to his chest. 'I know one place she isn't – that's in the old mine where someone had tried to drop that German fella.'

'Austrian,' Stephen said automatically.

'The flowers leave a powerful trace, and there was no scent of it on that bugger Swithun's clothes. I think she might be in one of the old deep places though.'

'Why?'

Casper shrugged. 'There was tang. Deep earth, not the stuff that is still filled with growing and dying, but old. Has a tang on it.'

'Shouldn't we get help, Casper? Mr Crowther said there are lots of old mines here. If lots of people were looking . . .'

He shook his head and sucked his teeth. 'If she lives, they might kill her and bury her more deeply if they know I'm looking. Let them think I'm running from Sturgess and thinking only of revenge for my own beating. That might give us time enough, and mean they leave her where she lies.' He frowned and looked hard at Stephen. 'You remember what that lad looks like?'

'From Portinscale? Yes, naturally.'

'Naturally, is it? Good enough. You ever see him, you keep back. But watch where he goes. He's keeping away, but he's not got the sense to go far, and their job on me is undone.'

'What were they looking for, Casper?'

'Something precious, and they've come close. Something I reckon might need shifting somewhere a little safer. Come on then, mickle kingling. Might be best if you go back to Silverside now and play at being a good lad. I have a mind to get you to do some serious business for me tonight, and the more polished and polite you are today, the easier it will be to get done. We'll talk on the way, then I must start searching every hole in these hills.'

⊷————⊶

Cockermouth was a proud little town, and Mr White was a proud little man. He attended the lectures in the public rooms whenever they were given, nodded his way through them and felt much wiser at their close, though he rarely remembered much of the argument presented. He could also be counted on to attend any of the public concerts held, in his emerald coat and a cravat he had learned to tie from a series of illustrations. He liked to be thought of as a man of fashion. When the musicians pleased him particularly, he was glad to say it was almost as good as London, which earned him respectful echoing from his neighbours. He himself had never been to London, but the most illustrious client of his firm, whose name he was always glad to bring into the most mundane of conversations, was there for some part of every season. He had once heard that gentleman say that such and such a player had a technique almost equal to the musicians in the capital, and this became Mr White's benchmark.

Mr White had hopes, he had expectations. His senior partner, Mr Hudson, had become rather broken down in the last few years since his son had been killed while off soldiering. Mr White was quite sure that in a few years more, he would have the firm's business to himself. He would then marry. He remembered that Miss Hodgekinson had admired the cravat and coat on several occasions. A woman of taste. He would improve his house – he had an eye on the sort of establishment he would like. It was at the bottom of the main street and occupied by Sir Lowther's law agent, whom he thought of as a model. It spoke of prosperity and propriety and was full of healthy-looking children. In such conjectures was Mr White employed while his senior partner and his clerk were about their own business in the town when he heard the street door open, and still smiling with thoughts of his future and the general neatness of it all, he left his office to see who had need of him.

It was a stranger. A woman, and alone. Mr White was surprised, and that surprise only deepened as he took in the details of the woman's dress and demeanour. Her riding habit suggested a gentlewoman of some means, yet the skirt was so filthy with the dust of the road one might have thought she had covered ten miles, and at speed. Her face was flushed and strands of her red hair that appeared from under her riding hat appeared to be dampened to her face with sweat. It was alarming. Ladies should always appear cool, fresh, and take trouble to remain so. Miss Hodgekinson would rather die than appear alone, in the offices of a professional man in such a state. The woman had a copy of the *Westmorland Paquet* in her hand. Mr White had an awful presentiment. Perhaps she was one of these women who had so badly mismanaged her domestic situation she had been forced to flee her husband. Or one of those foolish creatures who, ignoring the wishes of her family and friends, had fallen victim to an adventurer. He began to prepare himself to be avuncular, kind but firm. If she had climbed into her marital bed lawfully, the law said she must stay there. He raised his eyebrows, hoping she would not add to her state of dishevelment by weeping.

'Good afternoon,' the woman said, her voice quite strong, but pleasant. 'Are you Mr Hudson? If so, I would be most grateful for a moment of your time.'

'Mr Hudson is away from the office this afternoon . . . madam. I am his partner here. My name is White – and you are?'

'How unfortunate,' the woman said, putting a hand to her damp forehead. Mr White felt a vague frisson of alarm. 'Perhaps you will be able to assist me. My name is Westerman. I wished to speak to Mr Hudson about this advertisement.' She held out the newspaper and Mr White took it from her a little gingerly. 'May I sit down a moment, sir? I have had a long ride, and this heat makes what is usually a pleasure a trial.'

Mr White bowed, which she obviously took as assent, as she dropped onto one of the chairs and began to fan herself with the back of her hand. He looked at the advertisement. He had been told that it had been placed, but in truth he knew little of the matter, only that it was bound up with The Most Illustrious Client, and beyond that Mr Hudson had kept the business very close, and responded not at all to his most studiedly casual questions. It had been an annoyance which he had put from his mind, and now this woman thrust it under his nose again.

'Where have you ridden from, Mrs Westerman?'

'Keswick.'

Twelve miles in the heat of the day. Perhaps the woman was deranged.

'Alone?' He did not try very hard to keep the shock out of his voice.

She shook her head. 'No. Mr Crowther and I rode together – perhaps I should name him Lord Keswick. Most people seem to here, though he does not care to make use of the title. He has other business in town. Can you tell me anything of this matter, sir? I ask because the gentleman mentioned in the advertisement was found murdered yesterday morning.'

There was a click and whirr in Mr White's head and the

realisation struck him like a long-case clock marking the hour. This woman was Mrs Harriet Westerman, whose involvement in matters of murder had made her the subject of great spilling of ink. Miss Hodgekinson had remarked, with her eyes downcast and a pleasing shudder, that the thought of a woman taking an active role in the investigations of such crimes horrified her. He had agreed. He remembered that her husband had been a Naval man. No doubt the sun of the tropics had turned her head, but had she really no family to take her under proper control? He began to think of what Miss Hodgekinson would say when she learned that this woman – he could not really think of her as a lady – had presented herself in his office in such a state and talking of murder. She would find it fascinating.

'Mr White?'

He was startled to find that Mrs Westerman was examining him with those green eyes, her head on one side, and he was disturbed to see something like amusement in her expression. He returned the paper to her and drew himself as tall as he could – not far, nature is cruel – and put his thumbs into his waistcoat.

'I could not possibly give you any information on the subject, Mrs Westerman. These are confidential matters . . .' Harriet began to protest, but he put up his hand. 'Confidential affairs that concern a client of ours, a most illustrious client.' He smiled down at her, soothingly. One could be kind. 'I am certain that those affairs can have no bearing on any unfortunate accident met with by Mr Wurst.'

Mrs Westerman studied him for a moment, then stood up sharply. Mr White found he was now forced to look up a little, rather than down. His smile disappeared.

'Hurst, Mr White, Hurst. And it was no accident. Very well. Perhaps you would be so kind as to tell your partner of my visit. I am staying at Silverside Hall.' Mr White had been pleased to exchange 'Good days' with Mrs Briggs on several occasions. What could that good woman be thinking, to have such a creature in her home? 'At least then Mr Hudson and your client will be aware that any further advertisements will be as unsuccessful as this one.' She turned on her heel and was gone, taking the dust and blood with her.

IV.4

AGNES COULD NOT say if she slept or woke. She had found enough of a nail coming through the wood to pick apart the rope on her wrists, though when she did, the flood of pain and cramp in her hands had been so bad, she almost wished she had left them tied. Even with them free she could make no impression on the barricade. She had found a piece of slate in the gloom and had tried to drive the new nails back out, but they had only bent over. She pulled at every join and seam, and filled her palms with vicious little splinters; she screamed herself hoarse and heard nothing but faint bird calls and the turnings of the wind in reply. At last she had crawled back down the tunnel to collect her blanket and bottle, and returned with them to the barricade to make her camp there. She wanted nothing more than to drain the water that was left, but when she shook the bottle next to her ear, it sounded like there was little enough. She was hungry, it gnawed at her. So for a little while she let herself have a cry, and let that turn into a sort of sleep and dreaming.

A footstep, now she was awake. She threw herself against the barricade and drummed on it with her fists and shouted. Silence, then a voice.

'Agnes?'

'Swithun! You dog! You son of a bitch, you let me out of here, right now! Right this minute! I'm going to pull out your eyeballs and feed them to your pig, you bastard.'

'Shush now, Agnes. Don't take on so. You ain't dead, are you?'

'Much thanks to you! You let me out!'

'If you don't hush up, girl, I'm just going to go away again. Now quiet.'

Agnes bit her lip and for a while everything went silent. She felt herself begin to tremble. The idea that he might have just gone again was more horrible than her anger.

'Swithun?' She heard his feet shifting outside, and the sounds of him sitting down. It seemed as if he was leaning against the barricade.

'It weren't my idea, Agnes. I never meant you harm, though you've never been nice to me.'

She sighed and sat down on the earth floor, leaning against the wooden planks herself. There was light and home and air on the other side, where he was looking and sounding all pitying of himself. In front of her only damp and dark. 'Why should I be? I know you are like your da. Nothing but nasty from you every day I've known you. Folks are looking for me, Swithun. They'll find me, too – then if you think people hated you and yours before . . .'

He was quiet a while. 'They are looking in the wrong place.

You normally do your wanderings down into Borrowdale, along that shore – everyone knows that.' It was true. The thought of her father and friends walking her roads, fearing for her, made her eyes hot. She was working so hard on not crying at the thought that she hardly heard him say, 'Good that they are. You'd be dead, otherwise.'

'What's your meaning, Swithun?' She heard a rattle; he was picking up pebbles and throwing them at the wall.

'Me and my da have a thing to do, and when we're done we are going to be rich. Soon as we have the money we'll be out of this stinking hole and away. When we're clear we'll send word where you are. That was my idea. He just wanted me and Da to kill you dead, and he said if anyone came sniffing round here before it's done, I'm to hit you over the head with a rock.'

She scrambled up onto her knees and tried to look through the chink between the boards behind her. 'Who said, Swithun? What you playing at?'

'Never you mind.'

'Was it your da you were with? Beating on Casper?' Silence. 'Did you kill him?'

The answer came quick. 'No, no. He's powerful angry though. But Sturgess is chasing him for killing that German fella, so he's gone away.'

'What German?'

Silence. Then, 'Laker's been killed. His girl's at the vicarage. She's pretty, not as pretty as you though, Agnes.'

'Was that your work?'

He sounded shocked when he replied. 'No! I'd never! No business of ours. Maybe Casper did for him. I saw him out walking with the daughter. Maybe he's going to marry her and go off and be a gentleman.' He sniggered. 'Your da said he's going to that witch woman in Rosthwaite for a finding spell, as Casper's gone. Though everyone knows she's half daft. Casper didn't go before he scared my ma to death though.'

'That's no hardship,' she said bitterly. 'Your ma's a bully and coward just like you are, and your dad.' She heard the noise of him scrambling to his feet again.

'Don't be like that, Agnes! Didn't mean you any harm! What you have to come charging in for anyway? I told you he said to us to stove your head in. It was only because we told him you were Casper's 'prentice he let you live. Then he said to put you in here and seal it up. Said he might have a use for you. Said we'd be able to send word when we were paid, and I will, Agnes. I promise. I like you.' His voice had become wheedling and soft.

'Who?' Agnes felt a little sick; she'd sensed his eyes follow her enough times, and just the touch of them was enough to make her skin crawl. 'Who you talking about, Swithun? And why did you say I'm Casper's apprentice when I'm no such thing?'

'Not saying, Agnes. Won't say. He'd do for me.' She felt his thin weaselly body lean on the wood. 'Casper's been standing over your shoulder since you were born. He knows you are a witch at heart. Everyone knows it too 'cept you. You magic men towards you, and curse them if they turn away.' She heard him shuffle round, and when he spoke again his voice was so close she knew it was only the thickness of the wood between them. 'When he comes, Agnes, tell him something useful. Tell him where it is. We couldn't find it at the Black Pig. He's worried Casper's given it to someone to keep. Thinks maybe as you're his apprentice, you'll know. Tell him something, Agnes. Or he'll kill you. He needs it. He wants it, then he'll pay us and be gone again.' Agnes felt the blood dancing in her brain. 'I know you haven't got it.' His voice became soft. 'Da let me make sure of that myself, while you were sleeping.'

Agnes tasted her empty stomach in her mouth, gritted her teeth, then turned again and put her back to the gate. 'I'm hungry, Swithun. Real hungry and my water's almost gone.'

'I'm not supposed to give you owt. So that when he comes you'll be wanting to talk. My da would kill me himself if he knew I was here.'

She swallowed and tried to speak slowly. 'Maybe you are brave then, Swithun. Just some water and a crumb – I won't tell. Honest. You've brought me something, haven't you? I know it.' She waited in the dark, trying to hear him breathe over the sound of her own heart.

'All right then, where's your bottle?'

She pulled it to her. 'Here, you'll just have to open the barricade a little. I shan't run.'

He laughed. 'I'm not that stupid. There's a little bit comes away here. I'll open that and you pass it out.'

She heard him scramble up and the sound of a nail being pulled, then a little bit of wood a foot or so long and halfway up the barrier came free and light tumbled in. Still faint though, so the barricade must be set back a fair way from the entrance. There must have been a gap in the old barn door they'd used to block the tunnel, and another plank had been tacked on as a patch. 'Come on then.'

Half-stupid, she passed up the bottle. His hand grabbed it away from her. There was a moment of silence, then something was tossed through the gap and landed at her side. She didn't move, then heard the sound of liquid being poured from one vessel to another.

'Fill it right up, Swithun. And stopper it tight, won't you? My hands are tied and if I drop it and it spills, I shall go mad with it.'

'Wisht, will you? I have.' She heard the top go in. 'You ready?'

She was. The moment his hand appeared, she grabbed hold of his wrist with both her hands and pulled with all her strength. He yelled and she felt his body slam into the barricade.

'Let me go, you bitch!'

'I wasn't sleeping! Knocking me senseless is the only way you'd touch me, dog.'

It must be hurting him. He was whining and struggling. She carried on pulling down as hard as she could. She aimed the flint she had palmed in one hand and ran it hard as she could down the length of his arm. He screamed like a rabbit in a snare. He gave a vicious wrench back and she stumbled; the arm writhed between her hands and her shoulder slammed against the barricade. She heard the cloth of his shirt rip and her grip fumbled. His other hand scrambled through the gap, she felt him grab a fistful of her hair and he pulled on it hard. Her head was yanked back, making her scream, and she lost her hold. The arm was out of the hole quicker than a snake heads under a rock. She fell to her knees, panting.

'You bitch! You hurt me! What did you want to do that for?' She closed her eyes in the darkness. 'I don't care if you rot. No one's going to find you. I'll never send word now. You're dead, you little witch.'

Her voice came from somewhere low within her. 'I'd rather rot than have any cause to thank you, Swithun Fowler, but before I die I'm going to curse you and your da with the worst words I know. You're as dead as I am. You just don't know it yet.'

She heard him get to his feet and his sudden gasp. She had scared him. 'Witch! Agnes Kerrick, all very fine and your daddy with his little farm. All very neat and nice, aren't you? But you're just a dirty stinking witch.' His voice sounded as if he was crying a bit as he finished. Good – let him cry! Then she heard his feet running back out towards the light.

She stayed where she was for a moment, then with a groan began to feel around the floor beside her. Her fingers touched the bread first. She tucked it under an arm, then crawled round again, her fingers shaking and sore, till she found the bottle. Stoppered. Full. She turned her back to the barricade again and tried to calm herself a little before taking her first bite of the bread, but still when she tore off the first mouthful and brought it to her lips her hand was shaking so hard she could hardly place it in her mouth. She had plenty enough to think on now.

IV.5

WHEN CROWTHER SAW Harriet enter the private parlour above the coaching inn in Cockermouth where the horses and their riders were to be refreshed for the ride home, he was nothing but angry. His visit to the bankers in Cockermouth had been a farce. There were no ancient clerks conveniently available to recall his father's depositing money there over sixty years previously. The banker who had remarked on the greasy notes to Mr Leathes was long dead, and had taken his speculations with him. Crowther had been embarrassed by the banker's combination of deference and confusion. The money could have come from anywhere, and he had wasted the better part of the day pursuing it. For this, he blamed Harriet. He would have written and then at least have been spared those curious looks and reasonable, but unanswerable questions, but Mrs Westerman had the bit between her teeth. He did not understand how he allowed her to sweep him away in these cases, against all judgement and his own self-interest.

The only advantage that this absence from Keswick offered was the opportunity it gave his nephew to flee. What matter his arrows were clean? No stranger or common footpad would have been able to come close enough to Mr Hurst to strike the blow. Could it have been fired from a distance? Possibly, but Mr Hurst would have had to contort himself considerably for an arrow to pierce him at such an angle if fired from a bow. Crowther shook his head. He had almost allowed himself to believe Felix's protestations of innocence. He suspected he had had some romantic notion that by saving this boy he might make amends for failing Adair. He had always been suspicious of such ideas, and once more felt he was right to be so. For the most part he had observed that men killed their friends and their families first. Mr Hurst had only one old acquaintance in town – Felix – ergo Felix had most likely killed him.

Crowther paused for a moment and examined the air above him, considering Miss Hurst. The daughter obviously had reasons to hate her father. Suppose the wound had been caused by a crochet hook or something like it? His brow furrowed again. It would have been narrower, and even if she had had the good fortune and strength to kill him, there was no possible way she could drag his body into a mine entrance and cover it with a rockpile.

Instead of ameliorating his guilt, he had simply added to it. He had allowed an innocent man to hang thirty years ago, and now he was encouraging a guilty man to go free. He was adding further gothic horrors to his own history, and had found that his only memento of his father was a murder weapon; he had failed to identify the corpse in the tomb, and to complete matters had made himself ridiculous in front of his bankers. Now here came Mrs Westerman. She had made no apparent effort to tidy her appearance, and despite announcing her visit to the solicitors to have been entirely wasted, had the sheer effrontery to look as if she had just produced a winning lottery ticket from her cuff.

As if she could hear the thoughts running in his head, she reached into her pocket and brought something out from it, her fist closed.

'I wonder if you can guess what I have here?' Either she had failed to sense his mood entirely, or, more likely, it was simply unimportant to her. He looked up at her from his seat by the window.

'I fear you mistake me for one of your children, Mrs Westerman.' She gave a small sigh and opened her hand. He looked. 'A pocket watch.'

'Yes,' she said, sweeping out her skirts as she settled into the other arch of the windowseat. 'I saw it in a shop window as I returned from that appalling little solicitor, and it has lightened my mood considerably.'

Crowther turned away to glower at the cobbles outside. A small boy looked up at him from the yard, and seeing his expression retreated further into his mother's skirts.

'I am delighted that this town has provided you with an opportunity to spend your pin money. The day has not been wasted, then.'

There was a long pause, and it was with a creeping sense of uneasiness that Crowther turned to face Mrs Westerman again.

'This, my lord, is your nephew's watch.'

'I don't understand you,' Crowther replied, but his tone was rather more careful.

'Perhaps not, Crowther, but if you can resist frightening any more of the children of the town for a moment, I will explain to you.' He waited, and after a pause she continued in slightly less clipped tones. 'As I say, I noticed it, recognised it and asked to speak to the owner of the shop. I then told him, a little tearfully, that it was my late father's and my brother had sold it to cover a gaming debt and begged him to let me purchase it again.'

'He actually believed you to be Felix's sister?' Crowther then came as near to biting his tongue at this point as he had in the last thirty years.

'Yes. He was most sympathetic,' she replied neatly. 'He suggested a price, I was shocked and said my brother had told me he had got only thirty shillings for it. He was sorry to see

329

me so deceived by this wicked youth, and fetched his account book to show me that the price Felix received for the watch was three pounds and ten shillings. I paid three pounds twelve shillings with a trembling hand, hoping my husband would not blame me for the expense, and we parted with mutual expressions of regard.'

'Mr Leathes already told us that Felix wanted to sell his watch,' Crowther said a little sulkily, then the significance of the amount came to him and he continued, 'My apologies, Mrs Westerman. Three pounds and ten shillings. Mr Hurst had three pounds and fifteen shillings on his person.'

She smiled. 'Indeed, the sums are too alike. And why would Felix give every penny he had over to Mr Hurst and then kill him? Even if he were driven to it, he would not leave his last coins on the corpse. If there was time to conceal the body, there would have been plenty to search it. Also consider this, Crowther. Mr Hurst obviously had no time to spend the money and, given his landlord was pressing him to settle his account, we must assume that he was murdered shortly after he received it. Though I cannot like him greatly, I do not think your nephew a murderer. You may escape assassination yet.' She paused and swung the watch from side to side. 'At least, I think it less likely you will be killed for your money. Your manners will always leave you in some danger.' Then, before he could speak: 'I do suspect Felix may have been the last person other than his killer to see Mr Hurst alive though. We shall talk to him this evening. At least we know he has not the blunt to eat anywhere other than at Silverside Hall.'

Harriet had been enjoying herself watching the glint of the silver watchcase and was now ready to receive Crowther's congratulations. He was silent and she looked up. To her surprise he was bent forward with his head low, supporting his forehead with his hand. She reached across the space between them and placed her hand on his shoulder.

'Crowther?'

He reached up his own hand, keeping his head hanging forward and she felt his fingers brush brief and dry on her own.

'Thank you, Mrs Westerman.' He sighed and straightened his back, then passed his hand over his eyes. 'I am most impressed by your ability to recognise the watch. I did not observe it.'

Harriet felt a blush warm her cheeks. 'I was considering a watch as a present to Daniel Clode to mark his engagement to Rachel, and I noticed Felix's the day we arrived, as I thought it might be just the thing Clode would like.'

The dinner-hour was long passed when they returned to Silverside. Harriet could only comfort herself she had sent word before leaving for Cockermouth that they would not join the rest of the party that evening. Felix was not in the house. The Vizegräfin informed them that her son had decided to experience the delights of the waterfalls at Lodore at dusk. Crowther retired to the old brewery and disappointed, Harriet made for the comfort of her private sitting room.

On her way upstairs she entered her son's rooms and found him and Mr Quince going over his Greek translation. Mr Quince still looked unwell but he was, Harriet thought, showing signs of recovery. The fact that he felt himself equal to instructing her son must demonstrate it. Mr Quince smiled, and told her that Stephen had been a delightful companion to him all afternoon, and Harriet closed the door on them wishing them a good night. She was not certain if she was pleased her son had chosen to stay close to home, as she was sure she should be, or slightly disappointed that he had not spent the whole day ranging over the hills with Casper, searching for the missing Agnes. She pushed open the door to her room wondering if it showed a lack of spirit on Stephen's part, and condemned herself for the thought.

She took a seat at her desk to start a letter to her sister and, having made her pen and twisted her mourning ring, began by asking Rachel for news of her daughter. She wondered if little Anne were sleeping peacefully in the nursery at Thornleigh Hall. To think of her youngest child was like pressing on some fresh bruise in her side. She thought of the look of fierce concentration her daughter so often had as she dreamed, the way her small hands became fists. What sort of mother might *she* make? What sort of wife, what manner of sister to the gentle boy bent over his Greek a little way along the corridor?

Harriet bit her lip. She could not unmake herself, and she could not regret that she had lived a life out of the normal pattern, but she feared what Anne and she might make of each other as the child grew. Harriet was afraid her daughter would become a stranger to her if she lived a conventional existence as a respectable wife and mother, but if she followed Harriet's path she would risk the censure of society and make herself as vulnerable to harm as an adult as she was now as an infant. Harriet would be forced to watch that happen, and blame herself.

Some hour or so later, Mrs Briggs came to join her in her

rooms. Harriet had been trying to write to her sister words that were honest, but that would not alarm or enrage Rachel unduly. She found herself concentrating on giving an account of their speculations as to the history of Crowther's father, but the whole was still so confused she more than once dropped her pen mid-sentence and folded her arms. The interruption was welcome therefore, but seeing Mrs Briggs's face at her door made Harriet realise she had once again deserted the poor woman to the Vizegräfin. Her mind was already full of guilty whisperings about her behaviour and fitness as a mother as she wrote to Rachel, so Harriet felt herself in a holly-patch of discomforting emotions. She was very glad then, to see no sign of reproach on the face of her hostess.

'Mrs Westerman, am I interrupting you?'

Harriet smiled. 'You are, and I thank you most sincerely for it. Please, come and talk to me for a while if the household can spare you.'

Mrs Briggs bustled in and took a seat near the desk, looking pleased. 'Oh I am glad! I have come to escape the card table. I believe the Vizegräfin could play picquet for ten hours in every day. If only she would pick up a book from time to time, it would improve her fortunes and her temperament, I am sure. I was forced to claim a headache, which would make Mr Briggs laugh, for he knows I have hardly had one since he married me. I all but fled my own house this morning to escape her requests for a game.'

'She does not play well, then, Mrs Briggs?'

'She does not! I can hardly think she and Mr Crowther are of the same blood at times – he so controlled and she so high-handed in her play. And did you hear that Mr Askew called on you this afternoon? He wishes to see you as soon as he might.'

Harriet nodded. 'We received his note. I fear I am too exhausted by our ride to pay an evening visit, but we shall call on him in the morning. He probably wishes to renew his requests to Crowther to give a talk on the atmosphere. It does continue so close.'

'So it does! And now with all these disturbances and strange storms, the people around us grow most uneasy. If ever there was to be a revolution in England, now is the time. One good preacher and I believe they would throw us all in the lake to quiet the old gods. And Casper having to hide from Mr Sturgess means he is not there to steady them. The vicar and his daughter do what they can . . . Have you heard of this girl going missing, and the Fowlers? You can feel the unease all over town. Everyone is looking about themselves and wondering.'

Harriet picked up her pen and turned the quill between her fingers. 'The girl I have heard something of; I saw Casper by the lake this morning and he mentioned it. I know nothing more of her than her name, however – and who are the Fowlers?'

'You saw Casper, Mrs Westerman? Now, why am I thinking that perhaps you have not found a moment to mention that to Mr Sturgess?' Harriet could hear the smile in the woman's voice and felt herself colouring a little so she continued to study the transparent body of her pen as she replied.

'Miss Scales thinks that Mr Sturgess is very quick to judge. She seems to believe that Mr Sturgess resents the fact that the people here are as likely to consult a cunning-man in their disputes as the magistrate.'

'Mr Sturgess has been a most pleasant neighbour, and it is

a shame this business keeps him from playing cards with the Vizegräfin. I am a great believer in Miss Scales's judgement, however,' Mrs Briggs said carefully. Harriet wished she had learned to weigh her words so well.

She stood and crossed to the empty fireplace, suddenly tired of her seat. 'You mentioned the name Fowler?'

Mrs Briggs turned towards her and nodded. 'Yes, father and son. It is said they have stopped sleeping in their own beds.'

'That must be who Casper suspects of beating him and searching the Black Pig. He would not give me their names this morning.'

'He had his reasons, I'm sure. But the matter of this girl troubles me greatly. She is a sharp young thing; her family are good friends of Casper.'

'How old is she?' Harriet asked.

'Sixteen, I think.'

Harriet was examining a painting above the fireplace. It showed a reworking of the scenery that surrounded them. In the foreground grazed a pair of the long-horned cattle the local people favoured, observed by a couple in peasant dress lolling on the grass. They were facing the painter rather than the picturesque landscape behind them.

'Might she not have run away with the younger Fowler?'

Mrs Briggs laughed. 'I doubt that! I know the young can develop some unfortunate attachments, but Agnes is a smart girl and Swithun and his father are a nasty pair. I've tried to offer them the means to support themselves in the past, but always they reward us with complaints and petty thievery . . .' Her voice tailed off.

Harriet was trying to work out the geography of the painting in front of her; if the small island in the middle distance was in fact the Island of Bones . . . She was suddenly aware that Mrs Briggs was getting to her feet.

'I shall leave you to your letter, Mrs Westerman. Do ring if you require anything, and Miriam will look after you.'

Harriet was expecting to have a longer conversation with Mrs Briggs, but the little woman seemed to have been invigorated with some new purpose and bustled out of the room with great energy. Harriet wished her good evening, wondered for a moment, then turned back to her letter with a sigh.

When Agnes heard the sound of footsteps in the tunnel beyond the barricade again she was feeling stronger. Her scalp was still sore where Swithun had pulled her head back, her shoulder was bruised and aching and her hands stung and complained whenever she moved them, but she had eaten bread enough to stop the pain in her belly and had water, though she would pay any price she could think of for a bucket to wash her face and her scrapes in. There were two beings outside: she could hear voices; one sounded like Isaac Fowler, Swithun's father. The other was much lower, whispering, and she could make out none of the words. Fowler sounded as if he was apologising for something. No doubt they saw the gap in the boards and guessed that Swithun had visited her.

'Put your arm out through the gap. We know your hands are free.' Fowler's voice.

'Why should I?' There was a pause, whispering.

'Because if you don't we will open the barricade and kill you.' His voice sounded uncomfortable and strange.

'Who you playing parrot to, Fowler?'

'Never you mind. Just do as you're told, girly.' Those words were his own. 'You won't get past us. It's too narrow, if that's what you're thinking. He's counting! Do it now, Agnes. He'll kill you soon as spit.'

She hesitated, but there was just enough panic in the man's voice to make her believe him, so she stuck one hand through and felt at once a rough hand grip her round the wrist and pull her up against the barricade. He was pulling hard enough on her arm to bring the side of her face to the wood, her cheek pressed to the gap, but she could see nothing but shadows. Something pointed and metal touched her face and she heard a creaking stretch. She gritted her teeth.

'He wants to know where it is. Who is guarding it now?'

'Why should I say? You'll just kill me anyway.'

Fowler answered quickly. 'No, Agnes. He's said he shan't.' One of his hands was still pulling hard on her wrist, but she felt, strangely, the touch of his other hand on her upper arm. He was patting her. The strange metal point traced the line of her cheekbone. She could feel it now at the corner of her eye.

'Why does he want it? It's ours.'

The patting on her arm increased and she heard that stretching noise again. 'He says it's *his*, Agnes, and he wants it back.'

'All right! Just make him move that thing off me – I can't think straight!'

There was a pause, the arrow moved up to her temple, shivering, then she felt the pressure behind it unwind and the cold touch left her forehead. She trembled. She had to say something.

'That German lady. Casper said it's not safe to keep it here.

He's asked her to take it away a while. She'll send it back when it's safe.'

A whisper, then Fowler's voice again. 'How could he know? Why her? Why would he tell her?'

She had had time to think on that. 'He knows things! He feels things coming, you know that. He's always been a step ahead of you, Fowler. He came to my father's place to tell me. And he likes her. They went to the Druid stones together, we all saw that. He felt their trust of her, he said.'

There was a long pause. She could almost hear her words being weighed to see if there was truth in them. There was a weakness there. Fowler might believe Casper knew something threatening was in the wind, but would the other man? Silence. She felt herself relax a fraction, then that cold tip was on her temple again and, hearing the rapid drawing of the bow, she whimpered. The grip on her hand was suddenly released and she threw herself to the ground. There was a sharp song from the bow and a whistling noise, then she heard a thud as the arrow shot into darkness beyond the barricade.

Isaac's voice was high and keening like his son's. 'You said! She told you! Why did you do that?'

There was the sound of a blow, and she heard Fowler grunt. Then a low curse. One set of footsteps quick into the darkness, followed by the scuttle of Fowler's feet, and his whining complaints fading up the tunnel. Agnes breathed in and at once felt her stomach clench. She stumbled into the far corner to vomit up what little there was in it, then crawled back to the barricade and lay there panting. She hoped she had done the right thing. She had thought of everyone she knew in the village, but they all seemed too vulnerable, too open. The

338

German girl Swithun had mentioned was at the vicarage, he said, surrounded by the protection of the gentry. Swithun and his father couldn't get close to her. The story of her taking it away made sense, and everyone had seen Casper being friendly towards the girl. Still, Agnes was afraid she had set something bad on her and was scared. She felt fat tears gather behind her eyes and all of a sudden she was shaking so hard her teeth rattled. She gathered the blanket around her and rocked back and forth. 'I'm sorry,' she said to the dark. 'I'm so sorry. I didn't want to die.'

Harriet was not absolutely satisfied with her letter, but she folded and sealed it in any case. On her way downstairs to the post tray in the hall she heard raised voices coming from the library. The door was closed, and although she could not hear the words distinctly, she thought those arguing were Felix and the Vizegräfin. The door swung open and she stepped into the shadows of the dining room a moment, then peered round. It was indeed Felix. He was in the drawing-room doorway, apparently delivering his parting shot to whoever was within.

'I have made my decision, Mother. 'We have been very wrong.'

The Vizegräfin now joined him in the light. 'Felix, listen to me! You shall be ruined! There is no proof – how could there be?' She placed her hand on her son's arm. He lifted it to his lips, then let it fall.

'You cannot dissuade me.'

For a moment the Vizegräfin looked up at him, her bottom lip quivering, then she covered her face in her hands and ran up the stairs, her shoulders shaking. Felix watched her go, then crossed the hall into the billiard room. Harriet emerged from the shadows, dropped her letter onto the salver in the hall, then returned slowly up the stairs.

From the collection of Mr Askew, Keswick Museum

From *The Universal Magazine of Knowledge and Pleasure*, December 1752

Extract of a letter from Paris, 15 October:

> *Reports reached us yesterday of the death of Edmund de Beaufoy, 7th Earl of Greta, and his wife whom he survived for only three days. His poverty after his exile and his grief over his brother's execution and the forfeiture of his property in Cumberland has been well-documented, but what is perhaps less known is that in his final two years of life, Lord Greta abandoned strong drink and instead drank deep of his religion. He developed the habit of spending many hours of each day in prayer at his lady's side, and it is believed that the fever which took both husband and wife was contracted moving amongst the poor doing works of charity. How much comfort this reformation brought him is difficult to judge: though his friends reported he seemed much more at peace in his final months, the last cogent utterance he gave on hearing that his wife had passed was thus, 'May she find Heaven; the rest of us shall burn together in Hell.'*

PART V

V.1

THERE MIGHT HAVE BEEN a moon silvering the lake, but the corridor outside Stephen's room was still so dark he could not make out the shape of his hand when he held it in front of his eyes. He groped his way very gently along the wall, brushing his fingers over the rises and falls of the panelling. This door led to the Vizegräfin's rooms, then some three yards along was the door to his mother's chambers. He paused there, and thought how simple it would be to turn the handle and go and shake her awake and tell her what he was about. It was only for a moment though. He knew his mother was clever, but she did not understand everything. Casper had given him a task and he'd perform it as he had been asked.

He continued to trace the panelling forward until it disappeared at the top of the stairs. The atrium of the hall let some of the moonlight in; shadows fell into ashy piles into the corners. Stephen thought of his friend at home, Jonathan Thornleigh, Earl of Sussex. He hated the dark. For the first time Stephen was glad his friend was not with him. Ever since

343

his own father had been killed, Jonathan's nights were full of monsters. He would have seen creeping cracked faces hiding under the stairs, and thought the witches would be waiting for him in the gardens.

Stephen crept down the stairs and turned towards the kitchens. The back door was unbolted, which he thought strange until he noticed the light coming from the brew house. Even as he watched, he saw Crowther's narrow profile cross the window. Stephen was comforted that Crowther was awake. He closed the door behind him and, quietly as he could, stole out among the shadows.

The moon just lightened the darkness of the path to the edge of the park. Stephen kept his hand tight round his wooden Luck and trotted down the slope towards Portinscale. The woods seemed to give off stronger scents in the night, and the polished leaves of the ivy glimmered the same silver as the lace on his mother's sleeves.

Harriet stared at the darkness. She could not think who would have killed Mr Hurst if it were not the young man sleeping a few yards away from her. Or Casper? There seemed to be no alternatives, so she must be wrong about one or other of them. She thought of the great many people there had been at Mrs Briggs's garden party. Any of them could have disappeared for half an hour, the arrows for the competition on their thigh, disposed of Mr Hurst, thrown branches over him then sauntered down for another ice. Mr Hurst and his daughter had come to Keswick to pursue Felix for debt. Too far, surely? Had they come by coincidence, and Hurst had seen in Felix a way to refill his purse? What then of this letter, and the advertisement from Cockermouth? That could have nothing to do with Felix, surely? It indicated some separate matter. She sat up and hugged her knees. Could Hurst have been behind Casper's beating, then Casper killed him in revenge? No one other than Sturgess seemed to believe that. She flung herself back onto her pillow with a sigh.

Stephen had received very precise instructions. He crept round the back of the Black Pig and, having checked the windows were dark and quiet, picked his way among the old barrels and broken wood to the grille of the game locker that gave onto the inn cellar. Beyond it he could see the shadows of dead pheasants hanging by their necks, their soft bodies still and warm, their heads falling forward like tired women at the edges of a ballroom. He took the padlock in his hand. It was the size of a coin purse, and light. From his bag he slowly removed the butterknife he had put in his pocket at supper and slid it into the top of the lock, then biting his lip began driving it in where the shackle clicked into its body. His fingers were beginning to sweat and just when he thought the lock might give, the knife slipped and bruised flesh at the base of his thumb. He yelped and the padlock knocked against the bars. He went very still, sucking at the sore spot and glad he had not purloined a sharper knife. He waited, frozen and listening, but heard only the shout of a vixen calling to her cubs and the soft shiver of branches.

Drawing in his breath, Stephen began to work at the lock again. This time he slid the knife in at a slightly different angle. It clicked brusquely and the shackle popped outwards. Stephen grinned and looked about him as if he expected the broken barrels to congratulate him, then slid the padlock free and put it in his pocket. The grating swung open. There was a fierce creak and Stephen gritted his teeth. Still nothing. He checked his bag was secure over his shoulder and crawled in among the feathery corpses.

Though Crowther was examining the body of Mr Hurst, it was the mysteries of his own past that went tumbling through his mind that night. His imagination was still filled by the portraits of his father and brother that Mr Askew had so proudly displayed to him. He heard some noise at the back of the house and glanced out of the window. It never became completely dark at this season when the moon was large. He could still see the hunkered mass of St Herbert's Island, dark on the dull silver of the lake. He thought of what he had learned of his father. Where had that first money come from? Had he managed to steal it somehow from the deserted possessions of Lord Greta? Then this follower of Greta's, the arsonist, had demanded it back in '45. Why not simply pay him off? Sir William was a wealthy man by that time. Instead he had killed the messenger and, most likely, found de Beaufoy's location from him before the murder and parlayed that information into more influence with his King and his government. Then events had caught up with him. When had Greta died? If he had learned that Sir William had betrayed his brother, Crowther could imagine that Lord expending all his last resources in pursuing him. After all, he had preferred to see Gutherscale burn than let it fall into Sir William's hands. And Adair – well, Adair was as practised as any weak character in believing what he wished. It would have been easy to persuade

346

him to lead his now reclusive father into the open, especially if Adair thought his father's seclusion was a result of grief rather than fear, and Sir William would never have admitted to his children that he was afraid.

Sighing, Crowther folded back his sleeves and turned to the patient body of Mr Hurst.

The taproom of the Black Pig smelled sour, but Stephen did not think it unpleasant. It was a manly smell. The wide fireplace gaped on one wall like an entrance to a great cave, the pint pots over it glinting jewel-like. Long clay pipes sat in a rack pinned up on the wall by a long piece of slate, covered in initials and chalk-marks. Stephen picked up one of the pipes, put it into his mouth and sucked on it, as he had seen Casper do. The taste was bitter and made the tip of his tongue sting. He set it back on the rack hurriedly.

He stood as near as he could to the centre of the room opposite the street door, and with his back towards the steps to the cellar and game locker, then looked up to count the roofbeams above him. The third. It was very thick and entirely in shadow. He stared at it and sucked his teeth, then gently lifted a stool from its place by one of the tables and set it under the beam. The ceilings were low in these cottages, designed to hunker down among the winds that swept over from Bassenthwaite. Setting his bag on the floor among the sawdust, he clambered up on top of the stool, standing slowly to feel where the legs might wobble on the flags. He was not afraid and was proud to realise he was brave, but then this was Casper's place, and he was here on his orders. The walls and hanging pots approved. He reached above his head and cupped the beam in his palms, looking straight ahead so as not to lose his balance and trusting his fingers to find the place in the wood.

There was the seam in the deep dark under his left hand. He felt along from it with his right, till his fingers felt the straight line going against the curve of the grain. His arms were beginning to burn, but he didn't dare lower them and shake the blood back into them for fear of losing the place. He began to pull very gently. The wood sighed, then suddenly gave. For a moment Stephen was afraid he was going to fall over backwards, but the stool stood firm under him. He took the rough panel in his left hand and reached back into the hiding-place with his right. He found it at once: the touch of leather under his fingers. He curled them round and pulled it out. Then: footsteps. Outside, on the road from Keswick. Stephen froze, afraid any movement would attract the attention of the passer-by. He could see right out into the road from where he stood, and should anyone look in from the road as they passed, they would be sure to see him. His white shirt would stand out like a flag in the gloom.

The footsteps came closer, someone walking quickly. Stephen remained absolutely still, the leather pouch still held above his head. The shadow of a man passed through the theatre of the window. Stephen willed him to keep walking and held his breath. The walker disappeared and Stephen heard the footsteps retreat. Not till they had faded completely in the stillness did he dare move again. He lowered the pouch and stuck it into his waistband with his arms tingling painfully. All he wanted now was to be gone. The wooden panel he worked back into its place as well as he could, then he knelt down to get off the stool and moved it back beside the table before he dared take out the pouch again. It was deep brown and stitched into a cross. He smiled. There had been no dragon perhaps, but he had it in his hands, the gift of the fair-folk, the charm of the valley, the Luck of Gutherscale Hall. His fingers touched the fastening. Would it be wrong to look? Casper had not told him not to, but then it did not seem right. It was more honourable, somehow, to hand it to Casper unopened. He lifted the case and tilted it to see what he could of the fastening. It was tied well and the string looked old and dirty. He returned the pouch to his waist, headed back for the cellar and game locker, then out into the night.

The padlock would not click back together again, and he was wondering what to do about it when he heard a door open and whispering. He crept to the shadow of one of the old barrels and peered round it. It was the man Casper had told him to look out for, and his mother. By the light of her candle Stephen could see Swithun's shirt was torn. It looked like it had blood on it. His mother did not seem happy to see him — she was shaking her head and he had his hands lifted. Then she stepped aside and let him in. Stephen wondered what to do. His first impulse was to run away, but then he could tell Casper nothing about where Swithun might be hiding. He waited. It was not long till Swithun came out again, in a clean shirt this time. Stephen watched as he tried to kiss his mother, but she shut the door in his face. Swithun hesitated and put his hand to his shoulder, then turned away and set out across the fields behind Portinscale. North. Stephen started to breathe again and touched the leather case of the Luck. He was certain it felt warm.

When he returned to Silverside, the light in the brew house

was still burning, and the back door unbolted. He tucked the pouch into his pillowcase and fell asleep dreaming of dragons.

It was only two hours later that the landlord of the Black Pig called for his wife. She found him by the game locker scratching his head and holding the padlock to the game locker in his hand.

'Have we had thieves again, Tom?' she asked, peering past him to where the birds swung in permanent gloom.

He shook his head. 'I counted. Nothing gone. Just saw the grate was open, and the lock broke and sat on the flag there.'

'There's peculiar.'

'Not the last of it either,' the man said. 'I found this sitting beside it – payment for snapping it, I suppose.' He opened his hand and showed his wife a rather dirty shilling.

'Casper been here, you think?' his wife said.

'Maybe, maybe.' He scratched his nose. 'Let's keep it close, Issy. No need to mention it, I'd say.'

She took the shilling from his hand. 'No need at all, Tom.'

Harriet left the breakfast table before either Felix or the Vizegräfin had made an appearance, and went to join Crowther in the old brew house. She found him stitching up the torso of Mr Hurst, and was reminded of the sailors mending the sails. He shared their combination of concentration and practised ease. He looked up at her.

'Is it morning?'

'There are windows, Crowther. How could you not notice?' She picked up the lamp from the table and blew out the candle. Crowther paused only to note that the light of the room did not alter considerably, and returned to his stitching. Realising that Crowther did not think the question merited a reply, she asked another.

'What did you learn from the body? I note you have not opened the skull.'

He cut his thread, and returned needle and scissors to the leather roll.

'I thought the coroner's men had better see the wound as it is first,' he said. 'Any word on when the inquest is to be held?' After she shook her head he lifted the sheet from where it lay over Mr Hurst's waist and drew it up over his face. 'Sturgess is taking his time about arranging it.'

'He is too busy chasing Casper around the hills, I imagine.' She leaned against the trestle table on the left of the space, then realised that on it lay the coffin and boiled bones of the Jacobite and straightened up again rather smartly. She was irritated to see that Crowther had noticed.

'I can tell you that Mr Hurst was not an entirely vigorous specimen. His liver was rather engorged and his heart clogged and fatty. If he came here to walk the hills, it would probably have killed him as neatly as that arrow did.'

'You are certain it was an arrow then?'

Crowther shrugged on his coat and smoothed down his sleeves. 'Something very like an arrow was driven into his brain from a low angle with considerable force. You know I am seldom certain of anything, Mrs Westerman, but I present my evidence.' He picked up a saucer from the table behind him. Harriet registered, rather uneasily, that the pattern was that of Mrs Briggs's breakfast china. On it lay a wooden splinter, some two inches in length and rather black. She looked up at him with her eyebrows raised. 'I removed it from the brain. The incline of the wound shows it was driven upwards.'

'Not fired from a distance then, if it was an arrow.'

'I can think of no scenario where firing from a distance would have caused this injury.' He paused, and only continued when she had nodded. 'I have taken a number of measurements. The puncture is roughly three inches in depth. Death would have been immediate.'

'How did you manage . . . ?'

He smiled and produced a folded paper from his pocket. Within were three quills, blunt at the end. At a point about three inches along each was nicked. Harriet was delighted. 'What an excellent idea! You introduced the quill into the wound . . .'

'And when I felt the resistance of uninjured matter, made a nick with the scalpel on the shaft. It also confirmed the angle. The results are consistent. I would also say that as far as I am able to tell, the wound does not narrow.'

'I supposed a thin stick of any sort, or the narrow end of a billiard cue . . .'

Crowther shook his head. 'Given the force required, I would think an unworked branch thin enough to match the wound would have shattered, and a billiard cue would have left a wider wound, do you not think? Aside from the fact one is more likely to have an arrow to hand in the woods close to where an archery competition is in progress, than a billiard cue.'

Harriet shrugged, conceding the point, but only to a degree. 'What if he were murdered elsewhere then transported some distance to his burial site? You have noted he did not seem the type to go traipsing in the fields for pleasure.' Crowther smiled slightly and Harriet found herself doing so in reply. 'Crowther, what else? And can you also explain to me how you seem so much more improved in spirits when you have spent all night with a corpse rather than when you actually sleep?'

'To the latter I can say nothing. To the rest, look at his shoes.' Harriet turned to the neat pile of clothing behind her and lifted the shoes. Leather, rather soft, and with large buckles on them. Shoes more appropriate for a drawing room than a country lane. They were dusty though around the toes, as they would become were a man walking on dry paths, and the heels scuffed. Dragged a little way, having walked.

'I see,' she said simply. Crowther seemed pleased with his night's work, but for all that she could not feel they had advanced greatly. She thought of the argument she had heard in the library the night before, and twisted her mourning ring.

She was still considering the matter when they emerged from the old brew house. Crowther turned to secure the lock, so it was Harriet who first noticed Felix standing a little way away on the lawn and waiting for them. As Felix stepped forward, he did not have any of his usual ease and he seemed unsure what to do with his hands. Crowther leaned on his cane and waited for him to approach them, but though Felix looked as if he wished to speak, Harriet spoke before he could begin.

'How were the Falls by moonlight, Felix?'

He blushed. 'I spent the evening at the Black Pig, Mrs Westerman. I was considering what I should do, and wished to do so away from my— away from Silverside.'

But Crowther, it appeared, was uninterested. 'When did you last see Mr Hurst, Felix? Do try and be exact.'

Felix opened and closed his mouth. 'I have come here to be

as frank with you as I may, and against my mother's wishes, so I shall be as exact as I can, sir. It was during the garden party. I left for a few minutes to speak to Mr Hurst before the archery competition. I had arranged to meet him on the path above Silverside at about that time.'

Crowther studied his nephew carefully. 'To give him the money that you had received from selling your watch.'

'Yes indeed, but how did you know?' Felix looked afraid. Harriet stepped forward and placed the watch into his hand. However much he had frightened her, she could not help feeling a little sorry for him now.

'Tell us exactly what passed between you,' Crowther said.

'I gave him the money, and told him it was all I had. Then he laughed at me. He liked laughing at me. I had played cards at his house for some months, and he enjoyed telling me how much he had despised me the whole time.'

'He was not angry?' Harriet queried. 'He had had a long journey from Vienna to Keswick for three pounds!'

'I expected him to be so, but no. He had been pressing since his arrival in the village, for a greater sum, but then it was as if he did not care, or was suddenly content to wait until I . . .'

'Inherited?' Crowther said icily. 'And exactly how much of my fortune have you spent already?'

Harriet interrupted. 'You were humiliated by him then. Angry enough to kill him?'

'I was, but I did not. I left him enjoying my dismay and returned to the party for the competition.'

'At which you performed badly, as I recall,' Crowther said. It was interesting, Harriet thought, that he had bothered to observe his nephew's performance at all.

Felix went rather red. 'I was not myself. I went onto the jetty to try and calm myself, then Mr Quince appeared at my side with a message from Mr Hurst's daughter. Then I . . . It was unforgivable, Mrs Westerman.'

'Was there something offensive in the message?' Crowther asked.

His nephew shook his head. 'Not at all. It was exceedingly generous.'

'Generous?' Harriet repeated.

Felix hurried on. 'She sent me her best wishes and said she hoped to see me during their stay. But having just come from her father . . .' He ran his hand through his hair and straightened his back. 'Sir, the nature of my relationship with Mr Hurst altered some weeks before my mother and I left Vienna. I owed him a considerable amount, far more than I could pay, more than I knew my mother could pay, despite your generosity. He promised at that time to put off pressing for payment until I inherited if I . . .' He paused and lifted his chin. 'In short, sir, I married his daughter. Miss Hurst is my wife. We married secretly in Vienna four months ago.'

'That poor girl,' Harriet said softly.

Felix flushed, but did not protest. He carried on speaking, studying the ground in front of him. 'A few days later, my mother received an anonymous letter informing her of the marriage, and demanding I support my wife. She was very angry, and before I knew it had bundled me away up here. Mr Hurst followed us. Lord knows how he found us – bribed the servants, probably. My mother has never learned how to keep the loyalty of her household. He arrived only a few days before you did, sir, and was demanding that I acknowledge Sophia.

He had the legal documents with him. I took them to your lawyer with the intention of having their validity checked, but I'm afraid my cowardice overtook me.'

'Do you still have them?' Crowther asked.

'Mr Hurst waited outside Mr Leathes's office – he did not trust me.'

'And when you emerged, Felix?' Harriet's small store of sympathy for the selfish, self-deluding boy had dried up entirely.

'I told him they were in order. I knew they were, in truth. He seemed in need of funds at once, so I told him I'd pawn my watch. I also said,' he had the grace to lower his eyes at this point, 'that I had hopes my long-lost uncle might advance me some money. We then arranged to meet during the garden party.'

Crowther was looking at him with disdain. 'And what did the Vizegräfin have to say to *that*?'

Felix remained staring at the ground in front of his feet. 'She told me she was sure she could persuade you to buy him off. She said you owed her that.'

Harriet heard something behind her. Miriam was hurrying towards them from the house, calling their names.

V.2

DOUGLAS DODDS WAS NOT a man inclined to alter a carefully planned itinerary because someone had been murdered. His business associates called him resolute. It was the word he thought of as he looked in his shaving mirror each morning. He saw his pale pink face, narrowed his pale pink eyes and called himself resolute. But he was also wise. That had been said of him too and more than once; he rejoiced in the description. At first then, when the news reached him that a gentleman had been killed in Keswick, he considered the tender feelings of his wife and daughter and wondered if they might give up viewing the terrible beauty of Borrowdale for an additional day in Ambleside, but a fellow traveller, to whom he had confided his worries, assured him that the murdered man was hardly a gentleman at all apparently, having left bad debts and a reputation for a foul temper at every coaching inn he had passed through. Knowing his own credit and manners were regarded as excellent, Mr Dodds found this reassuring. When his new acquaintance added that the man was also a foreigner, Mr Dodds's wise fears were done away with entirely and his resolution returned. Many people, otherwise reasonable and hospitable, might find a dozen reasons to kill such a man.

As he drained his glass and called for another, and another for his good friend here, whose name he had yet to learn, Mr Dodds began to think that the killer had done a public service by removing such a sorry character. He found himself therefore on the following morning ordering accommodation for his family at the Royal Oak with a sanguine mind.

As the luggage was being taken down and stowed by Mr Postlethwaite's neat-looking servants, Douglas Dodds's feelings were soothed again by his landlord's description of the murdered foreigner, and he agreed his death was probably due to some unpleasantness that had followed him out of Europe like a bad wind. Mr Postlethwaite then added that he had nothing against the young lady, however, who was generally liked, and carried herself almost like an Englishwoman. Mr Dodds had not heard there was a young lady in the case. On enquiry, he learned that she was now staying at the vicarage until such time as her father could be buried, and that a collection had been started in the village to provide for her travelling expenses back to her native country. Mr Postlethwaite indicated a large jar hanging in a corner of the room from a convenient beam.

'All sorts are putting their pennies in,' he said, and tucked his thumbs into his waistcoat. 'Child of Nox the carpenter, who I know has fed himself on weeds more than one season, dropped a penny in there this morning.'

Mr Dodds was touched, touched and proud that even the most humble of his countrymen proved themselves such fine examples of feeling and charity. While his daughter and wife searched among the luggage for Eliza's sketchbook, he reached into the coat pocket where he kept his travelling money, and with a significant and friendly smile to the landlord shook a guinea into his soft palm, then, with his good English chest swelling, he stepped over to the jar and dropped the coin in through the narrow neck. It landed fortunately, glittering at the edge of the jar where it would be most visible. He turned and fancied he saw shining in the face of his host a sense of satisfaction much in tune with his own.

When his little party arrived at the museum, however, the first wrinkle in the day appeared, like the lone dark cloud on the horizon just when the picnic meats are set out on the lawn. The museum was housed in a neat, two-storey building of rather more modern construction than its neighbours, with a short flight of scrubbed stone steps lifting to its front door, but the door was shut. Mr Dodds knocked. Mr Dodds received no reply. Mr Dodds was confused. The advertisements stated, and

Mr Postlethwaite had confirmed, that the museum was open to the viewing gentry from ten o'clock in the morning. Mr Dodds withdrew his pocket-watch and studied it. He looked up to see the time displayed on the town clock. His watch was confirmed. The hour had struck some twenty minutes previously. He raised his fist to the street door and knocked again. Again no answer.

Eliza tripped down the stone steps and approached the window, shading her eyes with her kid-gloved hand.

'Oh Papa, I think I see . . .' As Mr Dodds turned towards her, she screamed and stumbled back into her mother's arms. Her sketchbook slipped. A number of her pencil drawings of the more charming ruined cottages they had encountered on their tour were in danger of getting dirty. Mr Dodds bustled down the stairs in some alarm and resolutely approached the window to see what had frightened the poor girl. On the floor, amongst the remains of a shattered display case, surrounded by glass, split wood and gleaming minerals, lay a man. His eyes were wide open, his head thrown back, his face waxen and his tongue protruding obscenely between his purple lips.

Eliza's sketches were always to lack a view of Derwent Water. Mr Dodds was back on the road to Kendal with his women white and trembling opposite him within the hour, and he felt the wheels could not rattle along fast enough, shaking off the dust of the low murderous little town in a furious and indignant spin. The last thing he saw as he left the Royal Oak was his guinea, glinting and swinging in the jar. The sight of it caught in his mind. It was like seeing a felon justly hanged and dead suddenly look up at him and laughing, wink.

The temporary servant of Mr Askew had never been trusted with a key to the museum. Harriet and Crowther arrived at the bottom of the steps to find Mr Sturgess instructing the Constable to break his way in with a crowbar. They looked in through the window as the wood of the frame cracked and broke around the lock, and the door swung open. Mr Sturgess started up the steps at once, and pushing his man to one side, entered the room at a dash.

'I hope,' Crowther said, turning aside, 'that Sturgess does not think he will be able to revive the man.'

Harriet shook her head. 'They were friends, Crowther. It is natural. But he must have seen what we did through the window. He can have no doubts.' She took his arm and they walked up the steps far more sedately, then turned into the main space of the museum to see Mr Sturgess knelt over the body, one hand on Mr Askew's chest, the other held over his own eyes.

The remains of one of the high display cabinets that had stood between the two tall street windows lay about the body. The glass doors had smashed, dusting the floor with glass that shined like a confectioner's dream of winter. The remains of the case itself lay beside their former owner like a companion on a tomb.

'Mr Sturgess?' Harriet said gently. He breathed deeply and stood up. He seemed dazed and lifted his hands for a second then let them fall.

'What horror. Poor Askew! He could be a troublesome neighbour at times, but he loved this place and this country. Do you think he suffered greatly?'

Crowther looked at the body on the ground. The wreckage

in the room showed that Askew had struggled, and the distorted face made it clear he had been strangled, which took some minutes as opposed to a knife in the right place or the up-thrust of some sharp object into the brain, but pain, panic and hopelessness left no marks on the body that Crowther could find with his knives and saws. He had no answer for the dead man's friend. It was Harriet who replied.

'While my husband lived, I heard many men tell stories of moments they thought they were about to breathe their last in violent times . . .' She hesitated, and Mr Sturgess looked up at her. 'They told me they were too busy fighting for themselves and their friends to feel afraid or suffer great pain. Perhaps that was the case here.'

Mr Sturgess turned away for a moment. 'Thank you, Mrs Westerman. You have given me what comfort you can.' He stood. 'Casper Grace must be found at once.'

'You persist in thinking Casper guilty of these crimes?' Harriet said. 'On what basis?'

He spun round to her. 'Madam, Grace is a charlatan and a madman. I have no doubt we shall find proof of his crimes, but his guilt is beyond doubt!'

'And the young girl who has gone missing? And what of these two men, the Fowlers?' Harriet asked, her tone still civil.

Sturgess put his hand to his forehead and spoke through gritted teeth. 'Mrs Westerman! When a young man leaves the area with a woman, I see no need to construct criminal conspiracy! The father is no doubt drinking the profits of his latest bit of thievery.'

'And the beating Mr Grace received?' Crowther added.

Sturgess turned on him, his arms outstretched. 'Why do you

support this delusional female, Mr Crowther? No doubt Casper cheated the wrong person with his tricks and has paid for it. Perhaps it was that which changed him from a local curiosity into a dangerous lunatic.' His breathing slowed. 'Now may I ask what business you have here?'

Crowther spoke clearly. 'I know of no other qualified surgeon with experience of such cases in the area. I shall make my observations and place them at the disposal of the coroner. And, Mr Sturgess, it is not myself who supports Mrs Westerman's delusions, as you describe them. It is the evidence.'

'Do what you will,' Sturgess said and left the museum.

Crowther walked carefully to the windows and pulled the wooden shutters completely across the glass, shutting out any curious faces beyond. He turned to see that Harriet had retreated to a high stool in the corner of the room.

'Mrs Westerman? I hope Mr Sturgess's rudeness has not distressed you. The man is an idiot. We have met other fools.'

She raised her head with a deep sigh, and tried, briefly, to smile. 'No, Crowther. Not Sturgess. Poor Mr Askew, I do not for a moment believe his death was a pleasant one. I fear we are become creatures to be fled from. All these deaths! That girl not found, two men missing from the village. These disasters cluster about us. I feel like Job, though I've no strength to praise God over these bodies. What did Askew ever do that he deserved *our* visitation?'

Crowther frowned. Her eyes had an unhealthy light in them and she was speaking more quickly than usual, even for her. He said cautiously, 'Mrs Westerman, unless you came down here in the night and throttled Mr Askew yourself, we bear no responsibility for this death.'

She spoke sharply. 'Yes, we do! Look the thing in its face, Crowther! Mr Askew is dead because someone wished to hide something from *us*.'

'You cannot know that.'

'Oh, I am certain of it. He called on us, he left word for us. I was too tired to call on him, and you were too busy with your knives. We have shaken something loose with our questions and it has fallen on this man's shoulders and knocked him down. We are like children throwing stones at a mad dog, only it is never us that get bitten. Only those with the misfortune to know us.'

Crowther watched the shadows on her face. Since her widowhood there had been one thing unspoken between them, one truth unacknowledged, one point of their last enterprise together that had been too tender for them to touch on. It was neither the time nor the place that Crowther would have chosen to speak of it, but it seemed his hand was forced. Crowther had thought on how the spymaster in London had known to send his assassin to James Westerman. He had considered the circumstances and come to a conclusion. But he had never spoken of it, not until now.

'You did not kill your husband, Mrs Westerman.'

She stood up quickly and turned her back to him. 'You know that I did, Crowther. You would have realised it the night James died. I believe it took me a little longer.'

'I saw the man who killed him.'

'Do not attempt to be so exact with me.' She turned towards him again. 'I am not a fool, Crowther. Did you really believe in all these months I had not worked it out too? James was murdered because I was chattering to an earl with a glass of champagne in my hand and said . . . and I know who overheard me. I know what the result was. You cannot protect me from that.'

Crowther crossed the space between them and placed one hand on her shoulder. 'Harriet . . .' She pulled away from him, but he took hold of her again and turned her towards him. Her head was bent forward and her shoulders were shaking. 'Harriet, my dear woman, do listen to me. You are right. It was your words that condemned James, but no one, no one would ever blame you for his death.'

She looked up at him. 'But they do, Gabriel! They do! They all whisper I have no business involving myself in such matters, that I bring shame on my family and friends. That horrid little lawyer yesterday will be saying the same thing, I could read it in his face. And *I* blame myself. How can I not? If I had only managed to keep my tongue still . . . I spoke carelessly, even knowing that there might be people in the room whom we could not trust. Let me take the blame when it falls on me. I am stupid. James, you would not have spoken as I did. God, my own husband! I loved him so, Gabriel. No woman has ever been as lucky . . .'

Her words trailed off into tears. Crowther kept his fingers tight around her thin shoulders as if he could keep her from falling into herself with the pressure of his hands. He did not speak until he felt her breathing slow, then said gently, 'Mrs Westerman, you are a remarkable woman, but you cannot take on responsibility for crimes not your own. Say this happened, and so this. Very well, that seems to be our task, but *you* have killed no one. Your husband would not blame you for his death. He would thank you for the service you have done for the men with whom he served.' Her breathing was becoming more even.

'Please, permit me to take some of the fault for your current distress,' he continued. 'I allowed a veil to be drawn over this. We never discussed why your husband was made a target at that time. I guessed, but I did not ask. And I should have realised by my advanced age that turning from what troubles us is no escape.' She looked up briefly at that with a crooked smile, and he returned it. 'I do not ask you to draw up a balance-sheet, but you have saved lives, you have served a greater good. How many deaths go unremarked, killers unpunished? Would you let the being who killed Herr Hurst, or Mr Askew, go free to murder again? Would you let Casper be taken off and hanged for the convenience of the authorities because you have decided that you should stop asking questions? Because of that little lawyer and his kind? Your husband married a braver woman than that. I wish to God I had had the pleasure of your friendship in fifty-one. I might have saved my brother from the gallows, had I known you then. Now dry your eyes, do! I need you to see this clearly.' He slowly released his grip.

Harriet pulled a handkerchief from her sleeve and began to wipe her eyes. She blew her nose and inhaled deeply.

'Very well, Crowther. Though I think I should retire to some nunnery when we are done with this business.'

'I doubt they would have you,' he replied dryly. 'I have never seen you stay still for more than half an hour at a time. Hours of silent prayer would be beyond you.'

He went back to the body again, then heard her follow him to the centre of the room. He heard her voice, and the tone was more like the woman he knew.

'As it happens, I was three years old in fifty-one,' she said quietly, and knelt down beside him.

Agnes jerked awake in the gloom, scrambled to her feet and called out, thinking some movement beyond the barrier must have woken her. Silence. She had spent most of the night too afraid to close her eyes. Then she could not be wakeful and frightened any longer. Sleep had taken pity on her. Since her waking at first light though, she had sung to herself whenever she was able, hoping that someone might pass by and hear her, but she could not help shutting her eyes from time to time, and whenever she woke, it was with this cold panic that someone might have passed the mouth of the tunnel while she slept, and left her here. She knew she would be looked for, but if Swithun was right and her people were looking on the wrong side of the lake, thinking she had lost her way in the storm, and if Casper hadn't seen her arrive in the rainstorm . . . She was sure neither of the Fowlers would be back now. She had a little bread left and a few mouthfuls of water.

It was a truth she knew of magic that each spell cast had a cost. She had been so angry at Stella that she thought she was willing to pay it, but now, curled and hungry in the darkness, she thought perhaps it was Thomas she should have been angry with, not the girl – and rather than get bitter and crooked, that she should have only held her head high and laughed at them. Casper had tried to take the hurt of the spell away from her by sending her up the hill with the poppet, but she had wandered away from it to see the fireworks. If she had stayed by them as she had been told, she would not have seen Casper being beaten, would not have been taken herself.

Drying her eyes, she then put her hands together and began to whisper church prayers. The hills would hear them, and know she had learned what she needed to know. She accepted her punishment then, and prayed for forgiveness. When the idea came to her it dropped like a stone into the cool centre of her mind and she opened her eyes with a gasp.

Crowther reached forward and twitched Mr Askew's collar to one side.

'Tell me what you see,' Harriet said.

Instead of replying he pointed to the neck and Harriet saw a thin groove across the man's throat, sharp-edged. It cut like a purple furrow across his windpipe. She bent forward, steadying herself among the broken glass with her left hand, then wet her lips and said, 'Too narrow and straight-edged for any rope, yet it was certainly wrapped round his throat. Leather perhaps?' She looked around the room and without waiting for him to reply, continued, 'Someone comes at him from behind. At some point in the struggle he grabs on to this display case and pulls it forward.' She paused. 'It might have saved him.'

Crowther nodded. 'But the debris from the cabinet seems to extend below him.' He lifted Askew's shoulder and the glass crackled under the body. 'He was pulled clear before the cabinet fell. His assailant obviously managed to keep his grip. A brave attempt though.'

'The noise must have been terrific,' Harriet said, getting to her feet again.

'Perhaps that is why the killer made no attempt to hide the crime, beyond partially closing the blinds, though perhaps Mr

Askew might have been doing that himself as he closed up his business. In either case the killer might well have left as soon as he was sure Askew was dead in case his neighbours came to investigate the noise.'

'You believe it was a man?'

Crowther rose to his feet and felt his knees complain. 'Probably. This required some strength, and Mr Askew was not a small man.'

She had ceased to listen to him but turned to the broken doorway. 'The door was locked. There must be another way out of this house.'

Crowther continued to stare at the dead man and the varied minerals scattered about him. Some still had their labels attached, written in Askew's punctilious script. *Black wad of the Borrowdale Plumbago Mines*; *Quartz with silver trace from the old mine above Silverside Hall.*

Crowther had not warmed to Mr Askew during their brief acquaintance. He did not like the hordes of cooing pleasure-seekers the man encouraged into the town with his fireworks and regattas, and had thought his understanding of the geology of the region was probably superficial at best. However, looking at the scattered minerals he saw the workings of a methodical mind. He had heard Mr Askew's maps of the area praised, and no one creates a decent map without difficult and detailed work. Examining the labels now, Crowther had to admit that to an extent Mr Askew had been a man after his own heart. He had sought to understand the world around him by breaking it into tiny pieces and giving each part its proper name, attempting to understand the whole by comprehending the detail. Such were Crowther's concerns in his anatomical studies, yet whatever expertise he had developed, he had never managed to arrive at an understanding of living human beings, their sensitivities and concerns. He wondered if Mr Askew had ever sensed a similar paradox. He had charted and measured each fold in the hills around him, ferreted out its history and its mineral treasures, its legends, but had he ever understood the place entire, how it flowed into its people, and how its people fed it in return?

Harriet emerged from the office. 'All windows are bolted, as is the door to the yard from that room back there.'

'The private apartments on the first floor?'

'There is a door at the top of the stairs, also locked. Only the front door has not had the bolts drawn.'

'But it was locked also.'

Harriet had knelt down by the body again, blocking Crowther's view.

'Was it not said that only Askew had a key?' she asked Crowther. 'It is not in his pockets.'

'Most likely the murderer took it with him.'

Harriet got to her feet again. 'Perhaps. Or perhaps we are dealing with sprites and ghosts, after all.'

Crowther crouched down again and continued to examine the body. 'What time is it, Mrs Westerman?' He heard the flick as she opened her pocket watch.

'A little after midday.'

'The corpse appears locked. I suspect death took place late yesterday evening, after the museum was closed, or his limbs would have begun to soften a little by now.' He looked above him and noticed a thin wire running from the top of the doorframe and along the picture rail, and up the stairs. 'Mrs Westerman, can you pull on that wire for me?'

She did so, and they heard a faint ring from behind the locked door at the top of the stairs.

'So,' she said, crossing her arms. 'Mr Askew had retired for the evening. He hears the bell, and comes down in his shirtsleeves, careful to lock his private door as he does.'

'A cautious man.'

'Indeed. He even opens the shutters a little to see who is on his doorstep. He is reassured and opens the door. It is only a few days past the full moon — what must he have seen?'

Crowther sighed and passed his hand over his eyes. 'He may have thought he saw me on the steps. Do you remember his request that you or I might call on him? I also promised to return those papers to him.'

'Whoever was there must therefore have been dressed as a gentleman,' Harriet said.

'He would have opened the door to Casper too, I am sure.'

Harriet shook her head, not so much disagreeing with him but shaking that line of conjecture away from her as it seemed to serve no purpose. 'He opens the door, and his killer need only take advantage of his surprise for a moment to step in and close the door behind him, then launch his attack.'

'What could Mr Askew have been so keen to share with us, Mrs Westerman?' Crowther rested his finger on his chin for a moment, then suddenly slapped his hand on the floor at his side.

'What is it?'

'That portrait! Askew was showing me a number of articles from his collection the evening before last in that office. Something seemed to surprise him, but I was distracted by my own thoughts, and did not enquire further. It was a portrait of Lord Greta in his later years – he must have seen something in it. I wondered if his call meant he wished to discuss it.'

In the office Crowther recognised the case in which the Greta relics were stored quite easily, but could not see any sign of the portrait of the last Lord Greta in his age.

'Either the killer took it . . .' Crowther mused.

'Can you recall the detail?' Harriet interrupted.

Crowther paused, irritated at having his thoughts broken in upon, but Harriet was too busy peering at the lurid oil of *The Luck of Gutherscale Hall* to register his displeasure. 'Or Mr Askew removed it to his apartments to examine more closely in private what he noticed in my company. It was an ordinary portrait – a man in his best apparel, bewigged and bejewelled.'

He had thought Harriet would take this as a cue to explore Mr Askew's rooms upstairs, but he saw she had stopped listening to him. Her green eyes were shining as she looked at the magnified jewels of the Luck. Crowther felt a flick of distaste. The habit of women to be attracted like magpies to things that only had a value in their ability to shine was remarkable.

'I've only seen Casper's plain little carvings. This is the Luck that was lost in 1715?'

'Yes.'

Mrs Westerman had an expression on her face half-dreaming, and half-excited. He recognised it.

'Lord Greta, his poverty and exile, his servant coming to your father even as Gutherscale smouldered, the lost Luck . . . Crowther, how much was the Luck worth?'

'Its place in the folklore of this area makes that impossible to judge. To the right collector, however . . .'

She frowned. 'No, not the thing itself. Too slow a thing to sell, too well-known in the area. I meant, what is the value of the jewels themselves?' She pointed at the painting. 'What would a trader in precious stones give for the Luck for their sake?' Crowther went still. 'Do you see, Crowther? Lord Greta fled the Tower for exile in 1716. Two years later, when your father needs it most, he procures enough ready money to purchase the land from which all his fortunes grew.'

'But how would my father come by the Luck?'

'I can't say, but in forty-six a Jacobite arrives at Silverside full of threats and your father takes him to the Island of Bones. Suppose he meant to take the Luck, but found it was not where he thought it would be and suspected your father. All that new wealth, the cottage become a grand house. He never leaves the Island, and Greta's brother and followers are betrayed. When your mother dies, rumours begin to circulate in Jacobite circles that your father was complicit in the betrayal. Your father is then murdered. Mrs Briggs mentioned a legend to me, that Lord Greta walks the hills in violent times. What if that belief dates from the time of your father's murder?' She began to pace in the room available. 'I hope Mr Palmer exerts himself on our behalf. I would gladly sign over half of Caveley to him for some more certain explanation.'

'I had thought,' Crowther said slowly, 'we were looking into the past and present, but if I am right, and something that Askew saw in that portrait of Greta led to his death last night, it is all one.'

Harriet growled in frustration. 'Oh, but what of Mr Hurst? If we believe Felix is innocent, who *did* kill that man, and why?'

'Remember also that Lord Greta died years ago, and far

away. But as to your speculation about the Luck, Mrs
Westerman, there is a rightness to it. Suppose Lord Greta hid
the cross, and my father somehow found it . . .'

A shadow appeared in the doorway and Crowther turned
to recognise Mrs Briggs's coachman in the doorway.

'Oh Lord!' he choked out as he looked down on Askew's
corpse, the lolling purple tongue.

Harriet stepped between him and the body. 'What is it,
Ham?'

Ham blinked at her. 'There is a message from Silverside.
A lawyer come to the house wants to speak to you and Mr
Crowther most urgently – a Mr Hudson. He followed me down
from the house hearing the business you are about, but given
the crowd, preferred to wait for you at Mr Leathes's house.
They are old friends, I understand.'

'I hope he is of more use than his partner. Thank you, Ham.
We shall join you directly. But what of poor Mr Askew?'

'We shall guard him, madam.' Two young people had
appeared behind Ham in the doorway. It was the girl who had
spoken. She had clear blue eyes and dark brown hair that
surrounded her face like a cloud. 'I was his maid, I'm Stella,
and he said he'd have me back when my ankle was mended.
This is Thomas.' As she spoke, Harriet took in the sheet over
her arm, the thick bandage around her foot. She glanced up
at Ham, who nodded.

'Thank you, Stella.'

Crowther looked the girl up and down. 'You may cover Mr
Askew, Stella. But I would be grateful if you did not begin
yet to prepare the body for burial. I must return to examine it
when we have met with this lawyer.'

She curtseyed. 'Yes, my lord.'

Harriet turned to the coachman. 'Ham, did you say something of a crowd?'

He cleared his throat. 'It's market day, madam. Everyone is here and word has got about. There are a number of persons outside.'

V.3

AGNES WAS AFRAID that the arrow would have broken and the head been lost among the stones across the floor, but perhaps the angle of the tunnel had saved it. She stood by the gap in the barricade and drew in her mind the line along which it must have flown. Into the deep dark. If she crawled off that way she might get lost in the blackness before she ever found it. The thought made her shiver. Better to die near this faint glow that still tasted of fresh air rather than go mad in the deeper tunnels. It would be so easy to be turned around, mistake her way.

She wondered if she might gather pebbles, or wood enough to lay herself a trail. Miss Scales had told her a story once about a man who stopped himself getting lost in a maze by letting a thread out behind him. She had none. Could she unpick the seams of her dress? She shook her head. The little bits of thread would be too weak and short, and she would be dead before she had the chance to make anything stronger and long enough to be of any use. She must trust to her luck and her prayers then. She got down onto her knees and crawled over to the far side of the tunnel. If she kept her left hand on the wall, and swept out with her right, she should be able to cover the ground where the arrow had most likely fallen. If the tunnel split again, if the wall to her left turned off . . . She would fret over that when she need. Putting her hand against the rough earth wall, she began to crawl forward, pausing every moment to sweep her right arm out across the ground with her fingers spread as if she were broadcasting seed in her father's fields.

As Harriet emerged from the museum behind Ham, she felt Crowther pause beside her and lifted her head. At the bottom of the steps a crowd had indeed gathered. She recognised the landlord from the Royal Oak and one or two of the other faces, but most were strangers to her. These were the weavers, labourers and craftsmen who lived on the other side of the velvet rope. At home in Hartswood she would recognise their faces, see them at church, visit their homes with Rachel when she went among them with her salves and ointments. Here they were as foreign to her as Saracens. For a moment they examined each other across the short distance that separated them. A couple of individuals seemed to be shoving Mr Postlethwaite forward. He took off his hat and looked up at them.

'Good morning, Mrs Westerman, my lord. Forgive us, but the word is that Mr Askew is dead.'

Harriet laid her gloved hand on the railing of the museum steps. It was strange how the people here moved between using Crowther's given title and the name he used. When they met him on the street they might be happy to address him as Mr Crowther as an indulgence to his eccentricity, but now, looking up at him and with the smell of blood in the air they reminded him in this way that his title still bound him to the place.

'Yes, Mr Postlethwaite,' he said. 'Mr Askew is dead.'

A sorry sort of whisper ran around the crowd. A girl turned towards the matron at her side and buried her head in the older woman's shoulder.

Harriet and Crowther began slowly to descend the steps and the crowd shuffled back a little till a sharp-faced woman with full lips and her dark hair escaping from under her cap spoke up.

'Is Sturgess saying our Casper did this too? Because he didn't. Didn't do for the other one either, however he laid him out. And Agnes Kerrick is missing. We need Casper to find her.'

Crowther turned to her. 'I do not know what Mr Sturgess thinks at this moment, but he wishes to speak to Mr Grace, as is natural.'

She tucked her hair under her cap. 'Wishes to carry him off and hang him in Carlisle, you mean.' Her cheeks were red. 'And we will not let him.'

The air was very still. Harriet looked at the faces around her. Only the woman was willing to meet her gaze. The others looked angry or afraid, but their eyes flicked to her and away as if looking at her scalded them.

Crowther spoke, clearly enough to be heard throughout the little crowd. 'I believe there is no evidence to hang Casper as yet.'

'Will that be enough to stop Sturgess blaming him though? How many men have hanged that did not deserve it?' The woman had come close enough for Harriet to taste her breath, sour in the haze.

Crowther looked at her very steadily. 'Too many. I assure

you Mrs Westerman and I will do everything to make sure that does not happen *this* time.'

She studied him a second or two longer, then took a step back. 'I am glad to hear you say that, my lord.'

Crowther made to move forward again, but felt a hand placed on his sleeve. A young man with wide eyes, his skin browned with field work, said, 'We need Casper, my lord. Don't let them take him from us. He is our Luck-keeper.'

Harriet frowned. 'What did you say?'

He looked embarrassed and tried to back away. 'Our cunning-man, madam. We need him.'

Crowther looked carefully into the faces around him. 'I will do all that is in my power, I assure you.'

He stepped forward and the crowd made way. There was a reluctance in their movements as they did so, and Harriet did not think all the whisperings were friendly, but move aside they did.

When Harriet found herself in the carriage and pulling away to travel the short distance to Mr Leathes's villa, she let go a sigh of relief.

'I thought they would scalp us, Crowther!'

He looked a little shocked. 'I doubt that – not today at any rate. But my class rules with the consent of the people, Mrs Westerman. If they decide they can tolerate us no longer, they will have no mercy in their revenge for the bill of petty tyrannies we have run up.'

She turned her head to take in the sight of Crosthwaite Church against the hillside. 'Luck-keeper . . . I have not heard the phrase before. Curious.'

'What are you thinking, Mrs Westerman? I fear my thoughts on the Social Contract are of no interest to you.'

She smiled. 'I like it when you talk like a revolutionary, Crowther. And I agree. But you are right, my mind has been picking at that phrase. What use is a Luck-keeper if the Luck is lost? Yet it must be if our speculations, wild as they are, about your father's wealth are correct.' She fell silent for a while, rapping her fingers on the leather of the seat beside her. 'Oh good Lord!'

'What is it, Mrs Westerman?'

'That chest of Mr Leathes that contained the letter warning your father! With the forced lock. Did you not think it a strange place to leave a letter? And it was covered in soil!'

'Hardly covered, but certainly dirty . . .'

'The Luck would have fitted in that, would it not?'

Crowther nodded. 'You make me recall that phrase of Lottie's when I asked her about the concealed strongbox. She said it contained nothing of value *by then*.' He closed his eyes.

'What is it, Crowther? You have thought of something further.'

'Mrs Westerman, I made very rare enquiries into my father's business interests. I knew he had discovered untapped mineral deposits on a parcel of land, so always assumed, when he said . . .'

'Crowther, please, explain before I tear my own hand off in frustration.'

'I did ask once on what our prosperity was based. He said it was founded on buried treasure.'

Old Mr Leathes was waiting for them by the garden gate

looking very solemn, and with no more than a bow, led them to the rear of the house, where a gentleman in his middle years was examining the aviary. He made the introductions, then returned to the house to leave Mr Hudson, Crowther and Harriet to examine each other to the trillings of his canaries.

'This is a matter of the greatest delicacy, sir, madam,' Mr Hudson said. 'I hope you do not think badly of me for emphasising that. I asked Mr Leathes if I might speak to you alone and without his walls, as even in the household of my old friend I fear that we might be overheard and someone might, in all innocence, learn something that should not be learned.'

He reminded Harriet of her father as she remembered him from her youth. A man, softly spoken and inclined to be agreeable, though his expression now was the same nature of worried concern that she remembered when her father had some hard duty of his office to perform.

'I think we understand, sir,' she said.

He nodded and put his hand to his chin. 'Thank you. First I must apologise for my *junior* partner. I suspect that he was uncivil. He knows nothing of the business of the advertisement and is inclined to resent it. As soon as I heard of the matter, I at once visited the personage concerned to see how far he was happy for us to take you into our confidence. Having done so yesterday evening, I came to you as quickly as I might.'

'You know, Mr Hudson,' Crowther said, leaning on his cane, 'that there has been another death. Mr Askew, the owner of the museum in this town, was found strangled this morning. It may be that whoever killed Hurst, killed Askew also. If you can tell us anything that might bring that man to justice . . .'

Mr Hudson kept his chin buried in his chest. 'I am aware. Remember I came from Silverside. I knew Mr Askew and admired his energy, though how his death is connected to this matter, I cannot say. I must tell you a story . . .'

'You have our attention, sir,' Harriet said.

'Yes, yes. The natural son of Viscount Moreland was travelling in Europe some years ago. He was a pleasant boy, but the man who had been paid to take care of him and guide him in his steps was taken ill in Vienna.'

'Vienna?' Harriet repeated. 'It is my understanding that Mr Hurst was a native of that city.'

Mr White nodded as if this had confirmed some thought of his own, and continued, 'The young man's tutor was confined to his rooms some weeks, and in that time his charge managed to lose a great deal of money at a card game held in a house off Rabensteig near St Rupert's Church.'

'How much?' Crowther asked. He had seen such things occur during his own years on the continent. Young men caught by smooth-talking strangers in foreign cities.

The lawyer looked almost tearful. 'It was a disaster. The boy's tutor was trusted by the family, and was charged with buying a wide variety of art and sculpture for their country house. He had therefore the letters necessary to draw on a small fortune from the bankers. His charge took those letters and drew on those funds to maintain his place at the table.'

Crowther noticed Harriet had become very quiet, and wondered if she were thinking of her own son, if he could be caught in such a way.

Mr Hudson carried on: 'The boy was distraught and took it upon himself, far too late, to find out something more about the reputation of the men to whom he had lost his father's money. He became convinced that the game had been crooked, and went to tell them so. He was challenged, and felt himself compelled to face the challenge. Even then he might have been saved if he had spoken to his tutor, but he was stubborn as young men are, and set out to prove his honour with pistols.'

Crowther studied the canaries in Mr Leathes's aviary, such small lives in their pretty plumage. He remembered bending over one tiny corpse, Mr Leathes guiding his hand as he made his first cut with a borrowed blade. 'He was killed by his opponent, I presume.'

'Murdered, sir,' Mr Hudson said. 'Murdered as certainly as poor Mr Askew. The devil he fought was a grown man. A man who had done military service. The boy was only eighteen and had never fired a gun other than in sport. His opponent could have shot wide but he shot to kill. I am sure he did so in order to escape with the money he had so dishonestly won. I call that murder, sir. As does the boy's father. The first the tutor knew of the business was when the body was returned to the lodging-house in a hired cab.'

Harriet worked her fingers into the brass wire of the aviary. 'And what became of the man who murdered him?'

'He fled with the money he had won, and we have had no trace of him since. Inquiries were made, naturally. We found something of the man's past, offered rewards for information leading to his discovery, but the moment he rode away from the scene of the duel, he disappeared. We let it be known in every large town in Europe that we were seeking him in the hopes that he would find himself among people who knew him under the name he used in Vienna. Men do not change.

I was certain he would find himself among the card tables again. For five years I have had a stream of correspondence across my desk from Paris, Rome, as far away as Moscow. Every similar scandal, any resemblance, any hint of a name. Each I have pursued to the best of my ability, and each time, whatever iniquity I discovered, there was no trace of the man I searched for.'

Crowther was still watching the birds whistling in their few square feet of comfortable captivity. 'What became of the tutor, Mr Hudson?'

The lawyer was silent for a moment, as if he needed to compose himself before speaking. 'The tutor was my own son. He did not forgive himself and would never accept that the fault was not his. He felt he had failed, and dishonoured me. He took a commission with the Sixteenth, and was killed in seventy-nine during the shelling of Fort New Richmond at the Mississippi River.'

'My condolences,' Harriet said quietly.

Crowther looked at the lawyer and said, 'You were advertising for Mr Hurst because he wrote to you offering you information about your fugitive.'

Hudson unfolded a letter from his pocket and passed it to Mrs Westerman, who released her grip on the aviary to take it.

I know where the man who shot the boy is. He is hiding in plain sight. I shall be waiting to hear from you at the Seven Bells in Cockermouth on the evening of Monday, 14th July and am ready to give you his current name and address when I have bills in my hand for £100. Gottfried Hurst.

Harriet looked up from the paper. It was quite plain, no return address, no date. It seemed Mr Hurst had decided not to use one of the sheets printed with the Royal Oak name that Mr Postlethwaite provided. 'A considerable sum. You kept the appointment, Mr Hudson?'

'Naturally. My client sent the letter to me as soon as he received it. I remained in the taproom of the Seven Bells from five o'clock in the afternoon until midnight, with the money ready. No one came.' His voice sounded hollow. Harriet thought of him during his vigil, the hope that his search might be ending, and his growing disappointment.

'Why did you think the appointment was not kept, Mr Hudson?' she asked.

'I hoped, Mrs Westerman, that he had only been delayed by some accident or inconvenience. I feared that he had been offered more money to stay away. By my advertisement I hoped to encourage him to believe he might ask for more. Even if the man I seek had fled, his trail might still reek enough to follow it. But I had no idea where Mr Hurst was precisely, so no idea where to begin until I heard from my partner where you were staying. Then I realised that Mr Hurst's information must be good.'

'How so, Mr Hudson?' Harriet asked.

'I had no success in tracing the man's movements *after* he murdered the young gentleman, but I had some in finding out about his past. The name he used in Vienna was von Lowenstein, but he was born Grenville de Beaufoy, only son of the last Lord Greta.'

Agnes's fingers touched something. Smooth, worked wood. She tried to pick it up, only to find it resisted. It had been driven into the soil, even after all this distance. It would have gone through her head and dropped her like a stone. She eased it out of the ground. That it had been meant to kill her was no fault of the arrow, and she had better plans for it now. She turned round very carefully and reached out her right hand to the wall. Good. The arrow she slipped into the waist of her skirt at the back to leave her left hand free. She began to sweep it back and forth as before as she crawled back towards the barricade, but this time she paused more often, plucking loose splinters and sticks from among the stones and stuffing them into her pockets.

Harriet felt unsure if she could speak. 'The son of Lord Greta is *here*?'

Mr Hudson raised his hands. 'We must assume so, or at the very least we must think that he has been here very recently.'

Crowther raised his eyebrows. 'Given the unfortunate demise of Mr Askew, I think we may assume he was also here last night. Do we know what age he is, Mr Hudson?'

'He was born shortly before the rebellion of forty-five.'

'In his late thirties, then. Any description of his person?'

'A gentleman speaking English, German and French like a native. Medium height.'

Harriet cast up her hands in frustration. 'I saw a dozen men of that age and height at the garden party at Silverside, all with a quiver of arrows at their side, and as many such at the fireworks, though I cannot answer for their linguistic abilities. No limp, sir? No disfiguring mark? Has he a wife, children?'

Mr Hudson shook his head. 'No duelling scars or obvious injuries I know of, madam. Though he may have acquired them, and a wife and children in five years of travel.'

'Do not despair, Mrs Westerman,' Crowther said quietly. 'There are only two good inns in town. We shall ask there if any of the gentry have been in residence since – when did you receive that letter, Mr Hudson?'

'In the morning of the twelfth of July.'

'Since before the eleventh then, who remain in residence or have left this morning and are of a suitable age. There can be relatively few.'

'Why did he not leave at once, having killed Mr Hurst? Why wait longer?'

Crowther did not waste his breath with a reply. 'Mrs Westerman, as you have already an acquaintance with Mr Postlethwaite, perhaps you might enquire at the Royal Oak. Mr Hudson, if you might make a similar call on the proprietor of the Queen's Head. I should like to spend a little more time with the body of Mr Askew.'

'And you will think on that portrait, Crowther?'

'Naturally, Mrs Westerman.'

V.4

WHEN HARRIET RETURNED to the museum, frustrated and disappointed, she found the main part of the museum being swept. The body had been removed – Harriet guessed that Mr Askew's office had become his mortuary. The girl who had offered to keep watch over the body was completing her labours and her friend was arranging the fallen rock samples on Mr Askew's counter. The girl looked up as she came in and nodded to her.

'Lord Keswick is in the back room, Mrs Westerman.'

Harriet began to unbutton her gloves. 'Stella, have you ever heard the stories of the ghost of Lord Greta walking the hills in times of trouble?'

She smiled. 'That was just old Farmer Willocks used to say that, madam, when he came into town for the market. He always had a story for the fire, and that was just one of them. He used to say the Northern Lights celebrated on the day Lord Greta escaped from custody, and that there was a witch in Thornthwaite Forest could turn herself into a hare, and he had a story of some bogle or other for every month in the year.' She chuckled and started the broom moving again, the glass cracking like ice in the pail on winter mornings.

'Did you hear the story? Is he living?'

'No, bless you, madam. There aren't that many like Lottie Tyers, who are too stubborn to die. We shared out the arvel bread for Willocks when I was right small. Twelve years ago, maybe. But I heard the story. It was the time of . . .' she dropped her voice a little, 'when the First Baron was murdered. Willocks said he was out in the evening seeing to his pigs, and he saw the ghost of Lord Greta on a black horse crossing Pow Beck. Then next day he heard there had been horrible murder done at Silverside Hall, so he reckoned he'd seen a bogle sent as a sign.'

'Where is Pow Beck? And how did he know it was Lord Greta?'

Stella snorted. 'Said he knew him by his bearing. And Pow Beck lies along the way to Braithwaite. I thought his other bogle stories were better, but he told the story of the ghost of Lord Greta enough times for it to drift around after we buried him.'

'You don't sound as if you believed him?'

It was the young man who replied. 'If Lord Greta's ghost came in times of trouble, he'd have been seen when the small-pox came. And if he came in times of murder, then he'd be outside the window now, wouldn't he?' His voice lowered a little as he finished, and Harriet found herself looking towards the shutter.

'Mrs Westerman?' She jumped a little and turned to see Crowther in the doorway to the office. Stella set to work again with the broom and the young man busied himself with the rocks. 'Perhaps you might join me?'

She followed him into the office trying not to blush, and as the door closed behind them, she asked, 'Did you hear any of that, Crowther?'

He nodded. 'Any news of significance from the Royal Oak?'

'Three gentlemen are currently in residence. Of these, two are of an age and have been here ten days or more. The first was having lunch when I arrived and was extremely surprised to be engaged in light conversation by a respectable widow. His name is Bloodworth, which gave me hope for a moment, but if he is a murderer, then I abandon all hope of ever knowing my fellow man. Charming, handsome, but I would swear him innocent. The second left this morning, a family man travelling with his two young daughters.'

Crowther looked up with his eyebrows raised, but Harriet shook her head. 'He was a man of enormous girth who, Mr Postlethwaite said, had to rest on his way up the stairs to his chamber. The thought of him dragging Mr Hurst's body into a cave and covering it with stones is impossible. Have you had word from Mr Hudson?'

'He left before you arrived, Mrs Westerman, but his information was much as your own. He is determined to widen his search and has taken horse for Kendal in hopes of finding his nemesis there.'

She looked at the body of the museum owner, lying across his own desk. 'Poor Mr Askew. Did he have any family?'

'His maid tells me there is a married sister in Cockermouth.'

'And have you learned anything more from his body?'

He nodded and indicated Mr Askew's left hand. She went to it and took the cold fingers between her own. The locking of the body was just beginning to pass; the muscles were still tensed, but she could open them just enough to observe the flesh of the palm. The skin was torn at the base of the fingers, though there was no sign of blood.

'I see it, Crowther. But I cannot pretend to understand.'

He looked at her as she cradled the dead hand. 'Those injuries can only, I believe, have been caused after death, since such abrasions should bleed. I believe some jagged object was torn from the hand when it was already clenched in death.'

She straightened, her green eyes clean and dancing. 'The struggle! Mr Askew had something in his hand that his killer feared might identify him?'

'That is my speculation, Mrs Westerman.'

'Then at some time in the night he realised it was missing and came back to collect it.'

'It was fortunate,' he said rather dryly, 'that the murderer kept the key to the front door.'

Stephen found Casper by his old camp. He had not expected to see the man himself there, but rather hoped to leave some secret signal for him that his mission of the previous night had been successful. He had not thought what that signal might be, and was standing by the firestone feeling rather lost when he suddenly found Casper at his side. He looked ill to Stephen's eyes. The bruises on his face were blossoming against the pale of his undamaged skin, and his eyes had the haunted air of a man who has slept little. Joe hopped down from his shoulder and hunched in the sun.

'You have it?' Stephen nodded and patted his waistband. 'Good lad.'

'You have not found her.'

Casper suddenly picked up the kettle from its place by the fire and threw it with all his strength across the camp. It clattered loudly against the rocks on the far side of the clearing. Joe fluttered up and cawed. Stephen remained very still. 'Nowhere! Nowhere! I know every mine dug on these hills since Queen Bess! Every nook and cranny of them! I've hammered and yelled at every seal to the mines. Any that are open I have crawled through like a rat and nothing! Nothing! And the nails on the barriers rusted and old each one. Where is she?' He dropped onto one of the stone benches and put his head in his hands. 'I lose hope, boy. Three days, and she is gone as a ghost! His clothes smelled of earth, deep earth. But nothing, nothing and nothing. They must have drowned her. Poor Agnes, poor clever Agnes.'

Stephen sat down next to him and put his thin arm across his shoulders. Casper turned towards him, and Stephen felt his forehead rest on his shoulder for a second. He smelled of air and sweat and tobacco.

'Can you use the Luck to find her?' He drew the case out

of his waistband with his free hand and placed it on Casper's knee. 'Is there not some magic?'

Casper wiped his face on his sleeve. 'Nay, youngling. If the Luck wishes her found, it will find its own way to do it. It guides and protects and punishes in its own way, not by simple men like me mumbling over it.' As he spoke he took the case in his hands and held it lovingly. 'I hope it may. Perhaps it tests us.' He was stroking the leather of the case. 'My da made this for it a long time ago now. The pox came in fifty-four, and everyone was so afraid. It is a foul way to die. They say it strikes those who fear it most, like a devil. The skin breaks and bleeds and people go wild and desperate in their pain, spitting and screaming till they are not man or woman or child, but some lost demon.' Stephen shuddered. 'My da did his duty. He covered the Luck and each night took it to every house where the pox was burning some poor soul. You ever seen it?'

Stephen shook his head.

'Pray you don't. Fever first, and cramps. Then they'd take to their beds and the pustules would come. Fat and seeping and the stink of them . . . they make you rot before you die, and so many their own mother wouldn't know them. The things they'd call out.'

'Did the Luck help?' Stephen said quietly.

'It calmed them, and calmed their people. We thought it had passed. Then my dad fell, getting from his bed in the Black Pig. I put it under his pillow, but he went hard anyway. Whatever sin he ever did, he paid for it then.' He turned and spat onto the ground, then handed the leather pouch back to Stephen. 'You take it, boy. It's safer with you for now – the magistrate might get me yet. Gentry you may be, but for now you are Luck-keeper of this place.'

Stephen nodded and placed it back in his belt. 'There's something else.'

'What, lad?'

'That man from Portinscale, the young one?'

'Swithun Fowler? Have you seen him scuttling about? What of him?' Casper's eyes had become bright and seeing again.

'I saw him as I was coming out from the Black Pig last night. He was leaving his mother's cottage and heading north. There was something strange about his arm. The sleeve was torn, and I think I saw blood on it. Looked like it was hurting him. It wasn't when we saw him the morning after you got beaten.'

'Was it now? North . . . is he hiding in Thornthwaite? We've visited all the old holes there, but I didn't have an eye out for a camp. Thought they'd have fled further by now. What holds them?' Casper reached down to where Joe was hopping and pecking at his feet. Stephen could feel the excitement in the man's bones. The jackdaw stepped daintily onto his forefinger and allowed himself to be lifted up. 'Arm hurt, hey? It wasn't us that did that, was it? What do we say to that, Joe?'

'Good, good!'

Harriet heard a knock at the museum's front door, then the sound of Stella greeting Ham. She stepped back briskly from the office into the main room. Even with her injured ankle Stella had made a fine job of clearing the space, and Harriet said so. The girl smiled.

'Thought I'd never heal, madam. But it's taking my weight

better and better now.' The museum looked as if it could be reopened within the hour, were it not for the body of the owner with his bruised and broken neck lying in the other room. Ham was looking flustered.

'Ham, you have been sent to us again! Is all well at Silverside?'

'Yes, Mrs Westerman, or I don't rightly know. Seems there might have been words between Mrs Briggs and the Vizegräfin, not my place to say, of course!' he added quickly, as if he had just admitted to the murder of Mr Askew himself.

Harriet smiled at him. 'Don't worry, Ham. But do you have some message for us?'

He looked startled again. 'Yes, madam, just that Mrs Briggs asked if it might be possible to see you at once.'

Harriet frowned. 'Mr Crowther and myself, Ham?'

'She just said your name, madam. She was right fretted to have missed you at breakfast and has been darting back and forth to the window looking for you ever since. Worse since we heard about poor Mr Askew, then that lawyer came and went looking white.'

'Hudson. White is the partner,' Harriet said a little distractedly. The last thing she had any time for at this moment was a quarrel between the women at Silverside. She and Crowther had hardly been given a chance to speak to one another. Then she thought of the unanswered summons of Mr Askew and sighed. 'One moment, Ham.'

She opened the door into the office once more. Crowther was still examining the wounds on Mr Askew's hand. 'You're going,' he said. It was a statement rather than a question.

'I am. Will you join me?'

He shook his head without looking at her. 'No, I shall spend a little more time here, then perhaps ask that man to break the door down into Mr Askew's apartments. I shall join you at Silverside later.'

The door closed and he was alone.

Mrs Briggs might have been keeping a close watch, but it was Felix who first appeared as Ham brought the carriage to a halt on the gravel path outside the house.

'Mrs Westerman!' he said, handing her down. 'I went to the vicarage to see Sophia, but I was not allowed into the house. Miss Scales said she would not see me.' He made his eyes wide and pleading. 'She said she was not seeing anyone, but that was not true! Mr Postlethwaite was allowed to pay his respects, and Mr Sturgess. It is only myself she will not see.'

'Does that surprise you, Felix?' Harriet said rather impatiently and tried to move past him, but he laid his hand on her arm.

'She wanted to see me before,' he said, his grip tightening. Harriet looked at him – a child, she thought. That poor girl has married a spoiled child with an ugly temper, and now she will be saddled with him till he drinks himself to death or a boar catches up with him. Or a murder of crows. Perhaps it would have been better if the marriage had been kept secret; at least then Miss Hurst might have had the chance to make another choice.

'She wanted to see you when her father went missing; she hoped to see you, no doubt, when her father was found murdered. Perhaps she thinks your visit unforgivably late.'

'But she is my wife!'

'She was your wife then too, Felix. And your wife when you left her with that monstrous father of hers and ran away

393

to England with your mother.' He turned pale, as if she had struck him, but did not release her arm. 'Now let me go.'

Ham cleared his throat. He was standing at Harriet's elbow and looking rather sternly at Felix. He rolled his great shoulders. Felix lifted his hand from her arm, and Harriet walked briskly into the house.

Mr Askew's apartments showed him to have been an orderly sort of man. There were a pair of armchairs round the fireplace in red leather and a number of well-stocked bookcases. The room was dominated, however, by Mr Askew's worktable on which he produced his plans of the surrounding countryside. Inks and stone for grinding them lay next to an astrolabe in a walnut case. The table had large candlesticks at each end, and though they were burned to stubs, Crowther could see Mr Askew used beeswax candles to work with. Again he had a rather painful sense of fellow feeling.

Of the portrait that Crowther had glanced at there was no sign. Rifling through the man's desk he found a great many cuttings from the newspapers advertising or reporting on his various entertainments, and boasting of the number of visitors of quality from many European countries whom he had welcomed into his museum. It had not been so when Crowther was a child. No one came here then, and the town had been miserable and poor. He picked up the astrolabe, which was beautifully made, and considered his father. The land he had bought he had used purely to create the wealth Crowther now enjoyed. He had cut down the timber, worked the last deposits he could from the mines and invested the profits elsewhere, where it could do no good for these people. For that, they had made him a peer of the realm. Mr Askew may have been an awkward man at times, but he had brought visitors and their money into Keswick, he had unpicked the history and geography of the area and made it available to his fellow men. Crowther had sneered at him, and now he lay dead among his exhibits, another bloody story among so many others.

Crowther closed his eyes briefly and put down the astrolabe. If Mr Askew's married sister permitted it, he would buy the instrument himself and place it on his own worktable to remind him. He remembered that Harriet had purchased a violin from the estate of another man who had died violently. Perhaps they deserved the reputation as carrion birds that some were keen to give them.

The notebooks Crowther found were full only of sketch maps and measurements. Mr Askew, it seemed, had not kept a journal of his thoughts. There was no note, no letter. Crowther leaned back in the chair and half-closed his eyes. He was trying to recall, in each detail, the portrait of James Westerman, Harriet's late husband, that hung in the drawing room in Caveley. It was a sort of exercise before he made an attempt on recalling the glimpsed portrait of Lord Greta. The oil of Captain Westerman showed him in a version of Captain's undress uniform – a vigorous, handsome man, with the sea churning behind him. It was painted, Mrs Westerman had told him, just before their marriage and shortly after he had achieved the rank of Captain. His barge bobbed off a little to the left in reference to his new position; he had his sword in front of him like a cane. The painter had given the impression of intelligence and humour to his expression. Crowther wondered briefly what the same painter would make of his own angular, ageing self. Would he be painted with a knife in his hand? Darkness behind him, his face made even more haggard by the candlelight by which he always worked? Well, such were his signs. Just as the barge, hat and sword were those of the late Captain.

Crowther opened his eyes again. He saw Mr Askew in front of him as he glanced up; the portrait had been almost life-size, and by the way Mr Askew had held it, it seemed he and Greta were looking at each other, turned slightly away from the viewer, one arm forward. A profile, and what were the signifiers there? A ring. The landscape behind him. On the waistcoat, an elaborate chatelaine. Crowther saw it, placed his hand on his forehead and thought. He had seen it before.

He stood up so quickly that Mr Askew's chair tipped over behind him.

V.5

London, the same day. Office of Mr Palmer in the Admiralty Building, Whitehall

MR PALMER SAW A great deal of correspondence cross his desk at the Admiralty; however, it was unusual to find an envelope addressed to him personally. His rather shadow-strewn professional career meant he was hardly acknowledged to be what he was, a man of growing influence and stature in that place. Usually those who wished to communicate with him did so in person or via some intermediary, rather than committing themselves to paper. Yet here was an express with his name plainly written on it, handed to him as the late afternoon began to settle into twilight. His first action on receiving the packet was to check the seal for signs of tampering, then having reassured himself on that point, he closed the door to his outer office where his clerks were busily at work and returned to his desk.

It might have been supposed that Mr Palmer would have had to find work elsewhere when the government of Lord North collapsed in the wake of the Yorktown fiasco, or when Earl Sandwich was replaced as First Lord of the Admiralty by Howe. He had not doubted the security of his position long. He knew too many secrets, secrets too old and varied to be spurned by any man of sense, and the new First Lord was wise enough to aim to win the favour of Mr Palmer rather than estrange him.

He opened the letter and looked first at the upright signature with which it was concluded. The look of suspicion left his face and was replaced with a smile. He turned back to the beginning of the letter and began to read. The smile became a frown. After some moments he set the paper down and turned his chair to examine the view behind him. It showed a busy courtyard in the heart of the capital, and beyond it the Mall. The heat of the summer had thinned out the Quality in Town and left the streets to men of business who could not afford to retreat to country air, and the poor who, with increasing desperation, dragged themselves up and down the streets trying to find enough citizens to buy their wares. The city stank and sweltered. The concert halls were growing dusty, the opera houses shut up. Only the pleasure gardens still gathered a crowd to walk in the evening and seek some cool in the shade of the trees, though the turf was yellowed and the musicians panted as they played. Mr Palmer saw little of what passed outside his window, however, and after a period of contemplation he stood and took up his coat.

He folded the letter into his pocket and passed through his outer office and down the main stairway. His clerks noticed his passing, but did not question it. Mr Palmer was forever coming and going with that look of concentration puckering the skin around his eyes.

Mr Palmer's destination was a modest house located off Whitehall and within five minutes' walk of his own office; however, it was almost an hour after leaving his office that he arrived there. He had spent some little time amongst the archives, then had made a brief stop at his own residence before coming here. It was not a place where one called without a gift of some kind. The gentleman who lived there had a taste for the antique and Mr Palmer had fetched from his rooms a reserved item from a portfolio of ancient maps. This portfolio he had bought at considerable expense some five years previously, and he had done so with the express intent of offering it piecemeal to the gentleman in Craig's Court.

The windows on the upper storey seemed oddly set, so the house had a hunkered, mistrustful look, like an old man peering sideways under lowered lids. His knock was answered promptly though by a clean-looking young woman, who greeted him with a smile of recognition.

'Mr Palmer! He will be glad to see you.'

'I hope so, Bess. Though I thought you might have shut up and fled the house in this heat.'

The girl stood back to let him into the dark hallway, and Mr Palmer felt, as he always did in this house, that he was disappearing into an ancient age. 'Lord, he'll never leave this place, sir. Can you imagine him being pushed around Bath in his chair and taking the waters?'

Mr Palmer had to confess he could not.

'No, the old spider will stay here at the centre of his web, twitching his strings.' It was said with a warmth and shake of the head that took all the offence out of the statement.

'Any interesting visitors since I was last here, Bess?'

She wagged her finger at him as if he were a boy half her own age. 'Now Mr Palmer, you always ask, and I always give you the same answer. Sir Gawen has visitors enough and they are interesting to him, and there let it lie. You shall find him in the upper parlour as ever. Shall I send the girl up with the decanter?'

Palmer nodded, and was beginning to climb the stairs when Bess spoke again. 'Mr Palmer, what would you do if one day I said to you, "Such and such a man had visited, and such and such another"?'

Palmer considered for a moment. 'I would suspect that revolution was in the streets and fear for the King himself, Bess.' She looked pleased with the response and left him to announce himself.

The gentleman that Mr Palmer had come to see was seated in his usual place in the dark upper parlour of the house, by the window with his chair turned so he could see the carriages and people passing the entrance to the yard. He was curled forward in his chair, staring out, his thin white hair hanging loose and unpowdered around his ears and his skeletal hands, rather swollen at the joints, loose in his lap. Opposite him sat a young boy, apparently engaged in reading the paper aloud by whatever light could crawl through the grime on the window. Palmer's knock had interrupted him. Sir Gawen turned towards the door, his great hook nose making his face seem more shrunken than ever by contrast.

'Palmer!' His voice was as cracked and lined as his face. 'You may leave us now, Edward. Come back and read the rest when Mr Palmer has finished with me. Go on, go on!' The boy jumped to his feet, crossed the bare floorboards and slipped through the door like a cat.

'How did you know it was me, Sir Gawen?' Palmer asked, as he took the seat the boy had just vacated. The hook nose followed him as he sat down and moved the paper to one side.

'I have heard you climb the stairs twice every week at least for five years, my boy. How should I not know you?' He chuckled, and looked out towards the street again. 'Though you are one of only three men that Bess will allow to enter this room unannounced, so the odds were with me.'

'Who are the other two?'

The old man laughed again. 'Have you brought me another map, sir? Pass it over to me then, while we wait for our wine and let me see how you value my advice. Fetch me that glass from my desk.'

Palmer laid the map across the old gentleman's knees, then went in search of the glass. It was a room that seemed to despise modern comforts, heavily panelled in black oak and apart from the desk and the two chairs by the window, almost entirely empty. Palmer had never seen Sir Gawen in any other room.

During winter evenings he might sit by the fire, but in summer he was always by the window, always in the same attitude, always, it seemed, in the same black coat and not quite white cravat. Palmer wondered if the garments had done all the ageing they were capable of and had now, like their owner, reached a point of decrepitude that would prove immutable until death. The image of Sir Gawen among the fashionable crowd at Bath occurred again to Palmer as he passed him the magnifying glass.

'What are you grinning at, boy?'

'At my own private thoughts, Sir Gawen.'

The man gave a bark of laughter and lifted the glass and map. His eye swam in its own yellow bile, suddenly huge.

The maid came in with a tray in one hand and a little table folded under her other arm. As Sir Gawen examined his prize, Palmer assisted her in setting it up, told her quietly to leave them and poured the wine himself before sitting down again.

'Well, well. Very fine. Now what have you to ask me? I know I must hand over some small part of my own private store for one of your little gifts. What do you wish to know? Old scandals in the French Court? I hear the Admiralty has come good at last, though a little late for Sandwich, and the treaty will be rather more advantageous to us than we first believed we could hope for.'

'You are well informed.'

'Of course, and you know I mention it to you because I am pleased with my present and have an old man's vanity. I wish to show you how wise you were to give it to me.' He laughed again.

'I enquire on behalf of a friend.'

'What friend?'

Palmer hesitated, then replied, 'Gabriel Crowther.'

'Ah! The anatomist who assisted you in eighty-one. Not state business then, if *he* has applied to *you*. No matter. On his behalf only, or is the harridan in the business too?'

'Mrs Westerman is mentioned in his letter.'

'Fine woman. Wish there were more harridans in the world. Bess is one, I tell her so to her face every day, and every day she tells me to thank God it is so, as no other would be able to manage with me. Where those two are and asking questions, you may be sure now there is blood in the water. Ask, and I shall answer for your sake and theirs.'

'Thank you, Sir Gawen,' Palmer said, glad the most difficult part of the interview was now at an end. He now only had to speak a word, then listen as attentively as he could. 'Greta.'

The man smiled again, revealing his blackened gums, and tilted his head back. His right hand tapped smartly on his thigh. 'Ahhh! Greta! The former Lord of half of Cumberland! Traitor and exile! How peculiar it is, the way one event leads to another. Pull at one strand only in history and all our world would be changed.' He reached forward for his wine. 'You know the story of his wife?'

'No, sir.'

Sir Gawen took a great gulp of the liquor and wiped his lips with the back of his other hand. 'Another harridan. If the Pretender had had ten like her, we might all be Catholics now, Palmer. Beautiful woman she was, by all accounts. Blonde hair, she wore very long in spite of the fashions, and a tendency to wear white. I saw her portrait once, and it was as near to being in love as I have ever been. When the news reached them at

Gutherscale Hall that King George was after him in 1715, he could not make his mind up where to run. He thought to hide himself in the homes of his servants, but his wife, on hearing of this, threw her fan at him and said "Take that then! And give me your sword!"' He shook his head. '"Take that!" she said. Naturally he had to go and join Foster and the other rebels then. Though if she had not thrown her fan, then Mr Crowther's father would never have become rich, or a baron, then Mr Crowther would not have trained as an anatomist, would not have been able to help you in eighty-one, then who can say? Our late successes at sea might not have occurred and our nation might have lost more severely on this treaty coming. All that and much more because a woman threw a fan at her husband.' He leaned ever further forward and beckoned Palmer towards him. When Palmer found his eyes were only an inch from Gawen's own the old man grinned again. 'See, Palmer? I am become a philosopher!' Then he rocked back in his chair and giggled.

Palmer smiled. 'Indeed you are, Sir Gawen.'

'Pah! But all this is known. You do not come to me, Mr Palmer, to discover things you could read in a lending library. What else?'

Mr Palmer took a more delicate swallow of his own wine and filled both their glasses. 'Mr Crowther and Mrs Westerman wish to discover what they can of Lord Greta's escape, and his life on the continent, and also the betrayal of his brother to the government.'

Sir Gawen's face became rather still. 'Do they, do they indeed? So they *are* in blood again, but old blood. Old blood.' He tapped his fingers on the map. 'You know this is the finest present you have given me since you started visiting me, Palmer?' The latter nodded. 'Naturally you do. Yet you give it in order to seek information for your friends, not for some crowning scheme of your own, or for your King.' He picked up his wine again and tilted it from side to side, letting the liquid reach almost to the brim before letting it fall back. 'Some of the guilty went unpunished in eighty-one, did they not? Do you sacrifice this treasure to make amends?' The glass tilted the other way. 'Or do you see, Mr Palmer, the advantage in putting these two rather unusual personages in your debt again?'

Mr Palmer said nothing.

'You went to the archives before you came here, did you not? It was after that visit that you decided to offer this treasure to me.'

'Yes, Sir Gawen. After I saw your name on the writ for Rupert de Beaufoy's arrest.'

The old man set down his wine. 'Your teacher cannot complain if you have learned your lessons well, Mr Palmer.' He stared at the map in his lap again, moving his hands across old, guessed boundaries, feeling with his fingertips for dragons in uncharted territory. 'Very well. We shall come to that when we must. Greta escaped to France from the Tower itself. It was his wife who managed the affair, dressing him as a maid and smuggling him out under the noses of the guards. They joined the court of the Pretender. They had managed to get away with some money, but most of that was spent in bribing their way out of the country.'

'Were your predecessors sorry to see him escape, sir?' Palmer asked.

A corner of Sir Gawen's mouth lifted crookedly. 'Not

altogether. He was a liked man among the people. It suited us better to see him skulk off to France in a frock rather than become a martyr. The crowd is fickle. Sometimes it is better to make them laugh at our enemies. Tell 'em he ran off in his wife's spare petticoats and they are less likely to make a hero of him.'

'And then?'

'He lived in some want in France. The Pretender and his son spent whatever money our enemies gave them on themselves and left the others to gather trifles. For over twenty years he watched his supposed King fail and flounder, and the Young Pretender become as spoiled and whining a brat as his father had been. Then his wife gave him a son when they had given up all hope of being so blessed. That was in forty-two. And this time his wife took the sword from him. She begged him not to join the Rebellion of forty-five, and as always her wishes were his guide.'

'So his younger brother was sent in his stead?'

'Indeed, with the few followers they still had. They got into the country quietly enough. We had grown a little too secure, having another George on the throne, I fear. Let that be a lesson to you, my boy. There are no such things as peaceful times. Only, when people such as you and I manage our business well, for a period they may appear to be so. We learned where they were. Something delayed them from joining the main force at the appointed time; they dallied longer in their hiding-place than they should have done. We found them in the house of a sympathiser not far from Preston. Swords were drawn, but no blood shed. The followers were transported. De Beaufoy was executed for treason in forty-six when the Rebellion had been driven back into the waters from whence it came.'

'And from whom did you receive the information about where de Beaufoy was in hiding?'

Again Sir Gawen smiled and stroked the parchment on his lap. 'It is a very fine map.'

'It is.'

'The rumour was he was betrayed by a servant who stole from him, then gave him up to the government.'

'I did not ask, Sir Gawen, what the rumour was.'

'You did not. Very well. We received our information from Sir William Penhaligon, as he then was.'

'Mr Crowther's father.'

'Indeed. He had come into possession of certain letters that revealed whose house they were sheltering in, so he said, and got that information into hands that could make use of it. Mine. And he was clever about it. He sent a servant with the message, and nothing written down. I can see that rogue before me, more sharply than I can see you, Palmer, in this gloom. A great thick-armed fellow who had ridden through the country without sleep till he reached my door. He had a mouth so full of the barbarous dialect of that place I could hardly understand him. He gave me the name of a house, said Rupert de Beaufoy was thought to be there according to letters intercepted, and added, only, "Sir William Penhaligon sends this message to his King". Then he was gone again.'

'You did not doubt the message?'

The old man shook his head very slowly. 'It was too fine a prize to be ignored. We knew of Sir William a little. He was a clever man and had already made enough friends among my friends. The information was good. We found it was time to bestow a new title in those lands. Sir William wished to purchase further land from the forfeited estates of Lord Greta. We arranged that he received an advantageous price.'

'And the rumour that de Beaufoy was betrayed by a servant?'

'Dropped into an ear or two. Allowed to fly uncorrected.'

Mr Palmer was silent a few moments. 'Intercepted. Was it not at the time of the Rebellion that Gutherscale Hall burned?'

'Not that I had leisure to think on it at the time, Palmer. But when we were secure again I had the same suspicion.'

'That Lord Greta had ordered that the Hall be burned rather than receive Sir William as a tenant.'

'Perhaps. And that either the arsonist was discovered, or was ordered to make some other threat against Sir William. If so, Greta underestimated Sir William and his determination to hang onto what Greta himself had abandoned.'

It was strange how quiet this room was, being so close to Whitehall and the hustle and show of the city. A silent ink spot in the centre of all that movement and display.

'Perhaps?'

Sir Gawen sniffed his wine. 'All these years, Mr Palmer, and now I find myself transparent. There was a man, much loved by Greta, whom we expected to find with his brother. A Kit Huntsman. He was not there, and we have never had sight of him since.'

Mr Palmer thought of the skeleton on the island and of the sharp lines of Mr Crowther's face.

'There is something more,' Palmer said at last.

'Rupert suffered the traditional fate of a traitor, you know. The King was adamant. Hanged, cut down when alive, disembowelled, then his limbs cut from his trunk. He lived a long while into it.' The haze in the streets seemed to have thickened. Sir Gawen no longer appeared so eager to look Mr Palmer in the eye.

'We have agreed it is a very fine map, have we not, Sir Gawen?'

The old man nodded. Palmer wondered whether, if he lived to such an advanced age, the secrets he held would bend his spine as they seemed to have done to Sir Gawen.

'We heard a rumour, a whisper that perhaps the story of the servant was no longer believed, and then . . . A man saw a face in the crowd.'

'When?' Palmer asked.

'The year of Lord Keswick's murder.'

'What season?'

'That season.'

Palmer breathed deeply, yet his blood still felt thin and hot in his veins. 'And no one thought to offer that information to the accusers of Lord Keswick's oldest son?'

'I did not. *I* did not. There was too much foul air trapped in the business to open it up. Do not play the child with me, Palmer. Would you expose so much, on so thin a scrap of rumour, to save the neck of a boy like Lucius Adair Penhaligon?'

Mr Palmer picked up his wine. 'Perhaps not.'

His companion nodded emphatically. 'If you must communicate this to Mr Crowther, have the decency to lie about when the information came to us. Say it was after the trial. We do not wish him an enemy.'

Mr Palmer drank. 'Very well. For that I shall ask you one last question. What happened then? What became of Lord Greta's son?'

'Lord Greta died two years later and three days after his remarkable wife, leaving his son a gentleman of dubious education and limited means. The son was a military man for a while, then made his way playing cards, but he was lost sight of after a scandal some five years ago. A grand game that ruined a young man. He was accused of cheating, and fought a duel though I have no doubt the accusation was accurate. He killed his man, and escaped with the fortune he had swindled. He went by the name of von Lowenstein at that time.'

'Had he other names?'

Sir Gawen drained his wine. 'His given one was Grenville de Beaufoy. There were times though when he liked to play the English gentleman of middling rank. Then we heard of him styling himself as Mr Sturgess.'

V.6

Silverside Hall

M RS BRIGGS TOOK HARRIET directly into the drawing room. 'Oh, I am glad you came, Mrs Westerman! So grateful. I do not know what to do. I thought perhaps your son might get a message to Casper for me, but I am not at all sure what I should say. I had to ask you – what should I say? It is a terrible, terrible slander if I am wrong.'

'Mrs Briggs,' Harriet said, looking her in the eye, 'I have not the slightest idea what you are talking about. Is this something to do with the Vizegräfin?'

Mrs Briggs had collapsed onto one of her sofas, produced a handkerchief and begun to gnaw on it. However, when Harriet finished she looked up swiftly. 'The Vizegräfin? What might she have to do with it?'

Harriet sighed and sat down next to her. Mrs Briggs took a deep breath. 'I may seem an idiot to you, Mrs Westerman, and if I do, I hope you will be kind enough to tell me so, as it would be a great relief.'

'Mrs Briggs . . .'

She held up her hand. 'Yes, yes. I know, I shall start at the beginning. When we were talking last evening in your room, we mentioned the Fowlers, father and son.'

'I remember,' Harriet said, cupping her chin in her hands.

'I told you I have tried to give them work from time to time, I think? Yes? Well, as it happens, one of those occasions was when we opened the tomb on Saint Herbert's Island. I had no idea that they might find anything to steal there.'

'The snuff barrel!'

'Precisely, Mrs Westerman.' She patted Harriet on the knee. 'If you remember, Mr Sturgess brought it to us.'

Harriet frowned as she tried to remember. 'He said they had been fighting, and were taken up before him as the magistrate.'

'Yes, yes. I began to wonder . . . and when you said that Casper thought they were the men that beat him . . .'

'I am not entirely sure I am following you, Mrs Briggs.'

'My dear girl, who might? I was so worried by what I was thinking I spent the whole night pacing my room and wondering at it.' She drew breath again. 'Mr Sturgess has always been passionately interested in the history and antiquities of the area. Such as the Luck.'

'Mr Askew said he made various contributions to the museum.'

'So he did, so he did. He tried to employ Casper to help him, but he is not the sort of man who sends fools after buried treasure. The whole village knows though that Mr Sturgess has a great interest in such things. I had thought that interest had waned, but then with Casper beaten and the Black Pig searched . . . Mr Sturgess is normally rather free with his fines and punishments and sending people to the Petty Sessions. I thought he had learned to be more merciful.'

Harriet bit her lip. 'I heard a man call Casper the Luck-keeper today.'

Mrs Briggs nodded quickly. 'I was here twenty years before anyone let that name slip in front of me. But those Fowlers, suppose they told Sturgess that Casper might have the Luck? They are stupid men, he could have threatened them with the rope or the prison hulks if he said the snuffbox was worth enough. Suppose they traded their necks for that bit of chatter, and then Mr Sturgess sent them off after Casper?'

'It is a grave suspicion, but it would make sense of his determination to have Casper taken up for the murder of Mr Hurst, and Mr Askew.'

'Just so, poor deluded man! To so compromise himself for the sake of a jewel! Oh, I pity him. I wanted to see if your son might warn Casper, and thought perhaps I might write a letter to Mr Sturgess in a friendly way, to suggest his enthusiasm might have overcome his good sense in his search for the heritage of this area.'

Harriet stood up. 'How long has Mr Sturgess been resident in the area, Mrs Briggs?'

Her hostess examined the air above her head. 'Let me see . . . it was when Mr Briggs first invested in the wine business on the continent, rather than simply importing what had already been grown . . . so it must be four, no nearly five years ago now.'

'I think it would be best if I pay Mr Sturgess a visit.'

Mrs Briggs put her hand to her mouth. 'Oh, Mrs Westerman, must you? He might be so ashamed. He has been such a good neighbour to us. And I might be terribly wrong.'

'I think I shall take Felix with me.' She began to walk towards the door, when Mrs Briggs's voice stopped her.

'But what of Mr Askew, Mrs Westerman? And Mr Hurst? Have your enquiries proceeded at all?'

'Yes, Mrs Briggs. Some.'

Agnes made the pile of her treasures as carefully as she might. There were the larger sticks she had found, then piled on top the splinters and sticks she'd managed to pull free from the more rotted joists that held the earth above her. On top of these she had bundled threads. They might not serve to lead her through the tunnels, but she had ripped the seam from her handkerchief and picked it apart with shivering fingers until she had this pile of thin stuff on top of the lighter twigs. In her left hand she held a flint, found and split in the darkness, in her right the arrow, its head pointed down.

Praying for sparks, she began to strike it down onto the flint.

When Casper had walked these paths to search the old shafts of Comb Beck, he had had no thought to look for the Fowler men. This afternoon he had found their camp easily enough, and seen enough of it to know they would return to it. A neat site by Masmill Beck, far enough from the path to be hidden. The beck had worked its way well into the slope just here. It had been easy to find slightly higher ground that offered the view he wanted, but where the rocks gave him some cover. What they couldn't provide he made himself, cutting down a branch from a rowan three yards off. The tree squealed behind his eyes, and he murmured his apologies. The white witch touched its trunk, and he felt it settle. Since Stephen had told him of Swithun's injury, her voice had become stronger. The black witch, Grice, who had been crowing over his failures till he could hardly know where he was, had slunk back a little. He was calm now, and moved with serious careful intent.

Now he lay behind the rocks, screened by the rowan but with good sight of the Fowler camp. He held his knife in his right hand. If either father or son came alone, he'd be able to subdue him and get sense out of him with no need of it, but if they came together he'd have to kill one quick to catch the other. He had no wish to murder any man but if needed, he'd do it easily. It seemed to him the Black Witch was struggling to have at him, but something prevented her. He flicked his eyes upstream. The white lady was sitting on a rock in the middle of the waters, her hair all glowing and gold. She raised her hand to him and smiled. He knew only he could see her, and her presence gave him comfort. He smiled then turned his eyes back towards the camp.

Agnes's eyes were wet with tears. She'd seen sparks jump, but they would not catch. For a moment she rested, then neatened the pile of threads and began again, striking metal and stone with a chant in her head of 'this time, this time'.

When the threads started to glow, she gazed at them stupidly a second then dropped the arrow and blew on them as gently as she could. One of the twigs began to catch. The thin light beyond the barricade was lessening. She began to tremble. What if all the light went before the smoke from her fire made it out of the tunnel's mouth? She tended the fire and cooed to it like a mother with a child. Then looked up to see the first smoke pulled through the gap in the barrier.

Harriet had taken Mrs Briggs's best saddle horse and Felix rode beside her on his own mount. He had grown sulky finding Mrs Westerman had no intention of explaining to him what they were about. She simply ignored his questions as if they had no more sense to them than the calls of the birds. As they reached Portinscale, Mrs Westerman suddenly reined in her horse and bent low in the saddle to speak to a woman with a basket on her hip.

'Miriam! Have you been in town? Have you seen any sign of Mr Crowther?'

The servant looked up with a smile. 'Yes, madam. I saw him not ten minutes ago a way ahead of me. He turned up into Mr Sturgess's house.'

Mrs Westerman's horse leaped forward and Felix spurred his own in pursuit.

The evening was coming on. Slowly the light was leaching from the air, and its taste began to change in Casper's mouth. The blooms of the day were closing, and the scents of darker flowers started to tendril out among the shadows. He felt no difference between himself and the trees and rocks around him; he was a part of the turn of the hill, just like the white lady and the black witch. The heavy air shifted with a faint sound: something was coming along the path, someone. He turned his eyes to where the white lady still sat like a mermaid on her stone in the stream. She put her finger to her lips.

It was Swithun. Alone. He looked about himself and ducked inside one of the rough covers, coming out a moment later with a large canvas bag which he began to stuff with his goods. Casper tensed his muscles and as Swithun bent forward to drive his blanket as deep and tight into the bag as he could, Casper swung down from his hiding place. As his feet touched the ground, Swithun spun round to find the evening air had split open and Casper before him. He cried out and Casper brought his fist up hard under Swithun's chin. He fell back onto the ground and Casper was on him, sat on his chest and pinning his arms to the earth with his knees. Casper lifted his knife so Swithun could see it, then brought it to his eye. Swithun stopped struggling at once. His long eyelashes tickled the point of Casper's blade. He shifted his weight onto Swithun's right arm. He groaned but so afraid was he of the knife he did not dare move. Casper lowered his face over Swithun's until he could taste the younger man's breath. He tasted the fear on it.

'Where is she?'

Swithun was panting like a fox cornered. 'I can't say. He'll kill me. Please, Casper! I'll send word. Please. You won't kill me?'

There were times when the evil that bubbled and stewed in

the black witch were of use. Casper let her speak now, through his own throat. His voice became older.

'I won't.' He moved the knife a little so Swithun could feel its point just on the bone of his eye socket, flicked away a strand of the boy's hair then returned its tip to the white and pushed just enough with the flat for the pressure to be felt. Swithun whimpered. 'But I'll put out your eyes if you don't tell me, and leave you to wander blind. Imagine the pain of that, Swithun. Think of the dark.'

'Sturgess's folly!' He said it fast; his body was shaking so hard it was as if he were fitting. Casper kept his face close, and blew gently on Swithun's eye so he blinked and his eyelashes touched the blade.

'That's nowt but a little dip for him to sit in. I'll do your left eye now, see if that makes you more inclined to be truthful.' He began to press.

'No!' Swithun screamed. 'I swear, it goes further back! He tried to mine! Some fella told him there was more copper there, when he first came. He tried it for three months.' Casper released the pressure a little and waited for Swithun to calm himself. 'It's deep enough; just on from where he's got all his shells it narrows and goes back. There's a barrier – she's behind that. I swear it!'

'And how come I hear this from you?'

'He brought in workers. Did it while he was landscaping his garden, like he was some fucking Lord. You were off somewhere.'

Casper thought back, keeping his knife where it was. There had been dark times now and again where he'd hardly notice a season pass, and come stumbling back to the village thin and hurting. It could be. And he would take no note of an out-comer prettifying his garden.

'Is she living?'

'Yes, yes, Casper! I swear! My da said Sturgess tried to do her, but he let go of her arm in time. I took her food, and water. We never wanted to hurt anyone, Casper. But he said we'd hang.'

'Sturgess? You tried to bargain with him?'

'He said we'd hang, I say! Over a snuffbox. Everyone knows he's always looking for the Luck. We had no choice! We didn't know it would come to this.'

Casper lifted his knife away and straightened, then shifted his weight to take the pressure off Swithun's injured arm a little.

'She do that to you?'

'Yes.' The voice was small, miserable. There was a smell of piss in the air.

'You brought her food? Your da helped her live?'

'Yes, Casper! We did! Swear on the Luck, we did!'

The black witch wanted blood. She always did. She wanted to see the knife go into the eye and watch the jelly of it burst. Casper ignored her. He felt the white lady standing behind him, her hand on his shoulder, and leaned back into her touch.

'That's earned you one chance, Swithun. One. Pack your stuff, find your da and then leave here. Don't do anything else. Whatever you've been promised, put it out of your mind. If you run now, you can live. I'll even keep an eye on your ma and you can send for her later if you want. But you and your da are banished from here. If you're ever seen here again, you'll breathe your last in those moments. You hear?' Swithun nodded.

'Swear it. Swear on the Luck you tried to take which sees and knows and remembers.'

'I swear it.'

Casper sprang up and was swallowed into the woods before Swithun even knew he was free. He rolled over, got to his knees and vomited onto the earth.

V.7

CROWTHER USED THE HEAD of his cane to knock at the door of Mr Sturgess's house. It was a convenient sort of place for a gentleman, with a long drive coming to a pleasant villa that would be perfect for a well-to-do parson and his family. Crowther was surprised, therefore, when the door was opened by the owner himself.

'Mr Crowther, what do you want?'

'Your maid's day off, Mr Sturgess?'

He looked rather flustered by the question, and annoyed. 'As you say.'

'There are matters I wish to discuss with you,' Crowther said. 'I am beginning to be of the opinion you were right all along, and these crimes must be laid at the feet of Casper Grace.'

Sturgess smiled more pleasantly, opened the door fully and gestured for Crowther to follow him. 'I am pleased to hear you are willing to see sense. Come in, we can speak in the study.'

Crowther followed him slowly. There were bare places on the walls, like the ghosts of the portraits in Mr Askew's museum, and a general air of neglect around the place that could not be explained by a maid only absent for one day. The study into which he was shown, however, was completely furnished. There were bookshelves down one wall and an imposing-looking desk with a chair behind it of antique style and almost throne-like pretensions, backed with a heavy dresser. One or two more modern, rather spindly dining chairs sat against the wall. There were a number of portraits. Crowther noticed another door leading to the lawns at the back of the house, and through the window to his left saw a pathway that he assumed circled round to the front. Sturgess had obviously noticed him absorbing the scene.

'This is where I conduct my official business. Every day at any time someone may be knocking on that door there asking for my assistance in some matter or other.' So this room is where you keep up appearances for the populace, Crowther thought, while the rest of the house rots. 'You wished to discuss Casper Grace, Mr Crowther? I take it, as you are alone, that you have not persuaded Mrs Westerman as yet?'

Crowther allowed himself a slight smile. 'When a woman takes an idea into her head, Mr Sturgess . . . especially a woman such as Mrs Westerman.'

The other man laughed and opened one of the drawers in his desk, removing a pile of papers that he began to sort into piles in front of him. 'I pity you! Still, I hear her husband left her nicely off. It might be worth putting up with a woman like that to increase one's fortune by such a slice.'

Crowther was looking at the items on the mantelpiece. There was a small gold cup amongst them which announced itself as the winner's prize of the Richmond Toxophilists Association. 'You are not wearing your chatelaine today, Mr Sturgess. I meant to ask you where you acquired it.'

Mr Sturgess began to sort his papers more slowly. 'It was made in Paris. I cannot imagine you wearing such a thing, Mr Crowther. Not really fitting with your monkish style, is it?'

'I thought I saw something similar to it in a portrait of Lord Greta Mr Askew showed me an evening or two ago. I do hope it has not been damaged.'

Sturgess turned his back and opened a drawer in the dresser behind him. 'Not beyond repair, I am glad to say. Though I was glad to retrieve the missing piece from Askew's body.'

'Do you know, Sturgess, you are the only man in Keswick who consistently calls me by the name Crowther? Every other body here slips in the occasional "my lord", but then you must loathe the idea of a Lord Keswick here even more than I. You are Lord Greta's son. Mr Hurst recognised you, blackmailed you.'

Sturgess remained with his back to him. 'Very astute, Crowther. I am. Apparently he saw me first on the morning of his arrival, though I did not note him. He slithered up the path into this room two days later, claiming acquaintance and discussing a business venture he had in mind and mentioned another interested party. It was quite blatant. Our paths had crossed in Vienna, it seems. Lord knows how he came to this backwater, but once he did I had to dispose of him before he realised I had not the means to outbid Viscount Moreland and that terribly persistent lawyer of his.'

'The tutor of the man you shot was Mr Hudson's own son. Now the lawyer holds you responsible for the death of his child in the last war, as well as the boy you shot. How did you know that Mr Askew suspected you?'

'Ah, that might explain it. Fathers and sons. I understand

it is often a close bond. Yes, poor old Askew. I saw him yesterday morning. I was asking after Casper's hideouts and the man could hardly look at me. I realised he knew something. I visited again in the evening to find out what it was, all friendly concern, and he was relieved to tell me he had recognised my chatelaine. I told him I had bought it at auction in Paris, having been told that it once belonged to Lord Greta. I told him it led to my first interest in this area. A neat romantic tale. We were getting along famously until I throttled him. He put up a good fight though. Just not quite good enough. I rather liked him, you know. He was a friend of sorts.' There was a click, and in a terrible instant Crowther realised what Sturgess was about. He sprang forward, but Sturgess had already turned round and was aiming the pistol squarely at Crowther's chest.

'Now, now Mr Crowther!' Crowther stopped, still too far away to reach him. He felt the ball of silver on his father's cane. If he could throw it hard enough at Sturgess in the instant he fired . . . 'Your father, Mr Crowther, was a murderous dog. He bought our land cheap and raped it. He would have had the Hall too if Kit Huntsman had not put a torch to it rather than see it so defiled. That act of bravery cost him his life, didn't it? Then Sir William sent my uncle to the executioner and let my father think for years that Kit had turned traitor. Your fortune should have been mine, Crowther. But as I cannot have that, I shall take your life. Kit was one of my father's favourites. I remember him a little.'

'Wait!'

'Goodbye, Mr Crowther.' His finger twitched on the trigger.

Crowther threw himself forward, already knowing he was too slow. Just then, something to the left caught Sturgess's eye out of the window and his face looked a little uncertain. Even as the powder burned in the pan the muzzle drifted in the same direction. Nevertheless, Crowther felt the force of the bullet strike him like a club and he fell back into darkness.

Casper saw the smoke as soon as he cleared the wall into Sturgess's private grounds. It curled weakly into the dusk from a carved grotto set into the side of the hill. He went running for it, not sparing the breath yet to call her name. The entrance to the grotto had been lined with shells, and a little fountain dropped a stream of water into the wide mouth of a granite fish. The smoke was thick.

'Agnes!' He paused, listening.

'Casper! I am here!' Weak and a way back.

He thrust his handkerchief into the fish's mouth and bound it sopping over his nose and mouth. Here was where the grotto turned into a tunnel. The smoke was powerful thick; in the darkness in front of him he saw the barricade, the base of it red and smouldering. He ran back then turned and threw himself at it. Where the wood had begun to char, it gave way. He could see a figure on the far side.

'Stamp out what flames you can, girl! I'm coming again.'

This time he let fly just to the right of where he had made a gap. A board cracked and fell away. He scrambled to his feet and pulled another of the glowing planks aside. Agnes fell out at once towards him, coughing and spluttering. He gathered her in his arms and made for the air.

To Agnes the evening had never smelled so sweet. She was still coughing and weeping with the smoke, but she was laughing too. Casper looked like a highwayman with his kerchief over his face, and it was funny to be carried as if you weighed no more than air. She was still giggling and gasping as she was set down on the grass and Casper beat the embers out that had clung to her skirts.

There was a shout from the house, and as they turned there they saw a flash of light in the window of Sturgess's office and heard the crack of a gunshot. Casper hesitated. Agnes struck him on the leg with the back of her hand as she crouched retching on the turf.

'Go on, Casper! Go on!'

Harriet hardly slowed her horse to dismount, leaping from her saddle with a grace Felix envied. He sniffed and looked into the shadows at the far side of the house. 'Is that smoke? I think something might be on fire.'

Mrs Westerman was hammering at the door with her fist. There was a sudden crack inside the house, and Felix slithered down from his own horse.

'Felix, break this door down.'

'Madam, I—'

'*Now*, Felix!'

Casper reached the window to see Sturgess standing over Crowther's body. He was reloading his pistol. Casper put his shoulder up to protect his eyes, smashed through the glass and stumbled into the room. Sturgess spun round and lifted his elbow as Casper reached him, catching Casper in the throat but dropping the pistol. Casper fell back. There was a bang at the front door, voices calling for Sturgess, Mrs Westerman shouting for Crowther. Even as Casper heard the front door give way, he

423

watched Sturgess run out of the side door. He rolled onto his knees, choking from the blow to his throat and crawled over to where Crowther lay. It looked bad, the blood was running hard. Crowther's eyes were half-open and he was breathing heavily.

'Oh God, Gabriel!' Mrs Westerman dropped to her knees beside him and took Crowther's hand. She was with another man. Felix.

'I shall fetch the surgeon,' he said. Mr Crowther seemed to shake his head, then nodded towards Casper.

'Very well,' she said quietly. 'Crowther prefers Mr Grace's care, Felix.' She was very white. 'Felix, we need bandages. Now. Go and rip a sheet from the bed.' The boy left as Casper pulled his shirt over his head and bundled it into the wound on Crowther's shoulder, pressing hard. He heard Harriet's voice again. 'Who is that?'

Casper turned round to see Agnes standing among the shattered glass of the doorway. She was black with filth, and her hands were scraped and bleeding. 'My 'prentice. Agnes, get a fire going in the kitchen. Hot water.'

She nodded and made for the door, staggering only once.

V.8

WHEN CROWTHER RETURNED, painfully, to conscious-ness an hour later, he found himself lying in an unfamiliar bed, and Mrs Westerman sitting by it, her green eyes on his.

'Welcome back, Crowther.' He felt the burning of his shoulder and closed his eyes again for a moment until the first wave of it passed. The flesh was on fire, though he was aware of a coolness at the surface, working in. There was a similar sensation on his shoulderblade. It was as if two cold hands were cupping the burning of the muscle and bone between them. 'Did the bullet pass through?'

'It did. And took some of your flesh with it. Casper cleaned the wound and made some temporary concoction to treat it. He is gone out into the hills now to find other weeds to make something more complex. You are now being healed with what could be found here, among Mr Sturgess's untended flowerbeds. It is his bed you are sleeping in at present, and we shall not risk moving you yet.'

He tried to raise himself a little and hissed as the wound burned and tore at him. Harriet passed him a water glass, and he drank. It tasted strangely bitter.

'Casper says this is what you are to drink,' she said.

Crowther took another mouthful. 'I hope the village's faith in him is justified.'

'As do I. Are you sure we should not send for a surgeon?'

He let himself lean back into the pillows. 'No, no. Casper will keep an eye on my fever. Just don't let him lay me out on the floor or stuff mistletoe in my pockets.' There were voices downstairs. 'Who else is in the house?'

'I hardly know,' Harriet said, and put her chin into her hands. 'The whole place is in an uproar. They think I am keeping watch on you, but really I am here to avoid the fuss. The family of that young girl had to be sent for, and arrived half-mad with worry. Remarkable girl. Resourceful too. She set fire to Sturgess's grotto, striking sparks with the arrow that was supposed to kill her.'

Crowther decided to pick the narrative out of that statement when the pain had subsided a little.

'Then, of course, everyone is trying to find a magistrate to take control of matters. Your sister apparently went into hysterics when she heard the news, and Mrs Briggs took the opportunity to slap her.' She paused, watching his faint smile. 'The Mr Leathes, junior and senior, and Mr Hudson are bent over Mrs Briggs's sherry, sent from the Hall with her compliments, two of her servants and half the contents of the kitchen. They are in the parlour trying to make sense of it all, and ignoring Felix.'

She fell silent. Crowther sighed heavily; he thought he read her frown with reasonable accuracy. 'Go on, Mrs Westerman. Say what you wish to say. I must face it at some time. Better now, I think, while I am distracted by the pain.'

Harriet looked a little indignant for a moment, then sat back and folded her arms. 'Very well. Crowther, I am so angry with you that if I had a pistol of my own I would shoot you through your other shoulder. Do not sigh at me!'

'The wound troubles me, Mrs Westerman.'

'Good! How *could* you be so foolish? You remembered something from the portrait, I presume – something that led you to Sturgess?'

'His chatelaine. Lord Greta was wearing it in the portrait. We thought he was concerned for his friend, but he was retrieving a broken piece of it from Mr Askew's fist.'

'Why did you not return to the Hall to tell me? Why come here on your own? You deserved to be shot.'

'Mr Sturgess's house lies on the way to the Hall. It was an impulse, Mrs Westerman.'

'Crowther! Of all the . . .' He smiled despite the fire in

his shoulder. It was not often he left Mrs Westerman speech-less.

'I do assure you, Harriet, it is very painful.'

'I am overjoyed to hear it! Really, how could you just *stand* there and let yourself be shot? Did he have a gun primed and ready?'

Crowther looked guilty at that. 'No, he had his back to me. I confess I was too interested in what he was saying to think what he was about until the last moment.'

Harriet was scowling at him. 'I thought he had killed you. If he had succeeded I would have gone mad, Crowther.'

He looked at her small angry face and said, very gently, 'My apologies, Mrs Westerman. I will endeavour to be more careful in future.' She placed her hand over his own and looked away as he continued, 'I am certainly fortunate Casper appeared when he did.'

'According to Mr Grace, you have the Luck to thank for that. He is quite sure it nudges events one way or another.'

The pain in his shoulder flared, and he felt her hand tighten on his own. He answered the pressure briefly and swallowed.

'The Luck? But do we not believe the Luck destroyed? Have you found out how it came into my father's hands?'

'It seems there is more than one sort of meaning of "destroyed". There is another visitor downstairs that I have not mentioned to you as yet. Mrs Lottie Tyers. As soon as she heard news of the shooting, and I do not think the word could have travelled any faster than the sound of the gun itself, she picked up her stick and walked over here. She is sitting downstairs and annoying the lawyers by referring to them as foolish young men. I shall send her up to you in a little while, if you are strong enough.'

He nodded and she took her hand from his and stood. As she turned, her green skirts spun behind her and she slipped through the door like a passing breeze.

Stephen walked very slowly, letting Mr Quince lean on his shoulder. Their stroll had been slow and faltering, and though Stephen had wanted to dash ahead he did not wish Mr Quince to feel abandoned so he tried to be patient and move steadily. The last light was soft on their faces.

Stephen wondered if Casper had found Swithun yet, and if Casper had managed to find out from him where Agnes was, but most of all he felt the weight of the Luck in his waistband. He was proud, but he hoped he would not have to keep it long. A secret was a heavy thing to bear, and he was glad not to have seen much of his mother that day. He felt Mr Quince stop: the tutor was peering up into the trees to where the higher path skirted the grounds of Silverside.

'Stephen, is that not Fräulein Hurst?' Stephen looked and saw a tall female figure in a dark green cloak moving along above them. 'Fräulein?' The figure turned and put back her hood. Stephen saw the familiar black hair. It was dark as Joe's back. 'Please do run up and ask her if she would be so kind as to come and speak with us,' Quince said. 'I wish to express my condolences.'

Stephen scrambled up the slope to the young woman's side. She smiled at him. 'Master Westerman, I hope you are well?'

'Please will you come with me and speak to my tutor, miss?' She hesitated. 'He has been rather ill, you know,' he added a

428

little pleadingly. She set down a small bag on the path at her side.

'Yes, of course. Will you give me your hand down the bank?'

Mr Quince brightened considerably as Miss Hurst put out her hand to him, but his kind round face was soon creased with concern. Miss Hurst was determined to see the ruins of Gutherscale Hall at dusk. Miss Scales had told her they were magnificent and her wish for some peace had encouraged her to make a late-afternoon walk round the lake. Mr Quince was worried that she might get lost in the dark or stumble and injure herself. She declared herself determined.

'I would insist on accompanying you, Fräulein,' he said, 'but I am tired even having walked round the gardens of Silverside.'

She shook her head briskly. 'There is no need, sir. I am quite capable of going myself.'

'Perhaps one of the servants from the house, if you'll allow me . . .'

'Please, no!' Her voice had become quite sharp, and as if sorry for causing poor Mr Quince any offence, she added quickly and more kindly, 'Dusk is coming on, and I am anxious to be on my way. Please do not worry over me, Mr Quince. I would hate to think you troubled at all on my account.'

Mr Quince's sickroom pallor was warmed momentarily with a blush. Stephen looked from one to the other.

'I can go with Miss Hurst,' he said. 'If you can return to the house without my help, sir.' It was Mr Quince who hesitated now. 'I know the way — you know I have been there lots of times since you were ill, sir. And we shall be quite safe if we go together. I am not afraid of the dark.'

Mr Quince looked at Miss Hurst with a slight smile. 'I would be much easier in my mind, Miss Hurst, if you would take Stephen with you. He can be a pleasant companion. Do not chatter at Miss Hurst, Stephen.'

Miss Hurst sighed. 'Very well, sir, if it will make you easier.' She proffered her hand and Mr Quince took it between his own. 'I am glad to see your health improving. We shall go now, Stephen?'

Mr Quince watched them make their way up the slope to the higher path. It was a hard thing to see his charge at the woman's side, since an evening's walk to the ruins in her company would have been one of the great occasions of his life. The pair disappeared into the trees, and he turned away feeling rather defeated, and through the lengthening shadows made his way slowly back to the Hall.

Harriet avoided the parlour when she left Crowther, and instead returned for a moment to the office. Crowther's blood was darkening on the carpet, his bloodstained coat and Casper's shirt tumbled and ripped beside it. She thought of her husband again, the way his blood had seeped through her hands, how he had looked at her while he lay dying. She stared at her hands curled in her lap. Her dress was damp in places where she had tried to scrub Crowther's blood from it in the kitchen and her cuffs were still marked. Some traces remained under her fingernails. She had felt blood run across her fingers too many times, she knew its smell and texture too intimately, too well. She felt the muscles in her arms begin to tremble and the world seemed to darken. When she heard the rap at the door she started, and turned away to wipe her eyes as it opened. It was Mr Kerrick, the girl's father.

'Will he do, madam? Lord Keswick?'

She nodded. 'Yes, thank you. I believe he will as long as there is no infection, though he is in pain now.' She tucked her handkerchief back into her sleeve and attempted to smile. 'How is your daughter? She is a brave girl.'

'We were so frightened, madam. Can't say as her mother will ever let her out of the front gate again. Thing is, we want to get her home and rested and fed, but she says she needs to see Casper first, and he's off on the hills gathering plants for the baron . . . She won't tell us why.' He sighed, and Harriet recognised the love and frustration of fatherhood. 'She's as weak as a kitten, but stubborn as ever she was.'

'Do you think she might speak to me? I would be happy to see her.'

His long face flooded with relief. 'Yes, madam, thank you, I shall fetch her at once.'

Harriet was looking out over the dark lawn when Agnes appeared in the doorway. She was still wearing her muddied skirts but had a clean linen shawl over her shoulders. It was dark red. She was obviously conscious of the bruises and cuts on her hands, and was trying to hide them in its folds.

'Come and sit here, Agnes.' Harriet sat in one of the spindly dining chairs and patted the one next to her own.

'I shall dirty it.'

'It is Mr Sturgess's chair. You may dirty it all you like.' Agnes grinned quickly at that and crossed the room to her. 'Now, is there something you want to ask me? Is it about Mr Sturgess?'

She shook her head. 'No, madam. Not that one. It is just . . . the German lady – she's all right, isn't she? Safe, I mean. No harm has come to her?'

Harriet frowned. 'Miss Hurst is staying at the vicarage with Miss Scales, Agnes. I am sure she is quite safe. Why are you worried about her? You heard that Sturgess killed her father, I suppose. He knew Sturgess's secret and was blackmailing him, I think. But I do not believe she had any part in the affair, and in any case Sturgess's secret is out now. Her father brought her here for other reasons . . .'

Agnes's fists continued to work in the folds of her shawl. 'He was going to shoot me. Put an arrow through my head. He wanted to know where the Luck was, and I was so scared. I said that the German lady had it. That Casper told her to take it away till all was safe again.' Harriet was quiet a moment. 'I'm so sorry, madam. I thought she'd be safest. I didn't know it was him, but I reckoned whoever it was they'd have a harder time chasing gentry.'

Harriet patted her knee. 'It was a good idea, Agnes. I would have done the same. Just the same. Go home now and rest. Sturgess has fled. Whatever his hope of finding the Luck, it is all gone now, I am sure. But I promise I shall send to Miss Scales. Perhaps Ham can make a bed there for a while, until Sturgess is taken or we are sure he is gone for good.'

Agnes smiled, and for the first time Harriet realised she was a very pretty child.

'Thank you! Thank you, Mrs Westerman. I will sleep easy, knowing that. Lord, I am so tired I could stay in my bed a month.' She yawned, showing her sharp white teeth.

Harriet delivered her to her parents and saw them ride away in Kerrick's cart just as Mrs Tyers was emerging from the kitchen.

'Mrs Tyers, you may see Crowther whenever you wish.'

432

'Very well. He must hear it all now, I suppose. You got help enough, my dear? Lord, this house is looking poor.'

Harriet nodded. 'Half of Keswick is here already, it seems.'

'Mostly lawyers though,' the old lady said, rolling her eyes. 'I mean people who can work and be helpful, and tend to Master Charles.'

'We have all the help we need for now, I think, Mrs Tyers.'

She narrowed her eyes and lifted her chin, examining Harriet carefully. 'You may call me Lottie, I think, madam. Very well, when I've done talking to Master Charles, I shall be on my way.'

'May I send someone to escort you, Lottie?'

'Nay, lambkin. It's hardly a mile. When I can't manage that on my own roads with ease, I shall get into my bed and let the Devil take me off at last.'

Harriet watched her climb the stairs with a smile. She would go to her at some time over the next few days and ask for her stories of Crowther. First, however, she needed to write a careful note to Miss Scales and send Ham to sleep outside Miss Hurst's door like a bulldog.

Stephen did not treat Sophia to another lecture on Austrian history on this walk. He could tell she was sad, and was still doing enough thinking and wondering of his own. They reached the ruins of Gutherscale Hall just as the sun was sinking. The haze in the air made for beautiful sunsets. To the south, Skelgill Bank began its steep black climb into the rose and gold sky; beyond Newlands Beck, Causey Pike and Outerside had become dark shadows. The last light struck the top of the pele tower through the trees, and the old hall was full of the voices of crows settling to sleep. They looked up at it together and it felt quite natural to Stephen to take Miss Hurst's hand.

'It looks so old,' he said. 'We could climb the tower, if you like, before we go back. You can see the lake from there.'

'That would please me,' she said, 'but Stephen, I am not going back.'

'I don't understand.'

'I wish to leave this place as soon as I might,' she said. 'I am with child. I want to go away somewhere. I will say I am a widow, and have my baby. I learned many things when I was at the convent; afterwards I shall go to some small town and teach the daughters of the gentry.'

'But you told Casper you have no money!' He blushed. 'I was near the camp when you came to talk to Casper. I haven't said anything.'

She looked a little shocked for a moment, then squeezed his hand. 'No matter, Stephen. Mr Sturgess knows my secret, I think. He came to see me this morning and was very kind. He said he knew I wished to carry something precious away from here and wished to help me. He has offered me money to slip away quietly. I think he brings it from someone less kind who wants me away from here. I am more easily bought off than my father.'

'I don't understand.'

She continued as if he had not spoken. 'I am to meet Mr Sturgess here in a little while. He will have a carriage waiting nearby. I shall disappear. It is for the best.'

Stephen did not like the thought of Sophia leaving, for some reason. 'But what of your father? Don't you want to see him buried?'

She put her free hand to her eyes and wiped something from them. 'He was not a good father. I must take this chance to get away. It is too painful to remain here.'

'But why?' He tugged on her hand.

'Oh Stephen, it is difficult.' She knelt down beside him and brushed his hair from his forehead. 'You will try to be a good man, won't you?'

He nodded, frustrated and unhappy. She stood again and said more brightly, 'Let us climb the tower and we shall look at the lake. Then perhaps you should go home.'

He began to lead her to where the spiral staircase began its old climb through the tower walls. He sighed. 'It is quite difficult to be a good man, if no one ever explains anything and just cries all the time.' He thrust his hands into his pockets. 'I shall wait with you. No one will worry about me for an age yet. Mr Quince knows where we are, and you should have a friend to say goodbye to you.'

V.9

HER NOTE WRITTEN AND Ham dispatched, Harriet had retreated to the kitchen to let Mrs Briggs's cook feed her, then realising her presence was making the woman nervous she returned to the study and sat drumming her fingers on Sturgess's desk and looking about her. Tucked under the desk she saw the butt of a pistol and hissed between her teeth as she bent down to retrieve it. It was a Light Dragoon pistol, impossible to shoot accurately with such a weapon, but at close range it was devastating. Crowther had been lucky beyond belief. She felt herself flush with irritation. How could he have been so foolish as to not see what Sturgess was about? She laid the gun on the table top. It was a fine example and well cared for. But then had not Hudson said Sturgess had had military experience in one of his former lives?

She stood and looked into the open drawer of the dresser behind her. The drawer was very deep. There was the case for the gun, and the powder and ball. He must have been very quick to load it and prime the pan without Crowther noticing, but then she had served long enough at her husband's side to see such weapons loaded and fired a hundred times. She would have recognised the necessary movements. Crowther, it was likely, was less familiar than she with such guns. The thought made her smile.

There was a knock at the door. She looked up, expecting to see one of the lawyers or servants, but instead saw Miss Scales hovering in the entrance with Ham beside her. Harriet felt a sudden cold dread in her stomach and her smile disappeared.

'Mrs Westerman, Sophia is missing.'

'Good God!' Harriet said, emerging from behind the desk. 'When? Did she take anything with her? Tell me all.'

Miss Scales was obviously distressed, but she answered calmly. 'She told me she wished to go for a walk while I was reading to Papa, late afternoon that must have been. I thought she must have returned and gone straight to bed, but when I went to her room after reading your note, it was empty. She had taken some clothes, I think, but not more than she could easily carry. It is difficult to say. I think she had a small travelling bag, and I cannot find it now but I may be mistaken.'

Harriet began to pace the room. 'Can we know what direction she took?'

'We saw some parishioners of my father's along the way and enquired. Miranda Dent is sure she saw her walking towards Silverside.'

'Alone?' Miss Scales nodded, and Harriet tried to reason herself out of her dread. No doubt Fräulein Hurst had regretted turning Felix away, and meant to try her luck at Silverside again. However unpleasant the Vizegräfin might be, Sophia would be safe there. Surely Sturgess would not make some attempt on her now, with the village ready to chase him down and his secrets exposed. He must be thinking only of escape.

But still . . . 'I am sure she will come to no harm, Miss Scales, but perhaps Ham, we should go and find her there?' The huge coachman nodded. 'Miss Scales, may I ask something of you?'

'Of course, my dear. Anything at all.'

'Would you be so kind as to take charge of Crowther's nursing until I or Casper return? Lottie is with him at the moment but when she leaves, I would be easier knowing he is in your care. He may develop a fever yet and should be watched.'

Miss Scales nodded and Harriet walked briskly into the hall and crossed it to reach the library. The circle of male faces looked up at her.

'Gentlemen,' she said with a nod. 'Felix – a word with you, please.'

He shot to his feet and joined her. 'Mrs Westerman, I have been kicking my heels for hours! I don't understand what is happening at all. Why did Sturgess shoot my uncle?'

She kept her voice very low as she replied. 'There is a chance that your wife is in some danger. She has left the vicarage and was seen walking in the direction of Silverside. Will you come with me to find her? I shall explain on the way, as best I can.' He did not manage to speak, but he nodded at least. 'Good.'

Harriet returned to the other room to collect her cloak and saw the pistol on the desk. She hesitated for a moment before picking it up and gathering ball and powder from the drawer, and re-attaching the ramrod to the barrel. Heavy as it was, she had no difficulty concealing it in the folds of her cloak. She did not want to spend the ride to Silverside arguing with Felix about the niceties of females arming themselves with such weapons.

As the darkness around them became complete Sophia tried to persuade Stephen to leave her to wait alone, but he remained adamant. He had a certain streak of his mother's stubbornness under his gentle ways. He had decided it was right to remain at Sophia's side and he would not be moved. Eventually she gave up trying to send him off and instead told him stories from the convent. Fairytales from the forests of Germany and Austria, folksongs that tricked his tongue and made him laugh. In turn he told her the stories he had learned at his mother's knee of her adventures as wife of Captain Westerman. Sophia was eager to hear all that he could tell, and as the landscape disappeared into darkness the time passed quickly. Then they heard voices below them. Stephen jogged to the edge of the tower and leaned over the edge. Deep in darkness below them he could see a lantern, and peering up at him the face of Mr Sturgess. He was with two other men but they were all in shadow. He called out and waved.

'We're up here, Mr Sturgess. Miss Hurst and I!'

'Very good!' Mr Sturgess said something to the men he was with that Stephen couldn't hear and they moved away. 'Wait there, Master Westerman! I shall come up and light you both down.'

Harriet found Mrs Briggs and Mr Quince in the drawing room in Silverside.

'Crowther's wound is severe, but he is conscious and lucid and in Casper's care. I think he will do,' she said in reply to their first urgent enquiries, then looked about her. 'I hoped to find Miss Hurst here. Is it possible she is closeted with the Vizegräfin?'

They were all confusion – no, Miss Hurst was not there. 'I saw her this evening. She wished to see the ruins of Gutherscale Hall at dusk,' Mr Quince said, and found himself the centre of Harriet's furious attention. 'Stephen went with her, as I did not feel I had the strength.'

'Stephen? Dusk has passed long ago, Mr Quince.'

His eyes darted to the darkness outside the windows. 'The news of Mr Crowther's shooting, I did not notice the time passing . . .'

'I assume Stephen has not returned?' Harriet asked. Quince shook his head. 'Felix, Ham, I suggest you arm yourselves, and fetch lanterns. We must go immediately.'

Ham left the room at once with a nod. Felix, however, hesitated. 'Mrs Westerman, surely you should allow us to go alone and remain here, till we return.'

Harriet did not bother to conceal her disgust. 'Go and arm yourself, Felix. We shall not wait for you.'

Mr Sturgess emerged onto the top of the tower and placed his lantern down at his feet. The thin light set the shadows of the crenellations and suns on the battlements dancing. The fallen corner of the tower though seemed to swallow the light entirely and pour out darkness of its own. Miss Hurst crossed to Sturgess and shook hands with him.

'I hope you have not had too uncomfortable a wait for us, Fräulein?' he said. 'I am sorry I was delayed.'

'Stephen insisted on waiting with me to wish me farewell, and we have passed the time very happily together. Is all prepared? Shall we leave at once?'

'Yes, of course,' he said with a smile and keeping a hold on her hand. 'If you will just give me the Luck, then you shall be on your way at once.'

Miss Hurst looked confused. 'The Luck, sir? I don't understand you. Forgive me, what can you mean? I have the little carving of Casper's — can you mean that?'

'Now, now Miss Hurst. We spoke of it this morning — the treasure you wish to take from the valley. That is the Luck. Give it to me now, dear.'

Stephen saw her try to remove her hand from Sturgess's, but though he was still smiling he held onto it fast. She put her other hand on her belly. 'I am with child, Mr Sturgess. Did not you know? My child is the treasure of which I spoke.'

'You stupid bitch!' Sturgess pulled her hard, spinning her round so her back struck the low wall behind her, then he laid the whole weight of his body across her and bent her over so her upper body curved over the darkness. 'I know he gave it to you!'

'He did not! He did not! Only one of his carvings!'

'Liar!' he roared. 'I know you have it! Give it to me now or I will cut that bastard whelp out of your belly this moment.' Holding her against the wall with his left arm, he pulled a blade into his right hand. It caught the lantern light.

Sophia screamed.

'Stop it! Let her go!' Stephen was on his feet and there was a black taste in his mouth. 'I have it, Mr Sturgess. I have it!'

They ran. Ham, Harriet and Felix, lightly and swift along the path between Overside Wood and Stub Hill. Ham and Felix carried lanterns held high, Harriet bundled her skirts over her arm, and her slippers scudded over the dry earth. They did not know they were watched for. There was a sound to the right, and in the same moment something came crashing down on Ham and he fell to the ground at once. Harriet and Felix turned to see two figures plunging out of the darkness, one with a club in his hand, the other a pistol. They all fired at once, and the air became as thick with flashes and powder smoke as at Mr Askew's firework display. The one with the club shouted and fell writhing on the path. Harriet heard Felix cry out and spin to one side as the force of the bullet caught him, carried him round and dropped him to the ground. The other was uninjured. He stepped towards Harriet and raised the butt of his gun. She froze, unable to do anything but wait for him to strike. She closed her eyes, then heard a gasp and opened them again. The man's expression had turned to one of surprise, the gun dropping from his hand as he fell forward, almost on top of her. There was an arrow sticking through the back of his left shoulder. She stared, still unable to move. A lumbering step and Mr Quince appeared on the path red and sweating holding Felix's longbow in his left hand. He bent over, panting, then looked into Harriet's white and frozen face.

'There were no more guns,' he said.

A scream, a woman's, opened the air behind them. Harriet turned towards it, then back to Mr Quince. 'Go, Mrs Westerman.' She ran off into the night once more.

'Give it to me.' Sturgess sounded much calmer all of a sudden, but he still had his knife raised, was still pressing Sophia over the wall. Stephen pulled the pouch from his pocket and held it up where the light from the lantern could reach it.

'Let her go first.' He was shaking.

'No, Stephen,' Sturgess said softly, and shifted Sophia in front of him, the knife at her neck. 'Bring it to me now, or I will cut her throat in front of you.' He pressed the blade into her skin.

'Stop!' Stephen yelled. Then he lowered his arm and took a step forward. 'Take it then.'

With all the strength and speed he could manage, he drew his arm back and threw the pouch at Sturgess's head. The man dropped the knife and, pushing Sophia away from him, grabbed at it as it spun by him in the darkness and caught it with his fingertips. Stephen dashed to grab Sophia's hand and drag her towards the stairs, but Sturgess was too quick for him. He got in front of the arch and swung his fist at Stephen, catching the boy on the side of his head and sending him staggering towards the broken corner of the tower. Sophia caught hold of him and pulled him away from the black edge and to her side.

Sturgess steadied himself and laughed. 'Not so fast, Master

Stephen. Let me see what you have given me.' He scooped up his knife. 'If it is another of Casper's wooden copies I shall be very, very cross.' He wagged the blade at them, then began to unwind the binding on the leather pouch.

Harriet saw the light on the top of the Pele tower and heard her son shout. Hardly able to think, she began to run up the stairs, feeling in her pockets for powder and ball. Her shoe slipped on the smooth stone and she fell heavily on her knee; the gun bounced out of her hand. It was so dark. She felt it again and grabbed hold of it, struggling up the remaining stairs, blinded by the night and her own desperate tears.

From where they sat huddled against the far wall Sophia and Stephen could only see the heavy gilt back of the Luck as Sturgess withdrew it from the pouch, but they could see his face change from delight to disbelief. He tossed the pouch aside.

'What is this? Where are the jewels, you little bastard! What have you done with the jewels?'

He threw the Luck down onto the stone. It clattered and spun, then lay there glinting gold in the lamplight. Sophia and Stephen held each other more closely, staring at the bald cross, its surface pitted and scarred. It was far more like Casper's wooden carvings than the cross in the museum picture. The same shape, but there were only indentations where the jewels had been.

'That *is* the Luck!' Stephen yelled. 'That is all there is!'

Harriet reached the last turn of the stairs. She poured powder down the muzzle, placed the lace ripped from her cuff across it and put the ball on top. She was shaking so hard she almost dropped the ball, then she pulled out the ramrod and pushed the charge home. Now she just had to hold steady enough to prime the pan. *Oh God, hang on, Stephen, please. Just another moment, just one more moment.*

'You lying little dog!' Sturgess crossed the space between them and lifted up his knife again as Sophia tried to thrust Stephen behind her.

'I'm not lying! That's the Luck! That's all!'

Sturgess hesitated for a second. Then there was a voice at the archway.

'Sturgess.' Harriet said it quite quietly. 'Get away from my son.' Stephen looked towards the arch and saw his mother, a pistol raised to shoulder-level. Her hand was very steady. Sturgess turned and took a step towards her. She fired at once, her arm straight. The force of it knocked Sturgess backwards; he threw out an arm, but it was not enough to save him. He stumbled, and for a moment they all watched as his feet scrabbled for purchase on the edge of the void, before his body went slack and he disappeared into the darkness. His cry was cut off, suddenly and completely.

Stephen yelped and stumbled towards his mother. She lowered herself to the ground to receive him and pressed him hard into her arms, rocking him, her eyes tight shut. Miss Hurst remained with her back against the opposite wall, her hands over her face. On the flags between them the Luck gleamed in the light of Mr Sturgess's lantern.

Casper's search for the herbs he needed to treat Crowther had taken him through the darkness to the high paths above

Silverside Hall. The land opened up to him as its own creature and he could move as sure-footed in the darkness as in the day. In the moonlight he gathered the comfrey, herb Robert and ribwort he needed to knit Crowther's shoulder together again, knowing them by the texture of their leaves, their scent and shadows. His own pain felt as if it had been lifted from him the moment he gathered Agnes into his arms and carried her from Sturgess's folly alive and whole, so when he caught the sound of the first shots coming from the path to Gutherscale he launched himself down the slope towards them like a fox who hears the pack behind him. He had not yet reached the path when he heard another crack from the tower.

He found Mr Quince, his hands all bloodied and tears running down his face, trying to stem the bleeding of both Felix and Swithun, and Ham attempting to raise himself onto his feet, his hand on the swelling bruise of his forehead. Felix's wound was flowing fast and his breath was coming in a fierce pant. Casper dammed it firmly with Felix's own coat and showed Quince where to hold it. Having done what he could and hissed at the gape one bullet had left in Swithun's belly, but unable to wait any longer, Casper was about to turn and run for the tower when he saw a light bobbing towards them. Miss Hurst was carrying the lantern. Mrs Westerman followed her with her son in her arms.

Miss Hurst at once dropped to her knees by Felix's side, a rapid stream of her own language at her lips. Mrs Westerman paused by Casper, but did not speak to him. Instead she let Stephen down onto his feet. He took the Luck from his waistband, its scarred body wrapped once again in its leather pouch, and handed it to Casper.

'Sturgess is dead,' he said. 'Mama shot him.' Casper glanced at Mrs Westerman and she nodded, so Casper took the Luck once more. Holding it in his left hand he placed the fingers of his right hand on Mrs Westerman's forehead. She flinched, but allowed it and shivered as he whispered something too low for anyone else to hear. Then he tucked the Luck into his waistband and released her.

Ham and Casper followed Harriet back to Silverside carrying Felix between them. It was on Casper's word they took him first; he judged Felix had the best chance of living through his hurt. It was slow progress. No one spoke and the only sound was of Felix's damp and catching breath. Silverside was a blaze of light and they found themselves greeted on the lawns by the servants of the place with lanterns raised and white faces. Felix they laid in his bed, leaving him to the care of Miriam and Mrs Briggs, and the hysterics of his mother. The last view of Mrs Westerman Casper had that night was through the half-open door to her rooms. She had her son on her lap, her face buried in his neck and was rocking him to and fro, though who gave comfort in that embrace, and who received it, Casper could not say.

Quince remained with Miss Hurst doing what they could for the Fowlers until Casper and Ham could come back with help and means to carry them. By the time they returned, Mr Quince had seen the man he had shot with the arrow die, his pinched, frightened face turned towards the lake. He had not bled much. Quince had crawled away from the body when the breath shuddered to a stop and the eyes became blank, and crouched on the path staring at the corpse till Ham and Casper arrived. He asked the man's name, and Casper told him in a low voice, placing his hand on Quince's shoulder as he did. All the while Miss Hurst calmly tried to make Swithun more comfortable, one hand on his brow, one on the padding placed over the ugly wound in his belly. His hands scrabbled in the dirt of the path. The servants Casper and Ham had brought with them carried torches, and by their light Quince watched Casper touch his fingers to Isaac's throat, then pull mistletoe from his bag, place a sprig of it in the dead man's mouth and close his lips over it. The Fowlers were lifted onto the blankets and carried to Silverside Hall.

Mr Sturgess was forgotten until after sunrise, so his corpse lay that night among the ruins of Gutherscale and the broken emblems of his family's great house, guarded by the crows.

L OTTIE SCRATCHED AT the door. 'Ruben?'

She thought she heard a stirring within and pushed it open a little, lifting her candle. There was a curse from the bed and her light fell on a tumble of blankets. Ruben Grace lifted his head. A woman was lying across him in her shift, her bare legs over him, her head, the brown hair all loose, scattered over his chest. Lottie breathed in sharply and turned her back. She heard the maid scurry under the blankets.

'What is it, Lottie?'

She remained bowed over her candle. 'There is something I must tell you. And in private.'

'Now?'

'Yes, of course now!' she hissed. She heard his low chuckle and the smack of a kiss delivered. She glanced swiftly back over her shoulder; he was cupping the girl's chin in his hand, and she was watching him like a greyhound watches its master. He swung his legs out of the bed and Lottie turned back to the candle, her face hot, and listened to him dress.

A moment and he touched her on the shoulder and passed by her across the threshold. She followed him and he pulled the door to behind them. He bent over the candle towards her.

'It's Sir William,' she said in a low voice.

'Does he ask for me?' He made as if to turn away and up the stairs to the upper chambers.

449

'No, no.' She put a hand on his arm to stop him. Another man would have asked her questions, hurried her, but Ruben stayed quiet and still, his attention complete.

Lottie drew in her breath. 'I saw the light under the door to his room, and I was going to ask him if he needed anything further this evening. You know how he has been up and pacing every night these last three days.' Ruben didn't speak, but simply kept his eyes on her face. 'I heard something – the door was a little open, so I looked in.' She licked her lips and stared into the candlelight. It fluttered and smoked. 'Ruben, did you ever see the Luck?'

His eyes widened. He placed one palm on the rough plaster wall between them, and leaned even closer. 'I did.'

She spread out her fingers. 'Was it a little bigger than this? With jewels in it?'

He nodded slowly. 'What did you see, Lottie?'

'The master bent over the table with a chisel in his hand. There was something that size, gold, on the table in front of him. I only saw for a moment, but there was a fat clear stone on the table near the door. And he was working away at another.'

Ruben's mouth set in a line. 'The bastard. That's the Luck.' He grabbed her shoulders and the flame shook. 'That's our Luck, Lottie. The Luck of the valley. I've been searching for it three years.'

Lottie drew in her breath. 'The dawn of the day he left this place Lord Greta rowed out to the Island of Bones. Sir William saw him, and told me of it that day. Between then and you coming here, I saw Sir William go there a lot. Always before anyone else was about, or late, and saying nothing.'

Ruben was frowning now. 'And you never thought to say anything?'

'I did not know you were looking! And he gave me a shilling to say nothing about Lord Greta going to the Island. Didn't seem right, and I didn't know what it might be.'

Ruben released her and put his hand to his chin. 'You are right, Lottie. Forgive me for speaking sharp.' Then, after a moment's pause, 'You must help me. Take off your apron. We must watch him from the shadows. You stay in the house, watch what you can from the door. I'll slip out the back and see what I can from the window.'

For a moment the instruction about her apron confused her till she looked down and saw it snowy in the gloom. He was gone towards the kitchen, treading as gentle as a cat, before her fumbling fingers had managed to undo the ties. Then she folded it, stuffed it under the settle, blew out her candle and began to creep into the dark.

They had a long wait of it. Lottie was pressed to the wall beside the office, never daring to look in, but listening to the sound of the chisel. At one moment there was a scrape and a curse from Sir William. Lottie thought her heart would burst out of her chest. She pulled her skirts around her legs and held her breath. The scraping started again, there was a final clink and the sound of the chisel being placed on wood. The office was full of drawers and cupboards and secret places a man might place his money or bonds away from the eyes and fingers of his servants. If Sir William placed the Luck in one of those, they might have to break every lock in the room to retrieve it.

Holding her breath, she inched closer to the hinge of the door, and put an eye to it. Sir William seemed to be looking directly at her, but she managed to fight the desire to flee. No, he was examining the jewels in the candlelight. His face looked set and heavy as he turned a diamond that looked to Lottie the size of a plover's egg in his fingers. Sharply, he set it down again and drew a little leather purse from a drawer of the desk. Then, one at a time, he placed the jewels within it. Lottie lifted herself on her toes; she could see the Luck itself, naked and golden, its surface full of ridges and hollows. Where the chisel had caught, it was scarred with short lines of brighter metal. Sir William put the purse back into his pocket, and picked up the cross. For a moment he looked around him, then with sudden decision took up his candle and stepped towards the door.

Lottie swung back into the shadows, flattening her spine into the wall and closing her eyes. Sir William did not look round but went straight to the front door, and from his candle lit the lamp that always hung ready in the hall. He pulled the bolts free and stepped out quickly into the night. Lottie gathered up her skirts and followed him. He had not pulled the door to behind him. She closed her eyes for a moment, and said her prayers, then followed.

The light of the lantern bobbed down the path to the edge of the lake. She kept to the shadows, stooped over and moving as quietly as she could. It was a dark night. Hardly a thread of moon, and that part obscured by cloud, and everything painted in dark greys. The path was silent under her and seemed to carry her forward.

Sir William stopped at the lakeshore, then she watched his light bob along the shingle, moving away from the path as she did so, but keeping him in sight. Lottie felt a touch on her shoulder and turned. Ruben was crouched beside her.

'He has it? I could not tell.' An owl cried out from the Island of Bones.

'He does,' she said as quietly as she could.

Sir William seemed to hesitate a moment. Then he reached into his pocket. A low winding wind shook the trees above them, and the clouds stepped away to let the thin moonlight fall on the man at the edge of the water. He took his hand from his pocket, drew back his arm, and threw. The light caught the Luck like a shooting star. It fell, and the waters swallowed it with a ripple. Lottie felt Ruben's fingers squeeze on her shoulder, he was as rigid as a pointer. Sir William waited until the disturbance on the surface had died away into the steady blackness of the water, then turned and made his way up towards the house. He passed so close to them Lottie could have reached out and touched him.

'What are we . . . ?'

'Shh!' Ruben said, his eyes still fixed on the surface of the lake. They heard the door to the house close in the distance, and the scrape of the bolts in the locks slipped down the slope of the path towards them.

Ruben stood up and walked across the shingle to the place where Sir William had stood. Lottie looked around, then hurried along after him. As soon as he reached the spot he began to undress, dropping his clothes on the grey stones, his eyes still fixed on the surface of the water like a man called to the rocks by the Sirens. Lottie turned away, and heard the gentle splash and gurgle of the water as he stepped in. When she turned back he was up to his waist, his white shift making him look like the ghost of a drowned man. As the water reached his shoulders he lifted his arms up into the air, then descended into the darkness. Lottie shivered and watched the spot where he had disappeared. The owl called again, and the surface of the lake settled as if Ruben had never been.

Lottie took a few steps forward, her hand held out. The cold waters met around her ankles icy and gripping. She could feel tears coming into her eyes.

'Ruben?' she called, her voice a whisper, rising. Her teeth began to chatter. 'Ruben?'

The surface broke. He half-swam, half-waded towards her, finally falling on his knees in the shallows. She splashed towards him, put her hands under his arms and began to haul him in. He panted and crawled with her up among the reeds, then collapsed onto his back. Lottie turned to look for his coat. His skin looked blue in the moonlight. She felt his hand grip her ankle; she turned back to him. He laughed softly at her, then lifted his right arm. The Luck. Scarred and dripping, it was held gleaming in his hand.

She reached for his coat and he sat up to let her sling it round his shoulders, then she crouched down beside him.

'He hurt himself, Sir William I mean, prying out the stones,' she said, after a little while.

'That I saw,' Ruben said, staring down at the Luck cradled in his broad dark hands. 'First bite the Luck has taken from him, and I doubt it'll be the last.' He traced the marks where the stones had sat.

'What wilt thou do with it, Ruben?'

'When I can get away she and I will walk the old ways together, Lottie, and rest together between the Druid's stones. Then I shall hide her, till we need her in dark times, and protect her as we may. This air is hers, this water and these hills and here the Luck will abide.'

EPILOGUE

A s soon as Casper thought it safe, Crowther was returned to Silverside. The Vizegräfin had insisted, in spite of her brother's advice, that Felix would be treated by a qualified surgeon. The latter rode over to Silverside from Cockermouth every day at great expense, but did not slow Felix's recovery too greatly. Swithun survived three days in the old housekeeper's room at Silverside Hall, but the wound began to stink. Casper brought his mother to him, and tried to ease him as far as his arts were able, but there was nothing much that could be done. He did live to see and know Agnes, however, who was brought to him at his request. He asked her forgiveness, received it, and it was thought that gave him some comfort. The night before the ravings took him at last, he caught at Casper's wrist.

'You warned me. I know that.'

It was all he could manage. Casper left for his bed, leaving him to his mother's care and grief. When the morning came Casper thought he could feel the haze beginning to lift; the air was fresher somehow. It did not surprise him then to find Swithun dead and laid out with his jaw tied, pennies on his eyes and salt on his chest. His mother was gone and they had no word of her again.

By the time Crowther was becoming impatient of his confinement, Harriet wanted nothing more than to retreat to her own room and never venture out again. She had found herself repeating the events of the past few days in front of the coroner and in public for some hours. Then there were a number of burials, ancient and modern, to attend. She could feel the hostility of the gentry who flocked to see her, and there was talk that a woman who had shot and killed the local magistrate should face judge and jury. Not among the people though.

The quiet and dignified testimony of Miss Hurst, as she was still referred to, Ham, and Agnes Kerrick did much to quiet this talk. Mr Sturgess's false identity was exposed, and when Harriet entered the coroner's court with no less a personage than Viscount Moreland at her side, who explained very frankly about the murder of his natural son in Europe, the gentry busied itself remembering they had never liked Mr Sturgess at all. Mr Palmer's letter arrived just when it was needed, covered in enough seals to frighten the local authorities and put weight behind Mrs Westerman's apparently wild assertions. The letter was subscribed with the signature and flowing titles of the First Lord of the Admiralty; Mr Palmer's name did not appear on it. Miss Scales and Mrs Briggs remained by Harriet's side whenever she went into public, and if the distrust of Harriet or the threats to her did not entirely disappear for some weeks, they were at least reduced to whispers. Even the vicar took the opportunity to support her from the pulpit, and although she suspected that his daughter wrote that portion of the sermon, Harriet was grateful to him.

Strangely, there never seemed to be any question of trying Mr Quince over the death of Isaac Fowler. Each such story requires a hero, and as Harriet was still regarded as rather dubious, and Crowther was too tainted by the crimes of his parent, Mr Quince became their chosen one. He found himself in front of the coroner too, and felt he was being egregiously thanked for shooting a man in the back. He resisted the charge of heroism as much as he could, and was made rather miserable by it. Where Harriet was heard with cold suspicion, he was warmly embraced. Harriet was too grateful to him, and too tired to resent it in any way. She laughed at him for looking guiltily at her, and doing so made her feel better in herself. After some controversy, Mr Sturgess's remains were placed in the Greta family tomb, and Kit Huntsman's bones found a place near the family he had served. Stephen attended both burials at his mother's side.

Miss Hurst returned to the vicarage. The Vizegräfin remained largely in her own rooms and Stephen continued to wander the hills with Casper and Joe, or with Mr Quince as his health continued to improve. Harriet wrote her letters and wondered if her sister would come to her, or refuse to ever meet her again.

The worst of these convulsions were over by the time, some three weeks later, that Crowther was recovered enough to leave his chamber. Harriet and Crowther were enjoying the clearer weather on the lawn of Silverside, seated side by side and watching the pleasure boats moving between the islands. The

Vizegräfin had been taking the air and passed by them with a cold nod.

'You have been having a number of conversations with your family, Crowther,' Harriet said when the woman was out of earshot. 'May I ask what conclusions have been reached?'

'I have reached the conclusion I was very wise to avoid my family as long as I have,' he said, 'and only wish I had managed to stay out of their way for longer.' She smiled. 'But I think you are asking about the future of my nephew's wife?'

'You are correct, sir.'

He sighed and shifted his shoulder; the wound was closing well, but he doubted he would ever be free of the ache or have the movement in the joint he once had. 'Miss Hurst has no wish to live with Felix, and given his behaviour, I cannot blame her.'

'The marriage was quite legal?'

'Oh, indeed. They are bound by law, I am afraid, just as they are by the child she carries. She came to see me determined to take another name and style herself a widow in some provincial town. There was a notion of her teaching languages.'

'And now?'

'I used my considerable powers of persuasion to convince her to use the name she has a right to, and take up residence in Bath. I understand the irony, Mrs Westerman, there is no need to grin up at me like that. I shall make her an allowance that will keep her in suitable style. It will be given out that Felix is making an extended tour of the family's business interests in the north. He will be allowed to visit her and the child frequently enough to keep up appearances, but make no further demands on her. He will be given a separate allowance, one I mean to monitor very strictly.'

Harriet turned away from him and looked down towards the Lake and St Herbert's Island. 'What does Felix say to that?'

'Felix, I think, has come to realise that his wife is a woman of sense and feeling. He may be in danger of falling in love with her eventually. I am glad of it. He knows he will have to become a different man to earn her respect. It might be the making of him. He will remain in England, therefore, for the time being.'

'And the Vizegräfin?'

'My dear sister. We have had a number of unpleasant interviews. She will return to Vienna and take up the pattern of her life there. She feels I have robbed her of a son now, as well as a brother. I fear if she were not my enemy before, she is now.' Harriet did not turn away from the lake, but let her hand rest for a moment on his sleeve. When she removed it, he continued, 'I am sure she knew something of the death of that Jacobite, Mrs Westerman. She would have been about six years of age at the time. It is clear she pressed to have the tomb opened, and I can think of no other reason why she might have done so, or perhaps my father said something to her after my mother's death. Possibly when my father sent her away to school. I do not think she was shocked at any point when I told her of what our father had done, and that makes me suspect she was in some way prepared.'

'Do you wish the scheme to move the tomb had never been proposed, Crowther?'

He considered a long time before replying. 'If you will forgive the romance of this answer, Mrs Westerman, I feel as if the haze has cleared from my own history just as it has lifted from the land. I hear reports that the harvest is looking promising.'

'There are poems to that effect in the latest number of *The Gentleman's Magazine*. What of your brother?'

'The vicar suggests a plaque in the chapel stating him innocent and commending his soul to God. That must suffice, I fear. Kit Huntsman's memorial stone will state he was murdered, but it will maintain a tactful silence as to who murdered him.'

'We could never, in truth, prove——'

'No, Mrs Westerman, but we do know. The rumours picked up by Mr Palmer's friends and the ghost stories of a deceased pig farmer are enough to convince me. Lord Greta murdered my father. However, it would have been satisfying to hear from Sturgess's own lips that his father murdered mine before you shot him.'

'My apologies, Crowther,' she said dryly. He smiled at her and she was glad of it.

'I notice that in all your dealings with the authorities,' he continued, 'that neither you, nor your son, nor Miss Hurst have mentioned the Luck. That is strange.'

'It seemed unnecessary. The gentry consider that Sturgess was turned mad by a fairytale. Let them think so. Casper has it once more.'

'And what has he done with it?'

She looked back towards St Herbert's Island. 'Mrs Briggs has abandoned her plan for a summerhouse again. Though the Gretas' bones will still have a home in Crosthwaite, their tomb will now remain on Saint Herbert's. The ruins are to be shored up and left as they are for the amusement of the Lakers. I have no doubt that Casper will make his way over to the island some quiet night and bury it there again.'

Crowther sighed. 'I asked Lottie how Kit Huntsman knew that my father had taken the Luck.'

'And?'

'Kit was the servant who rowed Greta out to the Island the morning he left to join the Rebellion. If my father saw them, Lottie guesses that they saw my father. She heard Sir William telling Kit in forty-five that he had only moved the Luck into the tomb for safekeeping, that day Kit came to confront him after burning Gutherscale. She knew it was long gone by then, of course, and fearing for my father, ran to fetch Ruben. He must then have discovered my father's crime, and the Black Pig was the price of his silence.'

Crowther thought of his father and the Jacobite opening the lid of the tomb, the Jacobite leaning in for the prize and finding instead a blade through his back, his body spinning away with the blow and the thin end of the blade snapping against the stone; then Ruben's arrival and the bundling away of the body among the ancient bones. His shoulder stung him.

High in the bright air above them a buzzard climbed the currents and called to the crags. Harriet watched it for a moment, wondering what it saw. 'So do the people believe that the cross in still covered in jewels, Crowther? Would they still have faith in its power, do you think, if they realised the precious stones were gone long ago?'

'Lottie told me that she supposes most still believe it is as it was, but they all know it is only fairy-wealth and so no good would ever come from trying to buy your way into the world with it. Apparently only gentry would be foolish enough to think otherwise.'

Harriet laughed quietly. 'And its magic? She still believes in it?'

'She said the Luck lost only its jewels, not its power, and asked me if we cut the lace from your cuffs and dressed you in plain stuff, would you, Mrs Westerman, not remain a remarkable and lovely woman?' Harriet felt herself flush. Crowther continued quietly, 'She told me it was not my father's fault. That the Luck wished to remain here, and called to him to avoid being removed by Greta or his followers, then paid him in evil coin.'

Harriet considered this in silence until movement on the path from Portinscale caught her eye, and she stood up swiftly. A woman in a brightly coloured skirt was moving up the hill towards them, a boy something over Stephen's age with her, and a terrier chasing around her as she walked.

Crowther could not turn so easily with his shoulder stiff. 'Who is it, Mrs Westerman?'

'Oh Crowther, it is Jocasta Bligh!' Harriet said, getting to her feet and waving. 'Casper's sister has come to him!' A stab of sadness struck her and she dropped her hand. She loved her sister too, not well always, perhaps. But sincerely.

'Harry!'

She looked up again: just rounding the corner she saw a man and woman arm-in-arm. Her heart soared. It was Rachel – she had come, and with her fiancé Daniel Clode at her side. They led a sturdy-limbed toddler by the hand.

'Oh, Anne!' Harriet cried, and Crowther watched her as she ran down the slope towards her daughter. He saw her swing her child into the air then kiss her sister.

Whatever their disagreements, it seemed they were forgotten

for the moment. Clode's warm voice carried up the path towards him. 'We are all come,' the young man was saying. 'We thought a show of force from Thornleigh Hall might be of use to you all. Graves, Jonathan and Susan, Mrs Service – the whole circus, all waving the family crest around like a good luck charm! The others are arranging our accommodation at the Oak, and Susan has already agreed to play at the re-opening of the museum. We had to come at once though and embrace you, Harry! Where is Mr Crowther? Is he up and about yet? Oh, I see him! Good-day sir. Is that Mrs Briggs at the door? Mrs Briggs! Delighted to make your acquaintance! No, we could not possibly dine with you here, our numbers are even more than you see . . .'

Crowther sighed. He used his father's cane to push himself to his feet, and turned to meet them.

Casper was sitting with the white lady on the slope above the Hall, sucking on his pipe and waiting for Agnes. The Luck was still in his waistband, but he could see it also between the white lady's hands. Only when she held it, it was lit with jewels again. The black witch was still in his mind, still hissing, but she was quiet for now.

The white lady shifted her long blond hair away from her face and pointed down the slope. Frowning, Casper turned to look. Far below them on the path to Silverside, he saw a movement of coloured skirts between the trees: a woman, with a boy and dog at her side leading a party of gentlefolk up the slope. He turned questioningly to the white lady, a broad smile already on his face. 'Is it . . . ?' he asked. She nodded. Casper jumped to his feet and began to run down the hill like a boy, with Joe flapping behind him. 'Jocasta!' he yelled as he went, and he heard his bird echoing him, and the white lady laughing.

HISTORICAL NOTE

Although *Island of Bones* is fictional and the characters invented, I have of course drawn a great many things from history and adapted them to my needs.

Students of the 1715 and 1745 Rebellions, and those who know the history of the Jacobites in the area will realise I have borrowed heavily from the story of James Radclyffe, 3rd Earl of Derwentwater (1689–1716) and his brother Charles Radclyffe (1693–1746). To make clear what I have invented, or culled from elsewhere, I thought it best to give a quick summary of their biographies here. James Radclyffe's residence was actually Dilston Hall in Northumberland. There is a plaque on the wall of the George, one of Keswick's great pubs, saying that the Earl rode to join the 1715 Rebellion from there, though by most accounts he visited the area only once and that in 1710–11. In *The Last of the Derwentwaters*, J. Fisher Crosthwaite, appointed a Trustee of the Museum in 1875, reports that James was *formed by Nature to be generally beloved . . . the poor, the widow, the orphan rejoiced in his bounty.*

There is no real evidence that his wife, Lady Anna Maria, threw her fan at him and demanded his sword, but the story is well entrenched in local folklore.

The Earl was captured at Preston, and executed in 1716. He was stripped of his titles and honours, and his estates confiscated. Disputes over their ownership occupied the courts for many years afterwards. His brother escaped the axe in 1716, but was an active participant in the Jacobite court in Rome and was executed in 1746, having been captured on his way to join the Young Pretender the previous year. James did have a son, John, but he died in 1731.

Lord Nithsdale, who was taken at the same time as James Radclyffe in 1716, did escape the Tower of London and execution due to the cunning of his wife, who disguised him in women's clothing. They lived in Rome till his death in 1744.

The first museum in Keswick was opened around 1781–2 by Peter Crosthwaite, who appeared to be advertising it and his regattas on the lake in 1782, though other sources say the museum was not established until 1784. Crosthwaite was a great map-maker and noted self-publicist. His museum was a 'cabinet of curiosities', and some of his exhibits, including the musical stones he began to collect in 1785, are still on display in the current Keswick museum. Also there when I last visited was Napoleon's tea-cup and an astonishing array of minerals, stuffed animals and various manuscripts of the Lake Poets. I wholeheartedly recommend a visit.

There are a number of 'lucks' in the area including the Luck of Eden Hall, the Luck of Muncaster and the Luck of Burrell Green. Some are the gifts of Kings and Queens, others came from hobgoblins and fairies. Apparently.

St Herbert's Island was the home of the saint who died in AD687. It is also said to be the inspiration for Owl Island in

Beatrix Potter's *Squirrel Nutkin*. To the best of my knowledge it has never been referred to as the Island of Bones. There was a summerhouse apparently built by the Derwentwater family, but that was on Lord's Island.

The strange weather of 1783 was caused by the eruption of the Laki fissure in Iceland, which had serious effects across Europe. Some of my descriptions of the weather are borrowed from Horace Walpole's letters of that summer, as is Crowther's theory that the haze was due to earthquakes in South Italy. The letter from Paris is genuine. There were serious hailstorms that summer, and a great deal of damage was reported in the newspapers from lightning.

For an account of folk-magic in the period, I recommend *Popular Magic: Cunning-folk in English History* by Owen Davies (2003).

For a history of Keswick, I recommend *Keswick, The Story of a Lake District Town* by George Bott (1994).

For an insight into the experience of voice hearers, I am very grateful to *Living with Voices: 50 Stories of Recovery* by Professor Marius Romme, Sandra Escher, et al. (2009), and the interviews available via the *Madness Radio* podcasts (*www.madnessradio.net*)

For an insight into the traditions of the area, please see *Life and Traditions in the Lake District* by William Rollinson (1974).

It is impossible to make use of all the legends, traditions, history and characters of the area in only one novel, but I've done my best. For my various errors and anachronisms, I can only apologise, particularly to the residents and historians of Keswick itself. Of course, this story is set before the Lakeland

Poets changed how we see the area for ever, but the great lovers of Wordsworth might want to note that the house Mr White so admires in Cockermouth belonged to the poet's father – and William would be one of the children he noticed there.

Read on to discover . . .

- A preview of Imogen Robertson's addictive new novel, *Circle of Shadows*
- An interview with Imogen Robertson

Circle of Shadows

PART I

I.1

25 February 1784, Oberbach, Duchy of Maulberg

DISTRICT OFFICER BENEDICT VON KRALL lowered his weight onto the stool with a grunt and lit his pipe, all the while watching the young Englishman sitting on the other side of the table. The man was leaning his head against the wall and staring blankly in front of him. The oil lamp sputtered and settled. He gave no sign of having heard Krall enter the room, but he seemed calm enough. Krall jerked his head and heard a shuffle as the guard retreated into the shadows a pace. The ties at the neck of the Englishman's shirt were loose, showing the hollows around his throat and collarbone. Krall thought of a portrait he had seen once at the palace of a young man, similarly perfect in looks. The high cheekbones, large eyes, full mouth – a strange mix of the innocent and the sensuous. Here, tucked under the Town Hall of Oberbach with its rough plaster walls and earth floors, they could, like that youth caught on canvas, be from any age, any time. The lamp between them sputtered again and the darkness crossed the young man's face like the wing of a crow, and away. The Englishman was twenty-five – twenty-six, perhaps. His smooth forehead was smeared with blood.

'Why did you kill her, Mr Clode?'

No answer.

English felt like a forgotten taste on Krall's tongue. The words were rusty with lack of use, but there they were, as soon as he called on them. For a moment he thought he caught the stink of the Thames at Black Wharf. He sniffed sharply and looked down. The Englishman's hands lay on the table in front of him, his bandaged wrists uppermost with dark blooms showing, the wounds declaring themselves, as if he were offering them up, asking for some explanation, but then his face was turned away. Not a request for enlightenment then. More an appeal. *See what you have made me do.* The palms of his hands looked very white. Not the hands of a working man.

Krall had had thick dark hair once, had it when he spent his years in London, learning trade, learning the language till for a while it was as familiar as his mother tongue. That was long ago, before war and worry turned his hair grey and cut deep lines into his forehead, around his eyes and mouth. Then, during his ten years as District Officer in Oberbach, he'd heard enough stories to turn his grey hair white. Women who'd smothered their bastard children; men who had taken a life over a game of cards, or lashed out at a friend to find a moment later that hell had chosen them in that second and they were damned. Nothing quite like this though. He blew the smoke out of his nose, feeling old.

'Tell me what happened,' he said more sharply. The floor and walls seemed to muffle his voice, steal it away from the air, so Krall brought his fist down hard on the wooden table, making the timbers dance.

It startled the younger man. He blinked and looked about the cellar as if seeing it for the first time. The cellar smelled of damp earth and wood-smoke. The air here still belonged to winter, as if the town were keeping some of the cold as a souvenir of the season passed.

The Englishman was still dressed in Carnival costume, in the chequered blue and yellow motley of the Fool. He seemed to notice this as Krall watched him, and rubbed the cotton with his fingers. His wooden mask lay on the table between them with its wide carved grin, a nose long and hooked like a beak.

'There was a party.'

Krall blew out another lung-full of smoke. 'Yes, there was a party. It is *Festennacht*, Carnival.'

The young man had a slight smile on his lips. He began to sing under his breath. *'Girl, come to my side, pretty as milk and blood.'*

Krall crossed his arms over his body. The singing scraped his nerves. He thought of the woman in white stretched out across the floor of the haberdasher's back room. Her blood-shot eyes, open and amazed. The slice across the wrist. The pool of blood shed by the Englishman before Colonel Padfield had beaten down the locked door and rescued him. The open razor, slicked with it.

'The woman,' he said loudly, trying to drown out the tune. 'Did you smother her? Did you smother her and then try to kill yourself?' The young man was still mouthing the words of the folk tune. Krall leaned forward. 'Listen to me!'

The young man flinched away. The song stopped.

'There was blood,' he said, and lifted his arms and wrapped them around his head as if fending off a beating. 'A man ...'

'What man?'

'Masked! He said he would help me. I did not feel ... Things were wrong. I was frightened ...' He suddenly gasped and his eyes widened. For a moment it seemed to Krall there was some sense there. 'Where is my wife?' Suddenly the young man had thrown himself across the table and grabbed at the lapels of Krall's coat. Krall heard a movement behind him and lifted his hand, telling the guard to keep back. The Englishman's blue eyes were glittering, feverish, an inch from Krall's own. 'Where is my wife?' There was a strange tang to his scent. Something floral.

'Mrs Clode is safe,' Krall said quietly. 'Release me. Release me before the guard knocks you senseless.'

The intelligence behind the young man's eyes seemed to fade. He looked at his fingers and gradually uncurled them, retreated to his stool. Krall exhaled, slowly. 'The lady dressed in white, Mr Clode. You knew her, did you not? You met at court, in Ulrichsberg. Lady Martesen. You were found with her body. Did you smother her?'

'There were fires everywhere.'

'Torches. For the Fool's Parade. Listen, Mr Clode. The lady in white.'

The prisoner looked up and met Krall's gaze. Again, the District Officer sensed a struggle for understanding, for reason. The man's lips began to move again. 'What is it?' Krall asked.

'Water ... water ...'

'You want water?' Krall twisted in his chair to nod to the guard. The Englishman grasped at his throat.

'I am drowning.'

'No, Mr Clode.' The Englishman stumbled upright, but at once his legs gave way. He spat onto the floor and hauled him-self into a corner, retching and gasping. Krall watched him, frowning deeply, but making no movement. He had seen men drunk, he had seen them mad with grief or rage. He had not seen this. Had the horror of the killing simply snapped the prisoner's mind? The man's breathing evened out. He looked up at Krall from his corner. 'Wake me. Please. I am dreaming. Wake me.'

The room became silent. Outside, Krall could hear singing – drunks banishing winter with schnapps and country songs of growth and fertility.

'Why did you cut her wrist before you sliced your own?'

The young man held his hands at the sides of his head and began to rock back and forth. There was something unnerving about the movement, its insistent repetition. There was no sense in this. Krall sighed and stuck his pipe into the hanging pockets of his coat.

'I cannot wake you, you are not dreaming.' Krall stood up. 'Mr Daniel Clode, in the name of the Duke of Maulberg I am arresting you for the murder of Her Grace Agatha Aralia Maria Martesen, Countess of Fraken-Lichtenberg.' He turned to the guard behind him. 'Get him out of that damn costume, and wash his face.'

An Interview with
IMOGEN
ROBERTSON

What inspired you to start writing?

Like most writers, I've been writing most of my life. I remember banging out short stories and poems on a manual typewriter from about the age of ten. Not good ones. I wrote a lot less during my career in TV until I signed up for a poetry workshop in about 2003. I learned a great deal there and also saw writing being approached as a craft to be worked at, rather than an attempt to channel some quasi-divine inspiration. I had a short story published in *Mslexia Magazine*, which was a great boost, and when I became a freelance director I spent time between projects working on prose.

What inspired me to take a real shot at writing was when I was one of the winners in the *Daily Telegraph*'s 'First thousand words of a novel' competition. The prize was lunch with the judges, who were so encouraging it was worth the weight of the steak in gold. I decided to try and finish the novel which became *Instruments of Darkness*, then I found my agent and signed a deal with Headline within a year. Now I get to write full time. I've been very lucky.

What do you enjoy most about writing?

The thirty-second commute! I love living in London, but I think if I were still travelling to an office in the middle of town every day, it might break me. Also it is great to be your own boss. I think I'm pretty much unemployable now. And I get to spend a lot of my time reading in libraries and calling it work. For *Circle of Shadows* I spent time in Germany, an automata workshop, Freemason's Hall and the great esoteric bookshops of London. Managed to claim all that was work too – nice work if you can get it!

How does the writing process work for you and how has it changed over the years?

I spend a few months each year on pure research, then start trying to get the outline of my plot together. That normally sends me back to the library on more specific quests. Then comes the writing when I am at my desk each day, and the characters start getting up and walking about. As the characters develop they often change the plot, so I rework my plan as I go.

Writing is a process of discovery. I am more confident in my work now than I was writing the first book. There are always problems as you write, but now I know that those problems can become opportunities to make the book better.

Which characters do you most enjoy creating and why?

I don't feel I have any role in creating them a lot of the time; they create themselves on the page. Sometimes the minor characters are wonderful to find. Someone like Mr Postlethwaite, the landlord of the Royal Oak in *Island of Bones*, just arrived panting and sweating on the page. Equally Adam Kupfel, the Alchemist who appears in *Circle of Shadows* was just waiting to be discovered in a corner of my mind, complete with his scars and smeared glasses. I remember being a bit sceptical when I heard writers talking about their characters 'just turning up' in this way, but it is true.

By contrast, Joshua Cartwright in *Instruments of Darkness* was very different when I started writing him. He was a coward and a bit of a creep, but when he was talking about his family he developed his own voice, and I went back to rewrite him as a more sympathetic, more fully rounded character. It's a real pleasure when characters grow like that. You ask yourself what this person's life is like and they seem to emerge from the fog, sometimes quickly, sometimes more slowly.

What and who are some of your favourite books and authors?

Jane Austen, Charles Dickens, George Orwell, Georgette Heyer, Dorothy L. Sayers, Patrick O'Brian, Terry Pratchett, Maggie O'Farrell, Roy Porter, Peter Ackroyd, Sarah Waters, Tom Holland, Amanda Craig, Lawrence Block, Virginia Woolf, Amanda Vickery, Jasper Fforde, Graham Greene . . . Favourite Books? Well, beyond the books by those mentioned above: *Emergency Kit* – a fantastic collection of modern poetry, *The Complete Poems and Plays of T.S. Eliot*, *Civilwarland in Bad Decline* by George Saunders, *The Idiot* by Fyodor Dostoyevsky, Walpole's *Letters* . . .

What the last really good book that you read?

I'm happy to say I read lots of really good books, but a recent one that stands out is Sarah Bakewell's *How to Live: A Life of Montaigne in one question and twenty attempts at an answer*. Beautiful, smart, funny. It is one of those books that makes you feel better equipped to deal with life and made me really appreciate Montaigne all over again.

If Instruments of Darkness *(or one of the other Westerman/ Crowther novels) was turned into a movie, who would you choose to play the lead characters?*

I've discussed this on my blog, as it happens. Stephen Dillane is a current front runner for Crowther and Naomi Watts has been suggested for Harriet. That would be very nice. I need to get George Clooney on set somehow too. Maybe he could take a cameo role, Shapin perhaps, then direct. Just a suggestion.

Can you tell us a little about what you are working on next?

I've just started work on a new book – not a Westerman/ Crowther novel, but a thriller set in Paris in 1910 and in the modern day. It's a new challenge, and one I'm very excited about. After that I'm glad to say I'll be returning to Harriet and Crowther for the fifth book in the series.

What advice would you give a writer just starting out in his/her career?

Learn your craft. Go to workshops, listen to working writers, take their advice and keep at it. Learn to be a constructive critic of your own work. And ignore anyone who says the way to a book deal is hassling agents or publishers at parties. You're much better off staying at home and working!

IMOGEN ROBERTSON

Circle of Shadows

DEATH AT THE CARNIVAL

Shrove Tuesday, 1783. While the nobility dance at a masked ball in a small market town, the beautiful Lady Martesen is murdered. Daniel Clode is found by her body, his wrists slit and his memories blurred and nightmarish. What has he done?

A DESPERATE MISSION

Harriet Westerman and Gabriel Crowther race to the Duchy of Maulberg to save Daniel from the executioner's axe. There they find a capricious Duke on the point of marriage, a court consumed by luxury and intrigue, and a bitter enemy from the past.

RIDDLE, RITUAL AND MURDER

After another cruel death, Harriet and Crowther must discover the truth, no matter how horrific it is. Does the answer lie with the alchemist seeking the elixir of life? With the automata makers in the Duke's fake rural idyll? Or in the poisonous rumours oozing around the court as the elite strive for power?

IMOGEN ROBERTSON

Anatomy of Murder

LONDON, 1781

The city seethes with rumour as the King's navy battles
the French. In one part of town, the privileged revel
in their wealth and celebrity. But elsewhere a body is
dragged from the Thames' murky waters. Is this an
ordinary drowning – or part of a treacherous conspiracy
betraying England's most precious secrets?

A DANGEROUS PURSUIT

Harriet Westerman awaits news of her husband, gravely
injured at sea, and seeks distraction. A passionate
believer in justice, she and reclusive anatomist Gabriel
Crowther agree to examine the dead man's body, risking
accusations of an unnatural interest in murder. With the
nation's safety at stake, personal reputation must yield to
the search for truth, but Harriet and Crowther do not
realise how dangerous their investigation will become . . .

Praise for ANATOMY OF MURDER:

'A labyrinthine mystery in the heart of a teeming
London, involving fashionable castrati, espionage and
bodies in the Thames . . . The city is evoked with a
Dickensian exuberance' *Independent*

978 0 7553 4844 2

headline
review

IMOGEN ROBERTSON

Instruments of Darkness

'Makes you want to read every word . . . the plot is serpentine and satisfying, with enough false trails and distractions to create a genuine mystery' *Daily Telegraph*

Thornleigh Hall, seat of the Earl of Sussex, dominates its surroundings. Its heir is missing, and the once vigorous family is reduced to a cripple, his whore and his alcoholic second son, but its power endures.

Impulsive Harriet Westerman has felt the Hall's menace long before she happens upon a dead man bearing the Thornleigh arms. The grim discovery cries out for justice, and she persuades reclusive anatomist Gabriel Crowther to her cause, much against his better judgement. That same day, Alexander Adams is killed in a London music shop, leaving his young children orphaned. His death will lead back to Sussex, and an explosive secret that has destroyed one family and threatens many others.

'Stylish, enigmatic and wonderfully atmospheric . . . a story of secrecy and shame, reason and passion, that resonates long after you reach the final page' Francis Wheen

'The doings of her characters may be darker than pitch but my lady's craftsmanship is beyond doubt' *Time Out*

'[An] extremely impressive debut' *The Times*

'Chillingly memorable . . . an extraordinary thriller' Tess Gerritsen

978 0 7553 4841 1

headline
review